Mission Rwanda

It takes more than a thousand people to undress a naked man.
— Old Rwandan saying

Therese Zink

*To Eric in gratitude for his personal tour of Rwanda
and best wishes to his new family,
Mutoni and Cyusa.*

Chapter 1

January, 1994

As the plane broke through the clouds, Ann stopped drumming her fingers on the armrest, interrupting the melody in her head. She marveled at the unbelievable greenness that stretched out below in all directions. With the plane's descent, brown ribbons appeared and widened into rivers that cut through a patchwork of fields and green mountains. The soft, rounded mountains resembled the Appalachians that Ann had visited as a child on a family vacation. But unlike the Appalachians, every inch of the mountainside was planted. A cap of green forest perched on a few of the higher ones—shelter for the native birds and animals who confined themselves to cramped living quarters or feasted off the farmers' crops. Ann would learn to identify the green patches: the emerald green of the tea fields, the sage and silvery eucalyptus groves, the stippled spinach tones of the banana trees. Patches of sweet and Irish potatoes, sorghum, millet, beans, and cassava plants marched their way up the terraced hills like a green giant's staircase.

The gray asphalt runway rolled out before the plane, which touched down with a whoosh from the jet turbines and a gentle rock. After a brief taxi, it parked a hundred feet away from the concrete block terminal.

Ann had arrived. At thirty-two, this was her first trip off the North American continent. A sigh of relief escaped from her lips as she peeled off her fleece jacket. She wouldn't need it in the tropical climate. She also hoped to shed the guilt and grief that had blanketed her for the past six months. The first layer arrived with the death of her niece, a drowning for which she felt responsible. The second involved the tortured death of her mother from pancreatic cancer. Maybe she was running away from the mess, but she had no choice.

Ann wasn't someone who spent much time exploring the crevices of her psyche. She preferred to "have her finger on the hold button." Ann smiled to herself as she recalled the words of the family medicine resident she shadowed in her third year of medical school. It was a horrendous call night. A delivery went bad due to a tight cord around the baby's neck. Ann resuscitated the baby and he was transferred to intensive care. Then the mom bled and bled—it seemed like gallons. The woman was as pale as a sheet and writhed in pain as the resident actually reached up into her uterus to remove the remaining piece of the afterbirth. After that fiasco they were called to the bedside of a cancer patient Ann had followed for most of his hospital stay. He was taking his last breaths and she was there when he died—the first patient she'd gotten to know well who died. The whole, horrible night left Ann emotionally and physically exhausted. She asked the resident how she managed.

"When the emotion of the situation is too much," the resident said, "I imagine an old push-button phone and jam my finger on the hold button."

Now, whenever things got tough, Ann always imagined herself pushing that hold button. It helped her cope. But she wasn't very good at releasing the hold button, especially when her feelings related to her own family traumas. Those feelings were locked somewhere deep inside.

She thought that some time away, caring for foreigners in an exotic place with problems bigger than her own, might give her perspective. She desperately hoped so.

She sucked in a breath and fingered the thin, gold chain around her neck. It held a locket that had belonged to her mother. Inside was picture of her parent's engagement, young and hopeful, their journey ahead full of promise. Her dad had given it to her before she left, trying hard to be supportive of her adventure. But at the airport he'd looked so forlorn and alone as she walked away. Perhaps she was abandoning him, but she was bushed. She'd been the family member who took a five month leave from the urban Milwaukee clinic where she worked as a doctor to care for her mother at home. A sliver of anger and resentment burned.

Another sigh. No time to sort it through, the passengers around her pushed into the aisles, retrieving their suitcases and coats from the overhead bins. Ann reached under the seat in front of her and grabbed her backpack, hoisting it over her shoulder. She buttoned up any reservations about her decision, focusing on the adventure ahead; she joined the parade down the stairs and onto the pavement. The hot, damp air smelled of grass, eucalyptus, and sweat. In the west, the slanted dying light colored the distant clouds blood orange.

Ann wiped her brow with her forearm as she showed her passport and visa and revived her rusty French. The equatorial warmth felt good, a contrast to the near-zero temperatures in Milwaukee. Her hair frizzed. After she heaved her luggage off the whiny turnstile, she paused to do a mental check— money tucked in her waist belt underneath her slacks, passport in her pocket, documents completed and ready for customs, a few Rwandan francs in her wallet. The Global Health driver would be holding a sign.

She breezed through customs and stepped toward the throng of black-skinned locals who waved placards with European names. Dark faces slick with sweat called to her—*Madame. Madame. Taxi. Taxi. Madame.* The other passengers dispersed into the crowd. Ann's pale skin broadcasted her foreignness. She swallowed her discomfort as she searched for the driver with a "Global Health" sign. Where was he? Someone was supposed to meet her. A scrap of paper with the phone number was folded in her wallet, but she'd have to find a phone and figure out how to use it.

A sea of ebony faces peered back.

Ann tried to lengthen her short breaths. Certainly, her driver was out there somewhere. She wanted to locate him before she had to walk into the dark multitude.

"Dr. Ann McLannly," a breathless voice called from the right and waved a white poster board with her name and the green GH logo, a stethoscope wound around an open palm holding a globe. Ann's shoulders eased as a tall man pushed toward her and extended his hand. His shake was firm and his smile broad. "Welcome to Rwanda." He touched his full Afro, then pointed to her frizzy hair and grinned again. "Like me, but red."

Ann smiled her relief, appreciating his effort at connection.

"Sorry me late. Much traffic."

Hot air rushed into the windows of the Toyota SUV as they left the airport. Ann tried to sit back and enjoy her new world, totally different from winter in Wisconsin. A few kilometers away, the driver pointed out the Amahoro Soccer Stadium, now home to the United Nations peacekeeping mission in Rwanda. White UN Land Rovers with the blue UN logo painted on the doors were parked on the field. The athletes' quarters housed the soldiers. In August 1993 the US, France, and the Organization of African Unity had brokered a peace agreement, the Arusha Accords, in Arusha, Tanzania, between the Rwandan government and a rebel group called the Rwandan Patriotic Front or RPF. Several hundred UN soldiers stood ready to oversee the peace.

The SUV wound through a maze of hills and streets lined with terra cotta houses and tin roofs. People gathered in front of their homes. Women prepared food and called to children as they hovered near outdoor stoves. Some collected laundry: shirts, trousers, skirts, and sheets that hung from tree branches or stretched across bushes. In a large grassy field, boys kicked a soccer ball that appeared homemade. Ann asked about it.

"Children make balls from garbage. Plastic bags, banana leaves with string," the driver explained. On the other end of the field, a boy with a large staff, about the same age as the players, tended a small herd of goats. The bleating of the goats and the cries of the scampering boys crescendoed then faded as the SUV motored on. Downtown Kigali, the capital of Rwanda, sported concrete-block office buildings that stood a dozen stories, many trimmed with bright primary colors. Billboards packed the round-abouts, advertising cigarettes, beer, and a radio station RTLM—*Radio Télévision Libre des Mille Collines*. It was promoted as the radio of the streets with call-ins, hip music, and rowdy disc jockeys.

A wooden sign with the green GH logo on a white background hung on the metal gate. Several embassies appeared to be housed across the street. On the corner, children in navy blue uniforms lined up in the school yard waiting to leave for the day. Nuns, dressed in a waterfall of black cloth, looked after them as parents and older siblings arrived to accompany the children home.

The smell of cooked meat greeted Ann as she entered the red-brick, two-story building that would be home for at least six months, the obligatory commitment for first-time volunteers. The spare setup surprised her, but this was Africa; at least she wasn't camping.

"*Bienvenue*," a woman with a Southern drawl said. "Welcome. I'm Sylvia, your new roommate." She extended a plump hand and smiled broadly. Her welcome seemed genuine. A t-shirt with the green logo stretched across her generous chest. Her bottle-blonde, Dolly Parton-like curls spilled to her shoulders.

She led Ann to the room. It had been years since Ann had had a female roommate. Luckily, the bedroom they'd share was spacious and Sylvia's side appeared neat and orderly.

True to her southern upbringing, Sylvia was hospitable as she gave Ann a tour. "We all share the bathroom." The "all" was elongated. "Some of our housemates were not well-trained by their mothers. Unfortunately, you can't pick your fellow volunteers." Although each volunteer had been assigned a shelf, shampoo bottles, combs, and razors were scattered around the old claw-foot tub and sink. A chest-high blue plastic barrel stood in the corner. "I just shove stuff onto a shelf. Staff cleans regularly, so hair and whiskers rarely plug the drain."

Sylvia spooled through her warning list in a southern drawl: "The commode seat shifts. Watch out. If your feet aren't planted on the floor, you'll land there. The shower dribbles. It takes forever, and I mean *forever*, to rinse off. But then, I'm a bit more buxom than you." Sylvia eyed Ann's flat chest. At five feet and just over a hundred pounds, most adults were larger than Ann. But Sylvia was probably pushing two hundred and she had at least six inches on Ann.

"Personally, I think it's easier to scoop buckets of water from the barrel and dump them. Just be careful about not getting it on the floor. Staff complains and the director will yell. He's a stickler about safety," Sylvia warned. "Safety in the house and in Kigali."

Ann swallowed hard as she took in the reality of what she'd signed up for. She loved a long, hot shower in the mornings, that's how she woke up. How would she adjust? Perhaps her decision to come was too rash. Perhaps she should have stayed and found the courage to face her family. She'd have to eventually. Her sister Coleen, the mother of the niece who'd drowned, wasn't talking to Ann. Her dad was pretty needy, alone for the first time in fifty years. Ann had taken a leave from work to care for her mother; none of her sisters could—they had jobs, husbands, and kids. After that, it was easy to quit work and sign up for the mission's six-month commitment. At the time it had felt easier than remaining in Milwaukee.

Sylvia continued, bringing Ann back from her reverie. "Jerk this chain to flush." She pointed to the ceiling, touching the chain. "Light bulbs are hard to come by." Above the sink a single bulb filled one of the light fixture's three sockets. "Guaranteed to smudge makeup. I hope you brought a flashlight. The city shuts off electricity in different *secteurs* on a rotating basis. We're near the equator. It's completely dark by six."

At least Ann had done something right. She'd purchased a headlamp at the last minute and stuffed a twelve-pack of AAA batteries into her luggage. Maybe she should have brought more. But Ann's sense of success didn't last long. Sylvia pointed to Ann's gold chain and locket. "Hon, you can't wear that here. Someone will rip it off your neck."

Ann gulped. It was the only memento of her mother she'd brought with her. Tears pricked her eyes as she unhooked the clasp, and carefully wrapped the jewelry in a tissue, tucking it into the drawer of her bedside table.

As she unpacked, Sylvia sat on the bed and filled Ann in on her history. "I grew up in West Africa," she started. "My parents were missionaries and I'm more comfortable in this culture than I am in the US. It's the missionary kid syndrome. Do you know about that?"

Ann didn't. She'd never met anyone who'd lived overseas, and the only place she'd traveled outside the US was Canada, to go fishing with a boyfriend, and Cancun, on a winter break, but that was hardly authentic Mexico. In hindsight, she wished she'd done a year abroad in college, but she'd been a gung-ho pre-med with no time for cultural dalliances.

"I spent junior high and most of high school at a missionary school in Nigeria, until my father got sick. Then we returned to Tennessee. My mother's family lives there. Daddy recovered, but my parents were killed in an auto accident during my sophomore year in college."

Ann flinched. "I'm sorry." Sometimes Ann was so caught up in her own pain that she forgot about the heartache of others. Sylvia had had her own share of hurt and loss.

Sylvia shrugged and continued, "I'm fluent in French." She described King Faisal Hospital, where she worked as an operating room nurse.

"Is that where I'm working?" Ann asked.

"I think so." Sylvia nodded and prattled on about how busy they were, how much she loved the Rwandan staff, how Ann's French would improve, how they were all one big family. She giggled as she described a UN colonel from Bangladesh with a charming British accent, the head surgeon, with skilled hands. "He's my crush. Well, to be honest, it's more than that." Sylvia blushed, then nattered on about the current political tension.

Ann's mother, herself a stickler for making a point and moving on, used to make a not-so-nice remark about one of Ann's talkative childhood friends— "the good thing about a radio is that you can turn it off." Ann wondered if she'd ever find Sylvia's off button. She was entirely too exhausted to hear all of this after traveling sixteen hours and almost eight thousand miles. She preferred to organize her underwear in private, thank you very much. But Sylvia was trying to welcome her. Ann told herself to calm down; she needed to make a good first impression. A friendly roommate was better than a cold and aloof one. Ann pressed her lips together and listened as best she could.

Sylvia's southern inflection jumped an octave as she told Ann a story she'd repeat every time she welcomed new expats to the compound or hospital. "I worked in Somalia. Hon, you have no idea what it was like. One morning we all woke up to our neighbors banging on our gate. 'Gather your belongings. The rebels are coming.' They were five blocks away. I packed the hard drive into my suitcase, opened the safe, and stashed the brick of money in my bra. I shook the guard awake. We made it out just in time. As we all sped away, I could see the whites of the rebels' eyes through the back window. They marched toward our compound with blazing torches, yelling and waving their machetes and the biggest sticks I've ever seen. Talk about fear. I could've peed in my panties."

Sylvia introduced Ann to the other GH volunteers as they returned to the compound for dinner. Two were from the US, the others French. They worked in agriculture, education, and community development. Ann described the GH surgeon recruiter she'd met in Milwaukee, wondering if he might be in Kigali.

She described him as prematurely gray and close to forty; the surgeon-recruiter had spoken at the Gesu church near the Marquette University campus in Milwaukee. It was mid November, an evening that had threatened either rain or snow.

Ann had attended because a medical school chum had sent her an email about international volunteer work as a potential next step. Paralyzed from the losses and not yet back to work, she felt desperate and directionless.

"Think about international work. It would be a change of pace. A chance to put your head and heart back together. Helping others always helps you. Global Health is a good organization," her chum had written. "I've heard the GH recruiter. He's passionate about the work."

The dark-walnut paneling and the smell of burning candles had created an odd backdrop to the kodachrome slides of relief activities in Africa. One slide Ann would never forget—a three-year-old girl, her ebony belly protruding like a watermelon, stared with a curious expression at a grenade that lay in front of her in the beige sand. The angle of the sun created a shadow, doubling the size of the grenade. Danger loomed large.

"Kwashiorkor, protein malnutrition," the surgeon had explained. "See the size of her belly. The edema in her feet. Lots of carbohydrates and no protein. The locals make gruel out of a local root that fills them up, but has no nutritional value. This picture was taken near our feeding center in Puntland, in Somalia. Doesn't she look like she is ready to pick the grenade up? If one of our staff hadn't run over and scooped up the girl, she'd be dead."

After the talk, Ann spoke to the physician. His nose was crooked, but his intense blue eyes, ice-blue like the marbles she'd played with as a kid, rimmed with steel, focused on her face. "Why did you start doing this work?" she had asked. It was as if no one stood behind her. She glanced away, embarrassed by his gaze.

"It's one of the best choices I've made," he said in his radio announcer voice, a timbre she could have listened to all day, all night. "It's a long story," he was saying. "Do you have time for a beer? I need to talk to the folks here. But . . ." He gestured. Nice hands, long fingers. "Then I'm free. I haven't had dinner." His half smile exposed a dimple on his chin.

Ann needed to get home. She was worried about her father, newly widowed. "I can't, but thanks."

Disappointment had flashed across his face.

Ann shook his hand, took a packet of information and left.

The next morning she mailed the GH postcard. A change of pace would be good. Trying to alleviate suffering was a worthy cause. That might be the antidote for her guilt, her sadness. She needed a diversion.

"I'd like to meet Dr. Blue Eyes, hon," Sylvia said and batted her own eyelashes.

Unfortunately, he was not part of the household or the hospital. ". . . I should've accepted his offer to have a beer," Ann said. "I can't remember his name, but he was headed back to Africa."

Chapter 2

There was so much to learn. The three-story King Faisal Hospital, where Ann would spend most of her time, sat like a beige box on one of Kigali's many hills. It overlooked a valley packed with mud brick houses painted brilliant colors: pink, blue, green, and yellow. The morning sun reflected off the tin roofs, creating a valley filled with glistening gems. Built by the Saudis as a gift to Rwanda in 1991, the hospital had closed after only two years due to dwindling government resources and insufficient staff. Rwanda schooled too few medical personnel and many had left the country because of the deteriorating quality of life.

Each week another affront disrupted what had been the status quo—a new roadblock sprouted up, a grenade was thrown into a crowd, political parades halted traffic, or a bomb destroyed an office building. Kigali General Hospital, located on the opposite side of town, was always packed because, despite the Arusha Peace Accords, fighting continued between the government and rebel forces. The UN had assigned the Bangladeshi medical platoon to reopen King Faisal Hospital.

Sylvia had a crush on the medical director, a skilled and charismatic surgeon who was a colonel in the platoon. He welcomed assistance from volunteer medical groups like GH. Non-government organizations (NGOs), such as the International Red Cross, restocked the hospital and had money to hire local nurses, doctors, and other support staff who were desperate for work. This created an important resource for the northeastern section of Kigali—jobs and a functioning hospital. In return, the neighborhood protected the facility.

Ann pushed through King Faisal's emergency entrance toward the end of her third week. The newness was gone. A clean ammonia scent filled the heavy air. Ann's clothes stuck to her body. She was adjusting to her own sweaty smell; it returned even though she'd doused herself with a bucket of cool water in the compound shower an hour earlier. The morning had started hot. Almost every morning did. Africa hot.

"Mwaramutse, good morning, Dr. Ann," Joseta said. She was nauseatingly cheerful in the morning, but Ann forced herself to return the greeting. A local head nurse, Joseta was the head of the emergency department, and a powerhouse at King Faisal. She had helped to plan the hospital's layout and worked for a year while Rwanda had the money to support the facility. When word got out that the UN hoped to reopen the facility, Joseta had approached them. She needed a job and they welcomed her knowledge.

Despite living in Rwanda all her life, Joseta sensed expats' discomforts and uncertainties. She offered reassurance, reaching out to each new aid worker, helping him or her avoid the *faux pas* everyone inevitably tumbled into. Kind, personable, and forgiving, she graciously helped the expat understand what he had done without shaming him too much. As a half smile crossed her face, she'd take the individual by the forearm, and walk him to the side of the room or suggest he join her in the break room. Then, fixing her gray-brown eyes on the expat, she'd explain the *shoulds* and *should nots*.

Somewhere in her fifties, Joseta was an attractive woman, full-breasted and broad-hipped. Like the other nurses, she wore a spotless white nurse's uniform, whiter than anything Ann ever managed in her automatic washer with bleach in Milwaukee. The degree of whiteness was even more amazing because a layer of red dust covered everything during January, the dry season. Passing motor scooters and cars blew up tunnels of dust that enveloped anyone on the side of the road, causing one to inhale and chew grime.

Joseta's vibrant headscarves, traditional headdresses worn by many of the local women, cheered the department on the most grueling days. A broad smile stretched between her full cheeks; her nose crinkled at the bridge when she grinned. "*Mumeza mute*, how are you?"

Ann had not had her coffee. She needed at least a half cup to think clearly, two cups to approach Joseta's cheerfulness. Ann hurried into the break room where tea and coffee—powdered Nescafe—were available. She filled a ceramic mug with steaming water and stirred in the brown powder. She'd been disappointed, expecting real coffee in Africa. She tried to savor her first sip, then carried her mug out to study the emergency department's chalkboard—central command. A dozen patients waited to be seen; the other physician, a Rwandan, had not yet arrived.

"There's a machete wound in bay six," Joseta said. "It's set up."

Ann left her mug in the nurse's station, and entered the exam room and greeted a tall, thin man who lay on the gurney, his feet extending a foot beyond the edge. Most patients were thin, in contrast to the staff whose body sizes confirmed steadier sources of income, hence food.

Blood-soaked white gauze circled the thin man's head, stretching to just above his closed eyes. He hummed a melody that resembled a lullaby. Ann spoke Kinyarwanda, the local language: "*Mwaramtse*, good morning." One of the Bantu languages, it employed the front of the mouth. She'd worked hard to learn the pleasantries.

He returned her greeting.

She glanced at the slip of paper that contained the patient's vital signs—stable—and pulled latex gloves from her white coat pocket. At home, every clinic exam room had three boxes affixed to the wall—small, medium, and large. Empty boxes were quickly replaced. Here there was no box; gloves were reused. Joseta and the other nurses washed them in tubs of soapy water and dried them on a string that stretched wall-to-wall in the utility room. The gloves were too big for Ann's small hands, but at least she had gloves. HIV was more prevalent here than in her urban Milwaukee clinic.

"*Que s'est-il passé?*" Ann asked what happened. Since Rwanda had been a colony of Belgium, French was commonly spoken. She'd learned not to pepper the patients with questions. If she asked one question then shut up, she usually learned what she needed to know.

The thin man responded in a flood of French, his hands and long fingers flying for emphasis, something about his neighbor threatening him with a machete for days. Then he folded his arms over his stomach and silently tracked Ann's movement to the head of the gurney. She unwrapped the gauze. The wound stretched like a hair band across his scalp. She grimaced, then performed a quick visual survey. His bloodstained shirt and baggy pants, held up by a piece of twine, were intact. He smelled of sweat and soil. His eyes, ears, and jaw were unharmed. He complained of no tender spots along the vertebrae of his neck. Red dust coated his skin and clothes. She carefully removed his red flip-flops; he wanted to hold them. His dusty feet and legs revealed old bruises and healing scratches, but nothing new. His heart and lungs sounded normal, his abdomen soft.

Joseta joined Ann and opened a brown paper package, handing her more sterile four-by-four gauzes. The hospital bought in bulk and the nurses labored to divide the gauze into small packs, wrap them in brown paper, and sterilize them in the autoclave. As a pre-teen, Ann had helped her father do the same in his veterinary office. That experience and living on the farm—delivering lambs, waiting for duck eggs to hatch, butchering sheep and chickens—had introduced Ann to the world of science. She'd set her sights on becoming a doctor from a young age. She'd focused on the sciences throughout high school and college.

Ann completed the exam. "What does he do for a living?"

"He farms a small plot on the outskirts of town. Sells produce at the market," Joseta said.

"You've seen him?" Ann asked.

"No, he told me."

Ann investigated the wound, palpating the depth with her gloved finger. Shiny, white bone glistened. This required a layered closure, first the galea aponeurotica, the protective skin of the bone. If she did not close that layer, the patient could end up with a hematoma and healing would be disrupted. A plastic surgery rotation during residency had given her confidence in her sewing skills. The number of injuries here had provided plenty of opportunities to develop them further. She enjoyed the work, even though the hospital was very busy.

Ann asked Joseta to inquire about the cause of the injury. There was another paragraph of rapid French.

"He's Tutsi. His neighbor's Hutu," Joseta explained. When the neighbor tried to steal his potatoes, the patient had fought back.

"How can you tell?"

Joseta set her hands on her hips. "He told me, but look at his nose—thin. Tutsi—thin nose, thin lips, usually tall and skinny, sometimes a lighter complexion." She pointed to her own nose. "Look at me. Hutu—broad nose, thick lips, stocky build, black skin."

Ann nodded.

Joseta continued. "The other ethnic group is the Twa. Pygmy people. They live in the jungle. You don't see many of them in Kigali."

"You're Hutu?" Ann clarified.

Joseta moved her head up and down as she handed Ann a syringe. "But my husband, Vincent, is a Tutsi."

"If there's intermarrying, what's the big deal?"

"Long story. I'll explain as you sew."

Ann sucked water into a 60 cc syringe and squirted it into the wound. Joseta positioned a towel and pan to catch the runoff. The irrigation got an artery pumping so Ann held pressure while Joseta slipped the needle into a holder then handed it to Ann. She tied off the bleeder, but struggled with the scissors. "These are dull. Can you find better ones?" Faulty equipment seemed to be the norm. It tested Ann's patience, not her long suit. She had not yet resorted to using her teeth, although she'd considered it a time or two.

Joseta slapped a clean scissors into Ann's palm.

"Merci." Ann pulled the gala together with catgut, a tan-colored, waxy thread made from bovines that the body's enzymes dissolved after three weeks. She closed the epidermis with black silk, which would need to be removed. At home, Ann would have used nylon sutures. Silk was old-fashioned, but it still worked. Some US or European hospital had donated cartons of silk and catgut.

While Ann sutured, Joseta snipped the thread and explained the Hutu-Tutsi rivalry. Belgians defined the Tutsi as a superior race because of their less "African" features. Belgian scientists measured facial features and skull size and issued an identification card to each Rwanda citizen, which defined one as legally Hutu, Tutsi, or Twa. By insisting on the identity cards, the Belgians stirred up the Hutu-Tutsi rivalry. The groups had had a more or less peaceful co-existence for centuries before the Belgians took over from the Germans after World War I. In 1962, Belgium granted Rwanda her independence and gave power to the Tutsi. After a bloodless coup, the power passed to the Hutu in the early 1970s. President Habyarimana and his wife, the real power broker, had remained in power ever since.

"Has he been good for Rwanda?" Ann asked.

Joseta paused for a moment. "He didn't have any money to fix up this place. Doors falling off their hinges, rusting metal bed frames, mattresses full of rats, insects. I scrubbed enough toilets to last me a lifetime." Joseta snipped the suture.

Ann took another bite with the needle, pulling the skin together.

Joseta continued. "I'll never forget the smell of mildew." She sighed. "The president owns a Swiss chalet in the outskirts of Kigali, complete with ebony woodwork and marble floors. He's not invited me to the swimming pool or tennis courts. You can figure out what I think." She clipped again.

"I hear you," Ann said and counted the stitches—twenty-four. "You're sewn back together, monsieur." Joseta applied a dressing and Ann moved on to the next patient.

A thin woman reached into her bra and retrieved a small plastic bag. She opened it and drew out a paper that she carefully unfolded and handed to Ann.

This was the medical record system. Since the hospital had been closed for more than a year, any records that existed were stored at home. X-ray reports, hospital discharge instructions, and pharmacy prescriptions, often several years old, arrived in a plastic bag, reserved for that purpose only. Patients pulled them out of pockets, purses, and, for most women like this patient, from inside their bras. The slightly damp ultrasound report described fibroids. The woman reported vaginal bleeding for three weeks. Her hemoglobin was low—six. Ann ordered blood and talked to the surgeon about a hysterectomy.

Midmorning a child gasping for breath arrived. Panic filled his eyes and his lips were dusky blue. The child was about the same age as Ann's niece Rosie. Ann fought the comparison, but the memory of that day came anyway.

The sun had reflected off the kidney-shaped pool outside her parents' home. "Rosie. Rosie." Ann panicked. She had left her five-year-old niece playing in the shallow end of the pool, but now she was nowhere in sight. Ann left her to attend to her demanding mother. Diagnosed with pancreatic cancer, she lay on the couch in the living room and had a bell that she rang when she needed something.

"Go have lunch with your friends," Ann had said to her father. "You need a break. I can manage things." Ann's sister Coleen, a psychologist, had to work and her afternoon childcare had fallen through, so Ann agreed to watch Rosie while she stayed with her mother.

Even though Rosie had taken swimming lessons, Ann had reminded Rosie to stay in the shallow end until she returned. Where was she? It wasn't like her to run off. Dread raised the hairs on the back of Ann's neck.

Ann stepped up to the edge of the pool. A small body with streaming blonde hair and in a royal-blue bathing suit was submerged in the deep end. Ann kicked off her flip-flops and dove.

Dripping wet, Ann laid Rosie on the cement. In her mind, she jammed the hold button on the old black phone with her pointer finger. With a trembling finger, she cleared Rosie's mouth and shook her small shoulders. "Rosie. Rosie." She felt her neck for a carotid pulse. Nothing. Ann's own pulse raced. She steadied her lips as she blew two breaths into Rosie's delicate mouth. Feeling for the flat sternum under the damp swimsuit, Ann began pumping on Rosie's small chest. One, two, three, four... After thirty compressions, she gave two more quick breaths. "Rosie. Rosie," she called, "Please, open your eyes."

Water dripped from Ann's thick red hair and trickled down her back. A puddle formed where her knees pressed against the coarse cement. She repeated the cycle—thirty compressions and two breaths. Her own heart hammered in her ears. Her breaths came short and sharp. She ignored the knot in her throat.

Ring, ring, ring. The bell again. What did her mother want now? Her mother would have to wait.

She needed help. 911. "Mom, call 911," Ann yelled in a shrill voice, her tears held at bay.

The damn bell again.

Calling for help was useless. Her mother couldn't hear her. She'd have to phone 911 herself. She'd have to carry Rosie with her. Ann sucked in a breath, swallowing a sob, as she prepared herself for the feat. Her shoulders and arms trembled as she leaned down to squeeze her lips against Rosie's. Two more breaths. She lifted Rosie and ran for the house. Rosie's limp body pressed heavy.

Maybe forty pounds. Sweat beaded at Ann's temples and her arms ached. Finally the screen door slammed behind her. The house was cool and dark, relief from the intense August sun. The bell again. Her mother stretched out on the couch, covered by a tri-color afghan.

"Mom, you'll have to wait. Rosie's not breathing," Ann screeched. "Not now. I can't help you now." Ann reached for the phone on the little wooden table behind the front door. She lifted the hand set and smashed the buttons. With the cord she couldn't go far. She locked her throat to steady her voice.

Message delivered, she knelt down on the rag rug in the foyer and delivered two more breaths and a round of compressions. She worked mechanically, her panic shoved away. She'd spent years perfecting the ability to respond with buttoned anxiety.

"What's happening?" her mother called from the couch.

"It's Rosie." Ann sniveled. "She was in the pool. She's not breathing. I called 911. They should be here soon."

Her mother stared from her perch on the couch. The bell sat silenced. "I'm praying," she whispered.

"We'll wait outside," Ann called. It would be easiest for the medics to find them on the porch. Her parents lived on a farm north of Milwaukee. The closest town was ten miles away. The rural ambulance service would take a while.

Ann lifted Rosie and pressed her forearm against the screen door's latch. The screen door banged shut as she set Rosie on the slider-swing. She braced herself and delivered another cycle of breaths and compressions. Then she repeated the assessment. No response. Still no breathing. No pulse. Ann started the sequence once more.

It was nearly fifteen minutes before the medics sped up the gravel lane, siren blaring and lights flashing. Two EMTs took over CPR as Ann heard herself describe the drowning to a middle-aged woman with lacquered red nails.

The ambulance wheels spit gravel as it roared away. Ann stood shaking. Her adrenaline pumped full throttle. She combed her fingers through her wet hair, trying to summon the courage to phone her sister. Feeling faint, she stumbled into the house.

Her mother sat speechless, dabbing her eyes with a tissue.

The cool air revived Ann as she looked up the number. She lifted the receiver to her ear, punched in the number, and in a tight voice asked the receptionist to interrupt the client's session. Her sister wanted Ann to meet her at the hospital, but Ann couldn't leave her mother alone, but her dad should return soon. Ann stared at her watch. It had stopped when she'd jumped into the pool.

Five days later, the family decided to turn off Rosie's ventilator.

"Oxygen," Ann called.

Joseta came running with a tank and an adult mask.

"Do you have a child's mask?" Ann asked.

Joseta shook her head. "This should do. I'll show you." Joseta flipped the mask upside down and the Rwandan boy accepted it, although the mask covered most of his face. The noisy tank made hearing and talking impossible. It was even hard to think. Joseta administered the epinephrine without being asked. She collected the details from the boy's mother in Kinyarwanda. "Insect sting," Joseta said.

Ann put her stethoscope on the boy's dark back. Wheezing, both lungs.

After ten minutes, the boy still struggled and Joseta suggested a second epinephrine and maybe starting theophylline. King Faisal didn't have a nebulizer.

Ann agreed, feeling a little stupid, wondering if Joseta recognized her insecurity. Part of it was the language, the noisy tank, the old equipment, the too-big mask.

The boy improved and Joseta suggested an injection of susphrine. "It's half the dose of the epi."

Ann nodded. Ann had used susphrine and theophylline during residency, but in the US it had fallen out of favor.

The boy's breathing returned to normal. Only an angry red welt remained on his right foot. As he left, he shot Ann a broad, toothless smile; his front teeth were missing. His mother thanked Ann several times. Ann nodded, feeling embarrassed about her awkwardness.

Ann bumbled through the remainder of the shift. She needed to get a grip; Joseta might not always be standing at her side, holding her hand. What was her problem?

At the end of her shift, Ann found Joseta sitting at an old metal desk in her office, finishing her documentation for the day. She thanked Joseta for her assistance. Joseta smiled and scooted her chair back, turning toward Ann. "I like working with you Americans. I thank Jesus for you. You're always grateful. You say thank you. You treat me like a partner, not a servant." She smoothed the skirt of her white uniform as she stood up. "Did I invite you to our party this Sunday? Vincent, my husband, just started a new batch of banana beer. I'm cooking goat stew."

Ann smiled. This would be her first authentic local activity. It felt like a vote of confidence that Joseta had asked her.

"A real African party," Joseta continued. "All our neighbors and you'll know people from the hospital. The UN colonel agreed to come."

Chapter 3

Ann rode with Sylvia and the colonel in a white UN Land Rover. Her solitariness mounted as she stood in Joseta and Vincent's front yard alongside Sylvia and Colonel Arif. They studied a tree that buzzed with weaver birds. Vincent held Joseta's hand as he explained the mating ritual. The brightly yellow-feathered males wove basket-like nests, chirping as they fluttered back and forth with blades of green grass in their tiny black beaks. Showing no sign of exhaustion after the day-long effort, the sparrow-sized birds sat at the small openings and sang, flipping their tails to attract their mates. About a dozen nests in various stages of completion hung from the branches. A few nests already held a dull brown female minding an egg.

"These boys work hard for their wives," Colonel Arif said in a British lilt. His milk chocolate skin and fine facial features, with thin lips, spoke of his Bangladesh origin. Sylvia, stout with blonde hair, and Colonel, comparatively small, his dark arm slung over her pale shoulder, looked like an odd pair of salt and pepper shakers.

"Thankfully, Joseta was easier on me," Vincent said and planted a kiss on Joseta's full lips. "Come try the banana beer." A tall, pencil-thin man, with gray hair cropped close to his scalp, wore brown trousers that hung from the belt that cinched his waist, causing his bright orange shirt to pleat out like an accordion.

Ann followed the two couples into the backyard where two neighbors shoveled red soil from a four-foot pit onto a growing heap near the house. Their wives talked nearby. The yard stretched to a grove of eucalyptus trees and contained a large garden. The men dropped their shovels and grunted as they bent over and heaved a large, black plastic vat onto the grass from the pit. Sweat stained their cotton shirts. Together they poured the contents through a sieve and into a large aluminum kettle. Moisture beaded on their brows. A breeze wafted with the spicy scent of eucalyptus, but offered little relief from the punishing sun.

Ann joined several other hospital staff in the shade of a small stand of banana trees, which served as a border between Vincent's yard and that of the neighbors. Vincent handed each of them a cold bottle of beer with a yellow straw. "*A votre santé.*" They clicked bottles.

"That's French. What's the Swahili?" Ann asked.

"*Maisha marefu.* Vincent held up a bottle. "This your first?"

Ann nodded. Banana beer was the local brew and Rwandan staff at the hospital had told her she had to try it.

Vincent gestured with his own bottle as he explained the process for making the beer. "The pit creates a slow oven for fermentation. Then we strain off the liquid. The mash goes into my garden. Great compost for the squash seeds I just planted." He looked out toward the tilled rows.

"What's the fermentation agent?" Colonel asked.

"Sorghum flour. I grind my own seeds."

"His secret is that he ignores it for a month," a neighbor said.

Vincent chuckled. "We've perfected the recipe over time. If it's too strong, we add a little water. Too weak, we boil it over the fire."

"Delicious. It's worth the wait," Colonel raised his brown glass bottle. "Beer is banned in Bangladesh."

The neighbor with a Yankee's baseball cap sampled the brew in the kettle. "It's a little thin," he called. "Come, see what you think." Vincent hustled over and stuck a yellow straw into the container. He nodded. Together, Vincent and the neighbors lifted Joseta's pot off the outdoor stove's grate and shifted the kettle of beer over the glowing embers. A neighbor picked up a wooden canoe-like paddle and stirred.

Vincent pulled a handkerchief from his pocket, wiped his brow, then removed his spectacles and rubbed them.

"Go take a turn," Sylvia said to Colonel. He hurried over to join the stirrers, who eventually handed him the paddle. Although Colonel gave Sylvia orders in the operating room, outside those walls it appeared that she was in charge.

Ann took her turn stirring the amber liquid. The well-worn wood felt smooth and warm in her hands and the over-ripe smell strained her nose, causing her to sneeze. The activity created perspiration, and soon dampness trickled down the nape of her neck and between her breasts. She handed the paddle to Sylvia, removed her hat and sunglasses, and wiped her brow with her forearm. She had lathered on the sunscreen and was careful to wear a hat to protect her fair, freckled skin. As a redhead she never took chances. Over the last month when she grew weary of the Rwandan heat, she remembered Wisconsin and the sub-zero winter temperatures this time of year, when the snow squeaked instead of crunched. She would stuff toe warmers in her boots if she was going to spend much time outside. On those frigid nights her dad locked the animals in the barn and fed them bales of sweet-smelling hay.

"Ladies, will you help me set the table?" Joseta called.

Ann and Sylvia covered a long wooden table with a navy blue cloth and anchored the corners with stones. More Rwandans wandered into the yard. A tall couple with three grade school-aged children, an older short, thick man accompanied by a younger man whose features resembled those of the elder, and another couple. Other expats from the hospital arrived. The *wazungu*, white people, were the only ones wearing sunglasses. Vincent welcomed everyone with a bottle of soda or beer, which he retrieved from the tub of icy water that was sweating in the shade of the banana grove.

A variety of dishes soon crowded the table: cooked collard-like greens, beans, rice, bunches of the sweet, miniature bananas. Neighbors brought food to share, which Ann hesitated to identify; she'd heard rumors of eating brains, maggots, and grasshoppers in Africa. Joseta invited the guests to eat. She ladled goat stew into plastic bowls, which Ann helped distribute. Vincent passed out more bottles of banana beer. Ann accepted one gratefully and took a long draw through her straw, the cool liquid pleasantly refreshing. She set it down, balanced her plate on her lap and lifted her bowl of stew.

The smacks and grunts of eating swamped all conversation. Guests sat in white plastic chairs. The children clustered together off to one side. Neighbors rolled *ugali*, a cornmeal dough, in small balls to wipe up the stew's juices and sucked it off their fingers as if it had the sweetness of mango or pineapple. Ann mimicked them, stuffing *ugali* into her mouth. It had the texture and blandness of a dumpling; it wasn't a recipe she'd take back to Wisconsin. However, her father would like goat, which ranked the most widely consumed meat in Africa and tasted like a combination of beef and lamb.

Not even a month yet and homesickness plagued her. The novelty had worn off and she now rethought her rapid exit from Milwaukee. Had she abandoned her father too soon after the death of her mother? She'd left so quickly. During orientation they'd warned about this period—a month into the mission the volunteer often felt disappointed and overwhelmed, the excitement with the newness vanished. Ann tried to focus on the conversation around her.

The baseball cap undid a notch on his belt and sighed. "Have you seen the venomous cartoons in *Kangura*?"

"That rag is pure trash," a neighbor remarked as he sprinkled tobacco onto a small piece of paper and twisted the ends. He handed the plastic bag half-filled with tobacco to the man on his right who also rolled a cigarette. They shared a match. Someone belched. Other guests helped themselves to seconds and thirds.

"They published the Hutu Ten Commandments," Vincent said. "Anybody see those?"

"No marriage between Hutu and Tutsi. Vincent, you're in trouble."

Vincent chuckled as he pulled a pipe from his pocket, packed it with tobacco, and lit it. The smoke smelled pungent, but sweet. "Joseta seduced me and she continues to after almost forty years." He pulled Joseta in close. She leaned over and kissed him on the cheek.

The baseball cap shook his head. "RTLM isn't much better. That station blames the Tutsis for everything. One radio announcer says, 'Hutus, kill the inyenzi, cockroaches. Squish them like insects. The time has come.'"

"We may be in for some hard times," Vincent said. He gestured with his pipe as he spoke. "They want to eliminate every last one of us."

The adults moved their chairs so they stayed in the shade under the banana trees. Some talked; others were content to sit. Each held a sweating bottle, periodically puckering their lips around the yellow straws. Several boys and one girl kicked a black and white soccer ball in the yard. As other families arrived, the children trotted over to the join the game. Soon several girls played too. When the ball landed in Vincent's garden he stood up and reprimanded them.

"He loves that garden," Joseta said.

It stretched about seven meters by seven meters with carefully tilled rows. The leaves of the plants rustled in the light wind, which liberated the spicy fragrance of eucalyptus once again. Vincent reported planting the trees fifteen years earlier when they had moved to Kigali from northwestern Rwanda.

Feeling satiated, Ann was happy to sit in the shade and listen to the conversations around her. It was fun to hang out with locals instead of her expat housemates. She'd grown weary with their conversations about work or life in America before their missions.

A tall, well-built African wearing aviator sunglasses strode into the yard with an air of authority. His gray shirt sported a white priestly collar. The mirror lens of his glasses reflected the cluster of guests. One of the neighbors offered his chair and ambled off. Vincent hurried over and handed the newcomer a beer. "Thanks for coming, Father."

"I had to take Communion to the sick parishioners. It always takes longer than I plan. Jean-Baptiste sends his greetings." The newcomer had the deep, melodic voice of a preacher. He pressed his full lips to the yellow straw, took a long suck, and his Adam's apple bobbed. He let out a prolonged sigh as he situated himself into his seat, stretching out his long legs.

"Doing the work of God, as always," Vincent said and introduced the priest as Father Innocent.

Innocent knew most of the neighbors and thanked the expats for their work at the hospital. Joseta carried over a bowl of stew and a plate of *ugali*. The priest spooned it into his mouth as if it were his first meal of the day while Vincent updated him on activities in the neighborhood. The conversation soon returned to politics. Innocent interjected his thoughts along with the others. Many expressed their concern about the mounting dissent, and whether or not the RPF rebels and the Rwandan government could coexist peacefully.

"Can the UN enforce the Arusha Accords?" someone asked.

"We are hopeful," Colonel said.

"Several hundred rebel troops have moved into Kigali."

"I don't know if President Habyarimana will share power," Innocent said.

"The US and many European countries manage."

"Last month they predicted his assassination," the baseball cap said. "He rules with an iron hand. If you aren't on his side, you might disappear one day."

The president had set up a new militia, the *interahamwe*. There was debate about why Rwanda needed a militia as well as an army. Reportedly the French had armed the militia.

"The French are still sticking their nose in our business," someone said.

"Several hundred rebels are a threat to the president," Innocent said with conviction.

As the baseball cap and Innocent argued, the neighbors wandered off, one by one. Some watched the soccer game that was in full swing. Others checked the kettle of beer boiling on the fire. Ann sat and listened, curious to understand the opposing factions.

Joseta and the other local women gathered around a younger version of Joseta who had arrived accompanied by a husband and three children. Joseta picked up the little girl and balanced her on her hip. The other expats clustered together, probably talking about the hospital; Ann had no interest in discussing work.

Soon, only Ann and the priest sat in the patch of shade. "You're from the US?" Innocent asked. He fingered the straw in his beer. His nails were neatly trimmed and the blue-black of his skin cut a sharp contrast with the pinkness of his palms and the bright yellow straw.

"Milwaukee, Wisconsin," Ann said. "It's in the upper Midwest."

"I know that region well. I spent a year in Chicago, at the divinity school."

"The University of Chicago? A close friend of mine studied there. What year were you there?"

"1980."

"Did you know Janet Bregar?"

He smiled. "We spoke French. She was in my study group."

A wave of relief rippled through Ann. Here in Joseta's backyard, in a Kigali neighborhood, in a tiny land-locked country in East Africa, sat someone who shared some connection with her home and her former life.

"What took you to Chicago?"

"The bishop of Rwanda had a friend who taught there."

"I visited Janet several times. She always took me to hear blues, some dive on the South Side."

"The Artist's Lounge."

Ann nodded. "I wonder if we met."

"I would remember." Innocent's head moved from Ann's face to her chest. She could see her reflection in his glasses.

Joseta walked up. "I see the two of you found each other. Ann is a physician and a very good one. Dr. Ann McLannly, meet Father Innocent Rwagasonza. Two of my favorite people. I thank Jesus for both of you."

"A physician." Innocent smiled and lifted his sunglasses to the top of his head, revealing large brown eyes with thick lashes. "You're Catholic? With your red hair and the last name McLannly, you have to be Catholic. An Irish Catholic. I see you like our beer." He gestured toward her with his own bottle, then looked up at Joseta who stood watching them, her hands folded across her bosom.

Ann shrugged. "A fallen-away Catholic. In the US, the Church seems to be on the wrong side of the things I care about. I don't go to mass much. . . But I shouldn't tell a priest that. I sang in the choir for a while."

"Ah, you like to sing?"

Ann removed her sunglasses then nodded. "I play the piano too."

"I'll bring her to mass with me," Joseta said and handed each of them a fresh beer before wandering away.

Ann was beginning to feel a buzz.

"Why did you come to Rwanda?" Father asked, placing his straw in the new bottle and taking a draw.

"I needed a change of pace," Ann said with a lilt, wanting to keep it light.

"You Americans. You run away from things. Run away from family. Run away from life. What are you looking for?"

Ann didn't know what to say. She shrugged and squeezed the yellow straw, lifting it and twirling it in her fingers.

"If Joseta says you're a good physician, then you are. She has high standards. Are you a pediatrician?"

"I am a family doctor. I care for children and adults."

"Ahh. That is good. Very near my church is an orphanage started by the Belgians. The pediatrician who helped out there just returned to Europe. The nuns are looking for someone to take his place. Would your organization allow you to look after the children?"

"I don't know why not."

"Maybe two or three times a week."

Ann liked the idea. It would give her some continuity with patients, like she'd had in her Milwaukee clinic. She loved children; she'd get to know them over time, care for their problems. Working in the emergency department and labor and delivery at King Faisal, she rarely saw patients more than once.

"Tomorrow, at the end of your shift, I can pick you up. What time are you done?"

The easy, sociable afternoon rolled on in slow motion. About fifty people came and went from the gathering. The crazy pace of the hospital and the politics of the GH compound felt like distant memories.

When a neighbor asked Innocent's advice about a personal matter, Ann joined her expat colleagues who were trying to avoid talking about work. Sylvia played to the naïve expats, a midwife and doctor who had arrived earlier in the week. She related her story about being chased out of Somalia by the rebels. By now, Ann had the drama memorized. Sylvia gestured with her sturdy arms and hands, pumping her legs in place as she described rushing around to collect their belongings. Ann listened politely, then quickly asked another nurse about her experiences prior to Rwanda. That nurse described an equally harrowing experience, a robbery in Bosnia in the middle of the night. Ann squelched the anxiety rumbling in her stomach with a swig of beer. "Is every aid assignment dangerous?"

The group stared at her, the new expats especially wide-eyed. Then, the new midwife shared a patient's story.

"You all, we're not supposed to talk about work. This is a party." Sylvia forced the midwife to take a swallow of beer. With good humor the midwife urged all to share in her punishment. This became a game—patient story, group sip.

Socializing and drinking was a Sunday afternoon tradition in Africa; the expats adapted effortlessly. Having grown up in Wisconsin where towns were marked with the presence of a bar, rather than a post office or church, Ann blended right in.

When the shadows of the eucalyptus and banana trees stretched across more than half the yard, Joseta shoved a tape into a tape deck attached to speakers. One by one, she encouraged the guests to dance. And dance they did. Adults with children. Men with men. Women with women. Men and women together. Ann danced with Innocent. They stomped, sweated, hooted, drank more beer, and ate more food. Laughter rang out, especially Innocent's deep chortle. No one held back on singing, but it seemed odd to croon along to top American hits in the middle of Africa.

Ann did not remember what time she left Joseta and Vincent's, or how she got home.

Chapter 4

The next morning Ann's head pounded, the sunlight burned her eyes and her mouth felt like she'd sucked on a hockey puck. She sat up, squinted, and pressed her fingers to her temples. It had been years since she'd nursed a hangover. She crept to the bathroom, guzzled a glass of water from her canteen and popped three aspirin. She recalled dancing with Father Innocent. Had she done anything that she should regret? She had vague memories of Sylvia, her roommate, helping her into bed. Ann prayed that she wasn't obnoxious.

The alcohol content was higher than she was used to. Vincent and Joseta kept passing out bottles; in the heat it tasted so refreshing. She should have refused, should have known better. But everyone was imbibing.

Sun poured into the bedroom window. Outside, the birds chirped and twittered, their calls unusually loud. A distant dog barked. Ann returned to her bed and checked the clock on the nightstand. Five minutes to dress, shower, and get to the hospital. She'd be late. Sylvia was already up and gone. In the bathroom, she dumped a bucket of water over her torso and soaped up, then rinsed with a second bucket, no time to fiddle with the shower. As she toweled off, she vaguely remembered agreeing to meet Father Innocent at the orphanage at the end of her hospital shift.

At five, Father Innocent's black pickup waited outside the emergency area. When he saw her, he waved and opened the passenger door. Ann slid in, wondering how to broach her behavior at Joseta's party.

He smelled of Old Spice. Squeezing her hand, he said, "Good to see you again, Dr. McLannly. How many patients did you heal today?"

Ann laughed. "I'm not sure about that, but we were busy. More and more injured patients."

They pulled out onto the main street. A parade of men in red and green shirts marched by yelling and shaking sticks and machetes. Some wore matching hats; others had trousers cut from the same cloth. They walked as if they owned the road. Innocent veered to miss them.

"Who are they?" Ann asked.

"The president's militia. The *interahamwe*."

They chanted, mimicking the announcer whose program was broadcast from loud speakers that hung on tall electric poles positioned along the street. Men and boys pumped their arms and shouted in Kinyarwanda.

"What are they saying?" Ann asked.

"Kill the Tutsi cockroaches, *inyenzi*."

"They sound so angry."

"It's RTLM, *Radio Télévision Libre de Milles Collines*, FM 106. They advertise on billboards around Kigali. People like their music. They talk politics."

They veered off the main drag and the chanting grew distant. "That doesn't look hopeful for the peace."

Innocent shook his head. "President Habyarimana has been good for the country. Rwanda is the Switzerland of Africa. I can't imagine that he'll share power with Paul Kagame and his Tutsi rebels. You heard the argument at the party. Vincent and I don't agree."

Ann wasn't ready to broach the party. She stared out the window.

A man shoved a bike fashioned from scraps of wood and an old bike tire up the hill. Two stems of green plantains, each almost as tall as the man, balanced on the handlebars and seat. He waved and smiled as they passed. Two women walked together. One carried on her head a burlap sack stuffed with grass, probably food for her cow or goats. The other hauled a yellow plastic jug, a gerry can, filled with sloshing liquid. A young child lay in the scarlet red shawl tied to her back.

Innocent stopped and honked in front of a bamboo gate with a blue and white sign the size of a license plate—Beauraing Orphanage. A Rwandan man with a toothy grin and a limp opened the gate. Innocent drove in. Purple, red, and orange bougainvillea climbed up the tall fence. The man chatted in Kinyarwanda and shook Innocent's hand, then Ann's. Innocent did not introduce her, but ushered her to the pink door. He knocked impatiently as he lifted his aviator-style sunglasses to the top of his head.

A dark-faced nun answered. All but her face and hands were hidden in the pleats and folds of her brown habit. "Father Innocent," she said. "You've brought a friend. The new doctor. Let me find the Mother Superior."

The fragrance of cooking onions and beans blanketed the stench of diapers. The laughter of children echoed from other rooms. Someone played an out-of-tune piano. A white-faced nun dressed in the same habit rushed up to Father Innocent, stood on her tiptoes and hugged him. He leaned down and kissed her on both cheeks. She looked fifty, but the prominent veins and thick joints of her hands suggested she was several decades older. "You must be Dr. Ann," the nun said. "Sister Mary Joseph." The nun shook Ann's hand firmly then kissed her cheeks, first the left and then the right. Sister Mary Joseph smelled of powder and the cloth of her headdress felt coarse against Ann's skin. "We are delighted that Father has brought you to us."

Father lowered his sunglasses and turned toward the door. "I have other obligations. I'll leave Dr. Ann in your hands."

Ann reminded Innocent of her curfew at eight.

A small girl ran up to Sister; folding herself into the dark skirt, she peeked out with a cautious smile.

Ann squatted down and said, *"Je m'appelle* Ann. What is your name?" She extended her hand toward the girl.

The girl covered her face and giggled. She grabbed hold of Sister's brown bead rosary and wound it around her small, dark wrist like a bracelet.

Ann asked the girl's name again.

The girl peered out. *"Je m'appelle* Michelle," she said and reached out to grab one of Ann's fingers. Ann twirled her forward and a laugh rippled from her small chest. It resembled the melodic call of one of the birds outside the compound window in the mornings. Dark blotches scarred the ebony skin of the girl's arms, legs, and face, remnants from some kind of rash, maybe chicken pox. She was thin, but not malnourished. A dozen pigtails fastened with red and blue rubber bands sprouted from her scalp.

"She has asthma, but she's doing better lately," Sister said.

Much to Ann's relief, the out-of-tune piano stopped, and other children streamed into the hallway flanked by two Rwandan nuns. Chatter and laughter soon overwhelmed the narrow space. The children ran up to touch Ann and reached for her hands, pulling on her skirt. Ann tried to steady herself.

"You have a way with children," Sister Mary Joseph said.

Ann wasn't so sure.

"Let me give you a tour," Sister continued and coughed, sounding like Ann's cat when she struggled with a hair ball.

The orphanage entryway opened into several rooms—a playroom, classroom, kitchen, dining room, and a dorm-style bedroom. The upright piano stood in the corner of the playroom. Children's drawings plastered two of the walls, which begged for fresh paint: black and brown stick figures with colorful skirts and shirts; pink hearts and orange suns. Most of the skies were white with blue clouds. One picture showed a gray cloud with rain drawn the size of sticks pelting a brown dog. Another picture showed a brown dog with a curling tail. Many of the drawings included some rendition of the dog. One depicted the dog with a broad smile displaying large fang-like teeth.

"You have a dog?" Ann asked.

Sister Mary Joseph frowned, clearing her throat again. "We did until one of the neighbors killed him. God bless us."

"I'm sorry," Ann said and she picked up Michelle, balancing her on her left hip. She was a little younger and lighter than Ann's niece Rosie. Michelle smelled of sweat and juice. She curled her fingers into Ann's hair and rested her head on Ann's shoulder. The joy of holding a child, a child who placed utter trust in her, triggered memories of Rosie, and Ann's other nieces and nephews. Between the two sisters, there were six, five without Rosie. Poor Rosie, now dead a half year, had been the youngest. A shiver convulsed Ann's shoulders. She inhaled to steady herself.

In the dormitory, at least two dozen cots lined the walls. Each sported a thin foam mattress. Above each one, mosquito netting hung from a hook in the ceiling and draped like a bride's veil. Relieved to see their compliance with the malaria prevention recommendations, Ann complimented Sister Mary Joseph.

"The pediatrician you're replacing was fastidious."

Michelle whispered into Ann's ear and wiggled down. She crawled under her bed and retrieved a cardboard box. Similar boxes were tucked beneath each bed. Michelle's box held the few belongings she claimed as her own—panties, two dresses, a long nightshirt, a sweater, a hairbrush. She dug beneath her clothes and pulled out a cloth bag, opened it, and retrieved a clear marble with a blue-green center. "*Je peux tenir le monde,*" she said and handed it to Ann.

"She says she has the world in her hand. I think she wants you to play with her. She'll keep you busy all evening," Sister Mary Joseph said. She asked one of the Rwandan nuns to entertain Michelle.

Ann returned the marble to Michelle.

As Sister led Ann to the medical room, she related Michelle's history. Michelle had arrived several months earlier, very thin, covered with scabies and open sores. "One of the market vendors brought her here in a wheelbarrow. We think her parents were killed. Or her father was killed and her mother couldn't support her, so she was abandoned at the market. God bless them. That's not uncommon. As you can see, she's very social, clearly has *joie de vivre*, the joy of life."

"Where'd she get the marbles?" Ann asked. The bag resembled one Ann had as a child.

"When the children arrive, they choose one toy from our trunk." Sister Mary Joseph said. Ann stood in front of a pantry off the kitchen. "Welcome to your office," Sister said. "My apologies, the space is quite small."

Built-in shelves, a straight-back chair, a file cabinet, and a bench wide enough for a small child to stretch out were crammed into the walk-in closet. The pediatrician had stocked the cabinet with band-aids, sutures, casting materials, ointments, and acetaminophen. He'd secured a nebulizer machine and a large box of salbuterol for asthma. An inventory list was tacked to one wall. Sister handed Ann a black binder with a page for every child, describing height and weight on admission and every month, a problem list, immunizations, and treatments received. The problems involved rashes and diarrhea; lots of doses of albendazole for worms, and lotion for scabies had been prescribed; some of the infants had cradle cap, dry skin caked on the scalp; more than half listed micronutrient deficiencies or malnutrition.

"Come. Bring the binder and we'll have tea." Sister led Ann through the kitchen and into her office that extended off the kitchen like a screened-in porch back home. A soft breeze ruffled the lace curtains. Ann settled into a straight-back wooden chair. Michelle scurried toward her and tried to crawl onto her lap. Several other children trailed behind.

"You have a shadow," Sister said and called the cook and her teenage helpers, asking them to redirect Michelle.

One of the teen helpers, dressed in a brown jumper cut from the same fabric as the nuns' habits, carried in a silver tray with a china tea service decorated with delicate pink roses and green leaves. Sister poured tea and offered Ann a cup and saucer.

"How lovely," Ann said, raising her teacup to inspect the design. Her mother had treasured a similar set and had given it to Ann's oldest sister.

"My grandmother's from Belgium," Sister Mary Joseph said. "These days it reminds me of better times." Sister Mary Joseph cleared her throat then sipped her tea. She described growing up in Namur, Belgium, studying at the convent, then joining the order, and accepting her assignment in Rwanda thirty-five years earlier. "Now, most of the nuns are Rwandan, but early on we all came from Europe. The Belgian nun who was here when Innocent arrived died last year. She was with the orphanage nearly forty years. God rest her soul."

"Father Innocent grew up here?" Ann had not realized that.

Sister Mary Joseph nodded. "He arrived as a young boy. When I came, he'd been here about a year."

That explained his commitment to the place and to the nuns.

"Fortunately, he still makes time for us. He's very busy with parish responsibilities. The bishop is grooming him for something important." The outside light was fading. Ann studied her watch as sister lit a kerosene lantern and set it between them on her desk. "We try to limit our use of electricity. We have a generator thanks to the pediatrician."

"He left big shoes to fill." Ann said. She set her cup in its saucer. "What do you expect of me?"

"Your predecessor came twice a week. That seemed adequate. It's best to have a routine. One of our nuns is a nurse. She can manage issues when you're not here." Sister took a sip of tea.

"Would I be on call?"

"Only in an emergency. Sometimes a new child might have problems that don't fit our protocols. Then we'd ask you to come in. Sister Francis Xavier, the nurse, treats all new admissions for parasites. If they have scabies, she takes care of that. We have a re-feeding protocol too."

Ann nodded. "What about lice?"

"Children don't get that here. Something about African hair is unfriendly."

Ann didn't know that. She asked where the children came from.

"As you know, there's been unrest between the Rwandan government and the RPF, the Rwandan Patriotic Front rebels. Despite the Accord, fights break out between the two groups all the time. People are killed." Sister shook her head. "For senseless reasons. Children are orphaned, or the remaining parent can't care for the children."

"What about extended families?"

"Of course, that's our first choice. But with the unrest many people have left Rwanda." Sister's voice grew hoarse, she paused for a swallow of tea. "Tell me about yourself."

Ann wondered where to start. The glow around the kerosene lantern seemed to grow brighter. Should she give the cliff notes version? Sister had a mother confessor quality. Before Ann knew it, the details about Rosie's drowning spilled out. Then she talked about her mother's battle with pancreatic cancer diagnosed just before Rosie's death. Sister listened quietly, watching Ann's face.

"Mother couldn't give up," Ann said. "She wanted chemo, although it was hopeless. She was so weak. She wouldn't accept hospice. My dad egged her on. Both hoped for the impossible, didn't hear, couldn't hear, about the slim chance of a cure. He couldn't take care of her by himself. My sisters have their own families, so I moved to the farm, their home. We had to carry her to the bathroom until she finally accepted a bedside commode. She refused a bedpan... She was angry until the end. He was too. A bitter end." Ann heaved a sigh. Her chest felt lighter. She had not talked about this.

Sister poured herself another cup of tea and freshened Ann's. "How kind of you to give up your work to take care of your mother." Sister encouraged Ann to continue.

"The funeral was a relief. Shortly after that I started the process for coming here. I had to leave. I probably should have stayed longer for my dad, but I just couldn't. . . I was so frustrated with him. Angry, really. Angry that he couldn't help her let go." She lamented. "I should call and check on him."

"Your sisters live there."

Ann nodded, then sipped her tea. It was cool. Sister was easy to talk to.

"God bless you. All that on top of the guilt about your niece. I can see why you wanted to leave." Sister patted Ann's hand. "God bless you, *mon amie*. I hope your time here gives you some peace."

Ann felt as if a burden had been shed; she'd dipped into the simmering emotions, but only for a moment. She glanced at her watch. "I should check the children." She stood up.

They walked through the orphanage and sister introduced Ann to each child. Ann glanced at the page in the notebook and wrote a few notes. The children were well cared for and happy. When she was done, she had a list of items to get from King Faisal, including amoxicillin.

Ann stared at her watch. It was quarter to eight. The ride home would take about fifteen minutes. She would be late. The director would ream her; he was a stickler about curfew. Near the equator it grew dark at six, almost exactly twelve hours of light and twelve hours of darkness. Given the unrest, the GH director prohibited the volunteers from walking outside after dark. Ann considered calling the GH vehicle to pick her up.

"Father will come," Sister said. "He always follows through, although as you can imagine, many things compete for his attention. God bless him. Time and punctuality are different here. Different from the US or Europe. Unforeseen circumstances arise."

Ann was learning to let go of her expectations about promptness. Everything started twenty or thirty minutes, even an hour later than the stated time. It was hard and at the same time liberating.

Father Innocent arrived at 8:15 and did not apologize for his tardiness. Sister pressed a small box into Ann's hand as she left. Ann climbed into the pickup, considering how to approach her behavior at the party.

The street lamps cast halos of light on the main road, which was filled with potholes. The government's money for road repair was long gone. No sidewalk paralleled the street in most places; instead, chunks of crumbled cement or mounds of eroding dirt served as the shoulder. A few men pedaled bikes with flashlights tied to the handlebars. One man wheeled his bike, a bulky burlap bag wedged between the front frame and the bike seat. No women walked the streets; it was good that Ann had waited. The men dressed in colorful shirts still milled around, but there were of more them. Several carried machetes. Others wielded mallets or clubs, which they waved above their heads as they shouted. In the darkness they crowded around fires burning in the gutter or inside a metal barrel. Burning plastic and rubber smells filled the air. The angry rant still blasted from speakers affixed high on the electric poles. It grew especially obnoxious near the round-about that headed toward the hospital. Some men wobbled as if inebriated.

Ann opened Sister's package—two Belgian chocolates. She'd share the treat with Sylvia. Despite her reticence, Ann sucked in a breath and took the plunge. "I need to apologize for my behavior . . ."

The vehicle veered around a pothole and Ann collided toward Innocent. She regained her balance. Had Innocent heard her? He said nothing.

In three blocks Innocent pulled to the curb outside the GH compound. The motor idled. He twisted toward her. "I don't want to hear your confession." He reached for her chin and pulled her face toward his, planting a kiss on her lips.

His lips were soft, his breath warm. There was the faint smell of cologne. Ann's heart raced.

"I'm continuing what you started," he said and kissed her again, this time a little tongue. Then, he lifted a stray strand of hair and tucked it behind her left ear, fingering the small gold hoop.

The streetlight illuminated the lower part of his face, revealing a half smile. His sunglasses still sat on the top of his head. Moisture dampened Ann's armpits. An awkward silence hung between them. Ann sputtered. "I liked the nuns, especially Sister Mary Joseph. Caring for the children will be fun."

Innocent touched a finger to her lips. "Dr. Ann, it is more than fun. You will be doing God's work. The nuns are good women."

"They, they told me you grew up there." She attempted to scoot toward the door, her hand reaching for the handle. Instead, she felt the edge of the cool, plastic seat. "Thanks for asking me. I should go. . . my curfew."

"Not so fast," Innocent said and pulled her in. He traced her wrist and wristwatch with his forefinger. His finger pad felt warm and soft. The half smile again. "You learned why I am fond of them, especially Sister Mary Joseph. Meeting you has been an answer to my prayers." He held onto her shoulder, still stroking the side of her face with his hand. "At the party you were endearing. A good dancer." He reached toward her hair once more. "I love your hair. Red is so unusual here."

Ann sat rigid, but relaxed the shoulder he touched. Why was she fighting his affection? She was attracted to him. It was possible to be attracted to a priest. But he was a priest. He had vows. At the party he'd told her he once had a girlfriend in Chicago.

She loosened the other shoulder, checking out what it felt like to accept his advances. She sank into the seat as he kissed her again. His lips were soft, his tongue moist, hungry. She loved kissing. But she did need to apologize. She pulled back and said, "I hope I wasn't obnoxious at the party. . . didn't do anything inappropriate. I am. . . I'm embarrassed to say I can't remember much." Finally, it was out.

He chuckled. "That's very African. Sunday afternoons and evenings are usually committed to drinking. You are doing as the Africans do. You fit right in."

Ann glanced at her watch. "I really need to go. It's way past curfew."

He squeezed her shoulder and let go.

Ann slipped out of the vehicle. The street lamp at the curb winked off. The electricity in their *secteur* was shut off for the evening. She sprinted through the compound gate, preparing her excuse for the GH director. She couldn't say she was kissing a local priest.

The director did not hear her enter the compound. Ann slowed her heaving chest as she crept up the stairs to her bedroom.

Sylvia sat on her bed with her headlamp spotlighting her toenails as she struggled to coat each one with maroon polish; the girth of the abdomen made it a challenge. A chemical odor filled the room. Sylvia's beam blinded Ann. "You're late, hon. Where've you been? I was worried." Sylvia adjusted her lamp to light the wall behind Ann.

"Did the Nose notice?" The GH director had a bulbous nose that resembled Andy Rooney's. Ann and Sylvia secretly referred to him by that appendage.

Sylvia nodded. "I told him you were in the bathroom. He says he needs to talk with you about your long showers."

Ann chuckled. "Thanks. As if you can shower with that worthless dribble." She sat on the edge of her bed. "I agreed to take care of the children at an orphanage that's not far from the hospital—Beauraing. Tonight was my first visit. My ride was late." Ann kicked off her shoes and then plopped across her bed. "I'm exhausted." She pressed her headlamp. It spotlighted the dust bunnies gathered under Sylvia's mattress, just beyond the braided throw rug.

Sylvia examined her fingernails, then replaced the brush and screwed the cap tight. She extended her fingers, waving them sideways and focused her gaze on Ann. "I need to talk with you." Sylvia's tone grew parental. She blew on her nails. "You overdid it at the party. Too much beer. The alcohol content is higher than we're all used to in the US."

"I know." Ann shook her head and studied Sylvia. "Tell me, did I do anything stupid? I honestly can't remember." She dropped her eyes toward the floor.

With some effort Sylvia swung her feet over the side of her bed, careful not to muss her nails, and scooted toward Ann. "What you did was foolish. I hope you learn from it. You may think you can relax and let go because that's what all the locals do. But in a foreign country, it's downright dangerous. People can take advantage of you. Situations change on a dime. If you can't limit your liquor, then don't drink. Do you hear me?"

Ann's face flushed. The room grew oppressively hot. Sylvia was the instigator of the stupid drinking game, should Ann mention that? She fingered the hem of her sheet and examined the stitching. Then she scrutinized the edge of the throw rug. She knew better. She didn't want to admit it, but Sylvia was right. Ann had had trouble with binge drinking in the past. She swallowed and looked up. "You're right. I was stupid," she murmured, "I'm sorry. Really, I'm sorry."

Sylvia continued to study her. "No need to apologize to me, hon. Just learn from it. You didn't do anything awful. I was your guardian angel. I kept my eye on you."

"What did I do?" Ann asked.

Sylvia widened her eyes. "You're a good dancer. The priest liked dancing with you."

"He told me that tonight."

"You danced with Colonel and the man with the baseball cap. His wife didn't like that."

Ann groaned.

"She cut in before the middle of the song." Sylvia held up her fingers as if counting Ann's sins.

"Don't tell me there's more."

Sylvia smirked and lifted another finger. "You kissed Colonel and the priest when you left. You hung on a little too long, so I dragged you away."

Ann rolled onto her back and ground her fists into her forehead. "Anything else?"

"Well, since you asked." Sylvia paused, her voice grew softer. "You threw up when you got home. Cleaning it up was no fun." She shook her head with a smirk. "And you snored like a pig."

"Oh, I am so sorry" Ann covered her face with her palms. "Never again. I promise."

"Just learn from it, hon," Sylvia said and resettled herself into the middle of her bed. She checked her nails with her headlamp. Appearing to be satisfied, she lifted her crossword book from her side table and paged through it.

Ann located her backpack and directed her headlamp inside. She retrieved the chocolates. "I have a peace offering." She carried the tiny box over to Sylvia. "Take one. They're Belgian. From the Mother Superior at the orphanage. A token of my gratitude."

Sylvia took one, opened the foil, and popped the candy into her mouth. "Merci."

Ann undressed. Her slacks and blouse smelled sour, so she tossed them in the laundry basket. She wrapped her cotton robe around her and went into the bathroom to shower, or rather, make the most of what dripped out of the spigot.

It was too hot to cover herself with the sheet. If they had electricity, the fan would push the hot air around. Often it felt no better than a panting dog.

Outside, insects peeped; one piped some treble note off and on in a rhythmic manner. Some night bird whooped. A small breeze fluttered the green curtains across from the foot of her bed.

"Want to play French Scrabble?" Sylvia asked. "I need a new puzzle book."

"Rain check," Ann said. "My brain is full and I don't want to play by flashlight."

"No prob. Sweet dreams, hon."

Ann pretended to be asleep. Instead she contemplated her history with alcohol. During college she'd partied, but when her grades suffered, she quit drinking altogether. She graduated from college with a 3.8. In medical school she abstained until after exams. Those nights Ann binged as did many of her classmates. Often her friends guided her home and tucked her in bed.

The man that she dated off and on, her boyfriend, although she'd always hated the term, was not a drinker. She'd met him after she started working at the community clinic on the south side of Milwaukee. None of their activities involved alcohol. He was a pleasant companion, someone to do things with, not into commitment, but he liked music as much as she. He did not have a college degree and her mother hated him for that.

One Friday night in August, after the death of Rosie and before she moved to the farm to help care for her mother, Ann guzzled a bottle of chardonnay alone in her condo. When she didn't answer her phone by midnight, her boyfriend called Ann's sister, the teetotaler who owned a bar and burger restaurant. The two of them went to check on Ann. They found her asleep on the couch, the embroidered silk pillow coated with vomit. She remembered little of the incident, except her sister's rage. "You're like me. Moderation is impossible. Quit drinking. You could have aspirated and died. You're a doctor, for Pete's sake. You know better. Dad would be dealing with your death, Rosie's death, and mom's cancer. Don't be so damned selfish." Later that week, Ann had started attending Alcoholics Anonymous. Maybe Sylvia was right.

Chapter 5

Ann stood in the back of the church with Joseta, waiting to talk with Father Innocent. The parishioners surrounded him, some patiently waiting their turn, others cutting in and vying for his attention. Innocent held court, standing tall and regal in his white vestments with a large red cross trimmed in gold. Overhead fans swirled around the warm air and the lingering incense and candle wax. St. Michael was one of the larger Catholic congregations located in Ann and Joseta's *secteur*. Most Rwandans, and Tutsis in particular, were Catholic. The red-brick structure stood on the corner not far from Joseta's and two blocks from the orphanage.

Father smiled, shook hands, laughed, and patted children on their heads. Clearly his parishioners loved him. When it was their turn, he leaned forward and kissed Joseta on both her cheeks. She thanked him for coming to the party. "I see you convinced the doctor to come with you," he said and shook Ann's hand, all business, no hint at what had transpired in his truck earlier that week.

Joseta nodded. "She's a good singer. I'm praying she'll be my regular Sunday mass companion. Vincent's not much of a churchgoer."

"You tell him he's always welcome. I'd be honored to have him join our flock."

"I need to get home to make him lunch."

Innocent and Ann talked a little longer. He maintained an appropriate demeanor and distance as she told him about a baby she'd delivered with spina bifida, a hole at the base of the spine. "Joseta took the child and wrapped it in a blanket. That was it. No resuscitation."

"Well, Doctor. That's how things are done here. It is different than in the US."

Ann nodded. "It takes some getting used to."

"When I studied in Chicago, I helped a family come to terms with the death of their father. A very sick man, hooked up to many machines. It was his time, but his children would not let him die."

"I call that death with a tube in every orifice," Ann said.

Innocent chuckled. "Orifice. I don't know that word."

"Hole. Mouth. Nose. Anus."

"I like that. It is, I think you say, crass, but true. A tube in every orifice."

Ann nodded and thought of her mother, her thin body surrounded with pumps and monitors. She, too, had tubes everywhere.

"We should talk more. I need to visit the sick, take them Communion. But I will be at the parsonage this afternoon. I'm there most Sunday afternoons. The view from my veranda is lovely. . . and private." He raised his right eyebrow.

Ann studied his face. He walked in both worlds, Rwanda and the US. But did she want to be romantically involved, surely he was hinting.

"It might help you work through some of the ethical dilemmas, help you adjust to the different ways of approaching things and we could. . . get to know each other." He smiled.

"That might be nice. I promised the orphanage that I'd check on a patient who had an asthma attack. Also a set of twins who just arrived. Maybe next Sunday." Ann had made commitments and she needed a little more time to decide how far she wanted this friendship to go.

"Next week it is." Innocent gave her a firm handshake, cordial, but professional.

The walk to the orphanage passed through a middle-class neighborhood. Sun-baked, mud-brick walls rested on squares of poured concrete. Each house had a small yard filled with brightly colored flowers, a fruit tree or two and a tiny garden patch. The plots were packed neighbor to neighbor, like a checkerboard. Wealthier families screened their windows and added a layer of plaster to the mud-brick, which they trimmed with colors as brilliant as the local birds—bee-eaters, trogons, and turacos. Poorer families could not afford window screens, but their doors and shutters were painted in gaudy, vivid shades.

The man with the limp and toothy smile greeted Ann at the bamboo gate. "I am 99. Who is you?" He stuck out his hand. "You come last week with priest."

Ann introduced herself and talked about caring for the children.

"That is good. They need good doctor." He accompanied her to the pink door and knocked.

Inside young voices sang *Frère Jacques* in rounds as one of the Rwandan nuns played the oak upright in the corner of the playroom. The piano had been tuned. The nun's fingers flew across the white and black keys. Another nun directed the children who sang, wholeheartedly, although off-key. *Frère Jacques* ended with a flourish and the nun switched to *Row, Row Your Boat*. Suddenly 99 stood next to Ann. He belted out the words, but sang horribly off-pitch.

"You tuned the piano," Ann said and asked if she could play. The melody of Chuck Mangione's song, *The Children of Sanchez*, flowed from her fingers. It was her current favorite. The high energy beginning was upbeat. *Da Da Da. Da Da Da...* Energy stirred in her chest and rushed into her arms and hands.

Ann played by ear. She could hear a tune and her fingers would begin to play the chords. She could also move her fingers on any surface—a table, her bed, her leg—and the melody and chords sounded in stereo inside her head.

The children jumped up and down and clapped at the end of the song. The Rwandan nun who had been playing asked Ann to teach her the song. One of the girls squeezed on the bench next to Ann and watched.

When Ann was finished, she checked on Michelle, who sat on her bed finishing a nebulizer treatment. Green snot dripped from Michelle's nose as Ann pressed her stethoscope against the girl's small chest—scattered wheezes. She'd need prednisone to treat the swelling in her airways and an antibiotic in case she had a bacterial infection.

Michelle showed Ann the book *Snow White and the Seven Dwarfs*. "*Muzungu*," Michelle said pointing to Snow White and then at Ann. She pointed to the dwarfs. "*Twa. Sept Twa, Indwi Twa*," Michelle said.

Ann scrunched up her forehead. "What's she saying? Seven what?"

Sister Mary Joseph walked into the dormitory. "She thinks the dwarfs are Twa, pygmies, people who live in the jungle," Sister said. "*Indwi* is seven."

Ann laughed. The girl knew a lot of English words. Ann's vocabulary was expanding too.

Sister insisted that she have tea in her office before checking the rest of the children. Ann pushed aside her hasty, check-things-off-the-list tendency and settled into the wooden chair. The room was warm, the lace curtains hung perfectly still.

"I see you've met 99," Sister said, fanning herself with a manila folder.

Ann nodded and sipped her tea.

"99 takes care of us." Sister set down the folder and lifted her teacup to her lips.

"I have a sister who's special. Her name is Irene. She's three years older than I. She has Down Syndrome."

"Ah, then you know the value of those who move a little slower. Nearly perfect human beings, unconditional love without judgment." Sister leaned back in her chair. "I have a wonderful 99 story. Someone taught him *incy wincy spider*. You know that song?" Sister pressed her thumb and pointer fingers together and moved them. "He loves the finger movements. Taught the children. They lined up outside under the roof when it was raining. Sang it in his broken English: '*down come rain and wash spider out. . .*' The laughter. They were soaked." Sister chuckled.

"I'll have to ask him." Ann's heart grew lighter. The activities at the orphanage provided a respite from her hospital patients, the different approaches to clinical care, something other than injuries. She was growing quite fond of Sister.

Chapter 6

S crubbed and gowned, her hair lassoed under a surgical cap, Ann painted the woman's pregnant belly with brown soap while she waited for Colonel. The sharp smell of betadine filled her nose. The clang of metal thudded against a sterile towel as Sylvia prepared instruments on a tray. Her eyes smiled at Ann above her blue surgical mask; Ann had entered Sylvia's domain.

Colonel entered the room. "This is yours," he said. "You need to know how to perform sections. Someday, you'll be working in some hospital where there is no surgeon. You'll save two lives."

Excitement rippled through Ann as she moved to the surgeon's place at the table and stepped up on a stool Sylvia brought her. At home, family doctors weren't allowed to perform C-sections, a combination of politics and turf on the part of the obstetricians. If only Drs. D'Ascoli and O'Brien could see her now. To date she'd assisted Colonel with five Caesarians.

"Inject the Ketamine," she said to the nurse anesthetist. The clock started.

Ketamine was cheap and did not suppress respirations. It could be injected into a muscle or given intravenously. It was the drug of choice in situations like this, although on occasion it caused hallucinations.

"Give yourself room. Sternum to pubic bone," Colonel said.

Ann's hands sweated inside her gloves. She sliced across the woman's taut belly, cutting to the outside of the navel, then she separated the skin. Colonel inserted the retractors. Ann lifted the omentum, the protective apron that lay over all the abdominal organs, and pushed the bowel away from the uterus.

"Remember, lots of room," Colonel said again. "You don't know what you'll find."

When a C-section was not an emergency, an incision was cut through the lower third of the uterus, a bikini cut, which preserved the uterine muscle and allowed for vaginal deliveries later. In an emergency, the slice was top to bottom.

The woman had arrived in the ED an hour earlier via tipoy—a bush ambulance. Two men carried the patient, who lay on a grass mat suspended between two bamboo poles. A larger patient required four people, one at each corner. They had trekked ten hours from a community in southern Rwanda. When they reached the outskirts of the city, a pickup truck gave them a lift. After laboring two days, the local birth attendant sent them on to the district hospital. Without a surgeon in attendance, they'd embarked on the trip to the big city.

"Remember to protect the infant. Use your other hand," Colonel directed.

The uterine muscle stretched thin, but strong. Ann inserted her left hand and cut with her right, cautious not to nick herself. The infant stared up at them, one leg extending through the cervix, the other folded underneath as if he were performing the tree pose in yoga. Ann pried the infant out, wiggling the leg free from the firm grasp of the swollen cervix.

"Suction, then cut the cord," Colonel said.

Ann squeezed the blue bulb suction into the infant's nose and mouth, then placed two clamps on the thick, pulsing cord and sliced in between with her scalpel. She sniffed back her tears.

"A little emotional?" Sylvia said.

A squirt of urine caught Ann's sleeve and dampened the front of Sylvia's gown.

"Nice timing," Sylvia chuckled and carried the boy to the ancient isolette, recycled from some first-world hospital decades earlier.

Colonel talked her through the steps as she removed the placenta, wiped the inside of the uterus and began to sew the uterus back together with absorbable suture. He complemented her as she completed each task. Sylvia anticipated her needs, slapping the necessary instrument into her palm.

"Now ligate her tubes," Colonel directed.

A tightness strapped Ann's chest. "Is that legal?" she asked. "We didn't ask her permission."

"Look, the infant lived. This is her fifth child. They've got their boy. With the section the wall of her uterus is weakened. If she's pregnant again and has a vaginal delivery, she could rupture. Then, her five children will lose their mother. You're doing her a favor. Besides Dr. McLannly, you need to learn."

Ann paused, should she refuse to do it? He wouldn't take no for an answer, she'd have to feign the need to pee or something.

"Time is wasting," Colonel said.

Maybe he was right. The rules were different here. Ann recouped her composure with an inhale. She focused on the field, tugged at the uterus as Colonel helped her identify the fallopian tubes, cut them, and buried each one into the uterine wall.

"Now close the fascia. Use silk. It's stronger than cat gut." Ann's forearms ached as she yanked the tough, fibrous layer. Across the room, the infant whimpered as staff cleaned and swaddled him. "Do your sponge and instrument count and close her up," Colonel said. "Well done! Excellent technique, Dr. McLannly."

He stepped back from the table and tore off his gown and gloves. Before he left the room he called. "By the way, I'm glad you recovered from Joseta's party."

Heat rushed into Ann's face. "I, I think I owe you an apology."

"Not necessary," Colonel said. "We work hard. We play hard." He walked out of the room.

As Ann sewed, the heat from the overhead light beamed down. Sweat moistened her armpits and trickled between her shoulder blades and she tried to zip up the worry about what she'd just done.

"Nice job," Sylvia said as Ann finished. "You have good hands. Compliments from Colonel are rare."

That evening Ann telephoned her dad. It was their first call since she'd arrived six weeks earlier. She'd sent off short emails. It was high time that she called. It had taken her a while to work up the courage. She'd bent over backwards to care for her mother. Neither her dad nor her sisters had acknowledged her efforts or her own feelings related to Rosie. Everyone rightly focused on poor Coleen, Rosie's mom.

"Annie, it's you?" His voice quivered.

"Do you have snow?"

"I can see grass," he said. "It's the first time all winter."

"It's hot here. Hot and dry. Still the dry season."

"Tell me about your patients."

"I did my first C-section."

Her father reminisced about the section he'd done on a cow shortly after vet school. The farmer and his wife had helped him because his vet assistant was ill.

"How are you doing, Dad?"

"Your sisters check on me. Little Irene stays some weekends. Last Saturday, she bowled 200, won the tournament. She was so proud. I think she writes you a letter ever few days." He always referred to her sister with Down syndrome as little Irene. Irene is short, but her body habits resemble Sylvia's. Irene is three years older than Ann. They had grown up together.

Ann's father chattered on. He seemed happy to talk. But when Ann's housemate, the teacher, checked on Ann for a third time and asked to use the phone, Ann said, "I have to go, Dad. I'll call you again soon. Next time it won't take me so long."

"I appreciate the emails too. I love you Annie."

Ann couldn't say it. The events were too fresh, and aggravated her like a splinter.

In her bedroom, she stared up at the mosquito netting. It swayed in the breeze that ruffled the green drapes. Finally she'd called her dad. She needed to make peace with all that had happened during the final months of her mother's illness. It was time to let go of her grudge. He and her mother had been married longer than Vincent and Joseta. Of course, it had been hard for Ann's father to let his wife die. Of course, he sympathized with his daughter who'd lost a child whose heart was also fractured.

Sylvia waddled in carrying a steaming mug of tea.

"Are you just getting home?"

"Long day," Sylvia sighed and pulled off her clothes. She slipped a loose cotton nightgown over her head and climbed onto her bed, lifting the tea to her lips. She blew. "Colonel talked about you after you left. 'She has the hands of a surgeon.'"

"It must be my piano playing."

Sylvia sipped her tea, then smoothed her new crossword puzzle book open.

"Does Colonel usually tie the women's tubes?" Ann had been mulling this over. It wasn't a topic to bring up to her father, a traditional Catholic; he certainly would have had an opinion. He and Ann's mother had gone on to have another child after Irene. That child was Ann.

"He has his ways," Sylvia said, looking up from her book. "I don't ask questions, but he seems to have some process for deciding."

At 8:00 p.m., the nuns on the corner began to sing their nightly vespers. They harmonized with perfect pitch, except for one scratchy alto. Their brick convent stood between the GH compound and the grade school on the corner. Ann passed the complex on the way to the hospital. During her first month, when the government had money and school was in session, the boys and girls, dressed in navy-blue uniforms, lined up on the playground upon arrival and at dismissal. Although school was discontinued, the nuns' voices still bloomed each evening. Ann found the routine reassuring.

She stared at a fly buzzing the mesh mosquito netting. An unsettled feeling sat in her chest as she studied the weave of the nylon net and listened to melodies. She wasn't much for analyzing things, but something she couldn't quite articulate caught inside her ribs like an incomplete breath.

Chapter 7

In the midst of the chatty parishioners and the lingering scent of incense and candle wax, Ann caught Innocent's attention. "This afternoon?"

Standing tall and regal, he nodded his head and winked. It had become their Sunday afternoon routine. Ann accompanied Joseta to eleven o'clock mass, then had lunch with Joseta and Vincent. Afterwards, she returned to the church and visited with Innocent in the parsonage. She treasured the talks, the comradery, her chance to check out impressions about Rwandan custom. They always spent a little time kissing, but she'd resisted more, despite his pressure. He was a priest after all, and her Catholic upbringing haunted her.

On that late-March Sunday, three men observed the street from the corner of the church yard. They talked and smoked, their machetes and sticks lay at their feet. Four more women conversed near the entrance, two with children fastened to their backs with colorful shawls. They stood just beneath the bell tower and the Jesus statue that watched over the church property from the front door. Usually the church was vacant at this time of the day; families gathered at home sharing food and drink. Sunday was a day of rest, time with family.

Curious about the activity. Ann stood at a side entrance and glanced inside. The aroma of perspiration hid any remnants of incense. Blankets and mats were piled between the benches and chairs. A woman nursed her infant, her back propped against the brick wall. Next to her, a toddler with a thick blue crayon gripped in her small hand drew pictures on a sheet of newspaper. A group of children played jacks on the tile floor near the altar. In another corner, a cluster of women sewed. Despite the children's chatter, the mood felt somber—no music, little laughter, no tolling bell. The parishioners seemed settled in for the afternoon, but why? What was happening? It didn't appear to be a service.

Everyone stared at Ann. A girl in a purple dress stood up, pointed and cried, "*Muzungu*."

Ann backed out. Damn her white skin. She hurried across the yard, knocked on the bright green parsonage door, trying to slow her breath.

Father Innocent answered. "Dr. Ann, did you run here?"

"What's going on?" Ann panted.

"Come in, come in."

His house smelled of cooked meat and the sweet, slightly burnt odor of roasted cassava.

"Things seem to be getting worse. We've had more injuries at the hospital. Why are folks hanging out at the church?" Ann asked.

Father Innocent shut the door. "My parishioners are nervous," he said. "This week, on the bishop's urging, I opened the church in the evenings. Parishioners come when it gets dark, spend the night, then go about their business at dawn. They've gathered earlier than usual today. If they feel safer in God's house, so be it. Come, let's make some tea."

"Maybe I shouldn't be here," Ann said. She still stood near the door.

"Relax, Dr. Ann. I have no obligations." He took her hand and led her into the kitchen.

His maid had left for the day. A wooden table with two straight-back chairs stood against one wall. A sprig of salmon bougainvillea filled a vase. Most Rwandans cooked on outdoor stoves, but thanks to the wealth of the archbishop, Innocent had an indoor stove, connected to a propane tank on the other side of the window. The fridge hummed. Innocent heated water. When the tea was ready, Ann followed him out to the veranda.

The view looked out on a pasture where a small herd of cows grazed. Beyond, a patchwork quilt of tilled fields climbed up the distant hillside. The moo of the cows was periodically punctuated by voices from the church, which stood ten meters to the right, but was not visible from where they sat.

Ann tried to push the activities next door from her mind as she blew on her tea. But the increasing unrest and the frequent street demonstrations were hard to ignore. She'd taken a side street to avoid the red and green-shirted men on one block. Innocent's perspective was different from Sylvia and her other expat colleagues, different from Joseta. They started with the weekly check in.

"I've been busy. Very busy," Innocent said. "Funerals, visits to the elderly, meetings at the diocese. The bishop says the current unrest is an opportunity to support the public experience of fear and uncertainty. We must buttress each other during these troubled times. That's why he asked us to open the churches.

Our Savior's death and resurrection teaches us that we are not alone. God is with us."

How typical of Innocent to respond to the needs of the parish. Ann sipped her tea, watching a cow nudge her calf to nurse in the middle of the field. "I've been mulling over an ethical issue for the past month," she started

Innocent smiled and nodded.

By now, Ann had done several C-sections with Colonel and he had instructed her to tie the tubes of every woman except one. That one was younger, delivering her second child. The procedure was never discussed with the patients. Arguing about the importance of permission hadn't worked, and since she was in the role of student it had seemed ungrateful to leave the operating room, but she wasn't comfortable with what they were doing.

"Tied tubes. What do you mean?"

"Sterilized. I've done if four times."

"Now you speak my language. Was her life at risk?"

"It's more complicated than that. It's a pattern. I'm not sure it's right."

"You violated the pope's teaching on birth control."

Ann set down her tea and folded her arms. "I know that, but put that aside. I want your opinion, not the church's teaching. Is it wrong to do it without asking permission in Rwanda? In Africa." She studied Innocent.

He looked at her and chuckled. "Africa is a continent with great diversity. In some cultures if a woman can't bear children, she's inadequate. It would be a reason for her husband to take another wife."

Ann rolled her eyes. "I don't think any of them were Muslim, if that's what you're suggesting. Colonel's point was that the women already had enough mouths to feed, and if they became pregnant again and had a vaginal delivery after the C-sections their wombs could rupture. The reality of that is pretty small." Ann reached for her tea and took a swallow. "At home we get written consent. In fact, a patient on public insurance has to sign a consent at least thirty days before the procedure is done. We worry about coercion. The not asking permission, it seems . . ." She searched for the word.

"Colonial?"

"Paternalistic." Ann had a hard time saying the word. The thought that she, someone for whom women's control over their own bodies was paramount, had been complicit embarrassed her. The realization harangued her like a jagged splinter. Why hadn't she seen it so clearly before.

But Innocent was off on another track. "White-skinned people have come to this region and told us what to do for decades. No one asked permission. Not the Germans. Not the Belgians." Innocent grew strident.

"Well, Colonel's not white."

"But his skin tones are lighter," Innocent said.

Joseta had told Ann that part of the historical Tutsi dominance over the Hutu was related to lighter skin shades. The Belgians had appointed the light-skinned Tutsis as their successors.

"He is a surgeon," Ann said.

Innocent nodded. "Unlike China, or Bangladesh, where he's from, we've not limited family size. It's against Catholic teaching."

"The Colonel's right, if you can't control fertility, you can't get out of poverty. But you agree, in Rwanda I shouldn't sterilize women without their permission."

Innocent gestured toward their view. "As you can see, we have an overpopulation problem. Just look at the hills. They are terraced to the top. Every possible inch of Rwanda is planted."

"Maybe the Colonel has his own campaign."

"Well, the bishop won't hear of it. You've seen the families on Sunday—five, six, seven children. But the tension around not having enough land to feed the population is growing. It's a big problem and adds to the current strife."

Ann mulled that over. "The Hutu were farmers and the Tutsis cow herders, nomads?"

Innocent shrugged. "Not really nomadic, more shepherds for their cows. The Tutsi monarchs took over the Hutus' land. The tension is longstanding. Population density has been a problem for a while. Did Vincent tell you about his battles with cows when he was a tracker for Miss Fossey?"

Ann shook her head. She'd slowly worked her way through Fossey's *Gorillas in the Mist*. She hoped to visit the gorillas before she left Rwanda. Reportedly you could show up at the National Park in northwestern Rwanda and purchase a ticket.

"The cows encroached on gorilla territory."

"I know cows got caught in the traps set for gorilla poachers," Ann said. "Once she painted a cow before releasing it and sending it home. People thought she was some kind of white witch."

"That was nearly twenty years ago. The population problem has only gotten worse."

Ann rested her head on the back of her chair. As always, Innocent had given her a lot to think about. Part of the political tension was about limited resources. Colonel had his own campaign against that—sterilize every woman who already had lots of children. It made theoretical sense, but smarted with isms—paternalism and colonialism. Ann needed to approach it differently.

A bird called from his perch in the acacia tree in the middle of the pasture. During the sun's zenith, the cows sought shelter in its shade. Now long, purple shadows reached across the grass. A man with a staff came out to round up his herd.

Ann's tea had grown cold. "I should go home. The Nose wants us home for Sunday dinner. We have a weekly meeting."

Innocent reached for her hand. "I like having you here. He stood up and pulled her to her feet, placing his hands on her shoulders. He leaned down and kissed her on the lips.

Ann pressed against his chest with her hands. "Not here. You have a church full of parishioners next door."

He touched her hair, running his fingers through it. "Well, let's go inside." He led her into his study, a small room furnished with a wooden desk, three straight-back chairs, and a bookcase. A high, rectangular window faced the pasture.

Innocent sat down in one of the chairs. "Come here," he said, pulling Ann onto his lap, he pressed his lips against hers as he stroked her hair.

Ann shoved away thoughts about what she was doing. He was a good kisser. Before she'd started these Sunday afternoon visits with Innocent, it had been eight months since she'd made out. She'd broken up with her boyfriend when she started caring for her mother, too busy to give him any time.

She lifted her hand to Innocent's shoulders. His firm deltoids filled her hands. She inhaled cologne, a hint of incense, and the faint tang of sweat.

Innocent's hands moved to her blouse and undid a button. His fingers walked along her sternum and the ribs above her breasts. His lips were soft and hungry, moving from her mouth to her chin and the hollow of her collar bone. Ann trembled. Her thighs prickled.

"You like this, Dr. Ann. I think you want more," Innocent whispered. He reached to her back under her blouse and deftly unsnapped her bra. He cupped her breasts with his hands.

Ann felt his groin rise against her leg. She sighed and tilted her head back as his moist tongue moved to the top of her left breast. She massaged his neck and upper back. She was losing herself; she needed to hold the line. They were going farther than they usually did. She needed to keep the boundary, but what was it?

Rap, rap, rap. A knock rattled the parsonage door.

Ann arched her spine. The air in the room grew cool.

"I can ignore it," Innocent said. His fingers thumbed her nipples, the cream-colored lace of her bra draped over his dark hands.

The knocking intensified to a constant pounding.

Ann recoiled. "Innocent. I think you need to answer the door. They know you're in here."

Innocent exhaled. "Ignore them. I'd rather do this." He mouthed her nipple. His lips were soft and warm, his tongue wet and hot. Her groin tightened.

The door pummeling continued and Innocent straightened. "Okay, okay," he said. "Stay here." His bare feet padded across the tiles of the hallway.

Ann stood and tried to regroup. She was getting carried away. She latched her bra and buttoned her blouse, tucking it back into her skirt. She ran her fingers through her hair. Their smooching had moved below the neck. What was her limit, the belt line? Her cheeks felt warm. Was she willing to perform fellatio? No. No. She should be going home anyway. Her watch read five.

She studied the spare room, trying to regain control. A lamp sat on the metal desk, which was neatly organized with piles of paper and a leather-bound calendar. The wooden bookcase had five shelves filled with six versions of the bible, a dozen theology textbooks, and a stack of notebooks. Another shelf was packed with paperback thrillers by Follett and others. On the bottom shelf at calf level sat a buffed wooden box that was intricately carved with inlays of lighter wood, creating an abstract design.

In the foyer, the male visitor spoke Kinyarwanda in a loud and urgent voice. Innocent responded in a calm, business-like tone. They bantered back and forth.

Ann moved to the bookcase and stroked the lid of the box—beautiful wood, maybe locally crafted. She lifted it with her pointer finger. A smooth, black object nestled in folds of a velvet-like cloth. The lid thumped against the back of the bookcase. Inside lay an eight-inch pistol with a chrome barrel, all black, the hand piece patterned. The design felt rough against her finger pad. She quietly closed the box. Why did Innocent have a pistol? Did he feel the need to protect himself? Was it a gift? If so, someone with money had given it to him.

The front door shut with a thud and Innocent's feet padded back in her direction.

Ann was standing near the desk when he returned. "What was that about?"

Innocent shook his head. "It's getting crazy."

"I should go. You have things to do. Dinner is at six. I have to. . ."

Innocent stepped up to her. "We were interrupted." Towering above her, he placed his hands on her shoulders. "I want to finish what we started." He kissed her on the lips and pressed her right hand to his groin, his palm moist against hers. His groin swelled against her hand. "Please undo my belt," he sighed.

Ann pulled back. "I really have to leave. Our team meeting."

He leaned down and met her gaze. His deep brown eyes held hers for a long moment. "I know you have to go. I will take you home, Dr. Ann. But I need you. I will keep asking."

"Innocent. You have vows."

"African priests are different," he said.

"I am flattered Innocent, but it is impossible. Take me home." Her face flushed.

"You're blushing, Dr. Ann. I can tell you want more too." He French kissed her again and then drove her to the compound.

Chapter 8

The Belgian establishment, Hotel des Mille Collines, Hotel of a Thousand Hills, stood on a hill, near the edge of downtown, twenty minutes from the GH compound. It served as a gathering place for foreign businessmen, local government officials, and expats from the UN and NGOs. It was a weekly excursion for the GH household. The Nose bought the beer, or sodas.

An imposing white brick wall surrounded the property, offering both privacy and protection. Neatly pruned trees, vines, and flowers filled the gardens. The lobby contained ceiling fans, rich, upholstered wooden chairs and couches, glass coffee tables, floor lamps with Tiffany shades and the reception desk, which was a masterful wood carving depicting a jungle scene. Tourists came just to gawk at the desk.

The outdoor bar opened to a spacious lawn with a large, rectangular pool, lit with underwater lights. The first time Ann went, she could not approach the pool. She asked her housemates to sit as far away from it as possible, at a table several meters into the manicured lawn. After a few visits, Ann breathed easier and realized how unusual the pool was in Kigali—large, clean and well maintained. Everything else around the city was falling apart.

That March evening, Ann and her housemates sat at a wrought iron table near the pool, nursing their drinks; Ann sipped Fanta and her housemates, the local brews, Primus and Victoria. A gentle breeze carried the scent of freshly cut grass and a late afternoon rain shower had washed away the day's heat. Ann sucked on the straw and ran her hands through her hair. The chaos of the hospital seemed far away. Lights twinkled like fireflies in some of the office buildings in downtown Kigali, while other sections of the city sat in complete darkness, a reminder that the schools had closed and the Rwandan government was growing increasingly dysfunctional.

An electric guitar and keyboardist accompanied a busty African in a miniskirt who belted out American hits with a French accent. On the sidewalk, near the band, several couples danced to Don McLean's *American Pie*. Ann was hoping someone would ask her to dance. Someone usually did, although none of her roommates ever danced. She eyed a group of soldiers in dark-blue uniforms who congregated around several tables on the other side, near the pool. The volume of their beer-fueled voices competed with the music as empty bottles began to crowd their tables. It grew impossible to ignore them; every guest on the patio monitored their activities.

The Nose returned to the GH table after talking with a group from the UN. "Belgian soldiers," he gestured with his head. "They should mind their manners."

"How can you tell?" Sylvia asked.

"Sam from the UN told me."

Ann felt a tap on her shoulder. She turned and a homely Belgian soldier asked her to dance. Finally. Now she didn't have to watch her housemates drink beer.

"It's her red hair," Sylvia said as Ann stood and took the soldier's hand.

When the band struck up Gloria Gaynor's *I Will Survive*, Ann stomped out the frustrations of patient care, raised her hands high above her head, and crooned along. She didn't need alcohol to fuel her good time. She'd always loved this song at med school parties, after exams. Forget her grumpy housemates. Forget judgmental Sylvia.

The soldier may have a homely face, but he could wiggle his hips. He was younger than she, freshly shaved, and smelled of cologne. When he spun her, Ann knocked a bottle off a nearby table, which crashed onto the concrete. The broken glass scattered. Ann tightened her hold on the soldier's hand to steady herself. A waiter appeared, scolded her, and swept up the shards. Her heart pounded; the Nose would chastise her if she called too much attention to herself.

The soldier invited Ann to join his table. She accepted, rarely refusing an opportunity to meet new people, and curious about what the Belgian soldier had to say about his mission. The soldier ordered her a beer and handed her a pack of *Intore* cigarettes. Ann fingered one and lit it from the hurricane candle centerpiece, signaling "okay" to Sylvia, who eyed her protectively, then scowled when Ann took a drag.

Conversation was impossible because of their proximity to the band. The soldiers continued to guzzle beer. When Ann waved away her beer, the soldier across from her happily accepted it. Ann leaned back in her chair to enjoy her cigarette; she allowed herself a smoke if someone offered her one when she was out. Sylvia always reprimanded her. Ann took a long draw, felt the calming effect of the nicotine, and watched the smoke float into the evening air.

A muscular Belgian soldier accompanied by a Rwandan woman dressed in a strappy top and stilettos strolled up. The soldier drinking Ann's beer whistled. The muscular soldier punched the offender, causing his strappy companion to tumble toward the table; bottles flew onto the grass and sidewalk. Ann stiffened, preparing to return to the GH table. A hotel manager dressed in a shirt and tie materialized and helped the woman right herself. He ordered the waiter to stop serving drinks. The soldiers hollered back at the manager, who asked them to take it outside. Someone tipped a second table; it thwacked the concrete and beer bottles and plastic glasses clanged and smashed, several careened into the pool.

Sylvia appeared behind Ann, grabbing her hand and telling the manager that she was with them. The manager glared at Ann as she reached for her cigarette before she stepped away. Soon security surrounded the soldiers and escorted them out of the bar. Through it all the band continued to play.

Ann reclaimed her seat at the GH table. The Nose raised his eyebrows but said nothing. Ann focused on her cigarette. Sylvia watched Ann, frowning and pinching her nose, mouthing something. Ann shrugged in response, took a final drag and stubbed out the butt. The band moved on to Simon and Garfunkel's *Bridge over Troubled Waters* as shouts and bangs reverberated from the lobby. Ann began playing the melody on her lap. The music transported her to a slow dance in high school with the hunk of the football team who had a thing for her red hair. That was a different life, sixteen years earlier.

Suddenly, Sylvia was pulling on Ann's shoulder. "We're leaving." The Nose led Ann and her housemates through a side exit, bypassing the lobby.

Their driver waited in the courtyard, gossiping with the taxi drivers about what had happened. "Look—Colonel Bagasora," the driver said, pointing through the windshield.

Ann and her compatriots turned to see a beefy man, dressed in a uniform, holding a cloth napkin over his right eye. He trudged toward an SUV marked with the Rwandan government logo. At his elbow strode Father Innocent, who helped him into the backseat of the vehicle and slid in next to him.

Ann's heart thumped. Her armpits grew damp. The nuns had said Innocent was well connected. Why should she be surprised? He hadn't seen her.

"Get in the car," the Nose yelled.

Ann settled in next to Sylvia, who was whispering about the priest, pointing to the SUV.

The driver rattled on in French. Reportedly the Belgian soldiers had trashed the lobby—furniture flipped and lamps shattered.

"Colonel Bagasora's a big wig in the Rwandan government," the Nose said.

"Ann's priest was with him," Sylvia said.

"He's not my priest," Ann said.

"Whatever, hon."

"I can't wait to hear what RTLM says tomorrow," the driver said in French.

The Nose nodded in the front seat. "I hope it wasn't a Belgian who punched Colonel Bagasora."

The next day *Kangura*, the local newspaper, reamed the Belgian soldiers for their behavior. It was a black mark on the international troops who had come to enforce the Arusha Accords. "Enforcing the peace but destroying the lobby of one of the finest hotels in town," was the lead line. The paper was considered an extremist rag, but any respectable newspaper would have labeled the soldiers' conduct in the same manner—poor judgment. The RTLM radio station ranted nonstop about the incident. Two of the Belgian soldiers were accused of rape. The blow to the Rwandan colonel was also reported as an assault against the Rwandan army.

The GH staff reminisced about the episode during dinner the following evening. Over beans, rice and *matoke*, Sylvia reminded Ann: "I rescued you. I was your guardian angel, hon. Again. Your red hair's a beacon for trouble. T-R-O-U-B-L-E."

For a moment, Ann heard her mother's shrill voice passing judgment. Ann swallowed her mouthful of beans and shrugged. She hadn't even had a beer. She forked *matoke* into her mouth and chewed the mashed plantain. It had the consistency of soggy paper. Sometimes it was served with peanut gravy. If not, Ann squirted on catsup from a little packet. Knowing her love for catsup, Ann's sister who owned the Milwaukee bar and burger joint had given her a gallon-size zip lock filled with catsup packs.

The Nose continued to hammer his team during dinner, using the episode as an opportunity to talk about appropriate expat behavior. "What we do is watched by others," he said.

Ann considered the hypocrisy. By the end of her first week in Kigali, she had figured out that the Nose was sleeping with their cook, an attractive Rwandan woman about half his age. This was contrary to what Ann had learned at the GH orientation. The *dos and do nots* in the field included no sex with local staff. The power imbalance was too great, the cultural divide too wide, not to mention the security issues, not to mention HIV, which was a growing problem in Rwanda. In spite of that Ann and the entire household were well aware of his escapades, thanks to the paper-thin walls.

As the Nose lectured them, shaking his pointer finger, Sylvia discretely rolled her eyes in Ann's direction. She'd moved beyond her accusatory attitude toward Ann. They were back on the same side; Ann silently sighed in relief. She needed an ally.

"As a result of this event, the Rwandan government has issued an 8:00 p.m. curfew," the Nose continued. "Our evening excursions to the hotel are over." He still wagged his finger as he glared toward Ann. "I expect you home by eight. No exceptions."

In their bedroom, Sylvia teased Ann about her curfew problems. "Did you see how he looked at you?"

Ann shrugged and pointed out the irony. "The Nose thinks his activities go unnoticed because he does it in the *privacy* of this compound."

Sylvia did the eye roll again then said, "I left a pack of condoms on his desk. He never acknowledged them."

"I hope he's using them."

"We don't need a screaming Rwandan-American infant in this place."

Ann made a face.

Sylvia sighed as she plopped down on her bed. "Do as I say, not as I do." She lifted her crossword puzzle book from her bedside table. "In the meantime, I'll keep my mouth shut and spend as little time with him as possible, unless he's buying the beer."

Chapter 9

Even Innocent mentioned the Belgian soldiers' activities when he gave Ann a ride home from the orphanage later in the week. ". . . disrespect for the people of Rwanda."

"You were there," Ann said. She sat in Innocent's truck and turned to look at him. Outside, light drained from the sky. "I saw you with the injured military man."

Innocent smiled in her direction. "If I knew you were there, Dr. Ann, I'd have asked you to check Colonel Bagasora's eye."

"Was he badly hurt?"

Innocent had returned his gaze to the street. He swerved to avoid the soldiers dressed in army green uniforms who marched in the street with no attention to the traffic. On the corner of the intersection, the RTLM radio blared from the mounted speaker. A jiving group of men and boys dressed in red and green shirts yelled and waved their machetes and sticks.

"What are they saying?" Ann asked.

"Kill the Tutsi *inyenzi*. Squash the cockroaches. They stole power. . . Bring us a cabbage head."

"A cabbage head?"

"A Tutsi's head."

Ann was silent.

"You know, it's the foreign governments who've armed both sides. The US is ultimately responsible. Your country is the largest arms exporter in the world."

Ann swallowed hard. This mission had grown complicated, even dangerous. She still felt safe at the compound and in the hospital. But she was witnessing the threats and menace local hospital staff reported. They talked of increased hassles from both the army and the *interahamwe* militia while going about their private business. One of the orderlies had not shown up at work. When co-workers checked on him, his family said he'd disappeared. A nurse had reported that her Tutsi husband had been beaten up. Another said her teenage sons were forced to join the militia. The expats seemed to be safe, but the Rwandans lived in fear.

The truck veered around a pothole, turned at the corner, and the Congolese music faded as they entered Ann's neighborhood. The embassy dwellings were lit, the front door lights burned brightly. Many had security guards stationed near their gates. This was a new development since Ann's arrival in January.

Innocent parked at the curb outside the GH gate. He turned to Ann and pulled her toward him, planting a hard kiss on her lips. The faint smell of his cologne tweaked her nose. His fingers combed through her hair and his tongue pushed against her teeth. His hand cupped her breast.

Ann pushed her palms against his chest. "Innocent. You can't," Ann tried to say, but his lips swallowed her words, his tongue exploring her mouth. Shivers erupted from where his hands pressed. He was fumbling with her button. She shouldn't be doing this; she'd promised herself to limit the kissing to above the neck, otherwise she lost herself. Why wasn't she resisting, reminding him of his vows? He tasted of mint. Heat grew between her legs as his tongue licked the top of her breast. She should tell him to stop.

Outside, the lamp above the GH security fence came on and the gate clanged open.

"The guard," Ann said. "Please stop."

He sighed. "I've been thinking of you since Sunday."

"I've told you. We can't," she said weakly.

"Says who?"

The new security guard that the Nose had hired approached Innocent's truck.

Innocent put a finger to her lips and sat back. "Do you know the Kinyarwanda saying, *Gutera akadobo*, 'throw the little bucket'?"

Ann laughed. "What are you talking about?"

"It refers to a Rwandan woman rejecting a man. *Aka* means little. *Gutera akadobo*, to throw a little bucket. *Gutera indobo* to throw a regular-size bucket. And if you are really rejecting someone it's *gutera ingunguru* to throw the oil drum." Innocent tapped his fingers on Ann's leg.

"*Gutera*," Ann said. "To throw." Her face felt warm.

"So how big is the bucket you throw at me?" Innocent squeezed her leg.

The security guard stood outside Ann's door and knocked on the window.

Ann thanked Innocent for the ride, slipped out of the truck, and hurried toward the compound door. The security guard stood at the open truck door talking with Innocent as she entered the house.

Sylvia stood by her bed folding several yards of colorful cloth. "I bought this for my aunt. She'll love the color and the print. She makes bags, the kind you throw over your shoulder to go to the beach."

"Lovely," Ann said, her tone distracted.

The nuns on the corner began to sing.

"You were almost late," Sylvia said. "After the lecture, you'd really be in for it."

"What was for dinner?" Ann pulled her blouse over her head.

"I bet you can guess."

"Beans, *matoke*, and rice," Ann said, slipping off her skirt.

"Did you see your priest?" Sylvia held the folded cloth against her chest.

"He brought me home. It's becoming difficult to fend him off."

"You slept with him? You're blushing." Sylvia aligned the ends of another fabric.

Ann shook her head. "No, no. He kissed me and I liked it. Then the guard came out."

"What's the big deal? A little smooching."

"I'm afraid of where it's leading. The kissing's getting pretty hot." Ann smoothed her hair into a ponytail.

"It's not like the Nose and the cook. He's not your boss. It'd be good for you, hon. A release. All the stress. We work hard. We play hard. That's how aid work is." Sylvia sat down on her bed.

"But he's a priest. He's got vows." Ann tightened her cotton robe.

"Africa is different."

"That's what he told me." Ann slipped on her flip-flops and moved toward the door.

"If you haven't noticed, it's more relaxed. You hook up. It's different. No one stays in one place long enough to make commitments. What you wouldn't do at home, might be okay here."

"It feels like a slippage to me, a moral slippage," Ann said, holding onto the door frame. "I'm not sure I'm okay with it. You, of all people, are supposed to remind me of my values. You kept me from doing something stupid at Joseta's party. And the hotel, the night the Belgian soldiers trashed the lobby. Don't give me permission to do something I'll regret."

"As long as he uses a condom, hon, I don't see what the big deal is. Colonel has made my time here tolerable, even pleasant."

Ann stood under the shower's dribble. It wasn't enough to moisten her hair and she desperately needed a shampoo. She filled a bucket from the barrel and poured it over her head. She shivered at the chilly smack, then repeated the procedure, imagining that she was washing away all the impurities, all her immoral thoughts as well as the grit.

Chapter 10

O n Thursday morning, Joseta was late for her hospital shift. It was not like Joseta to pull a no-show without warning. Something was wrong. When she had not arrived by 10:00 a.m., one of the staff left to check on her. In the meantime, another nurse triaged and the chalkboard filled quickly. Ann assessed a teen bludgeoned by some stranger with a baseball bat, set and casted his arm, and evaluated him for a skull fracture. He was lucky; he'd avoided a broken nose, but he'd have a shiner. She x-rayed his arm but couldn't order a CAT scan of his head to look for internal bleeding. King Faisal did not own a machine; in fact, no such machine existed in all of Rwanda. But, practicing low-tech medicine sharpened her clinical exam skills. She did a careful neurological exam, observing the movements of his eyes in all directions. He seemed a little sleepy and he vomited twice, so she admitted him for observation. She diagnosed a child with malaria. As she clipped the final suture on a machete wound, Joseta arrived.

The orderly had found Joseta sitting at her kitchen table, crying and dazed. Her eyes were red and puffy, and she'd forgotten her head scarf. Ann was shocked to see the sparseness of her gray hair. Joseta settled on a stool in the corner. Several nurses surrounded her. One pulled the plaid curtain for privacy. Another rubbed Joseta's shoulders.

"What happened?" someone asked.

Her husband had been arrested before dawn.

Ann swallowed her horror. Sweet Vincent detained. She gritted her teeth.

"*Mfasha*, help me Jesus." Tears welled in Joseta's eyes. She exhaled, removing her hands from her face and interlacing her fingers in her lap. She stared around her as her tongue moved inside of her mouth as if she were trying to loosen her words. Finally, she spoke in a halting tone. "Someone banged on the door. . . It was dark. But the birds were singing. Loud knocking. I thought they'd break down the door. They had guns."

"Who are they?"

"The police." Joseta shook her head, blubbering words. Then she pounded her fists into her thighs. Tears streamed down her face.

"Are your children okay?"Ann asked. She wanted to hug her, but Joseta sat stiffly, staring at her lap. Ann did not want to offend her. One of the nurses positioned herself in front of Joseta, clasped both of Joseta's hands in hers and said, "Tell us."

Joseta shook her head. "All I remember is the sound of their shoes on the gravel as they left. Oh Jesus, help me, please. My poor Vincent." The police had awoken Joseta and Vincent from sleep. Two officers demanded to see their identity papers. Vincent's stated "Tutsi" and they locked his wrists in handcuffs and marched him out of the tiny house with a gun to his back. Joseta had called her neighbors and her daughter.

When she finished recounting the details, she wailed a low-pitched moan that sounded from deep in her pelvis. The nurse sat with Joseta, holding her hands, saying nothing.

It was the wail that shook Ann. She wondered what could be done. In Wisconsin, a white co-worker had been attacked on the way to work. Ann had called the police, who arrived within minutes. The officer took the report, photographed the victim's swollen wrist and black eye. The system worked for the most part, less so for blacks. But if a police officer was aggressive or unfair, you could complain to his supervisors, to the courts. There was a process. But here?

Eventually, Joseta's sobs shifted to whimpers. The nurse who sat in front of Joseta hugged her. One by one the nurses followed suit. They whispered in Kinyarwanda.

When Ann took her turn, she searched for words. "Vincent will be okay; justice will be done; we'll figure this out." Ann's mouth felt dry, her throat tight. The phrases were hollow platitudes. He could be thrown in jail. He could be executed. Nothing was certain. All Ann could think to say to Joseta was: "I'm sorry. I am so sorry." Joseta's muscular arms encircled Ann.

Beyond the plaid curtain the pandemonium of patient care drummed on. A doctor yelled orders. A child cried. Wheels squealed as someone rolled a gurney away. Ann wanted to erase Joseta's morning, reshoot the scene, and write a different ending. How would Joseta go on without her Vincent?

Nearly three months in Rwanda and the numbers of injuries perpetrated by the police, the Rwandan army, and the *interahamwe* had increased. Ann had heard the stories as she sewed lacerations and casted fractures. It wasn't clear who could be trusted. Up to this point, the victims had been anonymous, patients she cared for at the hospital, the family of co-workers she didn't really know. But Vincent was different. She'd spent an afternoon at his home, drank his banana beer, and eaten food at his table at least a half dozen times. The insanity that stirred the pot in Rwanda had struck too close to home.

Staff offered support. "Joseta, take some time for yourself." Someone handed her a cloth to wipe her tears.

"I think it's better if I work," Joseta said, her lower lip quivered. "It will take my mind off . . ." She began to weep again. "I love him so. We met as teenagers. I don't know if I can live without him," she blubbered on in halting phrases. "Each morning, he brought me something from his garden. A cucumber. A tomato. This morning, I looked at his chair and started to talk, then realized he wasn't there. Oh Jesus, please help my Vincent." Holding the cloth to her face, she sobbed.

One of the Rwandan doctors looked in. "Is there someone who can help? Anyone with connections?"

"What about Father Innocent?" Ann asked.

"I tried. He didn't answer," Joseta said as she dabbed her eyes.

"I'll try to reach him," Ann said.

Another nurse had a brother-in-law with some contacts. She promised to call him. That nurse brought Joseta a cup of water, then rubbed her back. A third held her hand and whispered prayers in Kinyarwanda. They hovered like a pride around an injured lioness.

Chapter 11

Easter arrived several days later, the first Sunday in April. Ann planned to meet Joseta at St. Michael Church and come for lunch as always. Despite the increasing unrest, Ann felt safe walking in the daylight. At 8:00 a.m. the militia members were still sleeping off their drunken stupor.

The lush green of the planted earth met the azure sky as the morning mist burned off. A warm breeze rustled the leaves of the tall eucalyptus trees that lined the main road, releasing a spicy fragrance that mixed with the smell of the soil. Garlands of leafy twigs and vines wrapped many of the entryways. Freshly cut green leaves were scattered up the walkways between individual homes and the street, special decorations for Easter. It was a day that suggested nothing bad could happen in Rwanda.

Ann passed many Rwandans walking to church. She was one of the few whites on the street. A woman with a child swathed to her back approached, holding out her hand. Ann smiled, but shook her head. Locals assumed she was wealthy with money to dole out. Compared to the average Rwandan, who made a dollar or two a day, Ann was. The deferential way staff approached her at work—waited on her, asked her opinion—troubled her. It was more than the usual doctor respect, maybe remnants from colonial days. Her white skin wielded unexpected attention and privilege. It all felt awkward and took some getting used to.

The same fresh-cut green leaves decorated St. Michael's sidewalk and boughs of silvery-green eucalyptus lay in the extended arms of the Jesus Christ statue that hung over the main entrance. Carved from wood and painted white, the icon with flowing robes cut a stark contrast to the dark-skinned Rwandans who packed the church. Inside bouquets of blooming branches filled vases near the altar and shed their sweet scent. The bell pealed, welcoming the worshippers. During the service, open doors on all sides of the church allowed ceiling fans to swirl the breezes that entered.

Worshippers dressed in their Sunday best. The colors and patterns of the women's wraparound skirts and matching blouses, kangas, were bold and brilliant. Some latched infants to their backs with colorful swatches of cloth. Men sported pressed shirts, some with ties; most smelled of cologne. The children were spiffed up in their best shirts and ties or dresses, their hair combed and their faces scrubbed. Parishioners squeezed into the wooden benches and several rows of folding chairs filled the back, more crowded than usual. Just like home, even the fallen-away Catholics showed up for Easter.

Ann was underdressed. The 40-kilogram luggage restriction had precluded her from bringing dressy clothes. After several months in Rwanda, the colors of her floral-print blouse and skirt had faded. She took a seat on the right side toward the front, the area where Joseta usually sat.

The choir belted out Alleluias. Ann drummed out the chords on the pew's ledge. During the third song, Joseta slipped in next to her. Her vibrant purple-and-pink print top and skirt distracted Ann from noticing the sadness in her eyes.

"Did you visit Vincent?" Ann whispered.

"Today is his birthday," Joseta said. "He's 56. I made his favorite meal. Curried goat. I took him enough for the week."

"You're such a good wife."

"He's thin." Joseta shook her head and then studied her hands. "I, I want to spend his birthday with him. We met on his birthday forty years ago." Tears filled her eyes.

Ann clasped Joseta's hand, her skin warm and moist. They continued to hold hands throughout the mass. Joseta's hip touched Ann's. Adjusting to the close personal space had taken a while, but Ann had come to appreciate it. It made her feel connected, like she was part of the community.

Everyone sang wholeheartedly, swaying to the music, even the young men. Some of the hymns had the singsong rhythms of Ladysmith Black Mambazo. Not knowing the words, Ann hummed along. She remembered the Ladysmith concert she'd attended in Milwaukee several years earlier. She'd bought an album and learned to play several of the songs. The call and response rhythms reverberated deeply, somewhere between her navel and heart. The air grew electric as if a summer storm beckoned.

A half dozen deacons and servers, dressed in crisp, white, floor-length robes, processed down the middle aisle toward the altar. Father Innocent followed, dignified and regal in his cream-colored and gold-trimmed vestments, moving with gravitas and authority. A server shook the thurible back and forth, filling the church with incense.

The Easter celebration outpaced the staid Sunday celebrations at Ann's Milwaukee parish, the one near the Marquette campus where Dr. Blue Eyes had spoken. There, it was barely spring and everyone would be bundled in thick coats, only a few would lip-sync the songs along with the choir. That choir's enthusiasm paled in comparison to the pomp and splendor of St. Michael's, who rejoiced with their entire bodies. They stood on risers in the front, jubilant, each adorned with some purple garment—a turban, tie, sash, blouse, or shirt.

But the Easter celebration stood in razor-sharp contrast to the growing dissent evident on the streets. Injuries had poured into the King Faisal emergency department all week. Kigali General Hospital, located on the other side of town, had started redirecting their overflow to King Faisal. Like Joseta, several more staff members reported the abduction of family members.

Somehow, on Easter, the worshipers put aside their worries and praised God in a manner Ann had never experienced at home. Perhaps prayer would ward away the danger. Ann shoved away her own weariness—exhaustion from all the patients she'd cared for and her uncertainty about the future.

At the consecration, Innocent's pink-skinned fingers lifted the bread and wine high over his head. He gazed upward at the transformed Eucharist. The loose cream-colored sleeves of his vestments slipped down past his elbows, revealing dark, muscular arms, his skin so black it seemed blue. His melodic baritone announced the Body and then the Blood of Christ. A sunbeam shot through a skylight, illuminating his face as he looked up with a reverent expression. His stately six-foot frame was surrounded by an aura like the Jesus in the painted, wooden Stations of the Cross that lined the brick walls of the church.

Everyone clapped. Innocent appeared to revel in the high drama of the service. The familiarity of the Catholic ritual, even though Ann rarely participated at home, had grown comforting over the weeks.

At the handshake of peace, the children scurried up to shake Innocent's hand. It took five minutes for him to touch each child. When he sang the "Our Father" his Adam's apple bobbed. At the end of the song, his eyes locked on Ann's. When she accepted Communion from him, he said, "The Body of Christ, Dr. Ann." A rush of heat moved through her. She fanned herself with her prayer book as she returned from Communion. Other parishioners did as well. Had Father Innocent affected them, too, or was the heat of the day and the two hours in church taking its toll?

Joseta and Ann sat in the backyard watching the garden and enjoying the warmth of the sun. Bees hovered among the blooming bean plants, whizzing from blossom to blossom.

"The garden looks terrific, no weeds. How do you have time?" Ann asked.

"I want it to be perfect when Vincent returns," Joseta said.

Ann worried about what was realistic; she'd not heard of a process for securing Vincent's freedom, but Joseta remained hopeful. A Pied Crow flounced his white-feathered breast and cawed from a banana tree. His friends flew from the neighbor's yard to join him.

Suddenly the sky darkened and a few raindrops fell, filling the air with the scent of rain. The tall branches of the eucalyptus trees shook their silver-backed leaves like tambourines and the long, thick spinach green leaves of the banana trees undulated. Drops fell with a deliberate drumbeat and splashed Ann and Joseta's sandal-clad feet. Soon, sheets of water washed their legs as the strength of the downpour grew. No longer protected by the roof's overhang, they hurried into the house.

A fresh bouquet of flowers perfumed the simple kitchen. Next to the vase stood a plastic statue of Mary clad in blue garments squashing a fat green snake with her feet.

"Let's start lunch," Joseta said and asked Ann to chop onions. "Christine and her family will be here in an hour. She's bringing some food." The rain pounded hard on the tin roof, making it impossible to carry on a conversation.

When the deluge ended ten minutes later, Ann asked Joseta about her visit with Vincent.

Joseta stopped and started several times. ". . . He's in the central prison. You've seen the building. It's monstrous. . . red brick with green metal doors. . . on the outskirts of town. The conditions are awful. . . They take turns sleeping. There's not enough room to lie down. . . I hate to see him there. Smelly, overflowing toilets. Unkempt men coughing all over each other. I'm sure it's filled with tuberculosis. I pray to Jesus to protect him." Tears welled in her eyes; she wiped her face with the back of her hand. "If they'd just realize it's all a mistake and let him come home. . . Easter. Easter is about hope. I pray Jesus is watching over. . . my dear Vincent." She stared at the potato in her hands. Her wedding band encircled her fourth finger. She stabbed at the potato with renewed effort, then dropped the peeler. It clanged in the sink. "Why, why didn't we put up more of a fight? If I had resisted, the police might not have taken him."

"If you had fought back, you might both be dead." Ann set her knife down on the cutting board.

Joseta clutched the edge of the sink and wept, the same low-pitched wail Ann had heard the day Vincent was arrested.

Ann tried to comfort her. For the last few days, Joseta had mustered a can-do demeanor, focusing on work, saying she was trusting Jesus to help. Now, she gripped Ann's forearms and sobbed; her hot tears soaked the shoulder of Ann's blouse. Ann inhaled the smell of Joseta's perspiration and tried to imagine what it was like to have the love of your life imprisoned; worse yet, to have no way to respond, to know that he was being mistreated. . . the powerlessness.

Joseta began to hiccup and couldn't stop. Ann handed her a glass of water. The hiccups persisted despite Joseta's slow sips. Ann tried to scare Joseta like her older sisters had done to her when she was a child. That provoked giggles, and before long Ann and Joseta were shaking with laughter, losing all control, gasping for breath. Just as Joseta reached for the dishcloth, Christine and her family entered into the kitchen.

"What's so funny?" Christine said.

The grandchildren surrounded Joseta, two boys and a girl who pulled on Joseta's skirts, raising her arms to be lifted up.

"Use your words," Christine said.

"*Nyogokuru*, grandmother," Clementine said. Joseta picked up the six-year-old and kissed her. Clementine flung her small arms around Joseta's neck.

The long skirt of Christine's traditional dress swished as she set bowls of food on the counter: *matoke*, peanut gravy and cooked cassava leaves. She was clearly her mother's daughter as the intonation of her voice mimicked Joseta's when she directed the boys to greet their grandmother before they darted into the backyard. Christine's tall husband opened the fridge and helped himself to a beer, then tended the outdoor stove.

Outside, the air was fresh after the rain; damp leaves glistened in the sun, cradling jewel-like raindrops. Ann wiped the outdoor table and chairs. The boys had recruited two neighbors to join their soccer game.

"Bless *Data*," Christine prayed as they gathered around the table. Joseta doted on Clementine, helping her cut her meat until Christine said, "Mama, please let her do things for herself. She is six years old."

Ann searched for conversation as they passed the food. It was a difficult time for the family. The children were not in school. Christine's husband was out of work and her nursing classes were indefinitely on hold. The mood lightened when the boys talked about the upcoming African Cup soccer playoffs. Then Ann got Christine and Joseta reminiscing.

"Do you remember the Christmas we climbed the forest to where *Data* worked," Christine asked. "I must have been a little older than Clementine."

"We made the trip every year," Joseta said. "Miss Fossey was a stern boss, but she threw a grand party at Christmas."

"I fell in the mud and my new dress was ruined. I'd insisted on wearing it. You brushed me off. Kissed the *owie* on my knee."

"I think you were seven that year. I'd just started nursing school."

"There was a huge Christmas tree. Dozens of wrapped presents. My present was a doll."

"She gave presents to her staff and all their families," Joseta said. "You played with that doll for years." Joseta smiled at the memory.

Clementine's eyes widened. "Do you have the doll?"

Christine looked toward Joseta who shook her head. "You wore her out. She fell apart and I burned her one day when you were at school."

"Did you?"

Joseta nodded. "One year we saw the gorillas. Do you remember? Maybe you were too young."

"How could I forget," Christine said. "One of the younger gorillas ran over to us. He grabbed a boy's new baseball and tried to eat it. Another baby gorilla came to play. They tossed it between them. When they grew bored, *Data* retrieved it."

"You saw the gorillas?" Christine's older son asked.

"You never told us that," said the younger.

"Your *sogokuru* worked as a tracker for many years. All of us were born in Ruhengeri, the nearby town." Christine looked at Joseta. "How old was I when we moved to Kigali?"

"About eleven or twelve."

"That's the same as me," the older boy said.

"We learned about the gorillas in school last year," the younger said. "I can visit them on a school trip."

Ann had progressed in Fossey's book. As far as she knew, Fossey's research continued after her murder in 1985. Since that time, the apes had become a valuable resource for Rwanda. Tourists paid to see them and the government was better about protecting their habitat.

Joseta seemed to forget her worries. Christine's husband reminded Ann of Vincent, tall and quiet, talkative after a few beers. Ann sipped a Fanta and one of the boys laughed at her orange lips. She felt like she was part of a family, the teasing and laughter reminded her of times with her sisters' families before the drowning of Rosie, before the awkwardness and icy distance. Later in the afternoon, Ann excused herself, having agreed to visit the orphanage where

Father Innocent had promised to meet her. They had planned to get together for their Sunday chat.

99 sat outside the orphanage, opening the pink door for Ann. Sister Mary Joseph had gone to visit friends in the country. The children in the playroom hovered around Michelle. No nun was in earshot. Michelle sat on the edge of a wooden stool gasping for breath. Her nostrils flared and strings of clear snot oozed onto her upper lip.

Ann dropped her backpack on the floor in a panic. "Is someone getting her a neb?" she yelled to no one in particular.

Underneath Michelle's baggy undershirt, the spaces between her ribs sucked in and out. Her lips were dusky, almost blue.

Ann ran to the medical cabinet and rifled through the drawers. Vials of saline and salbuterol sat in a box in the middle drawer, old-fashioned medications for an asthma attack, no longer used in the US. Thankfully, the pediatrician had secured a huge supply. Ann grabbed one of each as well as the nebulizer machine.

Back in the playroom, Ann called for help, quickly squirting medicine into the chamber. One of the nuns came running, connecting the tubing and flipping the switch to on. The nebulizer hummed like a vacuum. Michelle whimpered, afraid of the noise and the mask. Odd, she'd used the nebulizer before.

Michelle's sobs grew high pitched as she fought the mask. Ann turned off the machine and soothed Michelle in French, holding the mask over her own face, but Michelle only howled louder and began choking.

Ann put her stethoscope on Michelle's back. She wasn't wheezing. Had she swallowed something? Ann stuck her finger into the back of Michelle's mouth sweeping the back of her throat.

Nothing.

She stood behind Michelle and wrapped her arms around Michelle's chest, just under the sternum. She thrust hard with an upward motion.

Michelle shrieked and a marble bounced across the floor. Another child chased after it, bringing the offending object back to Ann, who accepted it in her sweaty palm.

The nun returned with a cup of water and helped Michelle take a sip.

Ann inspected the marble before tucking it into her pocket. It was clear and had a green-and-blue center—*le monde*. Michelle had played with it the day Ann met her.

Ann caught her breath as she wiped her forehead with the back of her palm. The racing adrenaline slowed with her heartbeat. She'd responded without hesitation, on her own. Her panic about managing respiratory distress which had started after her niece's drowning was suddenly gone. The anxiety hadn't even reared its head. She hadn't even doubted herself. She exhaled a slow breath.

"Shall we do immunizations?" the nun who was also a nurse asked.

Ann quickly regrouped, remembering that the batch of measles vaccines had arrived. Half the orphans needed to be inoculated and she'd agreed to do it on Easter when she didn't have the pressure of her looming curfew. One nun hunted the children, another assisted, seat-belting the victim in her lap with one arm and steadying the arm to be injected with a large hand. The first child was a handsome boy who was missing his left foot, reportedly mangled in a car accident. He didn't flinch. This would be easy.

Victim number two, a girl, was positioned. She belted out a cry that would have shattered the crystal chandelier in the entryway of the orphanage if there was one. Ann jumped back, just avoiding a needle prick. A needle stick would mean a trip to the hospital for anti-virals and that would shorten her time with Innocent.

Ann quickly inoculated the wailing girl, then washed her hands thoroughly. The girl's howl caused a chorus of distress as the other waiting children joined her. They drowned out the singing in the playroom. Ann and the nun pushed on. The cacophony continued, worse than a chicken house upset by a mongoose.

Three o'clock came and went; there was no sign of Father Innocent. Ann organized her cabinet, did some small tasks that had been on her to-do list. She tried to call the parsonage—no answer. She told herself not to take it personally; he was a busy man, probably doing a favor for the bishop. After all, it was Easter.

The assistant superior, a Rwanda nun, stood outside the medical room. She introduced a coiffed Caucasian woman as Madame Durand, the French Ambassador's wife. Madame's hair was styled in a smartly cut bob and her long, red nails jabbed Ann when they shook hands.

"She's here to adopt a child," the nun said. "She has questions I can't answer."

Ann glanced at her watch. "I was supposed to meet Father Innocent, but he didn't come. I have to be at the compound by six," Ann said.

"My driver can take you home," Madame said. "Where do you live?"

Ann explained.

"No problem," Madame waved her fingers, the diamond on her ring finger at least a carat.

"Can you also protect me from my director whenever I run late?"

"Shall I have the ambassador call?" Madame smirked.

"That might work." Ann laughed. "My director is French."

"She's looking for a girl, preferably without health issues, maybe a toddler," Sister said.

"I lost a child in France and we've been unable to conceive. My husband is quite busy. With the unrest, I am heading home. I thought it would give me something to do." Madame flicked her nails with her thumb, one at a time.

"I'm sorry," Ann said. She wanted to add, "have you thought of volunteer work?" but held her tongue. Madame was close to her age, far too coiffed to be the kind of mother that got down on the floor to play with her child. But Ann's mother wasn't like that, and Ann had turned out just fine. She should quit being so judgmental.

Sister carried a list with the orphan's names, presumed birth dates and the day they arrived at the orphanage. Ann studied the medical binder. "Maybe Ellie."

They found Ellie stacking wooden alphabet blocks in the corner of the playroom. She was a well-nourished and good-natured three-year-old. Other than a Franc-size bald patch on the right side of her scalp, Ellie was pretty with smooth, milk chocolate skin.

"What about her head?" Madame asked.

Ann glanced at Ellie's page. "Probably from a case of tinea, a kind of fungus. Her hair may grow back."

Madame touched Ellie's cheek, then pried open her lips as if she were purchasing a horse. Ann shuddered and bit her lip, but remained silent as Madame scrutinized four other girls in the same manner. Michelle scampered toward Ann, wearing her lime-green flip-flops. She clutched Ann's leg.

"Who's this?" Madame asked. "She's darling."

Ann handed Sister the binder and bent over to pick up Michelle. "She has asthma," Ann said. "And she just swallowed a marble."

Madame made a quizzical look.

Ann's chest tightened as Madame touched Michelle's hair and examined her teeth.

"Do you know about asthma?" Ann asked, wanting to dissuade Madame.

"I worked as an LPN before I married," Madame said.

Maybe Ann was being unfair. Life for Michelle would be much better at the Ambassador's house. She'd have plenty of clothes and toys and would never go hungry. She'd get good medical care. But would she have enough love? Selfishly Ann wanted Michelle to stay at the orphanage so she could see her. Maybe she should adopt her.

Madame circled back through the rooms, her pumps clacking across the tile floor, looking at the children they'd discussed. Ann trailed behind with Michelle in her arms. Michelle played with Ann's hair.

"I think I want her." Madame said, turning and pointing.

"Her name is Michelle," Ann said, giving Michelle a squeeze.

Michelle giggled.

Madame smiled at Michelle. "Let me talk with my husband. I doubt you have a picture."

Sister shook her head.

"I guess I could ask him to stop by."

On the drive to the compound, Madame's driver was courteous. The land cruiser knocked through the potholes with the same jarring jolt as the GH Toyota and Father Innocent's truck. But the air conditioner and seat belts functioned, making the ride in the gigantic car just as bouncy, but cooler and safer, and much more pleasant. Ann shouldn't be so selfish; Michelle would have a much better life. With the increasing turmoil, there were no guarantees in Kigali.

Chapter 12

A few days later, everyone gathered around the Sony television after dinner to watch the African Cup of Nations soccer match. Hospital staff had talked about the semifinals all day: Nigeria versus Côte-d'Ivoire and Zambia versus Mali.

The living room was stuffy and the Nose narrated the plays. Ann had no patience, so she went to her bedroom to read; she preferred baseball anyway.

She sat on her bed, her legs stretched out. The street lamp outside her window cast a puddle of light on the floor that grew and shrank as a gentle breeze ruffled the drapes. Nighttime insects chirped. Fossey's *Gorillas in the Mist* made Ann think about Vincent—was he one of the trackers described in the book?

Downstairs her housemates cheered. The Zambia team was new; many of the earlier team members had been killed in an air disaster. The Nose and most of Ann's housemates rooted for them. Ann leaned back against her pillow and focused on Fossey's meticulous detail about the personalities of the gorillas.

Suddenly, a loud explosion rattled the house. The family photo on the bedside table fell forward and crashed to the floor. Ann vaulted from her bed. Did the stove's propane tank explode? The TV? No smell of smoke. Ann sprinted downstairs. The television still blared in the living room. Her housemates sat speechless, glued to the box. Their faces seemed to twitch in the dim dazzle of the screen.

A reporter in front of a large microphone, dressed in a dark suit coat and red tie said, "In a few minutes we will have scenes from the airport." An emergency bulletin marched across the bottom of the screen. "The plane carrying the presidents of Rwanda and Burundi was shot as it landed at the Kigali airport. There are no known survivors."

Ann and the others watched the airport photos play again and again: the lights of the approaching plane, a red flash, and the falling ball of fire. Later the news reported that the two presidents were returning from a meeting in Tanzania where they'd met with regional leaders about implementing the Arusha Accords. It was Habyarimana's private plane, a gift from the French president.

"Who would do that?" the teacher asked.

"Someone who thought the president was serious about enforcing the peace," the Nose said and went to his office.

"You all, I can't watch this anymore," Sylvia said and mounted the stairs.

Eventually, Ann went to ask the director what this meant for their work. The Nose had the phone against his ear and studied a note pad with scribbles. The cook carried in a cup of tea.

"How bad is it?" Ann asked.

He shook his head. "The plane crash has set off a killing spree."

"The hospitals will be packed."

"You can't go tonight. They don't want our vehicles on the road. The UN will pick you up tomorrow."

Ann nodded. She didn't know how she felt as she climbed the stairs. It had all happened so fast. She just wanted to be alone.

At 8:00 p.m., the melodious voices of the nuns who lived on the corner did not sing. Perhaps they were glued to their television set as well.

They began vespers at 9:00 p.m. Their lovely voices harmonized with perfect pitch, as if nothing had happened, except for the scratchy alto. The normality of their evening prayers reassured Ann and she found herself humming along. Sylvia sorted clothes in the wardrobe.

Bang.

The blast ripped through the night. Nearby. In the neighborhood. Ann jumped, tearing the page in her book. Her hand flew over her mouth. She froze listening, waiting.

The nuns' singing continued.

Bang. Bang.

A scream. The hymn continued with fewer voices. The richest soprano was missing.

Sylvia stared toward the drape-covered window, then back toward Ann. Her mouth frozen in a perfect "O." She clutched an armful of underpants to her chest.

Two more blasts.

A baritone voice shouted from somewhere outside. Only the off-key alto carried on. The baritone sang several bars, then laughed.

Silence.

A vice gripped Ann's gut. "Did you hear that," Ann mouthed, her eyes riveted on the green drapes.

"The shooter can carry a melody," Sylvia whispered.

They remained frozen, waiting. Seconds elongated into minutes. Then Sylvia set her clothes on the bed and stood on her tiptoes, reaching for her luggage on top of the wardrobe. *Kerplunk.* The bag crashed to the floor.

Ann flinched. She restrained a hiss. "What are you doing?"

"I am out of here," Sylvia rasped.

Ann couldn't think that far ahead. She shut her book and crawled under her bedsheet. Curled into a fetal position, she hugged her pillow to her chest and tried to slow her breath.

As the minutes ticked by, dogs howled. Gunshots exploded in the distance. The darkness spooled out, eerie and forlorn. Despite her weariness, Ann found it impossible to sleep. She tried to drum notes, but the melodies wouldn't fill her head. Her heart thudded in her ear as it rested against her pillow. She changed her position for the umpteenth time. The curtains hung motionless. The electricity was out and the blackness loomed around her bed. The only light was the face of her watch when she pushed its button. 11:02, 12:31, 2:00, 2:35.

Sylvia's bed squeaked as she flipped back and forth, more restless than usual. Outside, a dog barked. A gunshot silenced it. Then another shot. Ann wondered what the daylight would bring. At 3:00 a.m., she gave up on sleep and tried to read her book by headlamp, maybe Fossey's gorilla descriptions would make her sleepy.

Sylvia sat up. "What are you doing?" she snarled.

"Reading," Ann said. "I can't sleep."

"You don't have the ceiling light on, do you?"

"Of course not. The power's off. I'm using my headlamp."

"I don't want to give anyone out there a target."

"It's pretty quiet right now."

"Have you looked out the window?"

"No, but I safety-pinned the drapes. I didn't want them to flap open in the breeze."

"That's why it's so frickin' hot." Sylvia punched her pillow and turned her back toward Ann. "Tomorrow, I'm going to talk with the Nose about leaving. I don't want to stay."

Ann didn't want to think about evacuation. She wasn't ready to face her family in Milwaukee. She'd signed up for six months; it was the beginning of month four. She needed more time to work through the baggage she'd carried from home. If they disbanded the mission, she could accept an assignment in another country. But what about Joseta, the orphans, the nuns, Sister Mary Joseph? Ann had responsibilities. She'd grown attached. What would happen to them; didn't she have an obligation to help them? Then there was Innocent. She treasured his friendship. His church would be packed with scared parishioners.

At dawn, a UN escort would drive Ann and Sylvia to King Faisal Hospital to start their shift. Who knew what would be waiting in the emergency department in the morning?

A sequence of gunshots blasted in the distance. Dawn had to come eventually. But did Ann want it to come? Did she want to see all that was happening outside? Dian Fossey had weathered life in her tin shack in the Virunga Mountains, accompanied by Rwandan guards and trackers she couldn't understand. Ann could persevere. She switched off her headlamp, fixed her pillow, and tried to sleep. She reviewed her favorite songs, but the tunes still refused to come. Her nightgown grew damp. She tied her hair on the top of her head to keep if off her neck. She needed to still her mind. She needed to sleep. She inhaled and exhaled deeply, and then for the first time in a long while she recalled the *Hail Mary*, a prayer she'd learned as a child. *Hail Mary. . . full of grace. . . Blessed art though among women. . . Pray for us. . .* Her body sunk into the mattress. . . *Now and at the hour. . .*

Chapter 13

In the early morning light, Ann's neighborhood appeared untouched. Even the convent looked unharmed from the front. Perhaps the darkness had made things seem worse than they were. But reality began to creep in at the round-about, near the turn into King Faisal. There traffic backed up because of a new roadblock constructed out of tree limbs.

A soldier waving a rifle shuffled over to the UN Land Rover. He reeked of booze and grunted through the open window, refusing to let them pass. While the UN soldier argued, Sylvia kept muttering "I'm so out of here" from the backseat. Ann sat in the front and tried to remain calm by counting the number of hospital windows she could see from where they parked. When the UN driver handed over a few cigarettes, the soldier gestured them on with the butt of his Kalashnikov.

Another soldier with the signatory light-blue UN beret was stationed outside the hospital. He collected weapons from patients before they could enter. A pile of machetes, clubs, and a few rifles lay on the ground.

Ann hurried through the chaos of the emergency department to grab a mug of coffee to drink while she studied the chalkboard. The iron smell of blood coated everything. A few staff scurried about trying to manage the onslaught of patients. The chalkboard was nearly full with injured men, women, and children waiting for care: lacerations, broken bones, head injuries, gunshots. Ann gulped down the bitter Nescafe, shoving away her anxiety, then she pulled her hair into a ponytail, wrote her initials next to a name, and grabbed the next slip of paper.

Her second patient, "a tall one," whose legs were chopped off to make him short, bled to death before she got to him. She grimaced as she touched his clammy skin, apologizing under her breath, while she covered him with a dingy sheet. As she moved onto the next patient, she shoved away her regret and began working mechanically. Sew the ear laceration. Cast the broken arm. Refer the gunshot in the leg to the operating room for debridement. She did not care for people, she managed cases. That was, until she came to a woman and her daughter who had been raped.

They huddled together on a gurney. Joseta had put them in the corner behind the plaid curtain so they had a little privacy. Ann struggled through the exam; the pre-teen daughter whimpered and her mother consoled her. Ann collected the evidence, wondering if it made any difference. Her college roommate had been raped and Ann had accompanied her to the emergency room. The compassionate care the physician exercised with her roommate was a factor in Ann continuing as a pre-med. She'd been struggling through Biochem at the time.

"You'll follow the usual procedures with the kit," Ann said to Joseta.

Joseta nodded, but took Ann aside later. "The police won't pick up the kit. They said they have enough problems to deal with." Dark circles surrounded Joseta's eyes. She'd arrived early, unable to sleep and worried about Vincent. Joseta had little confidence in the police; they had abducted her husband.

When Ann had another rape case later that morning, she collected evidence; she felt compelled to, but she was less reassuring with the patient about its value. Civil society was disintegrating before her eyes.

Joseta wanted to visit her husband in prison, but one of the Rwandan nurses discouraged her. "The RTLM announcer says he'll pay a price for every Tutsi head. 'Bring me the cabbages and I'll give you francs.' You're just asking for trouble, Joseta. Give it a few days."

By noon, Ann and the other physicians broadened the triage categories to fixable, emergently fixable, and unfixable. Spending too much time on a patient with a gunshot wound meant patients with simpler injuries piled up.

The unfixables were moved to the side and one orderly checked them. When they died, they were transported to the morgue. What would happen after that was unclear. In Rwandan tradition, family members claimed the body and took it home for a proper burial. But entire families had been hacked with machetes or clubbed to death. *Do the best you can*, Ann told herself as she shoved her feelings into the same compartment where her unresolved feelings about her family still simmered.

The air hung thick. The floor grew sticky with body fluids. Ann saw more death than she had during her five years of practice in Wisconsin.

Father Innocent appeared at 4:00 p.m. at the emergency entrance. He looked fresh, dressed in his short-sleeved black shirt with its priestly white collar. The hint of a smile broke across his face when he saw Ann. "Dr. Ann, Sister Mary Joseph asked me to bring you to the orphanage. There are many new children."

"You're safe," Ann said and hugged him. She hung her white coat in the break room for someone else to use and followed Innocent out the door. "I've been worried. You didn't come on Easter."

Innocent did not apologize as he helped her into the truck.

"What's happening?" Ann gulped as she buckled her seat belt. It was the first she'd sat down all day. "It's been crazy, so much death, so many injuries."

Innocent squeezed her hand as the pickup's motor purred. Beyond the turnabout, men dressed in colorful outfits crowded the street and sidewalk. They flashed their machetes, making it impossible to pass. Angry chanting blared from the speakers, the rant unchanged—"Kill the Tutsi cockroaches."

Innocent resorted to side streets. Six blocks from the hospital, orange flames enveloped a house. Ann rolled up her window when she saw the billowing black smoke. The smell of burning plastic and wood seeped into the car, burning Ann's eyes and throat. She discovered a bandana in her backpack and held it over her nose.

Innocent gripped the steering wheel as he maneuvered around a bike; its rider lay on the street in a pool of blood, his skull slashed open like a musk melon. Shoes and thongs sat along the roadside, as if their owners had stepped out of them, shedding all encumbrances to flee. Those who did not escape lay carved up by machetes or bludgeoned with sticks.

Ann watched from her perch, taking in the scenes like a reporter, unable to take in the true horror. Her years as a physician had taught her to buckle her reactions much like she had her seat belt. "How long will this last?" she asked. Innocent was so focused on driving that he did not respond.

The usual fifteen-minute walk stretched into a twenty minute drive. At St. Michael Church, men and boys jammed the yard. The front door stood wide open as women with infants strapped on their backs crowded inside with the girls and younger children.

"There are more than last week," Ann observed. "Many more."

"This morning the parishioners didn't leave. More arrived at dawn," Innocent said. "The bishop encouraged us to keep our doors open. God protects the church. The schools are welcoming families too."

When they finally reached the orphanage, Innocent parked at the curb.

A tall man in khaki pants with a light-blue beret opened the bamboo gate and approached.

"I don't recognize him," Ann said. "But he's UN."

"Look at his leather boots. There's a hole in the right one," Innocent sneered. "The UN peacekeepers not only dress poorly, but they are unarmed. What good can they do?"

Ann was surprised at Innocent's denigrating comment. So what if the soldier had a hole in his boot; at home one of her patients had cut a hole in a shoe to manage a bunion because he couldn't afford wider shoes. The stores in Kigali had had empty shelves for weeks.

Ann slipped out the truck's door. "Give me an hour," she called.

Innocent rolled down his window to talk with the guard.

Inside the orphanage, the din roared louder than usual. "I'm so glad you're safe. We're so happy you've come. We've been praying constantly," Sister Mary Joseph said, welcoming Ann with a hug.

Ann collapsed into Sister's generous bosom, taking in the smell of soap and powder. They smelled vaguely familiar. For a brief moment she forgot the day's horrors.

"*Que Dieu soit loué*," Sister said. "Thank the Lord and bless Father Innocent for bringing you. He's a good man. Let's have tea."

Extra mattresses were spread on the floor in the dormitory. Children cavorted down the hall and in and out of the kitchen. A few sat quietly by themselves, staring off into space.

Ann followed Sister Mary Joseph into her office. One of the Rwandan nuns carried in a tray with tea. Sister served Ann, then poured milk, and stirred a teaspoon of sugar into her own cup. She asked about Ann's day.

Ann savored the warm, milky liquid as she struggled to put words together. How could she describe their triage system—fixable, unfixable?

Sister interrupted her thoughts. "The prime minister and her family escaped from their home. But she and her husband were murdered at the UN compound this morning. Her four children are here."

Ann winced.

"People keep bringing us children. We've never been so full."

Ann's teacup clinked as she set it on the saucer; her hand shook. The orphanage would not be a respite this afternoon. It would be like the hospital, more patients, more damage from whatever was happening. She braced herself.

"Some of the new children refuse to talk," Sister said. "I think it's because of what they've witnessed. God bless them." She fingered her prayer book. "God bless all of us. We'll need Him to get through this."

Ann ran her thumb along the edge of the desk, trying to steady her hand.

She'd run all day. Her adrenaline still pumped full throttle. "Father Innocent's church is packed with parishioners."

Sister cinched her lips. "People are afraid. In some neighborhoods, men with machetes and sticks are going house to house. The Hutus seem to be targeting the Tutsis."

"That's what Innocent said."

"There's been gunfire all day. The BBC says that the moderate politicians are being targeted. The prime minister was one of the first. She was a key negotiator in the Accords." She paused to swallow a sip of tea. "I don't know how long this will last. We had uprisings in 1992, but this seems much worse."

"Where is the Rwandan army in all of this?"

"They're blaming the Tutsi RPF for shooting President Habyarimana's plane."

Out the window, the muted light of late afternoon was replacing the day's brightness as the sun slipped to the lip of the distant hills and the cook fed sticks into the outdoor stove. The sweet smell of roasting cassava wafted in; while it was pleasant to sit, Ann needed to work. "I should start seeing the new children," Ann said. "I just have an hour. My curfew."

"I'll ask one of the nuns to introduce you to the new children," Sister said, then coughed and swallowed a mouthful of tea.

The tea had quieted the gnawing in Ann's stomach. She'd felt too nauseous for lunch, besides, there wasn't time. Thankfully, she'd found two granola bars in her backpack in the middle of the afternoon.

She worked quickly, but tried to be gentle. The prime minister's children were between three and ten years old, two boys and two girls. While Ann examined them, the second youngest kept asking for her mother. The youngest refused to speak. They'd sustained no physical injuries, but Ann worried about the emotional toll, witnessing the murder of their parents. Ann had arrived bruised with her own problems and pain. But the tragedy she had seen that day now filled her head and rubbed out her own losses like chalk on a slate board. She recalled her fourth grade teacher who complimented her, encouraging her to excel; Ann worked harder because of that teacher. She felt the same gratitude for Sister Mary Joseph and vowed to help her, to weather this unrest, to come out on the other end.

Gunshots detonated in the distance while Ann worked. When yells and shouts sounded nearby, Ann lifted the curtains to peek out of the dormitory windows. The UN guard shooed four teens with sticks away from the gate.

The last three children had been collected by the UN guard on his way to the orphanage. One was beaten with a mallet and suffered from a head injury.

A large black-and-blue patch covered his cheek and forehead. The nine-year-old slept on his cot, but responded when Ann called to him.

"He vomited once," the nun told her.

Ann diagnosed him with a concussion. A few weeks earlier she would have admitted him to King Faisil for observation, but now he'd get better care here. "Can someone do neuro checks during the night?" she asked the nun. Then it struck her—if the boy's status changed there was nothing more to do. "Forget it," Ann said.

The nun shrugged. "I'll do whatever you want."

Lavender light painted the sky as the hour edged toward six. The smells of cooked squash and beans filled the house. The children crowded around the table in shifts, youngest first, older ones later.

Innocent had not returned. Ann would be late for curfew and the Nose would be furious. "I need to go," Ann said. "I hope Innocent is okay."

"He'll come," Sister Mary Joseph said and insisted that Ann stay for dinner.

First, she called the compound to tell them she would be late, then she and Sister ate in the office. The food was bland and monotonous. Eating had become functional. Images of childhood peppered her mind: gathered around the Formica kitchen table, her sisters picking at their dinners, her mother telling them to clean their plates—the poor starving children in Africa would be happy for a meal. Tonight, many children in Rwanda would go to bed without supper.

An hour later, Innocent finally arrived. He was distracted and in a hurry, and declined dinner. They drove in silence as Innocent veered around the potholes and struggled to avoid the men with torches marching in the street near the hospital. Ann sat with her hands clasped in her lap, taking in the scene with short, sharp breaths. It was as chaotic as their afternoon drive, but the veil of darkness increased the eeriness, especially where the fires burned in the gutters. Their smoke filled the air with a putrid smell, causing Ann's eyes to water.

Several new roadblocks had sprouted up. The pickup slowed and Innocent rolled down his window, speaking Kinyarwanda to the soldier. He reached in his pocket and extracted a card from his wallet. The soldier shined a flashlight and laughed; the stench of his boozy breath filled the car.

Ann stroked the strap of her backpack, worrying the edge like Greek worry stones. Tears clogged the back of her throat. The Nose had reprimanded her when she'd called. He said that he wasn't responsible for her safety if she didn't follow the rules. Now she was dependent on Innocent and this drunken soldier who kept flipping Innocent's ID card back and forth, then called another soldier over to examine it. The new one appeared equally intoxicated. They both scrutinized the ID.

Innocent argued in Kinyarwanda. Finally, the first one waved Innocent on, but the truck's motor sputtered and stalled. Ann panicked and pulled her backpack to her chest like a shield.

Innocent pumped the clutch and cursed. The motor grunted several times. In front of them, two men dressed in the *interahamwe* colors tugged open the roadblock, a two-by-four hammered with upright nails. Finally, the truck's motor turned over and they lurched forward. An object flew against Ann's left heel. She reached down to see what it was, and felt something cold and smooth, almost pipe-like—the barrel of a gun. She wrapped her hand around it and pulled it forward so she could see. The pistol she'd seen in Innocent's study. She dropped it, swallowed hard, and sat upright, nudging it back under the seat with her shoe. She decided to say nothing.

At the GH compound, Ann turned to thank Innocent. She reached for Innocent's right hand and noticed that his left was wrapped in a bandage. "Did you hurt yourself?"

"Just a scratch," Innocent said.

"I can check you inside…"

"I'll be fine."

"Are you sure?"

Innocent nodded. "I'll try to pick you up at the hospital about the same time tomorrow." He squeezed her forearm.

"Be careful," she said and opened her door.

Innocent held onto her hand. "My offer still stands."

Ann paused, her emotions swirling—the chaos on the road, the gun, the offer. She nodded, then prepared herself to face the Nose who called to her from the gate.

Chapter 14

The Nose gave Ann the predictable lecture about curfew, wagging his finger the entire time. She apologized and thanked him for his concern. Exhausted, her tears rose to the surface, but she managed not to cry.

Ann's housemates stared at the television. Sylvia acknowledged Ann by patting the cushion on the couch next to her, then squeezed Ann's forearm when she sat down. "You in trouble again?" she whispered.

Ann nodded, appreciating the friendly touch. She fought back tears, wiping her eyes on her forearm. She tried to watch the news.

The BBC switched between street scenes and a reporter with a grim expression who stood against a nondescript ivory-colored wall, perhaps his hotel room. He spoke in British English about the murder of Prime Minister Agathe Uwilingiyimana and her husband. "Groups of soldiers are moving street by street and house to house. We have reports that there is a list of Tutsis and moderate Hutus. One by one, the soldiers are checking them off. With both the president and prime minister dead, Rwandans are wondering who will take over the government."

"This is getting really awful," Sylvia said.

Most of the killing was confined to the Kigali area. An estimated 8,000 had been murdered. Hundreds were taking shelter in churches and schools. Hospitals were overflowing. The RPF, the Tutsi Rwandese Patriotic Front, had launched a major offensive in Kigali to end the killings and rescue 600 of their troops. Their troops were based in the city as part of the Arusha Accords.

The teacher, sitting on Ann's other side, shifted on the couch. "I want to go home."

"Headquarters hasn't given us anything definite," the Nose said. "Look, President Clinton."

"I'm *not* staying," Sylvia said and folder her arms across her breasts.

The teacher looked toward her and nodded.

Ann felt ambivalent. It was crazy here, but she had nothing to go home to. At the orphanage she'd felt committed to helping the nuns, but she might not have a choice. GH could just tell her what to do.

Clinton's face filled the screen. "We are watching Rwanda carefully. The situation is very tense. There are a sizable number of Americans living there. We are doing everything we can to stay on top of the situation and are taking all the appropriate steps to assure the safety of our citizens."

The screen went black. Everyone dug flashlights out of their pockets or backpacks. The room gained an eerie cast as one by one, a half dozen handheld lights illuminated the shadowy face of its owner. It could have been a scene from a horror movie. The dim beams of light emphasized the dips, hollows, and protrusions of facial structures, creating a room filled with talking skulls. Ann's housemates talked about wanting to be evacuated. Eventually, everyone gathered their belongings and made their way to their bedrooms.

Ann lit a candle in the bedroom and climbed onto her bed with her book. Guns sounded in the distance. The ceiling fan stood silent. The drapes hung pinned together and unmoving. The room felt like an oven. It was too early to go to sleep.

Sylvia entered the room and stripped to her underwear. She mopped the sweat from her brow and neck with a large, white handkerchief as she bustled around the room retrieving her suitcase and throwing in her slacks and tops. She recited parts of her Somalia rebel story as if Ann had never heard it. "When I got home, my great aunt had fallen and broken her hip. She was in a nursing home and was really cranky. I got out safely, but returned to a real mess. I hope everything's okay this time. I don't want to face another crabby relative. It was a horrible homecoming; after all I'd been through."

Weary and impatient with Sylvia, Ann fanned herself with her book, then flipped it open to the folded page and tried to read.

Chapter 15

Ann paced on the dusty tile floor in Sister Mary Joseph's office. "Should I stay?" At breakfast the Nose had informed them that Europe and the US were evacuating their citizens, but an experienced GH manager from France was coming to take his place. If anyone wanted to stay, they could. Sylvia said that she was already packed. Ann wasn't sure. She'd made a six-month commitment. She'd barely begun month four. She wasn't ready to face her sister at home who had not responded to her emails. The need in Kigali was greater than ever, especially at the orphanage.

Outside Sister's office, the sun angled low, highlighting swatches of the terraced hills in the distance and creating plum-colored shadows in the backyard. Ann stared at the houses between the tiny fields. Everything appeared deceptively quiet. What about the residents of those houses, were their loved ones rotting between the rows of tea? There hadn't been a gunshot since she'd arrived.

The hospital had been so chaotic that by mid-afternoon they had sent patients away. There were too many injuries waiting to be seen, no more beds in the inpatient wards and no space in the waiting area. Men, women, and children rested on gurneys and mats lining the hallways. The Rwandan army had confiscated a truck transporting supplies and medications, so Colonel had spent much of the afternoon on the phone, pleading with the UN commander to protect the shipment that was coming in the morning. His voice was peppered with anger; everyone was on edge.

Innocent did not show up at the hospital at the agreed-upon time. When he was not there by 4:30, Ann panicked and phoned the parsonage. The line was dead. She convinced one of the ambulance drivers to drop her off at the orphanage. As they passed St. Michael, she searched for Innocent among the parishioners who spilled out into the yard. Men still stood guard along the fence with machetes; their numbers had tripled. She didn't see Innocent or his vehicle. Was he okay? At the orphanage, it was a relief to see the UN soldier with the hole in his boot and walk through the pink door.

Ann's 6:00 p.m. curfew loomed; her orphanage rounds had to be abbreviated. She found Sister Mary Joseph sitting at her desk studying a spreadsheet. Sister ordered tea as she twirled a pen between her fingers. The kerosene lantern created pools of dancing light on the desk and ceiling. Ann asked about Sister's plans.

"The mother-house in Belgium is allowing me to stay. I've been here so long they'd have to pry me out with a crowbar. God bless Mother Superior." One of the cook's helpers carried in the tray with tea. Sister tapped the end of her pen on her desk.

"Were you a smoker?" Ann asked. "The way you handle your pen... I'd love..."

Sister Mary Joseph angled away from her desk and pulled an Intore pack from the top drawer. She pushed it toward Ann.

Ann grabbed the pack. "I don't really smoke. Only when I'm stressed."

Sister shot her a smile.

"When I studied for exams in school," Ann continued, as she freed a cigarette from the pack and handed it back to sister. "I could smoke a pack... Do you have a light?"

Sister tossed a pack of *Hotel des Mille Collines* matches in her direction.

Ann picked up the matches, stared at the cover. "You frequent the hotel?" she asked and struck a match. The smell of sulfur.

"The manager helps us out."

Ann took a drag. The end glowed. The smooth paper felt pleasant in her fingers, soothing. She was a tactile person, having something to do with her hands had been her favorite part of the awful habit. She studied Sister. "When did you start smoking?"

"As a teen. I was wild."

"Really?"

Sister nodded. "In another life. A child of the sixties. I drank, smoked, sowed my oats. We protested the Vietnam War, listened to the Rolling Stones, the Beatles. They all toured Europe before coming to the US."

"You were a hippie."

Sister smiled.

Ann shook her head as she puffed hungrily, twisting away from Sister to exhale.

"I caused my mother a lot of worry. When she fell ill, I came home, cared for her. I was a good daughter. She wanted me to join the convent. I did."

"Do you smoke now?"

Sister raised her eyebrows. "Jesus forgive me. Every now and then." She held her finger to her lips and made a half smile.

"Sister Mary Joseph!" Ann said shaking a finger toward Sister. "With your cough, you absolutely shouldn't."

Sister lifted her shoulders and dropped them dramatically. "These are stressful days."

Ann nodded and stubbed out her cigarette. In the kitchen, the cook and her helpers prepared dinner. The murmurs of their conversation and the clanging of pots were a comforting backdrop. The distant crack of gunfire punctuated the cacophony in the kitchen.

"This morning the GH director talked about a French woman, Margaux D-something. She'll be taking over as director. Do you know her? She's worked in Rwanda."

Sister nodded. "Margaux Dupont. God bless her. She's a good woman. Strong, opinionated. You'll like her."

"It sounds like the entire American embassy is leaving. Do you know any Americans who are staying?"

Sister cleared her throat and picked up her pen, tapping it on her desk. "Michelle left this morning with the French ambassador's wife," then, she began coughing violently. She pulled a white handkerchief from somewhere in the folds of her habit.

Michelle was off to a safer life Ann told herself. She was not surprised; the woman was fascinated by Michelle's charm. It had hooked Ann too. She would miss her. She sniffed back a tear.

Sister regained her composure, tucking the hanky away, as she reached into her desk drawer and extracted a small, black leather address book. "There's a man with the Seventh Day Adventist group. His name is J something. . ." She flipped through the dog-eared pages. "John Friend. John's been here for over a year, very dedicated. God bless him. He often brings me children and helps secure supplies. He's coming by tomorrow. Asked what I needed. I'll mention you when I see him." She coughed again, took a sip of tea, then scribbled the address and phone number on a scrap of paper. "The phones are in and out. I'd drop by."

"Do you think I'm stupid to stay?" Four months earlier Ann was ecstatic to arrive and leave her troubled life behind her. Now she was considering whether or not she should stay. Most of her GH compatriots were packing. They were afraid. But she felt some obligation to the orphanage, to Joseta, and to Innocent. It actually seemed easier to stay. She just wasn't ready to face the loose ends at home.

Sister studied Ann, then slowly moved her head from right to left. "God bless you, *mon amie*. You're just committed."

"With you and Innocent, I don't really feel afraid. And maybe I'll like Margaux and John."

"We need you here. We are fuller than ever. I don't see any of the children leaving. Michelle got out just in time."

Ann glanced at the piano, no time to play. She evaluated the new children quickly. In the foyer, a little girl with doe-like eyes and a skin infection that Ann diagnosed as impetigo hugged a pink pig and sucked on its ear. Next to her a child with pigtails stacked wooden blocks around a gray whale, creating a tower six-blocks high. Some expat had delivered a suitcase filled with Beanie Babies. The nuns distributed them to the newer children. Sister handed Ann a dolphin and a whale. "You might encounter a child who needs one of these at the hospital."

Ann cautiously stepped over the block construction. The young builder eyed her wearily.

Thankfully, the Nose had sent the GH vehicle to pick her up. Sister hugged Ann. "I'll pray for you and your decision," she said. The smells of powder and sweat filled Ann's nose, fragrances that reminded Ann of her mother.

Chapter 16

Suitcases and backpacks were stacked near the front door of the GH compound. None of Ann's housemates had even considered staying. The familiar smells of dinner—beans and potatoes—drifted throughout the house. Ann found the Nose organizing his office. "Thanks for sending the driver," she said.

He gestured toward a chair.

"I want to stay," she said.

"Really?" The Nose eyed her.

Ann nodded. "I want to help out at the orphanage and the hospital. I'm needed. I can make a difference."

"You're committed for a first timer." He folded his hands on a pile of folders.

"When is Margaux arriving?"

"She's got a seat on the French plane that is coming to evacuate the expats. Should be here tomorrow."

"Will we keep our SUV and driver?"

The Nose leaned on his desk; he wore a pinched expression and seemed to search for his words, directing his gaze toward the wall. Had Ann said or done something? Was it her work at the orphanage? Her repeated violations of curfew? Was he upset because the GH vehicle had picked her up? Usually when he was angry he stared her down. She'd never seen him like this. He looked like an embarrassed little boy.

Beyond the office, voices murmured. Luggage bumped down the stairs and skidded across the tile floor, then landed with a thud somewhere in the front room. Finally, the Nose said, "I want to take the cook with me."

That was all, the woman he was sleeping with. Of course. Relief washed through Ann and she nodded her head slightly. "But what does she have to do with the driver?"

The Nose pursed his lips and continued. "The driver who takes you to King Faisal is her husband."

Ann had not expected that.

"If you continue to employ him, it will be easier to take her with me. You're giving him a reason to stay, a job, money. Their boy can stay with him. If he's got something on this end, she'll come with me."

Whatever. Ann had lost all respect for the director. If he wanted to take his mistress to the US, that was his business. "How do we settle this?"

"I'll tell the driver that you and Margaux need his services. I can't imagine it'll be a problem."

As if on cue, the electricity shut off. Business conducted, Ann fumbled for her headlamp and stumbled up the stairs to her bedroom. The yellow halo of candlelight reached into the hallway. The fragrance of the burning candle mixed with the chemical scent of nail polish. Sylvia sat on her bed carefully painting her nails purple, babbling an inaudible string of chatter. A purple sweat suit for the morning's departure was draped over a chair. Sylvia would look like an eggplant. She seemed as relieved to leave as Ann felt happy to stay.

A pile of condoms sat on Ann's bed.

Sylvia smiled wryly when Ann thanked her.

Ann felt guilty about her earlier judgments.

"I trust you'll make good use of 'em, hon."

Ann would miss Sylvia's odd Southern-belle-meets-liberated woman-meets-missionary-kid ways. "You've been a good roommate. I'll miss you."

Just as the birds began to chirp, Ann pulled herself from a dream about wandering the streets of Kigali with stray dogs and orphans. A banging at the compound's gate, followed by the call of the security guard, rattled the compound awake. A deep voice shouted "US marines."

Their ride had arrived earlier than expected. The marine would take the group to a bus that would drive them across the border to Burundi where US and European planes would collect their citizens.

All scurried to dress. Ann pulled on a t-shirt and shorts, splashed water on her face and stumbled down the stairs to say goodbye. The electricity was still shut off so coffee was not an option until the cook built a fire in the outdoor stove.

However, the cook stood in the living room with her duffle. The marine shined a battery-powered spotlight in her direction, creating an atmosphere of interrogation. He said something about "expatriates only," then hoisted a load of luggage into his arms and marched through the front door. A rush of cooler air entered.

When he returned, he barked, "I said expatriates only."

The Nose hoisted the cook's duffle over his shoulder, threw his other arm around the cook, and ushered her toward the door.

"Did you hear me?" The marine's light blinded everyone in the room. "We're evacuating expatriates. Show me your passport."

The cook froze in the beam of light.

"Show your papers," the Nose urged. The cook fumbled in her bag and pulled out a fistful of documents.

The marine took them and dropped them on the ground. "I don't have time for games. We have to get to the bus."

Sylvia and the others scurried out the door. The Nose and cook followed. The marine glared and yelled after them. "Are you deaf?"

The Nose stopped on the walkway. He pleaded with the marine. He offered to pay the cook's way.

The marine kept repeating "expatriates only," the volume of his voice increasing until he was shouting.

The sky brightened. Ann watched with revulsion as the Nose begged like a child who wanted something he could not have.

The cook took a step away. "*Va-t'en!*" she said. "They come for you, not me."

The Nose dropped her duffle and hugged the cook.

After a brief embrace she shoved him away and shouted in French, "They're not here for us. They're here for you. *Va-t'en*, get out of here!"

The Nose took a step toward her, then turned and marched to the van without a word.

The marine heaved the last suitcase over his shoulder and followed. His light beam bounced up the walkway.

The cook returned to the house. She and Ann stood in the morning's gray light. "Bastard *muzungu*," the cook murmured.

The hair prickled on the back of Ann's neck as the cold reality of what she had just witnessed crashed over her like a bucket of frigid water. The US wanted to ensure the security of *their* citizens. No one else mattered. The cook and the other Rwandans who had labored to make the expats lives work here did not matter. The Rwandans understood things in a way that Ann did not, did not want to. It was different for her, different for the other Americans. The US did not care about Rwanda or its citizens.

Since she was staying and Margaux was coming, the compound staff would have jobs. *Wazungu* presence was important for the Rwandan staffs' security. Ann knew without a doubt that she'd made the right decision. She and John Friend, Sister Mary Joseph's friend, would be the only Americans left in Kigali, maybe in all of Rwanda.

As day-glow filled the east, the roof lights inside the van outlined the silhouettes of the Nose and the other expats. As they pulled away, no one looked back. No one waved. The red brake lights grew smaller. Ann decision to stay was final. The metal gate clanged shut and the security guard secured the latch.

The clear morning yielded to rain. At the hospital, patients lay two and three to a gurney as more injured men, women, and children arrived. Many were too far gone to help. Ann's shoes stuck to the linoleum floor, coated with body fluids and mud, as she scurried around the ED. The odors of blood and sweat hung thick in the rooms. Outside, it drizzled, the sky blanketed with angry gray clouds that appeared impenetrable.

Mid-afternoon, Ann and Joseta stood in the supply room, both searching for something. They'd barely spoken all day. "Have you heard from your husband?" Ann asked.

Joseta shook her head. "I've not visited him. Too dangerous. But thank Jesus, after work, one of the nurses and her husband will go with me." Her gray-brown eyes were vacant.

Ann nodded, wondering how to respond. Could she say, "Be safe"? Could she even wish that, given all that was happening? "I'm praying for you. Praying for Vincent," Ann said, then she asked if Joseta had heard from her children.

"Christine and her youngest, Clementine, moved in with me last night. Her husband and sons are missing," Joseta said. Her voice was flat as if she'd just purchased potatoes at the market.

"Missing." Ann cringed as dread washed over. How could Joseta's Jesus ask more of her.

Joseta continued on without a flinch. "Christine got home from work and the front door stood wide open. Her husband and the boys were gone. My granddaughter stays with the neighbor next door. She was fine. The neighbors heard commotion, but knew nothing more. We don't know." Joseta collected what she needed and walked out to the triage area.

Ann stood with her mouth open, holding a bottle of antibiotic pills in her right hand. Only six days earlier, she'd spent Easter afternoon with Christine and her family. The boys had laughed at their mother's gorilla stories and enthusiastically filled Ann in on the details of the upcoming soccer match. Their father was a kind, quiet, and respectful man, a lot like Vincent. He'd held Clementine on his lap and comforted her when she'd taken a spill while trying to play soccer with her brothers. How could Joseta shoulder these losses? What about Joseta's other children who lived outside Kigali?

But Joseta was already triaging the next patient. She paused to straighten her head scarf. The chalk squealed on the slate as she printed the name and complaint. She worked through the triage routine mechanically: interview, record vitals and essential details on the half sheet, then notations on the chalkboard.

Ann's chest felt leaden as she observed Joseta. This was too much pain for a human to bear. Is this how one coped? Keep moving, keep stepping forward.

Ann's losses—the drowning of her niece and the unsuccessful resuscitation leading to Ann's guilt and shattered confidence, her mother's battle with cancer, the family disagreement about how long to continue her mother's treatment, the bitter death. It had been exhausting, devastating. But what Joseta shouldered outweighed all of Ann's troubles. Did her troubles even matter; how could one compare? She'd discuss it with Innocent the next time she saw him.

Chapter 17

Margaux looked from the files she was sorting in the Nose's office. She took a long draw on her cigarette and blew the smoke to her right in a slow, steady stream. Then she rotated her head and her thick, gray ponytail flipped back and forth like a horse swatting flies. Small creases radiated like a starburst around her dry lips. "Getting here was a travel nightmare," she said. "We were delayed at takeoff, had some malfunction over the Mediterranean, then flew back to Paris. At that point I bought a bottle of scotch at the airport." She let out a hearty laugh and continued. "We changed planes, and left again." She sucked on her cigarette. The orange tip glowed. "We stopped somewhere in North Africa to refuel." She ticked through the details in a hoarse voice, thanks to her cigarettes. She pushed the pack of *Impalas* toward Ann.

Ann accepted. She'd had a hectic day. She stared at Margaux's yellow-stained fingertips. She wouldn't make smoking a habit. She'd just have one now, before dinner. It would taste good. It would calm her. The exit of the expats had increased the workload at the hospital.

Margaux tossed a lighter in Ann's direction. "So what was Michael like as a director?"

"Who's Michael?" Ann asked. She clicked the lighter and put the cigarette to her lips. She loved the feel of the paper on her fingers.

"My predecessor," Margaux said, making a quizzical look. "Was he that unmemorable?"

"Far from it. We never called him Michael. He was the Nose to most of us."

"The Nose?"

"Have you met him?"

Margaux shook her head.

Ann laughed. "If you had, you'd understand the nickname. He was a stickler about security."

"Considering the current situation that was wise."

Ann nodded.

"His memos seem thorough, but some of the expats gave him low marks on their evaluations."

Ann exhaled. Should she tattle? The clatter in the kitchen suggested that the cook was preparing dinner.

"How should I read your silence?" Margaux took a drag on her cigarette and set it in a makeshift ashtray, a jar lid.

Ann raised her shoulders and dropped them. "Well, his philosophy was 'do what I say, not what I do.'"

"In what way?"

Ann lowered her voice to a whisper. "He slept with the cook."

"Against GH rules." Margaux tightened her lips.

"I don't want to get him in trouble. This is my first mission."

"Say no more," Margaux said as she narrowed her eyes and smashed her cigarette into the lid.

That evening they had dinner like a family. The GH driver, his wife the cook, and their six-year-old son gathered around the wooden table covered with reed placemats. They conversed about their days: the driver trying to secure a generator, the cook doing household chores and home schooling their son, Ann's work at the hospital, and Margaux's travel escapades. The Nose had not permitted the Rwandan staff to join the expats at meals. Ann much preferred Margaux's inclusiveness. Having staff live at the compound along with the expats was the safest option given the circumstances. Ann asked Margaux about inviting Joseta to stay with them as well.

"We offer some security for the Rwandans," Margaux said. "It's the least we can do."

After dinner, they set up the satellite phone Margaux had brought with her. They could use the phone to make calls and get email and would no longer be dependent on the increasingly erratic and inoperable local services. When they were finished, Ann called her father.

"Annie. I'm so glad it's you." His voice quivered. "I've been worried."

"Is there much about Rwanda in the news?" Ann asked.

"Roméo Dallaire. Have you met him?"

"Heard of him," Ann said.

"He's a Canadian Catholic. The head of the UN mission. I read in the

Catholic Telegraph that he asked the UN for more soldiers, but Madeline Albright said no. She thinks the US should focus on Bosnia."

"You get more news than we do." Ann swallowed to manage the catch in her voice. "It's bad. Really bad."

"Are you okay?"

"I've never seen so much death. . . kids, little babies." Ann sniffed, trying to lock back her tears. Hearing her dad's voice weakened her resolve, maybe she should have left with the others. The words tumbled out along with the tears— the hospital, all the injured patients, the orphanage, and the abandoned and parentless children. Ann cradled the phone and blinked against the moisture in her eyes, wiped her cheeks with her forearm. Crying would worry him.

"Oh, Annie. We miss you here. All of your sisters ask about you."

She clenched her jaw and in a tight voice, she reassured him. "I'm just tired. I'm sorry." He made her promise to call later in the week, sooner if she needed him. She would always be Annie, his little girl, the youngest.

Ann sat alone in her bedroom; the room felt huge without Sylvia. A half-dozen unused crossword puzzle books were piled on Ann's bedside table. Ann's tears started again when she saw them. She hadn't cried for months. She sobbed into her pillow, gained control, then remembered a kindness from Sylvia, or something funny someone at work had said, and wept again. Outside, large military trucks collected their citizens, rattling the buildings as they passed. Distant gunshots pierced the darkness. Tonight they seemed more noticeable; perhaps it was the absence of Sylvia's chatter. Maybe Ann was stupid not to leave. By now, Sylvia and her compatriots would have reached Burundi, boarded the plane, and would be flying to the US.

Chapter 18

The chalkboard was full. Patients waiting to be seen packed the wooden benches of the waiting area. Some leaned against the wall, adding oily smudges to the whitewashed wall, which already had a gray cast. Others curled up on the yellow linoleum floor, worn to black along the heavily trafficked pathways. The room reeked with body odor. Babies whimpered. In triage, Joseta rushed from patient to patient. When Ann came to ask her something, Joseta said, "Did I tell you that Kigali Hospital was raided last night."

"Raided?" Ann shuddered. Kigali General Hospital was located on the other side of town, very near downtown.

"At midnight, the security guards were held at gunpoint with Kalashnikovs. The *interahamwe* checked identity cards. They murdered all the Tutsis," Joseta explained, her tone perfunctory.

Ann was speechless. "I… I thought… hospitals were safe."

"They stole medications. Kigali General's closed today. That's why it's so crazy here."

Early in the afternoon, the UN negotiated a temporary ceasefire between the Hutu-Power Government and the RPF so that the patients at Kigali General Hospital who were still alive could be transferred to King Faisal. Ann was asked to help. "The UN Land Rover will escort you," she was told.

She had remained in Rwanda to do what needed to be done. She ignored the butterflies in her stomach as she stuffed her backpack with additional gauze, needles and syringes, a bag of IV fluid, and a vial of morphine. A siren went off in town, signaling the beginning of the ceasefire. The ambulances had one hour to transport patients between Kigali General and King Faisal.

Ann climbed into the ambulance, a van with a stripped interior that was equipped with one stretcher and a rudimentary first-aid kit. A threadbare carpet covered the metal floor. Ann leaned her back against the side wall, bracing her feet against the frame of the stretcher. It did not come close to the padded seats, state-of-the-art lights, monitors, and radios she knew at home. In residency, she had assisted with a number of transport flights between small towns in rural Wisconsin and the Milwaukee County Hospital. The ambulance helicopter was well-equipped, even had surround sound; the pilots took requests. On one trip, a Chopin piano concerto calmed an anxious farmer.

The driver clipped a strobe light to the van's roof and leaned on his horn. The blaring horn replaced the siren. The backseat roof light was burnt out so Ann was thankful for her headlamp. The setup was the kind of contraption you'd see in a cartoon sketch—strobe flashing, gangly driver, and blaring horn; in the back, the dead bulb, the worn carpet, and the doctor with her headlamp trying to prevent the stretcher from falling over on top of her. The caption would read: "Emergency aid in Africa."

Thanks to the UN, the trip progressed quickly. They bumped in and out of the potholes, were waved through checkpoints and slipped past roadblocks. But progress slowed when they approached downtown. Houses smoldered. Some bikes and cars stood abandoned. Dead bodies lay everywhere and the stench grew atrocious in the heat of the day.

Several office buildings lay in shambles; others were pockmarked with bullet holes. A steady stream of pedestrians clogged the main road out of town. Women swaddled young children to their backs, balanced bundles on their heads, and clutched yellow plastic gerry cans in their hands. One woman carried a large, purple plastic bowl filled with cooking utensils and a squash on her head.

The ambulance maneuvered alongside the refugees and in between the bikes, motor scooters, and the few cars leaving Kigali. The bikes and scooters were packed high and wide, one had tied a chair to the handlebars. What would the man do with a chair when he reached his destination? What was special about that chair?

The driver blasted the ambulance's horn when the stream of people widened into his lane. The refugees squeezed to move out of the way, but on the overpasses there was little room. The survivors—mothers, fathers, children, grandparents, aunts, uncles, and cousins—fled Kigali, trying to stay alive. Like turtles they plodded along, carrying everything they owned. Would the gangly van driver squeeze them off the road, run over their sandal-clad feet? Where was the safe harbor? No one appeared to be hysterical, but clearly they were on a mission; their destinations may have been uncertain, but their intent was evident—leave behind all that had been destroyed, all that had been lost, carry what remained with you. Their faces were expressionless. Ann had seen the same vacant look in Joseta's gray-brown eyes.

Kigali General sat in a valley not far from Hotel des Mille Collines. As they neared the hospital they came to a pyre of charcoaled corpses spewing black smoke and surrounded by barking dogs. The stench of gasoline and barbequed meat strained Ann's nostrils and brought tears to her eyes.

In anatomy class, tendons and ligaments were connected to muscles and bones; the pattern made sense. Every cadaver was unique, one person's coronary vasculature might vary slightly from that of another, gallbladders hung from assorted locations on the liver with differing arrangements of the vessels and ducts, but all in all a predictable pattern existed. A surgeon learned to look for the variations and operate. Open the skin, cut out the diseased organ or repair the blockage, tie off the vessels, and close the skin. The problem usually solved.

Outside the van window, nothing made sense. People were fleeing their homes. They feared for their lives. Their loved ones had been killed. Those still alive could not even bury their dead. The dogs had become aggressive and ravenous.

The Kigali Hospital was a bloody mess. Clotted bodies of the dead still lay at the scene of the crime, growing putrid and bloated in the heat of the day. Ann kept her wits about her; she had remained in Kigali to help. There were no straightforward solutions to the problems, but she could be a cog in the wheel. She accepted two patients and helped transfer them to the stretcher in her van. Soon they bumped back toward King Faisal.

The patients were young, a woman with an infant suckling her breast, her other breast hacked off. The second, a teen with a leg amputated because of a wound infection, had an intravenous line dripping into her forearm. Her back and arms revealed scars as if someone had played tic-tac-toe. Ann wondered at the humanity of the perpetrators. What human could do such things to another human being? Her patients were either Hutu or had been hidden during the raid.

An early afternoon drizzle soon slicked the road, causing the van to skid and swerve as it climbed the hill toward King Faisal. The teen sat up and screamed. Ann tried to calm her. She touched her shoulder, reassuring her. Ann ran her fingers over the rough linear scars on the teen's forearm. "*Nta kibazo*," she said, "don't worry." The teen still panicked, her thin body shaking, so Ann injected hydroxyzine into the IV. While not ideal, it would help her sleep. Within minutes the teen had quieted. Ann steadied the cot as the rear wheels skidded in the mud. Ann found herself reciting the *Hail Mary: Holy Mother of God pray for us. . .*

As she unloaded her patients at King Faisal, the rain softened. The warm droplets washed away her sweat and dampened her worry. She breathed in the freshened air. Both she and the patients had arrived safely. She did not mind her rain-soaked scrubs. It was like a baptism.

Chapter 19

The Sunday after the killings had begun, the church bells in Kigali did not chime. Many worshipers were already camping inside the churches. Yellow gerry cans lined the brick walls and cooking fires smoldered in the church yards, fueled by torn-apart tables and chairs that had been collected from the nearby, abandoned homes. The unmistakable smell of roasting cassava, mixed with the scent of wood smoke and unwashed bodies, permeated the neighborhoods. Families shared food; it was the Christian thing to do. The only partiers who slept off their binges were the *interahamwe*. They did not staff the roadblocks until late morning. By early afternoon, they were well on their way to intoxication.

Ann and Joseta skipped church and spent the morning moving Joseta and her daughter into the GH compound. It would be safer and the house had plenty of empty rooms. Joseta had been reluctant to leave her home and move into the church with the other parishioners; she liked her privacy.

Joseta's neighborhood was quiet. The rainy season had moved in and thick clouds threatened a downpour. In the front yard, the weaver birds' nests still hung in the large tree. Breeding season appeared to be over. The fledglings had hatched. A few birds lingered, chattering and flitting from branch to branch. No male wove a nest. Only one carried insects to a brown female sitting on an egg. Ann wondered if the female had a hopeless task. Had the current unrest affected the ranks of the weavers? Were the few who remained protecting the village? Had the others flown off to build homes in a safer tree? Perhaps they, too, had left Kigali.

Ann helped Joseta collect her things. Vincent's pipe was tucked next to his Bible. Joseta fingered them both and held them to her breast. She didn't cry. Ann wondered if it was possible to run out of tears. Joseta hadn't talked about Vincent for a while. Ann asked about him.

"One of the nurses at King Faisal has a friend who works in the prison," Joseta said as she slipped Vincent's things into her red cloth bag. "He thinks I can pay some money to get Vincent out."

"Like bail?"

Joseta nodded, her expression grew wistful. "My prayers may be answered."

Hope. It was hope that pulled Joseta through. Hope guided one through the jungle of uncertainty and improbability. Ann had hoped that her niece would open her eyes, hoped she'd breathe on her own. Ann's mother and father had hoped they could beat the cancer.

Before closing the door and locking up, Joseta walked through a final time. She touched the bed that she and Vincent had shared and made the sign of the cross. After a moment of silence, she said, "We bought this from the neighborhood market when we moved to Kigali. You may have seen the shop. It was still open when you arrived."

Spooled wooden bed frames had stood against the canary yellow wall of the store. One assembled bed sat near the entrance. The colorful striped mattresses were stacked in a tall pile near the door. Sometime in March, the shop was ransacked. Shortly after that, it closed. In hindsight, the tall, thin owner was probably Tutsi.

They finished the move just as the afternoon rains started. Rain spattered the window glass, creating a steady drone. Joseta and her daughter Christine said little as they settled into the GH compound; they preferred to share one room. Clementine skipped from room to room, looking out every window. She tapped the beds and dressers, humming some melody, trying to decide which room she liked the best. Three of the five were already occupied by Margaux, Ann, and the driver's family. When Clementine was settled into her room, Ann presented her with the Beanie Baby dolphin. Clementine petted the gray toy and rubbed it against her cheek. Shyly she thanked Ann. *"Mwakoze cyanne."*

Joseta's statue of Mary was already displayed on the wooden table beside the bed she'd chosen for herself. Joseta had more than hope; she had faith, a deep faith. Her faith resembled that of Ann's father.

Ann telephoned her father. Frequent contact seemed best until things settled down. Something was healing between them. Maybe all the loss she was witnessing helped her appreciate the family she still had, even if she was angry with them, even if her sister would not answer her emails.

It was morning in Wisconsin. He read snippets from a front-page *New York Times* story on Rwanda. "It covers more international news than the *Milwaukee*

Journal." Ann's mother had loved the Times and had insisted they subscribe to Sunday's edition. Her father had continued the subscription. "They say that thousands are dead. Is that true?"

"I don't know, but it's a lot."

"Are you sure you're okay, Annie?"

"I'm okay."

Her dad grew silent, "Be careful, Annie" he said. "Sometimes the horrors you witness can haunt you. Did I tell you about the apartment building during World War II?" Ann had heard the story many times. He and his cronies had awoken in the middle of the night to a deafening blast that shook the bedsprings and rattled the crucifix on the wall above their beds. In the morning, they learned that the front of the house had been blown off. Luckily, they'd been sleeping upstairs in the back. Ann's mother had talked about her father's screaming fits. Years later he still woke up yelling in the middle of the night. As a child, Ann had wondered what her mother was doing to her father. In medical school, Ann diagnosed it as post-traumatic stress disorder, PTSD.

On the BBC that evening, the newscaster reported that the killing was spreading throughout Rwanda. Joseta and Christine watched, their faces stoical. Joseta had said little about her other children. "People across Rwanda have sought shelter in schools and churches," the reporter said. The footage on the television flashed to an African priest dressed in white and gold-threaded vestments standing at the pulpit. "In Cyangugu prefecture, Monsignor Thaddée Ntihinyurwa preached against the killing of civilians."

"Where's Cyangugu?" Ann asked.

"In the south," Joseta said.

"Do any of your children live near there?"

Joseta nodded as she pressed her teeth into her lower lip.

Ann imagined that Innocent had had a similar message. St. Michael must have had little room for the Sunday worshipers who were not already camped between the benches. Three days and she had not seen or heard from him. Hopefully preaching kindness from pulpits all over Rwanda would halt the horrors that had overtaken the country. At least the rain would wash the streets clean.

Chapter 20

Several days later, Ann passed St. Michael church on the way to the orphanage. It had been five days since she had seen Father Innocent. Ann sat inside the SUV and searched the yard, crowded with parishioners, for Innocent. Men with machetes patrolled along the fence. Above the door the white statue of Christ extended his arms heavenward. Even though Ann remained inside the vehicle, people noticed her. Several boys ran up and banged on Ann's window yelling "*muzungu*" and holding out their palms. With that the driver gunned the motor and the vehicle skidded away from the curb.

At the orphanage, 99 stood at his usual post accompanied by the UN soldier in his light-blue beret. They greeted Ann with, "God bless," and nursed Cokes. Coke was impossible to find on the street; the nuns had secured quite a stash. The soldier pulled a box of Chiclets from his pocket and offered one to Ann. She accepted gratefully.

Before Ann started her rounds, Sister Mary Joseph invited her into her office with a furrowed brow. "We have a problem," she said and fingered the rosary beads at her waist. "Let's talk over tea."

After tea was served, Sister said, "There's a rumor that our orphans are on the list to be murdered."

"What?" Ann squawked, setting down her cup. She sat up in her chair as a buzz blared in her head. "Are you sure?"

Sister restated the concern.

Ann's muscles froze. She couldn't move, blink, or breathe. Finally she stuttered, "I can't believe it's come to this. Are the perpetrators insane?"

"I don't know if it's retaliation for the behavior of the Belgian soldiers or what." Ten Belgian soldiers had tried to protect the prime minister the day after the president's plane was shot down. The soldiers were captured and eventually killed. The murders were well-publicized, demonstrating the potential for retaliation for any interference with the current government. The prime minister's four children now lived at the orphanage. Sister continued, "Over the last four years, we've been left alone during periods of unrest, even in 1992."

Ann gulped. "What can you do?"

"Find people with influence to lobby Colonel Bagasora, and pray," Sister said.

"Father Innocent?" Ann asked. "He probably knows the Colonel."

"God bless him, yes. But we haven't seen Innocent for a few days."

"I've been worried," Ann said. She described her drive by the church.

Sister set down her teacup and clasped both of Ann's hands in hers. Sister bowed her head and led them in prayer. She recited the *Hail Mary*, the *Our Father*, then a spontaneous request for an intervention for the safety of the orphanage and the children and their friends, especially Father Innocent.

A gunshot echoed in the distance but neither woman flinched; it had become a common punctuation during the day's activities.

A dozen new children awaited Ann's attention. The nuns had scrubbed the blood splatters from their hair and skin, but terror haunted their eyes.

Chapter 21

Ann struck a match and inhaled as she put fire to her cigarette. She puffed, then exhaled. She imagined the nicotine diffusing across the single layer of cells that separated the alveoli in her lungs and her blood. Real or imagined, she felt calmer.

After dinner Margaux often sat out back, smoked, and watched the dying embers of the cooking fire. The eucalyptus wood they burned had a pleasant pungency. A tall brick wall surrounded the twenty foot by twenty foot yard, much smaller than Joseta's yard, but enough room for the cook's garden. A light breeze released fragrance from the stand of eucalyptus that towered in the neighbor's yard, mitigating the smoke that lingered from the pyres scattered around Kigali.

It was a pleasant way to unwind from the day and Ann often joined Margaux, allowing herself one cigarette.

"Did you hear about St. Michael Church?" Margaux asked. Dogs howled somewhere in their neighborhood.

"That's the church Joseta and I attended?" Ann said, making a quizzical look.

"The parishioners were murdered sometime before dawn."

Ann gasped. "I. . . I just drove by there yesterday." Her cigarette dropped into the grass. Her breaths came in short and sharp spurts.

"Several churches and schools met the same fate," Margaux added. The end of her cigarette glowed.

"What about Father Innocent?" Ann asked. "No one's seen him." Ann bent over to retrieve her cigarette and burned her thumb picking up the butt. She stomped on the smoldering grass.

"He's not so innocent," Margaux said.

Ann twisted her face in a puzzled expression as she sucked on her thumb.

"He handed his parishioners over to the killers," Margaux said. "The director of the International Red Cross thinks he's working with the *interahamwe* militia . . ."

Ann remained silent, licking her burnt thumb, but Margaux's words fell around her ears. *No! No!* Ann wanted to scream. Impossible. It couldn't be true. Only a rumor. The nuns had said nothing about . . .

Margaux continued, ". . . several priests and ministers around Kigali invited their parishioners into their churches as a setup." She swirled her glass of whiskey and took a sip.

Ann rubbed her upper arms vigorously, trying to get warm. "Does Joseta know?" Ann had suggested she take shelter at the church. Thank God Joseta, her daughter, and granddaughter had not. Thank God they'd come to the compound.

Margaux shook her head. "I didn't tell her." After a final drag on her cigarette, she tossed the butt into the fire and quickly lit another. In the evenings, she often smoked a half a pack nonstop. She offered her Impalas to Ann.

"It just doesn't sound like Innocent." Ann said, accepting the pack. Her hand shook as she pulled a cigarette from the foil. She put it to her lips and worked to steady her hand as she struck a match. She'd already had her cigarette for the evening. It was a nasty habit. She wanted to manage her stress in healthier ways, but tonight she had a good reason for one more. The familiar smell; the comfort of the smooth paper against her lips.

"This is an organized effort," Margaux said and fingered the rim of her glass.

The silence hung heavy between them, magnifying the volume of the chirping insects, the yowling dogs. The nicotine burned but soothed Ann. She exhaled. A rifle blasted somewhere beyond their neighborhood. "The orphanage is being threatened. The nuns want people with influence to talk to Colonel Bag-something. Do you know him?"

"Bagasora. He's a general now. Was promoted with the president's death."

The embers in the fire pit glowed orange and red, shimmering like gold as a breeze dusted off their ashy covering and blew Ann's hair free from its clasp. The smoke curled toward where they sat. Ann stood up. A bat fluttered high overhead.

"I've met him before," Margaux said, leaning away from the smoke. "After the RPF attacks in the fall of 1990, citizens in the north left their homes.

Technically, they weren't refugees because they didn't leave Rwanda. IDPs, internally displaced persons." She cleared her throat. "Bagasora approached several NGOs about setting up a camp." She continued to fan the smoke away from her face. "We had several meetings and he committed a dozen troops to help us organize a camp in the northeast."

Ann walked to the other side of the grate. "Would you talk with him?"

"You should talk with him. As an American doctor he might pay attention."

"I've never been political."

"We can go together." Margaux took a swallow of her whiskey.

"How?" Ann asked, fiddling with her cigarette, rolling it between her fingers, studying the filter as she grappled with the task thrust in her direction. She flicked cigarette ash into the fire, then stomped her feet, still chilled.

"Best to drop in at the parliament," Margaux said.

"I wonder if I've seen him. All of the staff used to go to Hotel des Mille Collines for drinks. Rwandan officials hung out there. I saw one injured."

"I think I have a picture of him inside." They smashed their stubs on the corner of the fire grate and tossed them into the coals.

Inside, Margaux lit a kerosene lamp and riffled through a stack of newspapers on the buffet. She pulled out an old edition of *Kangura* and handed it to Ann.

General Bagasora was a beefy man dressed in full military uniform, sporting a sober expression. "I remember him from the hotel. Someone gave him a black eye," Ann said. She did not mention that Father Innocent had accompanied him.

"I'm sure there were repercussions for the perpetrators."

"Belgian soldiers," Ann said.

"Murdered."

Ann nodded and picked at her thumbnail. "But I think the General was a patient at the hospital last week. Is that possible?"

In between patients, Ann studied King Faisal's inpatient log—a large, leather-bound book filled with the inked names of patients, fifty to a page. She ran her finger down the list from the week before. The hospital had 150 beds, but some beds held two, even three patients. The current census consumed several pages. The name, date of admission, admitting diagnosis, date of discharge, and discharge diagnoses were meticulously printed by a compulsive secretary in blue ballpoint, although the secretary had told Ann that some of the names were manufactured to disguise the admissions of prominent Tutsis.

"General Théoneste Bagasora" was printed neatly. Diagnosis—kidney stone, left against medical advice. She'd evaluated him in the ED. Certainly Ann could pay him a follow-up visit. She mulled it over as she saw patients.

She decided that she needed Colonel's blessing to visit General Bagasora and use the name of the hospital. Late in the afternoon, she caught Colonel outside the OR; these days he ran from one case to the next. She explained her dilemma, keeping her voice low since patients and their family members waited nearby.

Colonel scratched his cheek and mused. "Large man, an important fellow in the Rwandan government. He asked that I see him personally, even demanded a private room. But as I recall, it was pretty straightforward, fluids and pain meds. I don't recall him passing the stone."

"Can I use the name of King Faisal? Take him some pain medicine. Confirm that he passed the stone?"

Colonel studied Ann. "You're a plucky girl. I like that about you."

Chapter 22

Margaux waited for Ann at the emergency entrance at noon. They planned to drop in without an appointment. It was the first time Ann had seen Margaux dressed in something other than jeans and a t-shirt. The straight blue skirt and blouse flattered Margaux's figure. Despite her two-pack-a-day cigarette habit, she looked to be in good shape for fifty-something. She wore her gray hair twisted into a bun and she'd applied lipstick. "You look great," Ann said.

Margaux flushed.

"No, really," Ann said.

"Please," Margaux said. She smelled of soap.

The GH driver motored the short distance to the government offices. A fine drizzle fell. The windshield wipers whined as they flipped back and forth. The surrounding neighborhood was largely destroyed. UN soldiers in their light-blue helmets labored to collect the corpses. A large pyre smoldered in a park on the corner. Margaux handed out several cigarettes at the one roadblock they encountered. It was the most permanent one Ann had seen. The soldiers had a little shack complete with a corrugated metal roof and a couch.

The stucco Parliament building sat on a rise. The once well-manicured flower gardens sprouted weeds; the grass was so long that her father would have baled it at home. The other government buildings that stood in close proximity also suffered from months of neglect.

An eight-foot chain-link fence surrounded the property. The Rwandan army patrolled the gate. Kalashnikovs rested against the brick guard house, their barrels pointed skyward. Ann leaned forward and flashed her King Faisal medical ID from the backseat. "I'm paying a medical visit to General Bagasora," she said.

The soldier examined her ID, flipped it over, and studied the back. He kept turning it back and forth and, just as she considered slipping him some francs, he harrumphed and waved them through.

Margaux and Ann strode into the building with their best air of official business. The placard showed that the General's office was on the fourth floor. Of course, the elevator was not in service, so they panted and sweated up the stairs in silence. On the third-floor landing, Margaux had a coughing fit.

A brass nameplate hung outside the door. The handsomely appointed office looked over the city. General Bagasora sat in a leather chair at a large, polished, mahogany desk. A thick middle-age man with a paunch and a wolfish smile, he chewed on his cigar throughout their entire visit. Certificates, awards, and photos of the general posing with various dignitaries hung on one wall. An air-conditioner trimmed with rust sat in the window frame on the far left, silent. The other windows were propped open. The modest breeze that entered did little to erase the stale, musty cigar smell. Ann recalled visits to her cigar-smoking Grandpa on Friday nights as a child. All their clothes reeked when they got home. Everything was tossed into the laundry.

"Dr. Ann McLannly from King Faisal Hospital," Ann said, extending her hand.

He stood and regarded her. He was at least six feet. Instead of a handshake, his palm touched hers.

"Margaux Dupont with Global Health. A pleasure once again."

He gestured for them to sit down. The chairs, covered in dark-brown leather, matched his swivel chair.

"General, I met you in the early 1990s. I helped set up the IDP camp, Keiko. After the RPF attack."

The General nodded, set his cigar in the ashtray on his desk, but gave no hint of recognition. Much to Ann's horror the ashtray was the palm of a gorilla, exactly what Dian Fossey had railed against.

Ann smoothed her hands over her green scrubs. She'd decided not to change out of them, thinking they might make her look more official; in fact, she still wore her stethoscope around her neck. "General, it is our policy to check patients who leave the hospital against medical advice. You were in a great deal of pain when you were hospitalized with what we believed was a kidney stone. How are you feeling?" She tried to be professional and direct, but display appropriate concern. Initially she looked him in the eye, then glanced away as a gesture of respect.

"I'm fine. The pain ended the next day." He picked up his cigar.

Ann nodded, trying to appear calm. Her heart raced and sweat trickled down the middle of her back. The waistband of her scrub pants grew moist. "I'm glad you are better. I brought you a few more pain meds, just in case— Hydrocodone. Colonel Arif Sengupta, the surgeon from the UN, thought it might be good to have them on hand in case you have another attack. You're a busy man."

The general palmed the vial and shoved it into the pocket of his beige trousers. "*Merci.*"

"Let us know if you have other problems, we know you have many responsibilities." Time to address the orphanage issue. Ann took a deep breath and plunged in. "I also wanted to ask you about the Beauraing Orphanage. We understand there are threats on the lives of the children and the nuns. I am the medical director." She gave herself an official title. "The nuns are committed. They take good care of the children. We are asking you to make sure they are not harmed."

A phone clanged in the office next door. It rang five times before a female voice answered, halting the drone of someone striking typewriter keys.

General Bagasora stared beyond them at some point on the wall, took out a lighter, and relit his cigar. The stream of smoke enveloped Margaux and Ann.

On the way over Margaux had told Ann that Bagasora was rumored to be the mastermind of the Tutsi murders, creating the list of Tutsis and Tutsi-sympathizers. He was in charge of the army and had conceptualized the *interahamwe* militia, having convinced President Habyarimana that he needed to finance a group of non-military men who would be loyal to him. The *interahamwe* were reportedly doing much of the killing, especially outside Kigali.

If all this was true, General Bagasora was ordering the murder of thousands, maybe tens of thousands, trying to wipe out an entire race. Did he care about what she had to say? Ann reminded herself that he urinated, defecated, likely had a wife and children, maybe a mistress or two.

The cigar smell was almost unbearable. The fluorescent lights buzzed. Voices echoed in the hallway. Suddenly the general's gaze met Ann's. "You know Father Innocent Rwagasonza?" he asked.

"The pastor of St. Michael Church," Ann sat up straighter, shocked to hear Innocent's full name. Her face flushed and sweat dampened in her armpits.

The general nodded. "He asked me to spare the children at that orphanage. He said that the nuns are good women. The director, Sister Mary Joseph, is not *ibyitso*. She is not a traitor who is saving Tutsi children."

Ann swallowed hard. She couldn't swear to that fact. But thankfully, Father Innocent had convinced General Bagasora that it was true.

Margaux bent forward slightly and spoke in a clear, steady voice. "These are innocent children and dedicated nuns. They raised Father Innocent. They should be spared."

General Bagasora eyed them for a long minute, then puffed on his cigar, leaning back in his chair. The chair creaked.

Margaux continued, "How will history judge you, General? It is your duty to protect the citizens of Rwanda. How will you explain killing innocent children when we are on the other side of all of this?"

The General moved his lips around his cigar, then stood up. "Thank you for coming. King Faisal provided good service. I'll remember that." He extended his hand toward them. His hand was thick and his shake was still limp and moist, like clasping a large, room-temperature fish.

In the SUV Ann and Margaux high-fived. "Nice job," Margaux said.

"I was so nervous, could you tell? I liked your appeal to his conscience."

"It was the only ammunition I had," Margaux said. "And I am glad to hear that Father Innocent said something on behalf of Beauraing. Perhaps the International Red Cross director is wrong."

Ann asked to drive past St. Michael; she needed to see for herself.

The eucalyptus trees blew in the gentle breeze unaware of what lay on the ground beneath them. Bodies blanketed the grassy lawn to the east side of the church. Many had fallen in defensive postures, a hand raised; others still gripped a stick or machete. Just outside a side entrance, the bodies were piled several thick, as if the killer must have stood at the door and bludgeoned them as they tried to escape. Was it her imagination, or did she see a head turn? A dog busily chewed on someone's hand.

The front door under the statue of Jesus stood ajar. A man in bloodstained trousers lay on the cement step; his foot acted as the doorstop. Overhead, one arm of the Jesus statue was hacked off; the other reached heavenward, draped with a woman's bloodied dress. On the walk that led to the parsonage a woman lie dead; her baby still clutched to her breast.

A wave of nausea gripped Ann as she whispered the rote prayers she'd learned in religion class. *Our Father who art in heaven. . . deliver us from evil.* Perhaps that was the purpose of rote prayer, like a mantra, it interrupted the troubling thoughts and images, stamped away the evil, filling one's head with other words and concepts, holy intentions, prayers for protection.

Except for the idling of the SUV's motor, they sat in silence. Was God listening? When trapped in her own private hell—Rosie's drowning and Ann's mother's illness—Ann had questioned the value of prayer. Nothing changed. She asked for things and God rarely came through. The pain and anguish, the desperation continued, maybe less acute because she'd grown distracted. Ann wasn't as certain about God as Joseta, Sister Mary Joseph, or 99.

And who was the God that allowed such awfulness? The senseless slaughter spread out in front of her. Someone at the hospital had accused God of sleeping in Rwanda.

Hail Mary full of grace. . . pray for us sinners. Despite her misgivings about prayer, the well-rehearsed lines flooded her brain. Like worry beads, her mind curled around the phrases. . . *now and at the hour of our death.*

Margaux broke the quiet. "There are no words to describe this."

The driver gripped the wheel and nodded. "I thank God that I work for GH."

Ann didn't see Father Innocent, but people lay several deep. He had talked to General Bagasora about sparing the orphanage. That meant he was alive. She did not want to believe the rumors about him. He wouldn't betray his parishioners. He was a man loved by all, who drew many to him and to the worship of God. She prayed for his safety.

Chapter 23

As April slid toward May, Rwanda slipped deeper into the rainy season and the pandemonium intensified. The international community ignored Rwanda; they said she should solve her own problems.

Outside Ann's bedroom window the morning mist hung thick. The folds of the night mingled with the day, blanketing the neighborhood with an ethereal quality. Ann's watch had stopped. Was it time to get up or could she crawl underneath the mosquito netting, between the sheets, and into her cocoon? The howling dogs were strangely silent.

Down the hall, Margaux hacked her five minute smoker's morning ritual. Ann had sworn off cigarettes since her meeting with General Bagasora. The aromas of coffee and porridge wafted up the stairs from the kitchen and Joseta and her granddaughter were talking in their room. The hour was later than Ann thought.

Fog also mantled the courtyard at King Faisal where locals had taken up residence on the north side of the property. The outlines of makeshift shelters stretched all the way to the chain-link fence. Much like at St. Michael Church, families arrived lugging pots and pans, bundles of clothes, mattress rolls and yellow plastic gerry cans. The community expanded daily. One NGO provided food. Another promised to supply tarps and tents to waterproof the stick-and-thatch structures.

Hospital officials did not chase the squatters away. In fact, the hospital administrator moved his family into a room on the hospital's top floor. Ann examined one of his children. Many staff followed his lead, bringing along their extended families. The actual census rose well beyond the 150 beds. In addition to the two and three patients to a bed with family members sleeping on the floor, some relatives slept on the balconies, and others crawled into the broom closets. When Ann made hospital rounds, she stepped over sleeping bodies and was careful to pinpoint the patient before she started her assessment.

Shortly after arriving on the morning of April 30th, she learned that the UN had arranged yet another ceasefire so patients could be transported between Kigali General and King Faisal. "This is a safer part of town," the hospital administrator explained. "We've not had the raids Kigali General has. We're lucky."

"All went well last time," Ann said.

Ann filled her backpack with supplies. Her patient had a broken leg and surgery was planned at King Faisal. Joseta handed her a vial of morphine and told her to tuck it in her bra. "If you get stopped, they won't look there."

When the siren screamed across town, the ambulance took off, trailing the UN Land Rover. The strobe light flashed on the roof and the horn blared. The ride was less bumpy than on earlier trips because the potholes were now padded with trash. People shoved their refuse into the street, now that garbage pickup services had ceased.

By 10:00 a.m., the sun had burned off the morning mist and the day grew oppressively hot. Ann dabbed at the perspiration on her neck as she watched out the small van window, holding back the beige curtain. She couldn't complain; after the extended grayness, she welcomed the sun. Dogs roamed the streets in packs, barking and growling, aggressively pursuing their prizes—a leg bone, an arm, a human foot. One group fought over a torso. Ann cringed when she identified that the rib cage belonged to a child, not a dog. She survived by honing her professional distance to a new level, not engaging her emotions too much. Maybe the memories would haunt her later, but at this point if she really let in the horrible realities, she wouldn't be able to function.

The smell of petrol and smoke had grown as familiar as the flocks of vultures, the buzz of flies, and the odor of decaying flesh. Would Ann ever get rid of the stench? She bent over and sniffed her forearm—the disgusting odor. It smelled more permanent than perfume; it penetrated her clothes, skin, hair, even her nails—maybe it was stuck in her nose hairs.

This time the ambulance pulled up to Kigali General's morgue entrance. Strange.

"*Bonjour*," Ann greeted her patient. The sheets on his gurney were stamped Veterans Administration, a donation. A fully extended crutch, tucked against the patient's buttock and wrapped with torn rags, served as the splint, a creative solution given his height. She pressed her hand into his groin and felt for his femoral pulse, then she checked for the pulses in his foot and ankle—doralis pedis and post tibial. A rhythmatic beat throbbed against her fingers confirming that the bones were properly aligned and his circulation intact.

The patient grimaced.

When she switched to English, she learned he was in a great deal of pain. The RPF Tutsi rebels had taken shelter in Uganda in the early 1990s after the war. Because it was a British colony, English was commonly spoken and most Tutsis from Uganda spoke English. The intravenous line was not clotted off, so Ann retrieved the morphine from her bra, drew it into a syringe and injected it.

The road was choked with traffic on the way back. They crawled along and were forced to stop at several checkpoints. Ann pinned the beige curtains so no one could see in, restricting her view.

Angry shouts surrounded the van as it jolted to a stop.

"Okay back there?" the driver called.

"All's fine," Ann yelled over the ruckus, grabbing the gurney to keep her balance. The patient snored peacefully, benefiting from the morphine, as she adjusted his sheets.

The volume of the outside commotion grew even louder when the driver rolled down his window. Ann could not understand what was said, but when thumps sounded on the van's back door the intent became clear. She pulled a roll of thick gauze out of her backpack and began to wrap her patient's head. She couldn't disguise his height, but she could conceal his facial features. She retrieved bandage scissors, sliced the name band off his wrist, and stuffed it in her bra.

The hollering and pounding intensified. A hammer slammed through the back window across from where she stood. Ann squeezed against the van's other side as glass sprayed everywhere. Hands groped inside, tugging at the curtains. The yelling grew a decibel louder and the pummeling increased. Ann's heart galloped. The van rocked back and forth—would they tip the van? Ann crouched, bathed in sweat.

She stood up to swat at the hands that reached in through the broken window. A hand tore the curtains. More banging on the back door, and suddenly it flew open. A tall, angry African dressed red and green screamed at her and propelled himself into the van. He tried to rise to his full height, but could not because of the cramped space. His left hand aimed a pistol at the patient's head as he glared in Ann's direction.

Ann stared into the face of Father Innocent.

His angry eyes could have burned through tin. Hatred spewed from his mouth. Spittle collected at the corners of his full lips. Ann barely recognized his contorted face. No one would have identified him as a priest. His left hand held the black pistol she'd seen in the bookcase in his study and on the floor of his truck.

Her heart pumped. Her breath came in jagged spurts. Should she acknowledge him? He didn't act as if he recognized her. She straightened, trying to look imposing. She inhaled and spoke in deliberate French: "*Mon patient est très malade*, my patient is very ill. He is in a great deal of pain. We do not have time for an inspection."

The hospital staffer, a thick Rwandan with piercing black eyes, who had sat in the front on the passenger side, jumped into the van and translated what she had said into Kinyarwanda. Innocent continued his rant. The pistol still pointed at the patient.

Would Innocent acknowledge her? Would he back off? Would he fire the pistol? Time stood still. Ann remembered to breathe, forcing air through her windpipe and into her lungs. Her mouth tasted like cotton. She stared at Innocent's hand, the blue-black skin and the pink palm closed around the gun.

After a deep inhale, she said, "Father Innocent, don't harm my patient. Please, by the grace of God leave us alone."

Innocent spun toward her. His dagger-look bore down, the charisma and intelligence she'd known scraped away. "If you tell anyone you saw me, I'll put this to your head." He shook the pistol. "*Gutera ingunguru.*" Then he focused his gaze beyond her, beyond her patient, and dropped his arm with the gun. He raised his right hand and blessed them with the sign of the cross. Then he jumped from the van, shouted in Kinyarwanda, and disappeared into the street crowded with red and green-shirted men. The hospital staffer followed, slamming the van door. Within seconds, the staffer had bounded into the van's front seat. The motor *vroomed*. Ann steadied herself as the van jerked forward.

With her buttocks wedged between the van's side wall and the gurney, she bent over, planted her hands on the bed's edge, and inhaled and exhaled against a wave of fear. He had threatened her. She busied herself, carefully picking up the shards of glass. They were hard to find, the clear glass lost in the white folds of the sheet and the patient's gown. A shaft of sunlight looked like a splinter of glass. Ann pricked her right pointer finger and put it to her mouth to stop the bleeding. She pressed her thumb and finger of her left hand together as she searched for all the broken pieces, collecting them in a recycled plastic bag.

She rechecked the patient's pulse and blood pressure and carefully unwrapped the gauze from around his head. Completing these tasks kept her mind off the panic that filled her belly. It had become personal.

When they reached King Faisal, she gave her report to the OR nurse, clarifying the time of the morphine dose and the patient's latest vitals. She said nothing about her confrontation with Innocent. She returned to the emergency area, walked up to the chalkboard, and checked off the next patient.

She worked. That was the best way to manage her shock. She repaired lacerations, cleaned abrasions, casted fractures, stabilized patients for surgery and declared others dead. For five hours she shoved away thoughts about her encounter with Innocent.

At 4:00 p.m., the hospital administrator sent her home. "You've put in a long day. You deserve some rest."

Ann asked the GH driver to take her to the orphanage. On the way they passed St. Michael Church. Three vultures perched on the parsonage roof. One picked at the entrails in its claws, the other two moved their ugly heads back and forth, appearing to monitor the activities in the yard. One glared directly at the GH vehicle and flapped its wings. Ann pulled her hand to her nose against the dreadful stench.

The UN guard opened the bamboo gate. He and 99 were sitting at school desks under a purple parasol sipping Cokes. 99 did not stand to greet her. The heat of the day made everyone lazy.

Inside the orphanage, the noisy play of the children was her welcome. Four boys played jacks in the hallway. In the playroom, Beanie Babies sat at a table with miniature dishes that looked to be a tea party. A Rwandan nun played the piano. Ann followed the hallway back to the kitchen and found Sister Mary Joseph sitting in her office. Sister ordered tea and offered Ann a cigarette.

Ann declined, settling herself onto the wooden chair.

"Something terrible has happened," Sister Mary Joseph said.

"I'm afraid. Innocent . . ."

Sister Mary Joseph nodded slowly. "We all expected much more from him." She rose and stepped around her desk toward Ann. Ann held up her hand; she needed some time, some space. The cook carried in the tea tray and Sister Mary Joseph poured, handing Ann a cup and saucer.

Ann set her rattling china on the desk. When the cook left, her words poured out. "He threatened me. He told me to tell no one. I have to tell. . ."

She related Margaux's suspicion, the rumors, and the visit to General Bagasora. How even then, when the general had mentioned Innocent's name, she had not believed it was possible, especially since Innocent had spoken on behalf of the orphanage and the nuns. She described the ambulance ride and the shock of staring into Innocent's face, the anger and hatred, his vile manner. Her voice grew stronger as she spoke. "I addressed him by name." She did not mention that he accused her of *gutera ingunguru*, rejecting him, throwing an oil drum.

Sister Mary Joseph sighed and made the sign of the cross. "We heard the rumors. We all expected so much more of him." She was silent for a long minute, cleared her throat, and then took a sip of tea. "He came to us with his name. He was born on the feast of the Holy Innocents, December 28th."

Ann rubbed the edge of Sister's desk, "I've heard of that." She took her first swallow of tea. It was cool.

"The feast day celebrates the children of Bethlehem who were murdered by King Herod after the birth of Christ."

Ann bit her lip; her eyes brimmed and she made her body rigid to keep her emotions in check.

Sister continued, "I am disappointed. Sad. I knew him as a boy. A brilliant boy with the chance to do so much good in Rwanda." Sister fingered the rosary that hung around her waist. "We desperately need the charisma and intelligence of someone like him. Do you know that over a dozen popes have carried the name Innocent? It's a name with such possibilities."

Ann stood up and walked to the window. "He was a great preacher." Gunfire sounded in the distance. She began to drum the window ledge. The distant hills looked so peaceful with their long, violet shadows creeping across the land as the sun slipped behind them. Her fingers played the notes of the birds' chirps: C, D minor, E, E, E. The fading light inched across the orphanage garden, obscuring the individual plants.

". . . the two of you were close," Sister Mary Joseph said.

Ann nodded.

"God bless you. Don't be too hard on yourself. He was a charismatic man. I am as surprised as you. . . at what he's done."

Ann continued to gaze out the window. She stood far away from that fateful day in August when Rosie drowned, five days later when they turned off her ventilator. So far and yet so close, the hole inside gaped open again—searing pain at Innocent's betrayal. It cut as sharp as a scalpel. The pain from her own failures had begun to fade, but now she brimmed with disappointment, anger, yes, there was anger, and something else. . . .He could hurt her.

She'd said enough. Her curfew loomed thirty minutes away, created for her safety. She needed to return to the compound.

Sister rose and hugged Ann, pulling her deep into the coarse cloth that covered her generous bosom. "Are there any children that need to be seen?" Ann asked, struggling to keep her voice even.

"Everything can wait until tomorrow," Sister Mary Joseph said. "Go home, take some time for yourself, *mon amie*." Sister cleared her throat.

Ann blinked back the dampness in her eyes.

Sister walked Ann to the door. "By the way," Sister said. "We've been left alone. The killers have passed us by, so far. King Herod hasn't bothered us." She chuckled. "In fact, the Rwandan army dropped off a supply of clothes and a crate of food for the children."

At the compound, Ann feigned diarrhea and rushed into the bathroom. She wanted a shower, a long, hot shower. She ripped off her clothes, stepped into the tub and twisted the faucet—the usual dribble. She filled a bucket and dumped it over her torso, then splashed another toward her pelvis. She had not told Sister Mary Joseph everything. *Gutera ingunguru.* Innocent had wanted her. She'd considered it, even liked his touch, his kisses, been encouraged by Sylvia to accept his advances—"the rules in Africa are different." But she'd said no. What a relief. She'd rejected him. But he was not letting her forget it. Goose bumps marched across her back and over her shoulders. She heaved another bucket of the tepid liquid over her scalp. He could hurt her. How should she keep herself safe? Another bucket of lukewarm water crashed over her head and face. Where were her lofty goals of helping people? She wanted the incense, the choir, and the holy feeling of Sunday mass, the courage to go forth and heal. Not this darkness.

She stepped out of the shower stall dripping and grabbed a towel. She patted her face and rubbed her hair. The boiled potato from lunch sat like a boulder in her stomach. Her mouth watered. She would be sick; she swallowed purposefully, holding the towel over her mouth and choking down the saliva and bile. She leaned over the toilet. When her bowels cramped, she squatted onto the toilet seat, gulping air to manage the spasms. She purged her lunch.

Someone rapped on the bathroom door. The house only had one bathroom. "Just a minute," she called. "Almost done." She huffed and rose to pour a bucket of water into the back of the toilet, pulled the chain suspended from the ceiling and flushed. She wrapped the towel around her like a skirt, pulled a t-shirt over her head, and wadded up her clothes.

In the mirror her pale face and bloodshot eyes stared back. Her hair lay damp and matted. She pulled out a spiraling gray hair near her part. The four-plus months of the mission had taken their toll. She hadn't left Milwaukee for this. She'd come to help, to forget her own pain. She couldn't return home yet. She wasn't ready.

Ann understood that she'd piled the heartbreaks of others on top of her own. She'd jumped from her own tragic play to a tragic opera, but she'd not yet figured out how to swim in and through the pain of human loss and suffering. How to let it transform her.

More knocking.

She opened the bathroom door and apologized as the cook's son hurried in, holding his crotch. The door slammed as she walked down the hall.

In her bedroom, Ann dressed. She wouldn't burden her housemates with the dreadful events of her afternoon. Besides, she couldn't stomach rehashing the details. She would tell Margaux that the orphanage was safe.

Ann wandered into the kitchen. Christine handed her a hot glass of tea. "Rough day?" Christine asked. "Dinner's almost ready." The tea settled Ann's roiling stomach. The familiar smell of beans and onions, sweet and earthy, rose from the metal pot.

Chapter 24

During the season of long rain, it could pour for days; a quilt of gloom blanketed everything and everyone. The weather only deepened Ann's gray mood. It was not the cold dankness of the Midwest; the temperature was warm, but nothing dried out, everything, including her underwear, smelled of mildew. When she crawled into bed at night, her sheets felt damp, as if she'd slept drenched in sweat night after night.

One rainy morning in early May the RPF rebels burst through the emergency entrance at King Faisal at 10:00 a.m. The tall, thin soldiers were not as well-dressed as the Rwandan army or the *interahamwe* who wore red and green shirts, but they carried rifles and pistols. They pushed past the UN soldier; what could he have done anyway, not being permitted to use his gun? They yelled in Kinyarwanda and English, causing quite a ruckus among the waiting patients.

Ann stood against the far wall, irrigating a woman's infected leg wound. She peered around the curtain that separated her patient's gurney from the rest of the room. A chill bristled across the back of her neck as she returned to her patient. Someone else could deal with it. Confronting men with weapons, armed men who were angry, tall men with pistols and Kalashnikovs was too much.

Joseta approached them. She planted her feet and held her arms akimbo. In an "I mean business tone," as if she were refusing to accept insolence from her teenage sons, she shouted "*Kuki*, why?"

The rebel who pointed the Kalashnikov at her chest lowered it a few centimeters. His peers stepped back. She had their attention. The audience of waiting patients fell silent. All eyes focused on Joseta.

One RPF soldier explained that they needed medications to care for their ranks.

"Put your guns there." Joseta pointed to a gurney. "Come with me." The half dozen men followed her into the medication room. She negotiated what they could and could not take. They pitched medication bottles, vials, and bandages into several jungle-green duffels, then after thanking her, they collected their weapons and paraded toward the entrance. Staff members gawked, frozen in place, hiding like Ann behind curtains and further down the hall. There was a collective gasp when the rebels walked out the door. Joseta looked around the room, shrugged, and went back to the triage desk.

The shelves would not be restocked for several days. Staff got by, borrowing medications and supplies from the hospital floors. Joseta had created a hidden stash with additional medical provisions. Ann cut corners, giving antibiotics for five days instead of seven.

But King Faisal could not sustain repeated attacks. Raids by the Rwandan army and the RPF had brought Kigali General to its knees. If this became the norm at King Faisal, they would have to close.

Colonel demanded another guard from UN headquarters; perhaps two would be better than one. "Why can't the guards use their weapons?" he yelled into the satellite phone. Of course, it was to no avail, maybe Colonel felt better, but the UN's hands were tied by the US and Europe. Colonel had resurrected a moldy and decaying hospital. Now staff hauled water, bargained for propane to run the generators, and cared for the burgeoning census. The 150-bed hospital had grown more unsanitary and dysfunctional. Over a thousand refugees camped on the north side, crowding into the field that stretched from the hospital's brick walls to the chain-link fence. Inside the fence laid a zone of safety, beyond it, anyone was fair game, especially at night.

The UN soldiers who guarded King Faisal strained to manage the hoodlums who wandered onto the hospital property. They collected machetes, sticks, and Kalashnikovs as best they could. But they were handicapped against the army, militia, and rebels because they could not use their weapons.

The long, rainy season drizzled on. No one dried out. Everyone plodded through the long days, internalizing the gloom. The roads and walkways grew slick with red mud. Pedestrians tracked it everywhere. King Faisal's yellow linoleum floors developed a red, grainy film. The cleaning staff struggled with an impossible task.

With limited supplies, the doctors and nurses became resourceful. A patient came in with a decayed tooth that needed pulling. Ann had no anesthesia and the OR protected their limited stash of Ketamine. The patient held his dark hand against his cheek and moaned. One of the orderlies told Ann to wait, he'd return with a remedy. In the meantime, Ann cleaned wounds, set fractures, started a nursing mother with cellulitis of the breast on antibiotics; at least she had the right antibiotic to treat the infection.

The orderly appeared a half hour later, breathless, his cheeks flushed and his trousers spattered with red mud. He pulled a bottle from a brown cloth bag. "*Urwagwa*," he said and untwisted the cap.

The sharp scent hinted at the local liquor's strength. Ann directed the patient to take a swig. Within a few minutes, he was snoozing against the angled back of the cot. He opened his mouth when asked. The putrid smell assaulted her. With the pliers she'd borrowed from the maintenance staff and wiped with alcohol, she grabbed the tooth and tugged. It didn't budge. Her hands and forearms ached. Disappointed, she pointed the tooth out to the orderly and stepped aside.

The orderly grasped the tooth, grunted, and jerked out the offending molar. The patient didn't wince, but a faint wheeze indicated that he was still among the living. Ann thanked the orderly, focused her headlamp into the patient's mouth, mopped up the blood, and probed the hole in the gum. The orderly peered over her shoulder. No porcelain chimed against her probe, no tooth fragments. She stuffed in a wad of gauze and pressed the patient's jaw closed, directing the orderly to keep watch so the patient wouldn't swallow the packing when he woke up. She hurried off to wash her hands before moving on to the next patient.

Ann twisted the faucet—nothing. It was such a habit—turn spigot, water followed. But they'd been without water for almost a month. She sighed as she dipped a cup into the water bucket, located the splinter of soap, scrubbed her hands, and wondered how much longer she could do this.

The hospital had acquired a rank stench only partially disguised by the cleaning staff's ammonia. The restrooms, in particular, had grown increasingly wretched. The toilets flushed if a bucket of water was thrown into the porcelain in the back, but often the water barrel was empty, and folks did not bother to flush. It was as if staff, patients, and their families were saying *life stinks, and there is nothing we can do about it.*

At lunchtime Joseta and Ann shared a bowl of boiled potatoes in the break room. "This is miserable," Ann complained. "I work here to make folks well. We have no medications. The bathrooms stink. Cleanliness is impossible. I don't think we are making much of a difference."

Joseta nodded, her gray-brown eyes heavy with exhaustion.

They chewed in silence. Ann worked up the courage to ask if there was any news about Vincent.

Joseta swallowed her potato and stared at the floor. "Nothing," she said. "I keep praying to Jesus."

Ann's bite of potato stuck in her throat. How could Joseta have such faith when God had been so cruel to her family? The platitudes: *I'm praying for you. God will provide. It can't get any worse. Trust God's plan.* Once upon a time, Ann actually believed them. Where was God now?

Colonel threatened to close the hospital unless the Rwandan army and the RPF rebels helped to secure the supply trucks. The army mounted a plastic bladder on the roof as a source for water. The RPF donated bags of food. When one side asked Colonel if he was treating the other, he diplomatically replied, "If you don't raid King Faisal, you and your soldiers will receive all the care you need."

A steady exodus continued to leave Kigali. Many wore brightly colored flip-flops on their feet, a rainbow of yellow, hot pink, royal blue, and Kelly green. Bikes packed with wooden boxes and crates and draped with yellow-plastic gerry cans were pushed, not ridden; there was no room for a rider. With the departures and killings, Kigali's population dwindled to half of what it was before April 6th. The BBC reported: "Tens of thousands of refugees from across Rwanda are fleeing into Tanzania, Burundi, and Zaire."

Margaux pushed back her plate, having scarfed down tiny portions of beans, potatoes, and *matoke*. Ann lamented running out of catsup a month earlier. She forked the bland *matoke* into her mouth and swallowed, looking across the table at both the driver and Joseta's families, who cleaned their plates.

Margaux swirled the amber whiskey in her glass, straight up. Ice was impossible to come by. "Headquarters asked us to transfer our operation to a camp in Tanzania. I want all of you to consider coming."

"You're closing the compound?" Ann asked. She was happy to leave the hospital, but what about the nuns, the orphans.

Margaux nodded. "Security is deteriorating." Margaux made eye contact with each person at the table—Ann, the driver and his wife, the cook, as well as Joseta and Christine. "There will be work for everyone." She smiled at the children. "Of course, the children are welcome."

Evangeline, Joseta's granddaughter, pointed to the potatoes.

"Use your words," Joseta said. Evangeline was a good eater and clearly the delight of her grandmother.

"Potatoes," she intoned.

Ann passed the bowl.

Margaux continued, "There's a steady stream of Rwandans crossing into Tanzania and Zaire. According to the UN, it is the largest and fastest refugee exodus in modern times. Food, water, shelter, and medical aid are needed. Pronto. We'll run one of the medical facilities at the camp."

"Where?" the driver asked.

"Near Basuko, an hour from the Rwanda-Tanzania border."

"River at border," the driver said.

"My sources tell me that a quarter of a million refugees have settled along the river." Margaux pulled a cigarette from her pack.

"So there's a source of water," Ann said.

Margaux nodded. "We'll live outside the camp in the nearby town." She lit the cigarette. "You'll be very busy."

"Tell me about the medical setup," Ann said, pumping her clenched hands. She wanted a cigarette, but she resisted. If she had even one after dinner, she'd be hooked again.

"We'll be one of three NGOs running a hospital and outpatient clinic. I'll hire Rwandan medical personnel who've fled to the camp. Doctors. Nurses. Lab techs." Margaux swallowed a swig of whiskey. "There'll be additional expats. An American surgeon will be the medical director. He thinks he knows you." She eyed Ann. "He owes you a beer or something."

"What's his name?"

"Edward Robinson." Margaux sucked on her cigarette and exhaled away from the table.

Ann raised her eyebrows and shrugged. Could this be the surgeon she'd met in Kigali? He'd asked her to join him for a beer.

"The trip takes a day or more," Margaux explained. "We'll take two vehicles." She looked at the driver. "I'm buying another Toyota. A truck will carry our supplies. There's room for all of you. I want to leave in three days." She dumped the ash from her cigarette on her plate. "Any questions?"

"It would be safer for us," Christine said, clasping Joseta's hand. "Mama, what do you think?"

Joseta lifted her shoulders, her face expressionless. "Let me pray about it."

Ann guessed that losing proximity to Vincent was a factor for Joseta.

"Think it over. Let me know in the next day or so." Margaux excused herself and carried her cigarette and whiskey to her room.

"I know you worked hard to restore King Faisal," Ann said.

Joseta looked at Ann. "The working conditions have to be better."

Ann nodded. "It would be safer for all of us."

Chapter 25

The same UN soldier, the one with the hole in his boot, sat underneath a broad, purple parasol in front of the orphanage. The rain had stopped, but the sun bore down. It was odd that 99 was not with him.

Ann pushed open the pink door; she no longer bothered to knock. How many times had she stood in the foyer, smelled the diapers, porridge and juice—the bittersweet scents that epitomized the orphanage. A dozen boys and girls crowded around her. One carried a book for her to read. Another handed her a doll. "Kiss the *owie*."

The children followed her to the piano. Two squeezed next to her on the bench. She lifted her fingers to the keyboard. *Da Da Da. Da Da Da...* the grand beginning to *The Children of Sanchez*. Playing became her focus. The music lifted her spirits. At the conclusion of the song the children applauded. "More. More," several called.

"I could play all evening," Ann said.

Someone asked for "the do, re, me song."

Ann's fingers found the keys. If only the rest of her life were so easy. If only the events marched out like the notes. If only the melody flowed without hassle, without worry. Ann played several songs.

"I should stop," Ann said. She needed to tell Sister Mary Joseph about her departure. The child on Ann's right began pounding out Chopsticks.

Ann found Sister Mary Joseph in her office reading the bible. "Where is 99?" Ann asked.

"He left for Tanzania yesterday," Sister replied. "God bless him."

"Can he make it?"

Sister shrugged, her eyes wide. "Someone gave him a bike." She poured tea and handed Ann her cup and saucer.

Ann stared at her teacup, the delicate china. "Margaux is moving our operations to Tanzania."

"You're going?"

Ann moved her head up and down. No one had the medical experience to replace her. King Faisal was too busy to send anyone; Ann had asked Colonel. "I, I feel like I'm leaving you in the lurch…"

"We'll make do," Sister said.

"I hate goodbyes."

"Drink your tea before it grows cold," Sister urged. "God will take care of us."

The nuns managed without water or flushing toilets. Thanks to the generator, they had limited electricity. They cooked on the outdoor stove and each day a group of older orphans collected wood from the eucalyptus grove at the edge of their property. The Seventh Day Adventist missionary from the US hauled water and secured the propane they needed for their generator. The manager at Hotel des Mille Collines delivered bags of beans and rice. Their gardener had vanished, so the younger nuns and older children tilled and weeded.

"Who will I talk to? Who'll keep me in line?"

Sister Mary Joseph laughed. "The camp will present challenges, but you'll do well. *Envoyer mon amour avec toi*, my love goes with you."

Ann traced the edge of the china saucer with her finger. "And… what about Father Innocent?" Saying his name made her shiver. "Have… have you heard anything?" She hoped she'd never see him again. She lifted her gaze to Sister's face.

Sister narrowed her eyes, a crease formed between her eyebrows. "I pray for him. Pray for his soul." She raised her hand to her forehead, touched her chest and made the sign of the cross. "Such a loss. Such a loss." She shook her head.

The nuns had prepared a care package for Ann. Inside a swatch of plaid cotton cloth was a score of Rodgers and Hammerstein musicals, a jar filled with tea leaves, and a plastic glow-in-the-dark rosary. "Where did you find the music?" she asked.

"I have connections," Sister said. "I trust you'll find a piano and when you play the songs you'll remember us. Pray for us."

"And the rosary," Ann said. "I had one as a kid."

"Hasn't every Catholic child?"

When she was a child, Ann's rosary had hung on Ann's bedpost during the day. At night, she tucked it under her pillow. When she couldn't sleep, the luminescent beads had offered comfort against the looming darkness.

Ann began her goodbyes. She hugged the cook and Sister Mary Joseph and told them to give her regards to the other nuns. The children lined up for hugs; there were close to fifty now. They did not understand that she was leaving for good, just as well. Ann pulled the door closed behind her, tears streaming down her face; would they survive as Kigali crumbled around them?

Chapter 26

O n May 11th, the GH caravan left Kigali at first light. The rain had stopped, but gray clouds hung low. Margaux had acquired a Toyota SUV from an NGO that ended its work and had green GH logos painted on the front doors. Margaux sat in the front of the new vehicle; Ann and Joseta shared the backseat with Evangeline, who played between them. Christine followed in another SUV with the GH driver and his wife and their son. A truck packed with medical supplies and bedding brought up the rear.

On the outskirts of the city, they motored up the hill near the soccer stadium. The field and bleachers were packed with makeshift tents constructed from white and blue plastic sheeting. Colorful laundry flapped between the goalposts. The cooking fires created a hazy smog that hovered over the field as though it were a large industrial city on a humid summer day. The smoke stung Ann's eyes. The cacophony of the refugees' voices as well as their goats, dogs, and cows grew thunderous, then faded as the Toyota SUV left the city.

The roadblocks were easiest to negotiate before noon. Fear swelled in Ann's belly every time they pulled up to a checkpoint as she worried whether or not they would run into Father Innocent. The driver, a newly hired, large, imposing Rwandan, slowly rolled down his window. Annoyed men from the army or the *interahamwe* peered into the vehicle and spewed Kinyarwanda. The driver responded with a hoarse whisper, never ruffled. Sometimes Margaux leaned over, pleading in French, occasionally handing over cigarettes or francs.

As the sun approached its zenith and the liquor flowed, the exchanges grew more irrational. If someone could just stop the availability of banana beer and *urwagwa*, the stashes should be long gone.

Although more than a month had passed since the deaths of the Rwandan and Burundi presidents and the start of the killings, dead bodies still clogged the roads in the smaller towns. Corpses killed with machetes lay in pools of dried blood, their skulls smashed as if they were pumpkins, their limbs twisted in contractions that spoke of their violent deaths, a hand raised to shelter a face, a mouth caught in a an unending scream. The driver swerved to miss them, but the SUV bounced over some like speed bumps. Ann cringed, imagining the crunch of bones. She struggled to relax her muscles, to loosen her shoulders, so the tension headache that pinched her temples would release. At times, she and the other passengers shook and flopped like clothes in a tumble dryer.

The SUV's radio burbled with a news update. Investigations of the Clinton's Whitewater scandal were underway. The 50-kilometer *chunnel* between England and France that allowed passengers to travel between the two countries in thirty-five minutes had finally opened after seven years of labor.

"How much farther?" Ann asked.

"Four hundred kilometers according to my map," Margaux replied.

Two-hundred and forty miles, four trips back and forth on the *chunnel*— the differences between the developed and developing world. They'd been on the road more than five hours, and given the interruptions and the condition of the road, they had at least five more to go.

Refugees paraded along the roadside like a chain of leafcutter ants. The women stood tall, almost regal, hauling ancient suitcases, potato sacks stuffed with belongings, and cardboard boxes, all balanced on donut-sized rings of cloth or reed that sat on their heads. Many had children swathed to their backs. Some walked barefoot; others wore sandals crafted from rubber tires. A few sported old running shoes; and others had the colorful flip-flops sold all over Kigali. Children, not more than seven or eight, carried their younger siblings or led a goat, cow, or donkey packed high and wide with gear. All proceeded at a steady pace as intentional as ants carrying their leaf fragments. By foot how many days was the trip?

Margaux continued to puff away in the front seat, blowing smoke that drifted throughout the vehicle. Ann chewed on a thumbnail and concentrated on the unpleasantness of the cigarette smell—she would complete this trip without smoking a single cigarette. Evangeline slept next to Ann, with her head in Joseta's lap. Joseta leaned against the headrest, snoring softly.

Ann pulled out one of the crossword puzzle books that Sylvia had given her. She worked all the short entries, words with three or four letters, where the letter of one word hinted at the answer. It was how she managed the scene outside the SUV, small glimpses, tackling manageable bites. Like the other aid workers, she had constructed a shell; she could not digest what was happening around her in its entirety. It was just too much.

The news reported that the Hubble telescope had proven the existence of black holes. Up to that point, their existence in the universe had been purely theoretical. Black holes—the absence of light, points where the universe collapsed in on itself. Negative force.

Ann stared out the window at the destruction: burnt homes and fields, lives and dreams ruined. All the killings planned and premeditated, the attempt of an elite group to hold power. Not unlike Hitler's regime with its collapse of all civility and humanity. What force kept the negative gravitational pull from swallowing an entire galaxy? Where was the edge of the hole, the edge of the insanity outside the window? Ann shuddered. How could she make sense of this? Was it even possible?

They crept toward a checkpoint. The driver's window rolled down and another boozy whiff, a spew of irritated Kinyarwanda. The irritated guard wanted everyone to get out of the vehicle. The driver negotiated in his patient whisper. When Marguax handed over her pack of cigarettes, the guard signaled and they motored on. Evangeline slept and Joseta pretended to do the same throughout the encounter.

Ann returned to the puzzle book. A seven-letter word, a surgeon's instrument. Ann should know that. Two "Ls." The air conditioner died and Ann fanned herself with the book and rolled down her window. Wafts of hot air carried the stench of decay. Evangeline stirred. Joseta sat up, looked around, patted her granddaughter, and closed her eyes. Ann held a bandana to her nose. The word was "scalpel". She scribbled in the letters.

"There's your cache for making liquor," Margaux said. With her cigarette, she gestured toward a stand of banana trees. Black, rotten fruit hung from the stems. Bunches had fallen into the grass and a flock of Pied Crows feasted on the bounty. A woven grass basket sat half-filled with fruit. Overhead, a family of vultures circled, indicating either animal or human remains. Produce lay neglected in the fields. Only the dogs and scavenger birds appeared to thrive.

Ann returned to her puzzle book. The hot breeze blew strands of hair free and she corralled them again with her tie. "Margaux, you should know this. What city in France is known for lace? Seven letters. It ends with an 'n.'"

"I'm horrible at crosswords. But that's easy. Alençon. A town in Normandy. Put that on your place-to-visit list. Very old town. Beautiful. Occupied by the Germans during WWII."

Ann printed in the word and looked for other hints that involved French. None. Four more left, hard ones. She closed the book. "Tell me about the surgeon. I think he recruited me."

"We've done several tours together. Bosnia, Liberia. Somalia. I can't remember them all," Margaux said. "He's an excellent surgeon."

"Does he have blue eyes?"

"*Oui, oui.* Prematurely gray. Very photogenic. He's good with reporters."

Dr. Blue Eyes, as Sylvia called him. The blue-eyed doctor Ann had met in Milwaukee. She'd forgotten that he was a surgeon. He'd asked her to have a beer, but she'd refused and kicked herself the next day. "What's his name?" She bent forward to hear the response and got a face full of smoke.

"Edward Robinson, Dr. Robinson."

It was a strong name.

"He's from one of the "M" states. Maybe Michigan. He loves poker."

"Poker?" Ann had played in college.

"It creates team spirit. He's a lot of fun." Margaux laughed, then coughed and threw her cigarette out the window. "There's a pediatrician too. His first mission."

Ann passed the next hour fantasizing a connection. Edward had engaged the audience. A good storyteller. He delivered the facts and made everyone beg for more. His nose was crooked, but his eyes were hard to forget—marble-blue, rimmed in steel gray. His eyes had held hers and she'd flushed. If he asked her to join him for a beer, he must have been interested. Ann hadn't really dated anyone since her mother's diagnosis. She'd had boyfriends in college, medical school, and residency. She'd not bothered to tell the last boyfriend that she'd volunteered overseas.

So what was Innocent? Her mouth felt dry and a sinking feeling settled in her chest. She'd welcomed his friendship. He'd been a confidant, a cultural interpreter. She'd anticipated their Sunday afternoon chats. Innocent was a good kisser, but she'd held the line. Then he had a side that had shocked her. Hopefully, she'd never see him again.

What would Edward be like to work with? He said he was headed to Africa. What had he done for the past six months? How would she describe her time in Kigali? He'd remembered her, asked about her. Would they be more than colleagues? She'd refused a beer with him once. Would she again? Would there be privacy in the compound? It had been a long time since... Stop. She was getting too far ahead of herself. For all she knew he and Margaux had a relationship. Margaux certainly liked him. He made her laugh and her cheeks had flushed when she talked about him.

As they neared the border, the clouds thinned and a stunning blue sky greeted them. Perhaps it was the absence of smoke and diesel fuel that intensified the color. The line of refugees thickened. The driver dodged adults and children and the occasional goat or cow. Of course, everyone was headed one way. Despite the stench of sweat and body odor, it was a colorful scene.

A locomotive-like roar filled Ann's ears. The churning brown water of the Rusumo Falls drowned out the car's motor as well as the animal noises and chatter. The Akagara River, which defined the border between Rwanda and Tanzania, shot through a steep and narrow stone gorge. The sheer gray rock walls glistened in the spray. Rainbows hung in the mist.

Then a bloated body catapulted over the cascades. Followed by another. Then another. One or two every minute. The lunch Ann had eaten flopped in her stomach.

The Toyota SUV crawled across the two-lane bridge that arched over the river. Refugees squeezed together to allow the vehicles to pass. Sweat beaded on the driver's forehead. He wiped it repeatedly, maybe nervously, with his forearm. People reached into the vehicle, sometimes grabbing inside. Ann and the others rolled up their windows. Her white, freckled arm was a stark contrast to the glistening blue-black and maroon-black skin of the refugees. The only *wazungu* in sight, Ann and Margaux beckoned stares, eye contact that lasted longer than a curious glance. Bold refugees knocked on the window glass and opened their hands. Margaux smoked incessantly, not considering the stench she created for the others. Ann's clothes hung heavy with perspiration and the stink of cigarettes.

Joseta made the sign of the cross and covered Evangeline's eyes. She held her lips close to Evangeline's ear and sang a hymn.

Corpses bobbed in the roiling waters as if they were sticks carried along after torrential rains. Voices cried out the stories of their slaughter. In another decade, this spot would be a spectacular place to lunch, take in the view, and reflect on nature's power and splendor—but in May 1994 it was a macabre scene.

For a few moments Ann allowed herself to replay all she had witnessed—the injured patients at King Faisal, the bodies stacked like bricks along the roadsides, the singing nuns silenced one by one, the grisly scene outside Innocent's church, the worried nuns and the children at the Beauraing Orphanage. She shuddered. It was too much—a very black hole, a terribly dark chapter in the world. Would anyone believe the horrors she'd seen? Could she even describe them? Her hand flew to her mouth with the memories and the puzzle book flopped onto the floor.

A melody played on the radio. Ann's fingers began to move through the notes. She didn't know the song. As she heard the high note, she stretched her little finger across her leg. Her fingers drummed out the melody and the refrain sounded in her head.

At the border crossing, Margaux collected their passports and folded Rwandan francs inside. No one was hassled. The SUV and truck followed behind them.

As dusk fell, the driver pulled up to a spartan hotel in Masulo, Tanzania, a small town several kilometers beyond the border. With exhausted jubilance, Ann and Margaux high-fived their arrival. Evangeline awoke with a start and joined in. The drive that should have taken four hours had stretched to almost ten.

Drs. Edward Robinson and Robert Pal waited for them in the lobby, looking travel-weary but happy to meet their team. "The taxi driver made a killing on us," Edward said and bear-hugged Margaux. The two doctors had joined up at the airport in Mwanza, Tanzania and hailed a taxi to Masulo. Edward shook hands with Joseta, Christine, and the rest of the local staff. Finally, Ann stepped up, extending her hand.

"Dr. Blue Eyes," she wanted to say, but held her tongue. They were bluer than she remembered. His hands were in the pockets of his suit coat as if he wasn't sure what to do with them. Then he smiled broadly. "You must have liked my talk." His eyes had an impudent twinkle.

Ann swallowed, suddenly at a loss for words, aware of her skin, slick with sweat and red grit, her hair was frizzed and windblown. She reached up, trying to tame her hair with her right hand. She was repulsed by herself. She wanted to say, "wait, I need a shower."

Edward didn't notice. His hands were out of his pockets and firmly placed on her shoulders. "I knew I'd see you again," he said. "Why not Africa?" He pulled her into his chest and kissed her on both cheeks. He was not as tall as her Milwaukee boyfriend. A faint smell of cologne lingered. "That beer, tonight?"

Ann stared up at the dimple on his chin. Promise bloomed as her exhaustion and self-reproach melted. He felt like an old friend, someone she'd known since grade school, and yet they'd only exchanged a few sentences that November evening, six months ago. She was different now, world weary.

"Or, how about dinner?" Edward added.

"After a shower," Ann said. "And I want to walk. We've been sitting for hours."

"We can accommodate that," Edward said.

The others crashed at the Kilwa Hotel.

A handful of dilapidated but functioning two-story structures lined the main drag—a bank, a government building, several stores, and a bar. The paved street was crowded with locals, the typical din of the evening gatherings Ann had experienced during the early part of her stay in Kigali, high energy but tranquil. Men, women, and children bartered with the shopkeepers who displayed their wares outside their shops. A tarp was piled with produce—squash, potatoes, and vegetables Ann was unable to name.

No RTLM radio blasted with angry rants. Police patrolled with guns, but chatted with the locals. Edward thought their proximity to the border and the strife in Rwanda resulted in what he considered to be "heavy patrol" for Tanzania.

The only *wazungu* on the street, Edward and Ann garnered the usual stares. Occasionally a beggar followed them; children ran up, wanting them to buy Chiclets or some other trinkets. Edward politely refused. It was an adjustment to walk without worry about safety, to smell smoke that was not laced with the scent of burning flesh. Ann ambled alongside Edward, trying to adjust. They retraced the half mile into town as Edward chattered about his recent experience with Sudanese refugees in Kenya. He became focused on toeing discarded bottle caps out of the clotted red mud that collected at the side of the road. He picked them up, rubbed them clean, and stuffed them into his suit coat pockets. He enlisted Ann's help.

The project grounded her. "What will you do with them?" she asked.

"Chips for poker." He reached for another cap, wiping off the dirt.

"Margaux told me."

"Ah, my reputation precedes me." Edward chuckled and slipped the cap into his jacket pocket. "Do you play?"

During the winter, Ann's family had played euchre and hearts on Sunday afternoons. She'd played pinochle in high school and learned poker in college. They had wagered pennies. It had been fun. Ann's mood lightened at the prospect. "I always wear my Brewers cap when I play cards. Who's your team?"

Edward shook his head. "I don't know much about that. Don't really follow sports. But I do know my cards. We'll have a weekly poker night." He leaned down and picked out another cap. "It builds team spirit. It's an easy way for expats and local staff to interact." He finished cleaning the cap and stuffed it into his bulging pocket. "Important for security. Margaux has quite the poker face."

"I can imagine the cigarette hanging between her lips as she contemplates her play." They snickered, bumping arms. It had been awhile since Ann had laughed. Some heaviness lifted.

The church at the edge of town glowed with light and vibrated with song. Except for the occasional tune on the radio, Ann had not heard music since the orphanage. Edward and Ann paused on the sidewalk, peering through the front door. The congregation sang a call-and-response, their bodies swaying to the music. Several children twirled in the aisles. The celebratory energy poured into the street and pulled Ann in closer to see the accompanist at the piano. The rhythm pulsed in Ann's body. The churches were largely silent once the killing had begun. Barking dogs, angry chanting, and gunshots had replaced the Sunday services. As she listened, some of her fatigue slipped away. A baritone joined the tenor who was singing out the call. He sent chills up her spine. She'd not thought about Father Innocent since they'd crossed the border into Tanzania several hours earlier. She spun and marched away from the church.

"Ann. Where are you going?" Edward called and rushed to catch up, grabbing her hand.

Out on the street with her back to the church, Ann struggled for words. "That baritone sounds like a priest I knew in Kigali."

Edward put his arms on her shoulders.

"The. . . the priest," Ann sputtered, "He joined the killers. Turned his parishioners over."

Edward massaged her shoulders. "Relax."

Ann's gaze fell to the ground. "Could he be here?"

Edward touched her cheek. He lifted her chin and looked at her intently. "The Hutu are in power in Kigali. I'd assume he's still there."

Edward's hand felt warm.

"You're really upset."

"Let's not talk about it." Ann closed her eyes and shoved away the grisly scene at Innocent's church—the arm of Jesus cloaked with the bloody dress, the door held ajar by the slaughtered man's foot.

"Ann. Annie. Can I call you that? Annie, are you okay?" He patted her cheek. "I lost you for a minute."

Ann shrugged. "Let's eat. I'm starving."

"Rwanda's behind you," Edward reassured. "Let it go. You'll go crazy if you don't." He swung his arm over her shoulders. Goose bumps rippled across Ann's back. They walked toward a bar that they'd passed in the center of town.

Edward's smell was pleasant, the faint cologne fragrance mixed with an earthy scent that reminded Ann of the closets in her childhood home, an old farmhouse outside Milwaukee. The pressure across her upper back was steady, comforting. She focused on that.

The lighting inside the bar was dim. Ann washed her hands in the bathroom, letting the water run, splashing some on her face and combing damp fingers through her hair, trying to flatten the frizz. Only then did she twist the faucet to off. How long had it been since she'd had running water, copious water, more than a dribble?

American hits from the 70s blasted from a cassette on the counter of the bar with a tinny, hollow timbre. Edward had chosen a booth as far from the music as possible. Ann slid onto the cracked vinyl seat. "I'm sorry. I'm not at my best."

Edward reached under the table and squeezed her knee. "No problem. You had a tough first mission."

He had ordered their food and two beers. She was too weary to refuse. Beneath the table, his knee settled near hers. He maintained a steady pressure, a pleasant heaviness. It grounded her.

Edward talked about growing up in Michigan with a father who was a high-octane surgeon. "I didn't know him as a kid. All he did was work. My mother says he found a blonde when he turned forty-five. His midlife crisis. Wife number two was a few years older than me. I didn't want to spend much time with him, although I did follow in his footsteps." He spoke in a clipped and direct manner as he fingered a thin leather cord that hung around his neck. The pendant remained hidden under his shirt. Ann wondered if it was a cross, although he didn't seem religious.

Edward emptied his bottle and ordered two more. He shifted his legs so he bookended her knees.

A warmth settled in Ann's groin. The beer was giving her a buzz. She needed to stop. One was enough.

Edward continued. "After my residency in Ann Arbor, I married my senior resident and we moved as far from St. Clair Shores as I could. We took jobs in Gladstone, a small community in the UP."

"UP?"

"The Upper Peninsula."

"Oh. So, where is your wife now?"

"We're not together." Edward started on his third beer and talked about his international missions over the past four years, the majority with Margaux as head of mission. He boasted freely about his surgical skills.

Ann had to ask. He'd probably divorced his wife, but what about Margaux? They'd spent a lot of time together. Granted, Edward's knees were pressing hers, but she needed to know. . . "Is there anything between you and Margaux?"

Edward stared at her quizzically.

"Romantic, I mean."

His brow furrowed and then he laughed, shaking his head with emphasis. "She tolerates my idiosyncrasies."

A wave of relief washed over Ann.

"A great head of mission. She's heads above the rest. Knowledgeable. Good at figuring out the context. Can sniff it out. Years of experience. Likes to be in charge. I tolerate her bossiness. This will be our fifth mission together. Five in four years."

"She smokes like a chimney," Ann said.

Edward nodded. "Her worst vice. And she's got the sexy voice to prove it."

Ann lowered her voice. "Like this?"

He imitated her and they burst out laughing, the kind that was contagious. As her laughter slowed, his increased, elevating hers. Her stomach muscles hurt and tears tumbled over her cheeks. Other patrons in the bar swiveled to stare at them. The waiter appeared at their booth.

"We're fine," Edward said and ordered two more beers. He chuckled as the waiter walked away.

"I'm done." Ann pushed her untouched second beer toward him.

"You're a cheap date."

Ann shrugged. She didn't feel like explaining.

Finally, the food arrived—plates of grilled goat, rice, and cassava leaves. Ann had not had meat for a while. She ate hungrily and Edward made fun of her.

Patrons came and went.

"Why did you start international work?" Ann asked.

Edward touched the cord around his neck and stared at a rowdy group of expats who had walked through the door and stood at the counter. "They're having fun," Edward said. But he didn't engage with them. Ann assumed they might be headed to the same refugee camp, but she was too relaxed to mention it.

Lucy in the Sky with Diamonds, a Beatles song, suddenly blasted from the cassette player. Someone turned up the volume and a group danced wildly in front of the bar.

If Ann wasn't so weary, she would have joined them. She asked her question again. When she'd met him in Milwaukee, he'd said he would tell her over a beer.

Edward looked at her. "It's a long story. Not tonight."

Fine, Edward was not ready to tell her, but she wondered what the big deal was. Before, he'd said it was the best decision he'd ever made. Ann tapped her fingers on the table and hummed along with the song.

When the song was done, Edward set down his beer. "You like that song," he said, a half smile on his face.

"I love music. I've missed it. The orphanage had a piano."

Edward leaned across the table and kissed her on the mouth. A wet kiss with some tongue. It took Ann by surprise, but she didn't pull back. The warmth in her groin stirred.

"I've been wanting to do that."

Ann flushed.

"And I left the girl speechless. A good sign." He kissed her again.

The dancing crowd grew larger and jived to another song, the volume turned higher, making it impossible to hear.

Edward sat back. "Let's go," he said and pulled money from his pocket. "My treat. I'm glad we finally had our beer."

Despite their fatigue, they'd talked for almost three hours.

On the street, Edward held Ann's hand and headed the wrong direction, but was appreciative when she corrected him.

Before they separated to their respective rooms, they embraced and kissed again. Edward lingered, exploring her mouth with his tongue. He massaged her shoulders with strong hands. She relaxed into him. He patted her on the buttocks, still kissing her. "Annie, I could get used to this," he said. He pulled back and took her face in his hands. "Remember refugee camp is refuge. You are done. The hardest part of your mission is behind you. We'll make a good team."

Ann tried not to disturb Margaux, who was snoring loudly in the other twin bed. The cement-block room was airless; the overhead fan clunked more than it whirred. Ann considered turning it off, but it diminished the noise on the street. She flipped back and forth on the thin mattress and ran from room to room in her mind. Soon she was drenched with sweat.

She rolled over on her back. Insects danced on the ceiling. Thankfully, the mosquito netting draped around her entire bed. The noisy fan and Margaux's snores were irritating. Ann needed to sleep. She thought of Edward and mused on the possibilities. He was moving fast, maybe too fast, but mission experiences were compressed and intense. She remembered his kiss. Soon, she pleasured herself. After coming she fell into a hard sleep.

Chapter 27

The roar of distant thunder and a riot of roosters woke Ann. At first, she thought she slept in her childhood bed, back in Wisconsin. When she forced her eyes open she saw scuffed walls—different from the floral-patterned wallpaper at home. Overhead a fan chugged. And a floating ghost... no, mosquito netting. Kilwa Hotel. Tanzania. Ann located her present reality. She needed to call her dad. He would worry. Maybe when they were settled at the camp.

Dinner with Edward. Rwanda was behind her. Tanzania offered new friends and colleagues. Maybe a new lover. Go slow. But she had a lot to look forward to.

Ann dressed while Margaux sat on her bed and hacked, sputtered, and spat into a wad of toilet paper for several minutes. At the GH compound Ann had heard Margaux's morning ritual. She sounded like a drowning frog. But Ann had never seen the ritual; gross hardly captured it. Ann vowed never to smoke again. Never.

In the hotel's dining room, they joined other guests for coffee and stale pastries. Margaux scolded Edward, "Hurry up and drink your coffee. Quit dawdling."

Outside, the smell of rain blossomed as large drops dampened the cracked pavement. A few dogs wandered in the empty street. They sniffed the garbage, touring the remnants of the evening's activities without the crazed demeanor of their Rwandan cousins.

The drizzle grew to a steady drone as the caravan left town. Local Tanzanians sloshed along the mostly unpaved road in rubber boots, beneath large, colorful umbrellas. Passing vehicles sprayed red mud. The refugees plodded along without protection, their clothes and belongings soaked by the deluge. The goats and cows grew dark and sodden, rivulets of water running down their legs. Chickens in cages fluffed out their feathers and hid their beaks under their wings.

By the time they reached the refugee camp, the rain had stopped. Called Batumba by the locals, the camp had sprouted up along the river about five kilometers outside the town of Basuko. The registration area and food distribution center were located at the eastern edge of the camp, about a hundred meters from the steel-pole skeleton of the GH medical tent.

Dripping rows of blue, turquoise, and white plastic tarps, strung between metal poles and wooden stakes, stretched across a broad, grassy plain as far as Ann could see. Homemade shelters, sticks covered with thatch, were scattered in between the tents. Intermixed stood a few more stable constructions assembled from sheets of corrugated tin. The spacing between the dwellings was close, with little room for planting a garden, or grazing the animals that had made the trek. Forested hills painted in vivid shades of green from the rain created natural boundaries, as did the river that widened into a lake at one point.

By late morning, a stiff breeze blew up, drying out the camp but spreading the stench of urine, feces, and vomit. Bleating goats and crowing roosters blended with the drone of human voices as adults and children emerged from their tents. Gray smoke began to curl upward from cooking fires, adding the scents of burning grass, wood, and animal dung. The gray clouds continued to hang low, threatening the return of rain.

A group of kids kicked a ball in an open grassy area to the west of the medical tent. A thin, light-brown-skinned man played with a dozen boys. The man wore a maroon-colored t-shirt with "Stanford" printed in bright white letters. Broken branches marked the goalposts. The children moved the ball up and down the appointed field deftly with their bare feet. Robert, the pediatrician, sprinted over to join the game. About five-foot-ten, with a paunch, Robert had a teddy bear quality, but was nimble on his feet, dribbling the ball with speed.

Robert and the man in the Stanford shirt looked overdressed in their name-brand running shoes. One of the younger boys angled in and tripped Robert. The pediatrician rolled on the grass, then rose to his knees and stood up laughing, his shirt and khakis stained with grass and mud. The children giggled and slapped each other on the back. They played a few more minutes, then Robert and Stanford tossed the ball into the group of boys and jogged toward Ann.

"Let-let me introduce Mahavir," Robert stammered.

"Just call me Stanford. It's easier," the young man said, pointing to his t-shirt. They shook hands all around. "I just finished my first year of med school at Stanford." His dark-brown bangs flopped like fringe into his copper-colored eyes. He was volunteering with Samaritan's Bounty, which ran an orphanage for the abandoned children in an old hotel near the river. He'd grown up in California and studied psychology as an undergrad.

"How is it?" Ann asked.

"Hard. I've been here a week."

"How-how so?" Robert stuttered, scratching his goatee.

"Hundreds of kids without parents. Many are too young to tell us their names. Some aren't old enough to talk. Some won't talk. I love kids, but such sad stories. Many are sick, malnourished. Every morning we collect the kids who died overnight. This morning there were a dozen." Stanford stared toward his feet and shook his head.

Robert threw his arm around Stanford. Robert's speech impediment did not keep him from talking. "We'll have-have to do something about that. You've got-got the makings of a pediatrician."

Stanford looked up and smiled. "Did you see the photo board near registration? Parents stare at it. They walk up and down, then turn away and shake their heads. Some check it several times a day." He rattled on. It was as if he'd had no one to talk to for the week.

Ann remembered the terror-stricken eyes of the newer orphans at Beauraing. The day before, as they crossed the bridge over the Akagara River, Joseta had covered Evangeline's eyes. This generation of Rwandan children would grow up with ghosts—horrors they'd seen and heard.

When the soccer game ended, the boys gathered several yards away, whispering among themselves. They ranged in age from five to maybe twelve; with malnourishment children were smaller. The shortest boy held a ball constructed from banana leaves and twine.

"*Venez*, come," Robert called and motioned with his large hand. "Look at this ball."

"They're really creative," Ann said. "I've seen plastic bags, vines . . ."

Robert squatted to the height of the younger ones, patting those he could reach on their backs and invited each boy to say his name. Two boys did not speak. Robert managed the entire conversation without stuttering. Perhaps he felt less pressure when conversing with the children. He had ridden in the other vehicle during their final road trip that morning. Ann hadn't spent much time with him, but from what she could see, pediatrics suited him.

Margaux and Edward joined them. Introductions were repeated. Stanford was delighted to have so many physician role models and resources. His team included several nurses, teachers, and college students on summer break. He described two other medical tents on the northern and western sides of the camp that weren't visible from where they stood.

"The UNHCR, the UN High Commission on Refugees, is estimating one hundred thousand refugees," Margaux said.

"Who came?" Ann asked.

Edward looked at her as if she were stupid.

"No, I mean Hutus, Tutsis?"

"We won't talk about those distinctions here," Margaux said.

Ann was stunned. "But how do we know if we are treating the good guys or the bad guys?"

"We treat everyone," Edward said.

Ann swallowed a silent sigh. How could she determine if Innocent might be here? She let it drop.

"The big international aid groups follow the refugees. They know what they are doing," Edward reassured.

Margaux lit a cigarette.

"My boss said that the refugees settled here because of the river," Stanford said.

"But it's polluted. I can smell it from here," Robert stuttered.

Stanford nodded. "Dead bodies. Lots of them." He crinkled his nose. "Someone caught a fish. In its stomach was a finger with a ring on it."

"Stories," Edward said.

"Really. I saw it with my own eyes."

"You were hallucinating," Edward said. "Too much bad air."

Stanford threw up his arms.

All gazed toward the river. No corpses were visible, but the thick smell of death was inescapable.

"Lots of work to do," Margaux said and sucked on her cigarette.

Stanford kicked the ground with his shoe. "I have a case to show you," he said. "Do you have time?"

"I have to work," Edward said.

Ann and Robert looked toward Margaux. "Go ahead," she said. "We're getting organized. It'll take us awhile. We have to talk with UNHCR."

The path to the orphanage wound close to the river for about a kilometer. Bloated bodies were caught in a web of tree branches. There the putrid stench grew especially potent. Ann covered her nose with her hand.

"I see what-what you mean," Robert faltered. "How do you get used to . . ." He stopped and heaved to the side, then pulled a hanky from his pocket to wipe his mouth. He proceeded along the path with his forearm over his nose and mouth.

"Believe me, it's amazing what you can get used to," Ann mumbled.

Where the river widened into a lake stood a three-floor brick structure with an intact tin roof. The mud brick walls of the former hotel were in good shape, but weeds had overtaken the yard. The fruit trees, laden with oranges and smaller mandarin oranges, begged for picking and pruning. In its day, the setting along the river with the grassy plain rolling toward the hills would have been picturesque, a place for respite.

"Home," Stanford said as he stepped on the cement of the veranda. He gestured toward the building. "We divided the kids into two groups. Under five are downstairs. Five to ten are upstairs. Expats live on the top floor."

"Where are the older kids?" Robert asked.

"Some other NGO cares for them." The trio watched as a young boy ran up to the side of the hotel and urinated. Stanford threw up his hands. "The kids pee and poop all over the place. We need to dig latrines."

"Are you immunizing them?" Robert asked.

"I think so." Stanford toed the veranda's cement floor, a scraping sound. "The World Food Program gives us food. And there's a priest from Kigali who brings extra bags. They have the WFP label too. His helper has a long scar on his right arm. The kids really like them. They hand out candy."

"A priest?" Ann said. Fear boiled up.

"I guess his parish closed in Kigali. He came here to help."

Ann didn't ask what he looked like, if he wore sunglasses. Kigali was a big city with at least a hundred churches. A number of priests and ministers likely came to the camp, some to take refuge. This couldn't be Innocent.

"Wait here," Stanford said and disappeared into the orphanage. Robert and Ann stood on the cracked cement veranda that faced the river. The breeze blew toward the river, so the strong smell was less noticeable. Someone had already planted flowers along the edge of the cement slab.

"I wonder if my grandfather stayed here." Robert said as he rotated 360 degrees. "He owned a tea plantation in southern Rwanda. Left in the mid-sixties when the Belgians turned the government over to the Tutsis."

"It looks old enough."

Robert nodded. "He told stories about his travels. Safaris in Tanzania."

"Did he talk about the apes?"

"I don't remember."

"Where was his plantation?"

"Near Butare. I can't help thinking. . . this is the kind of place he'd visit for a holiday. With the falls and all." Robert scratched his goatee. "I want to look around before I go home."

"Don't plan on touring in Rwanda. It's a mess."

"I forgot you just came from there."

"I wanted to see the apes," Ann said. "That won't happen."

Stanford returned carrying a boy who looked to be about seven. Across the front of the boy's ragged shirt was a piece of duct tape with "Harry" printed in black marker. "He doesn't talk," Stanford said. "I named him. Look at this hole." Stanford pointed to the boy's forehead. "It leaks fluid... but it doesn't look infected. Do you know what it is?"

Robert bent down to make eye contact with the boy, introducing himself in French. He stroked the boy's chin, then stuttered. "He's so thin."

"Everyone's thin and dirty," Stanford said. "Their clothes are grimy. We wash them and they fall apart. At least he has something to wear."

Harry's shirt and tattered shorts bagged over his scrawny body. His bony legs and arms stuck out like twigs. Ann had seen worse. The cloth appeared brown and polished, the dirt ground in. The sore above his right eyebrow oozed clear yellow liquid. The boy twitched as Ann touched the area.

Robert reassured Harry, then asked in French, "Does it hurt?"

The boy said nothing, just stared at Robert.

"I don't think he speaks French," Stanford said. "He seems to hear. See how he watches the speaker. I've heard him mutter some words, maybe the local language."

"Does it bother him?" Ann asked.

Stanford nodded. "Sometimes." He lifted the boy's shirt. "Here's another."

Ann examined the second hole near the boy's left shoulder blade. His shirt had a large, damp stain over the area.

Robert held up the boy's shirt. "I did an infectious disease fellowship in New Orleans; I think it's a larva from a fly." He was silent a moment then blurted out "bot fly."

"You're right," Ann said. Ann described her roommate, the teacher, who'd developed welts after a picnic. "I was convinced they were chiggers. The bites itched like crazy. I put her on prednisone and antibiotics. A white worm with tiny red spines emerged three weeks later. I put it in a glass jar and took it to the hospital. Joseta took one look and told me what it was. She told me to iron my clothes."

"Should I?" Stanford asked.

"I guess the heat of the iron kills the eggs the flies lay on the laundry drying in the sun."

"Gross!" Stanford said and crinkled up his nose. "The eggs must enter a break in the skin?"

"Makes you want to wear a body suit," Ann said. "If you remove the worm, do it carefully. If you leave any part inside, the body mounts a reaction. A red, itchy bump."

"Yuk," Stanford said.

"My sentiments entirely," Ann said. "Do you have Vaseline or duct tape? Nail polish works, too, but you don't look like the nail polish type." She chuckled.

"Every good camper has duct tape, but I have Vaseline too," Stanford said.

"Bring your Vaseline. We'll asphyxiate the buggers."

They carried Harry to a chair on the veranda. When Stanford returned with his jar, Robert steadied the boy and Ann dabbed Vaseline over both holes. Within minutes tiny air bubbles rose. She squeezed the lump in the skin which Harry tolerated without a grimace. "He's had this done before." She apologized and pressed again. Out popped a fat, white larva about a centimeter in length.

"Sweet. How'd it fit in there?" Stanford asked.

"Your first tropical medicine lesson," Robert stammered. "You won't forget this."

Before returning, Stanford gave them oranges to eat and showed them how to rub the peel on their wrists, an alternative to the stink. On the way back to the medical tent, the flies swarmed them. They crawled into Ann's ears and nose, making her sneeze. Flies stuck to her eyes and mouth, sucking at the moisture. She swatted at them, eventually tying her bandana around her nose and mouth for the duration of the trek. They'd never been this obnoxious in Kigali. Robert waved his hands across his face, buttoned up his shirt, and held his hand and wrist over his mouth and nose.

Stanford smelled his wrists, unbothered by the flies or the stench that grew potent near the river. He described his month-long in-service at Mother Teresa's orphanage in Calcutta during college. "I guess I developed a stomach for stuff like this." He waved his arms broadly. "The garbage in the streets was pretty awful."

The refugee photos at Ann's GH orientation were sterile compared with this reality. The actual smells, sounds, and images were overpowering, almost unbearable. Ironically, Kinyarwanda had only one verb for feeling, tasting, hearing, touching, and understanding—*kumva*. Rwandans speaking English often said "I touch it" or "I hear it" when referring to food. *Simbyumva* meant "I don't hear it," "I don't see it," as well as "I don't understand it." How could one word—*kumva*—possibly accommodate all Ann was experiencing, and another, all she did not understand?

Chapter 28

The UNHCR struggled to register the flood of refugees. They organized the camp in *secteurs*, reflecting the communities back in Rwanda. The *burgomaster*, the head of the *secteur*, like a mayor, helped with food distribution and security. Registration allowed for a fair distribution of supplies—more mouths to feed, more food, more bedding. Documenting who was in the camp was imperative for security. They hired Rwandans to sort through who belonged to whom. Neighbors were asked to care for the unaccompanied older children in their neighborhoods and to look after the widowed women. Unassigned children and households without a male could be overlooked in food distribution lines or preyed on by more aggressive refugees. Unclaimed younger children were sent to the orphanage where Stanford worked. Eventually all the orphans would be photographed and their pictures tacked up on the large poster boards so parents could try to locate their lost children.

By the second morning, the white canvas medical tent stretched across the long metal poles, and stakes secured the sides. Margaux paid refugees to unload the supply truck. "I'm contributing to the economy," she explained. "These men used to provide for their families. Now they need cash and something to do." If rural, they had tended gardens and small herds. If urban, they may have taught school, or run businesses such as carpentry, sawing wood, or taxi services. To suddenly have nothing to do, to be dependent on handouts, was difficult. The money allowed them to purchase additional supplies for their families from the Tanzanian merchants who were already reaping the benefits of the booming economy.

These merchants wandered through the camp hawking their wares—pots, food stuffs, yellow gerry cans filled with liquids: beer, oil, and kerosene. A few bold ones stopped by the medical tent to see if any of the expats had interest. Margaux purchased grass mats, which would serve as patient beds in the inpatient ward. After that purchase a stream of Tanzanian merchants visited the medical tent.

Refugees gathered outside and Joseta sent them away while she and the GH expats organized the inside. The temporary structure would function as an outpatient area and a small hospital. With the help of the Rwandan health professionals in the camp, they planned to staff it 24 hours a day. They divided the tent into triage, the ambulatory clinic, the ED, the inpatient ward, labor and delivery, and a break area for staff. The small laboratory was stocked with a microscope and the equipment to do hemoglobins, blood sugars, malaria smears, urine dip sticks and pregnancy tests, as long as the kits lasted. An adjacent tent was set up for surgery and recovery.

During the afternoon of the third day, Ann and Robert started seeing patients. Ann cleaned her hands at one of the hand-washing stations, pulled her stethoscope from her backpack, and walked to a gurney in the outpatient area. A familiar man sat on a cot, his toothy grin stretched across his thin face.

"Dr. Ann?" he lisped; his English was staccato, but understandable.

"Do I know you?" A Yankees baseball cap obscured his eyes. His t-shirt advertised the 1990 Tour de France.

"99," he said, reaching for her hand and shaking it vigorously.

Ann's faced flushed. "Of course. I can't believe it. How did you get here? It's so far."

"God bless. God is good. Good to see you, Dr. Ann. I pray I see you again. My prayers answer." His smile stretched so wide it looked as if his face might crack in half. Then, he frowned and pointed to his feet. "Help me." His feet were bound with strips of dirty cloth.

"Did you walk the whole way?" Ann asked.

"I have bike, but someone take her. Then I walk."

Ann shook her head as she unwrapped the rags. His body odor was pungent. How did 99 avoid the predators along the way? Like a duck with oiled feathers, harm seemed to roll away from him. As she undid the dirty cloth, her stomach turned. His soles were blistered and a long gash extended up the back of his left calf and oozed pus. It should have been sutured. Ann searched for what she needed to clean his feet, her first chance to test their setup.

She carried over a bucket with water and a bar of soap and helped him wash, then soak his feet.

"You have Coke?" he asked.

Ann shook her head, appreciating his simplicity; it reminded her of her sister Irene. "I'll see if I can find some." Coke managed to distribute their product everywhere.

"Who's this?" Margaux asked, coming over to check on Ann.

Ann made the introduction.

"How did he get his name?"

"The nuns at the orphanage said 99 was as perfect as any human being could be. His only defect is that he likes Coca Cola. I can't believe it hasn't rotted out his teeth."

"I need Coke," 99 said.

"I'll work on finding some," Margaux said and shook his hand.

Ann counted antibiotic pills into a plastic bag and explained how to take them. She wrapped 99's leg with gauze and a recycled ace bandage, then gave him a pair of clean socks in lieu of going barefoot. "Come back tomorrow so I can check you."

"God bless you. God bless." 99 lisped, then limped toward a lone acacia tree that stood a hundred meters away in the heart of the camp.

Many patients presented with wear and tear lesions from the trek— abrasions, burns, blisters. Like 99, some suffered old machete wounds that should have been repaired when they were fresh. Thousands had fled. Some stood tall and pencil thin, the typical Tutsi body habitus. Others looked more Hutu. Margaux had warned not to think about ethnic labels, but Ann could not help wondering whether or not Father Innocent might appear someday. Could he be the priest that carried extra food to Stanford's orphanage? If so, what would she say to him?

Chapter 29

I'm done with this game," Scar said and scooped up his bottle caps with his big hand. He tossed the bottle caps toward the ceiling and they clattered like hail on the wooden table, definitively ending the poker round.

Ann jumped. Scar had done well taking a round with a pair of queens and another with a set of three tens. She wasn't sure what had pissed him off.

The thick keloid scar glistened in the low light of the naked, overhead bulb. It ran from Scar's shoulder to his wrist and served as a reminder to all that his right arm had been filleted years earlier.

"I won't have my staff behaving like this," Margaux said as she rose to her feet. "Especially in front of the children." She smashed her cigarette on the plate that served as her ash tray. "Come out to the veranda with me. Now." The screen door slammed behind them.

Those around the table eyed each other warily. "Shall we continue?" Edward took a swig of beer, collected the cards, and shuffled. He dealt two and then three cards to each player.

Their first poker night had started out pleasantly enough. Poker was a new game for the Rwandans, so Ann and Edward had diagrammed the different hands on a piece of newsprint and taped it to the dining room wall. Edward invited the guards to join them. Scar had done so enthusiastically.

They played the first rounds with the cards face up. Edward had acquired quite a stash of bottle caps, having paid the children in town to collect them. Evangeline, Joseta's granddaughter, and Emit, the driver's son, were given

Tanzanian schillings to scrub them. "I'm cultivating entrepreneurs," Edward said.

When it was Ann's turn to deal, she'd spiced things up by teaching everyone Indian. Edward grumbled, but Ann had persisted, laying the cards facedown and directing everyone to stick the card on their forehead without looking. Ann went first, removing her Brewers' cap, licking her thumb, touching her forehead, then pasting the card on her brow. From what Ann could see, Emit's jack was high and Evangeline's four was low. "You bet on what you think you have," Ann said.

The children's eyes darted in all directions, followed by giggles.

Scar was the first to bid. He studied everyone's forehead, then slid his bottle cap into the center. Scar's card was a ten. Everyone tossed in a cap except Edward. "Indian is an insult to poker," he said. He folded his hands across his chest and pretended to sulk, fiddling with the leather cord around his neck.

"Knock it off," Ann said. "The kids like it."

"Watch your manners with the medical director," Edward quipped.

More sniggering from the children.

"I need luck. Robert, rub my head?" Evangeline scurried over to Robert's side. He gladly patted her head, then Scar rubbed her head, and she scrambled into her mother's lap.

Ann shoved two caps into the center, raising Emit.

"What should I do?" Emit asked.

"Hold," Edward said.

"That's not fair," Ann said, sending a pout toward Edward. "Now, everyone look at your card." Both she and Emit had jacks. Emit held a club and Ann the two-eyed jack of diamonds. "Mine's higher," she said. "Sorry, Emit. Diamonds are a girl's best friend."

Edward rolled his eyes and swallowed a swig of beer. The Rwandans missed the pun.

Scar dealt the next hand, asking Emit to help him. He seemed to enjoy the kids. He raised Ann three. The driver and Christine bowed out of the game, which meant Evangeline did as well. Margaux, Robert, Ann, and Edward stayed in. Now Evangeline and Emit stood near Scar watching his cards.

"Full house," Margaux said, laying down three tens and two nines. Ann spread out her straight and moaned. Robert had a pair of jacks.

Scar put down three kings and two queens. The grin across his face was priceless. Emit mimicked him. Edward folded his cards and pushed the pile of caps toward Scar. Emit climbed onto Scar's knee and helped him rake in the heap, counting each one. He stopped at *dix-neuf*.

The game continued, filled with teasing and laughter. Edward served another round of *Tanzabeer*, the local brew. Ann stuck with Fanta. Margaux offered her cigarettes to the group; only Scar took one. Emit bounced on Scar's knee as Scar lit up.

"Let's look at our cards," Scar said and balanced his cigarette on the corner of the table. Christine hurried to the kitchen and returned with a plate.

Margaux sipped whiskey from a coffee mug and reminisced about playing poker on the French Riviera with her husband when she was young and pregnant. "Seems like a lifetime ago." He was a professional card player. She described his sunglasses, how he barely lifted his cards, and how he usually convinced the others at the table that his cards were better than what he held. "My daughter and I believed we were the loves of his life. She was ten when I learned he had another family. That ended the marriage." She chuckled, a throaty cackle. The whiskey made her chatty.

Everyone was cordial until Margaux bolted up and slammed a spider on the back of Ann's chair with a copy of *The Economist*.

Ann jumped, laughing nervously. "I thought you didn't like me raising you."

"I hate spiders," Margaux said and apologized.

Scar drummed his fingers on the table and tapped his foot. Edward dealt next and asked him to stop. The drumming ceased, but the foot tapping continued. Margaux tilted her cards slightly to see what she had, discarded three and knocked. Robert, Ann, and Edward stayed in. Scar lost that round with a straight to Margaux's four of a kind. That was when Scar jumped out of his chair and exploded.

Margaux had hired Scar and five other Rwandans to provide security at the compound. They worked twelve-hour shifts and two took duty together. They did not carry guns. Scar had wanted to join the poker game; the other guard remained outside making rounds and watching the road.

On the veranda, just beyond the common room, Margaux and Scar's conversation started out in hushed tones. Within minutes, Margaux was shrieking. "*Vous etes virez*, you're fired. Gather your belongings and leave. Now. You are not welcome here." Everyone at the table turned to look out the window. In the lamp glow, Margaux stood with her arms folded, her lips pursed. "I am watching you leave. Now."

"I want some caps," Emit whined.

Evangeline whimpered into Joseta's bosom.

"It's well past bedtime," Christine said. "The children are tired."

Edward had lost all his caps. "Off to bed. All of you," Edward said. "Same time next week."

Parents carried their whining children off to bed. As Ann and Robert cleaned up, Margaux stomped through, firing a perturbed look in Edward's direction. She picked up her whiskey and clomped off to the bedroom she shared with Ann. When the dining area was returned to its order for the morning, Robert pleaded exhaustion and went to his room. Ann and Edward retired to the veranda to watch the moon rise.

Five days had passed since they had shared dinner in the border town. Since then, they'd had little time to talk. He and Margaux had been preoccupied with negotiating terms with UNHCR and the other eleven NGOs involved in the camp, signing memorandums of understanding, organizing the medical facility and living arrangements, and hiring Rwandan staff. Ann had been buried in patient care.

"Do you need to check on Margaux?" Ann asked. She stood gazing toward the road and the orange moon, which hung like a saucer behind a tree. A truck motored by, moving in and out of the spotlight near their gate about fifteen meters away.

"She's a salty old bitch. Don't tell her I said that. She'll fill me in if and when she wants to." Edward sat down, stretched out his legs, and patted the white plastic chair next to him.

The truck's headlights illuminated the surrounding trees and bushes as it negotiated the speed bumps positioned in front of the school. The hum of the engine was punctuated with two noisy *kerplunks*. Once the truck passed, stillness returned. From where they sat, they could not even hear their housemates in the back. The church service was over. After ten, the local bar muted their music.

"This'll be a nice place to live," Edward said.

Margaux had secured an old schoolhouse in Basuko, a sleepy town in western Tanzania, until the refugees settled on the nearby plain at the bend in the river. The NGOs followed, setting up residences in hotels and the other vacant or minimally used buildings. The town was five kilometers from the refugee camp.

The evening air smelled of damp earth. The neighbor's goats, who grazed the roadsides during the day, complained about their constricted nighttime quarters, their bleats a forlorn pleading. Ann played with her hair as she sat down next to Edward. "You and Margaux have your rhythms."

"Yep," Edward said and took a swallow of beer.

"Why did she fire Scar?"

"She learned he's up to no good. One of the other NGOs thinks he's responsible for hassling women when they collect wood in the forest."

"Hassling?"

"Rape."

Ann gasped and her hands flew to her mouth. "We're better without him." No crime was worse for a woman. She'd seen too much rape in Kigali. She sighed noisily and continued. "The kids liked him. Was he sincere or manipulating them?" Ann began drumming her fingers across her trousers.

Edward shrugged. "Guess we don't have to worry."

As Ann's fingers moved, a church hymn filled her head—*God is My Shepherd*. It was one of her father's favorites.

Edward reached his arm across Ann's shoulders. "What are you doing? Are you nervous?"

Ann stopped mouthing the words. "I told you that I play the piano. When I move my fingers through the chords, even without a keyboard, I can hear the song in stereo."

"You're weird."

"Just wired differently."

Edward mussed her hair. "Some real unique synapses in that brain."

"As a kid, you think everyone is like you." Her fingers marched out the finale and she leaned back against her chair.

Edward squeezed her shoulder and pulled her in. "I enjoyed our dinner. It feels like ages ago." He brushed her lips with his.

Ann liked the closeness but not the beer. "You smell like a brewery. If you want to get to first base, go brush your teeth."

"There you go with your sports metaphors." He leaned back and pulled a plastic box from his pocket. "Chiclets. Want one?"

"Sure."

He handed one to Ann and popped one into his mouth.

They kissed. The evening rolled out with possibilities. The moon climbed beyond the tree and tiny diamonds blossomed in the inky black sky. Only the neighbor's goats bleated their discontent.

Edward came up for air, tussling Ann's hair. "When Robert's on call, stay with me."

Chapter 30

uild it and they will come" was as true for the GH medical facility in the Batumba Camp as it was for the baseball field in Iowa. Despite the threat of rain, the line of refugees snaked the equivalent of two city blocks. Ann's watch read 7:15 a.m. This would be a long day. She shouldn't have stayed up so late with Edward. Ten Rwandan nurses and five doctors, all refugees in the camp, stood under the canvassed foyer of the tent, hoping to be hired. Their clothes were worn but clean, their hair and bodies scrubbed free of the dirt and grime that crusted most of the waiting patients.

"*Mumeza mute*, how are you?" Ann entered the tent and greeted the woman registering patients. She had worked as a community health worker in southern Rwanda. She and two of her five children had survived by hiding in a papyrus swamp during the day and digging potatoes to eat in a nearby field at night.

A dozen cots and gurneys lined the canvas walls of the emergency area. Ann's first patient stuck a black foot in her direction. The sweet, putrid smell of gangrene made her want to vomit. The *interahamwe* had sliced the woman's Achilles tendon to keep her from running away. The damaged blood vessels and nerves compromised the viability of the foot. Ann made her first referral to Edward.

Her next patient was a family of seven all scratching their arms and legs. Tiny crusts in the web spaces between their fingers and toes suggested scabies. Of course, they shared bedrolls. Ann sent them to the pharmacy area with a prescription for benzoyl benzonate and instructed them to hang their bedding in the sun. After she moved on to the next patient, she remembered that this was the rainy season and wondered how well the family could comply. She found herself itching the rest of the morning and worrying that the family would return in a week with the same complaints.

Midmorning Robert called Ann over. "How-how do you get used to this? I'm overwhelmed." He grimaced. Dark patches dampened the armpits of his scrub top and his sandy brown hair clumped at the nape of his neck.

"Pace yourself," Ann said, scratching behind her left ear. "One patient at a time. You'll burn out if you don't." She looked at her watch—10:30 a.m. "Let's take a coffee break."

"But-but look at the line."

"This is Africa."

Robert followed Ann into the break area and perched on a stool. The refrigerator buzzed nearby. Ann plugged in the electric teapot and spooned a heaping teaspoon of Nescafe into each cup.

"Only powder?" Robert asked.

"I complained to Margaux," Ann said, "but she said the real stuff is too expensive." Ann poured steaming water into their mugs.

"Tell Edward to sweet-talk her." Robert stirred in a teaspoon of powdered milk and two teaspoons of sugar and sipped his concoction. "I'll be glad when the Rwandan physicians join us."

"Looked like plenty of applicants."

"I have a patient with classic kwashiorkor." He tripped over the first syllable of the word. "Protein malnutrition. I can feel his liver. I've never seen it before."

"Let's finish our coffee."

"There are new guidelines in the works at the World Health Organization. Intravenous fluids have fallen out of favor."

"The nuns at the Beauraing orphanage were up on that. They had an oral feeding protocol."

The boy with kwashiorkor had long, thick lashes that framed large chestnut-colored eyes, which sunk into his skull. They tracked Robert's every move. He looked like a little old man and that became his nickname. Robert's big hands were amazingly nimble and gentle as he examined the child. No tears leaked from Old Man's eyes when he cried and sores crusted the corners of his cracked lips. Prominent ribs, without baby fat, corseted his small chest. He grabbed onto Robert's finger with a perfectly formed, but tiny, swollen hand and would not let go.

"He's close to two by his teeth," Robert said.

"He's a fighter," Ann said. "She probably quit breastfeeding him when the baby was born."

"Typical kwashiorkor." Robert pointed out the rash on his buttocks and thighs that flaked like paint. His belly protruded like a melon.

"Where's the medical student? We need to show him to Stanford."

"Cicely Williams, a Jamaican pediatrician, described the disease in the 1930s. I read her *Lancet* article. No eversion of the eyelids, so it's not Vitamin A or B deficiency. The skin lesions aren't typical of pellagra, a deficiency of C. This is clearly protein malnutrition."

Ann stared at Robert aghast. "You must have textbook pages filed in your brain. What a phenomenal memory."

"Welcome to my world," Robert stammered, then laughed, scratching his goatee.

Problem-solving was one way to cope, but Robert's ability to laugh at himself made him fun to work with, his stammer tolerable. There was something very likeable about him.

Old Man's mother wore a t-shirt with *Des Moines Demons* in blue block letters on the front and a *Blue Cross/Blue Shield* logo on the back, a donation from some Iowa softball team. The soles of Des Moines's feet were worn away much like 99's.

"I can't believe she can walk," Ann whispered.

The woman spoke a little French and from what Ann and Robert could gather she'd traveled for a week or more, abandoning her dead infant somewhere along the way. She'd carried this toddler on her back and had started breast feeding him again. However, she probably had not secured enough food or water to make much breast milk.

In French, punctuated with pantomiming, Robert explained to Des Moines that they would supplement her breast feeding with a cup or spoon. Robert started an antibiotic and pulled a knit hat on the boy's head. He retrieved a yellow- and orange-yarn afghan that some church group had crocheted.

The box had arrived on the supply truck. The return address read Branson, Missouri. Ann imagined some grandmother with knuckles gnarled from arthritis, meticulously looping and pulling the yarn with a plastic crochet hook. The bright colors blended in perfectly. Although muted from dirt and wear, the refugees' clothes were vividly colored. Did the church ladies have any idea that their box of crocheted blankets would warm a starving Rwandan child? Maybe so, maybe like Ann their mothers had told them to eat all their vegetables for the starving children in Africa. They'd probably said the same to their children.

Ann washed and dried Des Moines's feet. She slathered them with antibiotic ointment and gave her clean socks. The woman clutched Ann's hand, "*Mwakze cyane*," thanking her profusely.

Ann's next patient was a girl with an infected bullet wound in her cheek. The bullet had entered her nose and now sat in the fat of her right cheek, just under her eye. If she survived, she'd wear her war injury for all to see. Ann made another referral to Edward.

In the early afternoon, a boy and his father brought their goat. "I didn't triage the goat," Joseta said. "But I think you can help them." Joseta did a phenomenal job of identifying the sickest patients as quickly as possible. The nanny goat had broken its front leg. She was the family's supply of milk. Ann thought of her father as she palpated the hairy, gray leg and cooed to the goat. X-ray was not yet available; a van with a machine was supposed to arrive the following week. The patient bleated her discontent as Ann wrapped wet plaster around the right front limb.

Toward the end of the day, Ann examined a young boy whose fever registered 39 degrees Centigrade, 102 Fahrenheit. She lifted his holey red t-shirt and pressed her stethoscope against his small back. Crackles sounded at the base of his right lung. She called Robert over and pointed out the rash—raised red lesions on the boy's chest and arms. "It doesn't look like measles."

"Maybe Kaposi's," Robert faltered.

"AIDS? I hadn't thought about that. I hear crackles."

Robert listened to the child's lungs with his stethoscope. "Pneumonia. IV antibiotics for sure. You don't need an x-ray."

"We can't do one anyway."

"I wish we could check for HIV." They admitted the boy to the hospital and discussed his treatment plan given the concern of AIDS.

At five, Joseta sent the waiting refugees home. Robert and Ann checked on the patients they'd admitted. The Rwandan physician who had covered the inpatient ward during the day had worked at Kigali General and fled to the camp with the other refugees. He would not make eye contact. The other Rwandan staff addressed him with an African name, but he insisted that Ann and Robert call him Philip.

The ward was stuffy and had the acrid smell of sweat and body fluids. Ann untied the flaps on two windows to allow in some fresh air. Together they reviewed the charts of all the patients since Robert was on call.

Des Moines lay in the feeding section, curled up on the grass mat, spooning her toddler. Both slept. "She hasn't fed him much," Dr. Philip said. "The nurses won't have much time to fuss with him overnight. You won't either."

Old Man whimpered, opened his eyes, and fixed his gaze on Robert. "I hope I can pull him through," Robert said. Dark half-moons lay under his eyes. Robert was heading into call already exhausted.

"We can't save everyone," Ann said.

"Maybe you've been here long-long enough to be comfortable with that." Robert said, his voice filled with frustration. He fingered his stethoscope with its tiny stuffed bear hugging the cord. It wasn't an animal familiar to Africa, but the kids didn't care. "Do you know how many orphans were dead-dead when Stanford and I made orphanage rounds?" Robert didn't wait for Ann to answer. "Ten! Ten died overnight." He shook his head.

"You might pass a feeding tube through his nose," Dr. Philip suggested.

Ann wished Robert luck and walked toward the SUV, feeling sticky with sweat and grit. She anticipated a long, hot shower; the reality would be lukewarm and rapid. Four short months ago, she'd felt the same as Robert.

After dinner, Ann joined Edward on the veranda. The clouds had scattered after sunset and a few stars were visible. The moon was not yet visible. In town, the evening church service competed with the American rock that blasted from the local bar. The songs were hits Ann had danced to in high school and college, but the bar's sound system added a tinny timbre.

Behind them, in the common room, their compatriots listened to the radio. Laughter and threads of conversation drifted out the window. Margaux assembled a jigsaw puzzle on the dining table with the cook. Joseta was working with Evangeline on letters and words. The driver and his son, Emit, played some kind of card game that required slapping cards on one of two piles. It reminded Ann of a game she and her sisters had learned as children.

Edward sipped a beer and talked about a case—a refugee hired to work as a security guard at the camp who was attacked while patrolling the latrines.

"Sounds like Kigali," Ann said.

Edward nodded but continued, intent on sharing the details of the case.

Despite her exhaustion, Ann tried to listen.

"A knife wound. I searched for the bleeder. The blood pressure fell. It took me too long."

A truck passed over the speed bump with the predictable clamor. Edward continued. "The scrub nurse is good. She pointed out the spleen. It was expanding. I removed it. Saved the man, but what a bloody mess." He shook his head.

Another truck idled near the front gate with a loud rattle. Edward and Ann stared toward the road.

"Bad muffler," Edward said.

The spotlight shone down on the truck. The inside light blinked on and silhouetted a stocky frame with a shaved head.

"That's Scar," Ann said. "He's talking to our guard."

"He's not supposed to. Margaux and I should check." Edward rose and summoned Margaux. Together they tromped out to the gate, shining a flashlight at the driver. Ann trailed behind. The gist of the conversation was that Scar was not welcome. He should not visit the GH guards while they were on duty. The truck roared on, the muffler scraping the speed bump.

"*Merci*," Margaux said. "*Il va me rendre folle*, that man is going to drive me crazy." She stomped inside the compound, mumbling something about Scar and his cronies. The screen door thud shut.

"What's going on?" Ann asked.

"Margaux says Hutus are here at the camp. Although she won't use that word. They're trying to continue what was started in Rwanda."

Ann shook her head. "They're after the Tutsis here? I don't get it."

"We'll need to be careful about neutrality."

"They talked about that at orientation."

Edward sighed. "We treat all comers regardless of their affiliation."

Ann mulled that over. She had hoped to escape danger by coming to the refugee camp. A week ago, Edward had talked about refuge—refugee. His arm pressed against hers, sticky but pleasant despite the humid air.

Another vehicle bumped passed. The music from the bar still filled the night. Dogs yelped in the distance, warning of some insult to their territory. Stars began to crowd the sky and the lip of the moon inched into the trees. Edward brought up his case again, worried that the on-call team might not give the patient enough attention.

"You could have stayed and watched him, helped Robert out," Ann said.

"I've been doing this too long. I know about burnout. Besides, I wouldn't be here with you." Edward squeezed Ann's hand. His fingers were warm and soft as he moved them up and down her arm.

Her lips quivered and her skin soaked up the touch as they sat arm in arm. The guard's boots clicked on the stone pathway between the schoolhouse and the road. Behind them the driver and Emit slapped cards and laughed.

Edward brushed Ann's lips with his. His breath tasted of mint. "I've been wanting to do that again." He nuzzled her neck.

Her nostrils widened with his musky scent and she felt a tightening in her groin.

"I have my room to myself tonight." He nibbled at her ear.

The bar's tunes became white noise.

As much as Ann liked Edward, as much as her body was responding, she told herself to go slow. He seemed like a good man. But it took time to see someone's warts. Ann sighed. "We need to talk."

"About what?"

"The sex talk, STDs, protection, you know the drill. You're a doctor."

"Aren't you the mood breaker" He mouthed into her ear, his breath hot. He lifted her hair with his fingers and his lips followed the curve of her clavicle.

After another heavy sigh, Ann pulled away. She sat up, trying to prepare her words about living and working together. On the road, the truck with the noisy muffler chugged by. It paused at the end of the school's walkway and a baritone yelled a string of Kinyarwanda. Ann recognized the phrase—"*gutera ingunguru.*"

She froze. Shivers erupted along her spine. That was Innocent's phrase— rejection with an oil drum. The voice was deep.

The sound of metal scraped asphalt. "That's Scar's truck again. The muffler," Edward said. "What did he say?"

"I'm not sure." How did she begin to explain? The truck had motored on. Would she feel any safer in Edward's bed? Could she even sleep?

Chapter 31

In the morning, Robert sat in the feeding area with Old Man in his lap. The muggy air hung thick. Nearby a half dozen patients were in various stages of waking up. Beard growth stippled Robert's cheeks and dark shadows now encircled his green-gray eyes, making him look like a clown with poorly applied makeup.

"How'd it go?" Ann asked. "Did you get any sleep?"

Robert shook his head.

Robert was investing too much. Eventually he would learn that he couldn't save everyone. He'd realize it, in his time.

"I put in the tube," Robert said. A small, clear feeding tube snaked out of the child's left nostril. Beneath the long, dark lashes his eyes darted from Robert to Ann.

"You started feeding him," Ann said. "Where's mom?"

"I think she went outside to wash up. She was here all night." He pointed to the mat on the floor next to Old Man's. "She slept; didn't feed him once."

An hour later, Des Moines had not returned. After orphanage rounds, Robert had patients to see, so he enlisted Stanford to begin to spoon-feeding Old Man. If the child consumed enough calories, they'd pull the tube. Robert gave careful instructions. "A teaspoon every five minutes. Use your watch."

Stanford sat tailor style with Old Man in his lap. He spooned diluted Oral Rehydration Solution, ORS, a salt and sugar solution similar to Pedialyte, into Old Man's mouth. Stanford had the eagerness of an unvarnished medical student, keen to please his instructors. Old Man's jaw muscles oscillated as he swallowed. His bright eyes took in the surroundings. In between feedings,

Stanford read a book about Rwandan history, sharing snippets with any expat in earshot.

Ann saw patients in the outpatient clinic; someone else staffed emergency. She checked on Stanford and the boy when she could.

"Did you know the Watutsi took over the Hutu's land and set up a feudal system?" Stanford asked. "The Belgians only continued what the Tutsi monarchy started."

"Be careful about what you say," Ann warned. "Even though we are in the refugee camp, tensions between the two groups are high."

Stanford looked from his right to his left with a furtive expression. Beyond the feeding area, a dozen inpatients slept on grass mats; more than likely no one understood English. The boy with pneumonia received antibiotics; his mother snored as she curled around him. Several post-op patients, including the woman whose foot was amputated for gangrene and the girl with the bullet in her cheek, received intravenous antibiotics. Others waited for their guts to recover so they could start to eat normally. An acute abdomen had a nasogastric tube threaded into her nose that was connected to a suction machine that made a grunting sound. A young girl, with a large liver and a positive malaria smear, sighed on her mat. A woman who had delivered twins, one born dead, the other, scrawny but thriving, suckled at her breast. She lay in the room sectioned off for obstetrics.

Stanford continued, his voice lowered to a whisper. "There was a minimum-height rule for attending school." Exasperation filled his face. "Can you believe it?"

"Talk to Robert about Belgian history. His grandfather owned a tea plantation. He said he moved back to Europe when Rwanda gained its independence in 1962, I think."

"It seems more complicated than ethnic hatred imported by the Belgians. It sounds like the struggle between the two groups is long-standing."

Father Innocent had made the same point. Ann had not thought about him all morning, and that made her feel relieved.

Ann scarfed down lunch, a boiled potato and beans, and walked into the camp to check 99. He'd not shown up for his recheck. A hot wind fortified the camp's stench and the morning's grayness had vanished. Ann counted her blessings as the circumstances of the refugees spread out before her. Women busied themselves around their tents, tending cooking fires, preparing food, calling to children; their faces drawn with worry. Dozens of children wandered unattended, more than half of the children were naked. Ann wished she had the box of t-shirts she'd donated to the Salvation Army before she left Milwaukee.

All her stuff, even the stuff she dumped in the trash when she moved out of her condo, stood in stark contrast to the refugees' meager possessions; she regretted not having the use of it now.

A group of boys ran with abandon, yelling, laughing, and kicking a soccer ball constructed from plastic bags and twine. "Play is the work of children," Robert had said. "It's so important for them." The boys appeared unaware of the abject poverty that was now home. One of the NGOs hoped to start a school to provide some structure in the children's lives. Two girls tried to join the game, but one of the larger boys pushed them away. Ann wanted to intervene, but was distracted by the children who surrounded her. Flies crawled on their faces and arms. The children reached to touch her with grimy hands, pulling on her scrub pants. She picked up her pace as her lunch catapulted in her stomach. She flushed and breathed hard. They were only curious kids; they wouldn't hurt her. The smallest girl called, "Muzungu," and trotted to keep up.

As Ann neared 99's acacia tree she consciously slowed her breathing. The tree's green canopy shimmered in the midday light. Beneath it stretched a broad circle of shade where a throng of children sang a song. 99's off-key voice rang out decibels louder than the rest as he limped among them, passing out some treat. The group following Ann fluttered in among the throng, the two groups coalescing like flocks of birds. She stood at the edge until the song ended.

99 perched on his stool and beckoned Ann with his entire arm. "*Mwiriweho*, good afternoon," 99 lisped. His camp was neatly organized with items strung to the acacia's branches. The mosquito net she had given him was suspended over his sleeping pad. Cooking pots were stacked near the fire pit. Today his t-shirt advertised Budweiser beer.

The children's faces were jubilant. Her earlier panic seemed foolish. "Who are your friends?" she asked.

99 smiled broadly, his crowded teeth showing in his grin. He introduced most of the children by name and asked those he didn't know to introduce themselves. He concluded with "Praise God" and introduced her as "Dr. Ann from medical. She take good care of you."

Goose bumps shimmied up Ann's neck as she recognized 99's goodness. He could praise the Lord for the company of dirty and unkempt children, in a refugee camp of 100,000 poor people on a plain that made stockyards seem fragrant.

Ann had chosen to come here. She'd not been forced to leave her home. She'd arrived at the camp in a cushy SUV; she'd not recently trekked four hundred kilometers. If she was in 99's place, she'd be in tears, feeling sorry for herself, arguing with God, asking Him to reconsider the hand she'd been dealt. But here was 99, grateful for what he had.

99 stuck his feet in her direction. Ann peeled off his socks and unwound the bandage. The children gathered around to watch, mumbling to each other. One little girl tried to help. The gash on 99's leg was improving, slowly.

"Are you eating enough?" Ann asked.

He pulled the plastic bag of pills from his pants pocket and counted them for her. He'd taken them properly. "You make leg better. I thank God for you," he said, then grinned.

"Good, you are taking your pills, but what about food? What are you eating?" She moved her hand from her lap to her mouth in a gesture of eating.

"No like beans. Bad beans." 99 contorted his face and shook his head. Some of the children mimicked him.

"Beans. Why?"

"People say bad. Make sick. Have mold."

Moldy beans. This was the first Ann had heard. She'd ask Christine. She might know something from her trips to the Basuko market. Ann redressed his feet. "I want to see you in two days. If you don't come to me, I will come here."

"You come here," 99 said. "Please play song. Sing song." He moved his fingers as if he played the piano.

"Here?"

99 nodded.

Why not? Ann dropped her backpack and sat down. She stretched out her legs and drummed out *Da Da Da. Da Da Da*, the grand beginning to *The Children of Sanchez* on her pack. The children stared at her. They could not hear what she heard, so she started again and sang the powerful notes. 99 hummed along and many of the children followed his lead. He knew the words. Ann stumbled over the phrases in the middle stanza which talked about hunger for more than food. Here it took on new meaning.

99 applauded and the children joined in. 99 raised his hands. "You have Coke?" he asked and gestured toward the children. "We all need Coke."

Ann shook her head and lifted her shoulders. Despite the futility of his request, she said she'd see what she could do.

She ambled back to the medical tent alone; her earlier companions remained with 99. It was too hot to run; sweat dripped down her back and she wiped her forehead with her forearm. Mangione did not have it quite right. Spiritual food was important, but faced with the destitution of the refugees in the camp, Ann no longer underestimated the importance of basic needs—food, shelter, clothing.

She had taken for granted all she had at home. Caught in her own pain, she had not been satisfied.

Chapter 32

The foyer was packed when Ann returned.

In the emergency area, Edward bent over a patient with a shaved head who gasped for breath. "Knife in the back," Edward said. "Dropped a lung. Do you do chest tubes?"

Ann hurried to his side. "Tube goes over the top of the rib. Vessels and nerves run underneath."

"Do it. Make your cut one rib below and tunnel up. For the seal." He explored the knife wound with his gloved finger. "I'll suture this." Edward injected Ketamine into the man's buttock muscle to manage his pain.

Ann pulled on gloves and quickly organized her supplies on the tray: iodine, chest tube, scalpel, and suture. She made eye contact with the patient to explain what she was about to do. She froze.

Scar stared back. Anguish filled his eyes. Scar, who was up to no good with the presumed rapes, whom Margaux had fired, struggled to breathe. The oxygen mask covered his mouth, but his panting was audible, even with the hum of the oxygen tank. For a moment, he seemed to mouth something.

Ann's pulse raced. Sweat beaded on her scalp. Her breath came short and sharp. She braced herself and swabbed the brown antiseptic on the chest. Scar was up to no good. She drew up the numbing medicine and slipped the needle into the skin. *Shove my feelings away. Remember neutrality.* She mechanically talked herself through each step. Inject the lidocaine. Slice the skin. Burrow up. Feel the pop of the chest wall. Aim the tube toward the patient's head. . . Scar's head. She sutured the tube in place and clipped the final suture, then her hands began shaking.

Fury burned in her chest. It scalded like acid. What else was Scar trying to do? Ann configured the chest tube's suction, plunging the other end of the tube into a jar filled with water. Air bubbles gurgled, signaling the function of the tube. The ketamine had taken effect and Scar's distress eased.

Ann tore off her gloves and frowned toward Edward's back. Mission accomplished. She'd done what she needed to do. Neutrality was hard. She'd done it, but she didn't like it.

At orientation, they'd discussed neutrality. "You do not judge. You care for the patient. Your job is to provide medical care." It had taken every ounce of professionalism she could muster. She'd set aside the realities of who he was and what he'd done. She saw Scar as a patient in need, someone who depended on her medical expertise, not her judgment.

Scar slept on the cot. Only a thin cotton sheet covered his groin. He was muscular. In addition to the long, linear scar on his arm, several small marks were scattered over his body, a starburst near his navel — a gunshot wound? What battles had he fought and survived? How did he do what he did? Why did he do it? Did he have that much hatred for women? Did he detest the Tutsis that much?

As dusk fell, Ann stepped around the corner from the lean-to shower and headed through the courtyard toward her bedroom. The crude outdoor shower was off the back at the one end of the u-shaped school building. A step above the bucket dump in Kigali, it offered a lukewarm stream strong enough to rinse Ann's thick hair. A shower curtain with Mickey Mouse and Minnie created privacy.

Christine conferred with Margaux near the courtyard's garden. The evening chorus of insects had begun, rasps and clicks with a steady D-minor hum. A flock of small birds fluttered from one of the fruit trees. Ann spun around when Christine said, "Father Innocent." Ann adjusted the towel wrapped around her wet hair as she joined the conversation.

"I was buying chickens," Christine said. "They sell them in the back of the market. I swear it was Father Innocent. He wore his sunglasses. The pastor at St. Michael Church in Kigali, Mama's parish."

Ann gulped, pulling her cotton robe tighter.

"I wanted to talk to him, tell him that Mama and I had moved. Mama was always so fond of him. I wanted to know if he was saying mass at the Catholic Church in town."

Ann shivered. Christine did not know the truth about Innocent. How to tell her? Ann cinched the belt of her wrap tighter.

"I called to him. He didn't hear me. Then Scar came around the building.

Evangeline and Emit ran to him. Before I could stop them. He pulled some candy from his pocket and gave it to them, then waved them away. He and Father Innocent drove off. An old, white truck with a motor that sounded awful. The truck bed flew open. A sack fell out. The kids and I went over to inspect it. WFP." Christine crossed her arms across her bosom.

Margaux removed the cigarette from her mouth. "Was the truck labeled?" She cleared her throat.

Christine shook her head.

"World Food Program has their own staff. They deliver food directly to the camp. I suspect that Scar and Innocent were up to no good."

Ann smashed a mosquito on her cheek and swatted another on her calf with her foot.

"I wondered," Christine said. "I waited about five minutes. When no one returned, I walked over and looked inside the old shed. It was filled with metal. I could smell it. You could feel the heat."

"Weapons," Margaux said and narrowed her eyes. She took a long draw on her cigarette and exhaled, turning her head away. "Where was the shed?"

"Just north of the market. It has peeling red paint and a tin roof. It's the largest in a group of three, maybe four buildings."

Margaux sighed and shook her head.

"Scar is a patient," Ann said. "I don't know if I should be saying this, but I just put in a chest tube. Someone knifed him in the chest."

"So, he'll be out of circulation for awhile." Margaux sucked on her cigarette.

Fixated on Father Innocent, Ann asked Christine how certain she was about seeing Father Innocent. She forced his name across her tongue.

"He's unmistakable, with his height and closely cropped hair," Christine said. "Not many people wear sunglasses."

"She doesn't know," Ann said to Margaux.

Margaux bit at her lip and nodded, then pounded the cigarette butt into the ground with the heel of her sandal.

Ann began to speak but faltered.

Margaux took over. "What Ann is trying to say is that Innocent is on the wrong side. He is. . . He told his parishioners to take shelter in the church, then handed them over. They were slaughtered."

The evening's coolness grew more noticeable.

Christine screwed up her face and moved her head from side to side. She exhaled forcefully and pawed the ground with her orange flip-flop. She looked away, then back at Ann and Margaux. "I. . . I don't think Mama knows." Christine bit her lip. "She'll be so disappointed."

Disappointed, Ann thought, more than disappointment, try furious, try... Ann's heart sped up. She and Joseta had discussed taking a shelter in that church. "I have to get dressed," Ann said abruptly. She'd ask about the beans later. As she walked toward her room, Evangeline appeared, demanding her mother's attention. Evangeline's hands were affixed to her hips as she babbled about something and stamped her flip-flop.

Chapter 33

The rain poured as they slid deeper into May. Nothing dried out. Everything reeked of mildew. Sitting on the veranda was out of the question. After dinner, Margaux, Edward, and Ann played Scrabble. Robert was on call. After the game, Ann followed Edward to his room.

She hadn't given it much more thought. But Edward kept asking, and she decided it was time to accept. She liked Edward well enough and they worked together well. Frankly, she'd not had sex for awhile and she wanted the release.

Edward and Robert's bedroom had windows on two sides; one bank faced the garden courtyard, the other, the field that rolled out to distant hills. Rain pattered on the roof, swelling to a steady downpour. Edward lit a candle, then lifted the mosquito netting and invited Ann onto his cot. They stretched out, but it felt impossibly narrow.

"This will collapse under our weight," Ann said.

"You're not that big." Edward laughed.

Thankfully, the rain drowned out any chance of Joseta and Christine hearing. Their room was on the other side of the mud-brick wall and the walls seemed paper-thin.

Ann insisted they pull the bedding to the floor. She pulled a condom from her pocket and laid it next to the mattress.

"I'm glad you're a girl scout," Edward teased.

She shushed him with a kiss. He tasted of peppermint toothpaste.

He pulled off his t-shirt. A simple gold wedding band, not a cross, hung from the leather cord around his neck.

Ann rolled off Edward and sat up. Was the wife still in the picture? She'd assumed they were divorced. A hollowness filled her chest as she tapped the ring. "What's this?"

Edward's lips tightened and he moved to his side, leaning up on his elbow, he fingered the ring with his free hand. He seemed to go inside himself. His playful mood vanished.

Ann held her breath, waiting. She wrapped the sheet around her. The downpour had softened to light pings.

"I owe you an explanation." Edward continued to stroke the ring. "But. . . I hate talking about this."

"Uh huh," Ann said. Her heart raced as she took more distance.

Edward sighed. "My wife and three-year-old son died in a car crash. I was the driver. I came out with only burns from the airbag and a broken nose." He stroked his face.

"I'm sorry," Ann said. She reached to touch him but pulled back. "How awful for you."

"I had a Chrysler, one of the few cars with driver-side airbag restraints at the time."

"When did it happen?"

"June 20th, 1989." Edward stared at some point beyond her.

Ann nodded.

Silence. The inward look. After a few minutes, Edward said, "I should have told you. It's been five years. . . still hurts like it was yesterday."

They sat looking at each other. The pings on the roof were comforting.

Somehow this revelation, this vulnerability made him even more attractive. "So that's why you started overseas work," Ann whispered.

Edward nodded slowly. "I couldn't stay where I was. I'm not terribly close to my family. Erica, my wife, and Dean, my son, were the only family I had."

"I've asked you on two, maybe three occasions. You always avoided my question."

He sat quietly, switching his gaze between Ann and the bedding between them. The mosquito netting hung from the ceiling behind them, moving ever so slightly in the breeze.

"I guess everyone who does this work has some kind of wound they're trying to heal," Ann said. She considered her own motivations. Rosie's drowning and her mother's battle with cancer. She'd not yet disclosed those. "Perhaps we're looking for pain greater than our own. . . to gain some perspective."

Edward shrugged. "Maybe."

Ann reached out and patted his hand. "I'm exhausted. Let's just hold each other. I don't need bells and whistles the first time."

"You never know." Edward blew out the candle.

"Come here," Ann said. She directed Edward to roll over onto his other side. She spooned him, skin to skin, her breasts pressed against his back. Their legs curled together, his longer than hers. She'd been yearning for this. In that position they fell asleep. Their breathing synchronized.

Someone shook Ann awake. A male voice was talking. "You're screaming. Annie, you were shaking me . . ."

Ann rubbed her eyes. "What?"

"I don't know. You started rolling back and forth and talking, then screamed. Something about . . ."

Ann's skin was damp; her heart thumped. "I was back home. . . trying to. . . trying to resuscitate. . . Rosie, Rosie, my niece. I was supposed to watch her. I left. . . She drowned."

"What?"

"Can I have some water?"

Edward found his water bottle and unscrewed the cap. Ann took a long draw, then wiped her mouth with the back of her hand.

Edward stared at her. It was still dark. The rain had stopped. Outside the window, the sky was packed with stars.

Ann recounted the story: babysitting her mother and Rosie, leaving Rosie in the shallow end to help her demanding mother, finding Rosie, CPR, the ambulance, the days that followed. She'd not shared it beginning to end with anyone in Africa in such detail. While she spoke, Edward listened. He handed her his t-shirt when tears welled in her eyes. He didn't touch her until she was done, then he opened his arms. "Annie."

She swallowed against the lump in her throat as she collapsed into his chest and wept. He said nothing, just held her until she was ready to speak. She lost all sense of time as she heaved out her regrets and grief. Her tears matted the hair on his chest. His cord and ring pressed against her forehead. It was still dark when she sat up.

"You talked about wounds earlier."

Ann nodded.

"What I don't understand is why you blame yourself. Sure, it happened on your watch. But you left Rosie to help your mother. Maybe you should have taken Rosie with you. Or told her to get out of the pool. But she knew how to swim. She was playing in the shallow end. You can kill yourself with 'shoulds.'"

Ann stared at him. The mattress supported her buttocks. The pillow felt soft against her knee. Edward's words surrounded her. She could hear his breath.

"I think you need to forgive yourself and move on."

"How do I do that?"

Edward shrugged.

Ann reached for him. They hugged, then kissed. His soft lips brushed her neck, pressed against her breast. Soon she felt Edward's erection. He rolled on the condom and stroked her between the legs. "Tell me if I hurt you. I don't want to . . ."

They lost themselves in body scent, the crest of the pelvic bone, the warm moisture of the hungry tongue and moans, moans of comfort and satisfaction.

Chapter 34

The grind of large equipment interrupted patient care the next morning. Ann looked out the mesh window of the medical tent and recalled her night with Edward, savoring the sweetness. Thirty meters away, the rumbling backhoe presented a stark contrast. It dug a gaping hole between the medical tent and the river that flowed another fifty meters beyond. A hiss of smoke belched from its smoke stack as a skid loader arrived with several corpses shrouded in cloth, dumped them, then sped off.

"What's going on?" Ann asked no one in particular.

Margaux stood outside the tent monitoring the activity. "I hired a Tanzanian company to dig a mass grave."

"What about the shovel brigade?" Ann asked. A group of refugees had been hired to dig graves.

"They couldn't keep up."

Ann walked outside, joining Margaux, who fiddled with her pack of Impalas as she inspected the work. She never smoked around the medical tent, but she usually had her cigarettes with her.

The large shovel dumped the red-brown earth in a growing heap. The skid loader returned with several more bodies piling them near the edge of the hole. "There was an issue with the desecration of some of the corpses," Margaux said over the drone. "Some not-so-nice things were being done to the corpses of a certain ethnic group. I'll leave it at that."

Ann understood--Hutus defiling Tutsis. A wave of indignation overwhelmed her as the pile of corpses grew. There was no end to the awfulness. Scar still lay on a mat in the inpatient area. She'd heard nothing about Father Innocent for awhile. She toed the red dirt with her sandal. Finally she said, "I have a hard time understanding neutrality when we are fixing up the perpetrators to go out and continue their crimes."

Margaux mouthed an unlit cigarette. "Neutrality is hard," she said. "And it is Global Health's policy, but I'll be frank. It has been a point of contention at the collaborative meetings because Paul Kagame, the leader of the rebels, has started accusing the NGOs of protecting the *génocidaires*."

Ann braced herself against the words. When the backhoe finished, the skid loader pushed the bodies into the hole. A series of thuds sounded; Ann could feel reverberations in her torso. Then the hoe grunted and the shovel sprinkled dirt into the hole.

No one back home could imagine the magnitude of disease and death. She'd shared her secrets with Edward last night, felt softer, but taking in the reality before her, fully admitting the lives cut short and the fact that her efforts might be contributing to the horrors, would paralyze her. She observed Margaux's nonchalance.

"Traditionally, families claim and bury their relatives, but there's no room in the camp." Margaux looked at Ann. "It's become a health hazard. Edward and I decided this was best."

"The wail is gone?" Ann said. Early on she had heard it. After the family dug the grave, they announced the loss with a wail. The other mourners joined in the cry, a haunting complex of sounds, imbued with emotion that resounded from somewhere deep in the pelvis. An unforgettable register, it commanded attention much like the emergency test that occurred on the first Wednesday of the month in Milwaukee.

Margaux continued to stare toward the grave still fingering the unlit cigarette. "I need a smoke," she said.

Ann buckled back the emotion. "I need to get back to work."

Later in the afternoon, Robert called Ann over to see a mother and her son. The boy lay like a sack of beans in his mother's thin arms. His lips were parched and cracked. The mother kept touching a damp cloth to his lips, but the boy's lips didn't move, no tongue thrusting, no swallowing. He was covered with sores oozing pus. "What do you think? Antibiotics and fluids?" Robert asked, his stutter more pronounced.

"I don't know," Ann said. "He's sicker than Old Man. I don't think we can commit that much time to him."

Robert's eyes met hers. His eyes glistened and he closed them, sucking in a breath. They settled the mother in a corner of the tent with a fresh cloth and a bottle of water. There she could minister to her son and be away from the other commotion. When they checked on her an hour later, she had left and the boy lay lifeless on the floor, the cloth pulled up over his face. It was so different from home where curing was the expectation and death considered to be a failure. Together Ann and Robert wrapped him in a sheet and Ann carried him to the stack of corpses for the day. Robert had seen too much; he couldn't do it.

Chapter 35

Des Moines, Old Man's mother, never returned. Both Ann and Robert were disappointed. Dr. Philip, the Rwandan physician, said that Des Moines probably had other children to care for and left when she knew Old Man was in good hands.

Stanford made it his job to work with Old Man daily. The boy progressed with his feedings and, after three weeks, he was spoon-feeding himself a porridge made from cassava and powdered milk. His cheeks began to fill out.

"He graduates today," Robert said. Raindrops beat on the tent canvas.

Stanford smiled. "His mat in the orphanage is ready."

"One of the lucky ones," Ann said, bracing herself for another day of patients dressed in soggy clothes and the inerasable smells of mustiness and body odor.

At the end of the work day, Robert carried Old Man to the orphanage. Ann accompanied him, having promised Stanford that she would come to see the latrines he'd been digging. The day's drizzle had stopped and the golden light of the afternoon sun bathed the reeds near the river. Dragonflies buzzed and flittered about, colliding and mating during free fall or while poised on long blades of green grass. But for the smell of the bloated corpses that lay trapped in branches along the bank or bobbed in the river, it was a lovely afternoon. Ann was delighted to dry out, although her clothes still smelled of mildew.

Outside the orphanage, many of the children wore clean, white dresses, some with blue and yellow stripes, others with a floral pattern. Stanford hurried up the path.

"What's with the outfits?" Ann asked.

"Uniforms for the orphans?" Robert joked.

Stanford laughed as he explained that the priest who gave them extra food had dropped off a dozen crates filled with linens.

A buzz filled Ann's ears. The priest again. Was this Innocent? She couldn't believe he'd converted to a humanitarian. Christine thought she'd seen him near the shed full of guns. But in Kigali, he'd lobbied for the safety of the Beauraing orphans at the same time that he'd carried out his heinous crimes. What motivated him? Thankfully, she'd not yet encountered him face-to-face in the camp. Stanford was still talking.

". . . sheets are useful, but no one uses pillows. This afternoon, I took a pillowcase and cut three holes—one for the head and two for arms. *Voila!* I solved our clothing problem! We've tried to wash the kids' clothes, but the rags just fall apart. And nothing dries in the dampness."

"You're brilliant Stanford," Robert stuttered.

"Another organization sent a box of high heels. Are you in need of footwear?"

Humor, try to find the humor. Ann forced a laugh. "I'd break a leg."

"We get the dumbest donations," Stanford said. "Hair dye and makeup."

Ann shook her head. "But, I'll place my order for a tube of lipstick."

Robert set Old Man down. He promptly joined a group of children drawing pictures in the dirt.

"He's a miracle," Stanford said.

Robert nodded like a proud father. "You were part of it."

They followed Stanford to the far side of the building where a fence constructed from sticks and wire surrounded a half dozen pits covered with wooden boards. "Our improved sanitation," Stanford said. "Now we have to teach the kids to use them." He grinned broadly. "Mother Teresa used to say: 'Small changes add up. If you can't feed a hundred people, feed one.'"

A chorus of young voices called to Stanford from the soccer field.

"Time to play," Stanford said and sped off toward the boys who kicked a ball. "Come join us . . ." trailed in his wake.

Robert raced off.

Their handmade ball appeared to be constructed from leaves and string. They'd embellished the goalposts defining the ends of the field—now tree branches secured with piled stones. Ann felt too weary to join them. She walked the perimeter of the orphanage and, ten meters beyond, twenty-one mounds of fresh dirt rose above the grass. The cemetery. Ann counted a mound for every day. The purple shadow of a cloud stretched across the area. A breeze from the river carried the scent of algae and bird life, laced with rotting flesh.

Chapter 36

Knock. Knock. Knock. The thumping blended in with Ann's dream, pressing on Rosie's small chest, trying to get her heart started again: one-one-thousand, two-one-thousand, three-one- thousand... A drowning victim is not dead until she's warm and dead. The body's processes hibernated at cold temperatures. When would the medics arrive? Arms aching. Pool water dripping from her hair... No. No. It was Christine's voice.

Ann bolted out of bed. The cement floor felt cool on her feet as she slipped on flip-flops and flapped to the door.

"What?" Ann whispered, trying to gather her wits.

"It's Evangeline. She's ill," Christine said.

Ann pulled her hair back and tied it with a bandana. "What time is it?"

"Noon."

Ann had slept four hours after being up most of the night with patients. She grabbed a shirt and followed Christine across the courtyard and into the bedroom Christine and Evangeline shared with Joseta. A gentle rain fell from the gray sky, no change while Ann had slept. Raindrops dampened her shirt and sleeping shorts and felt pleasantly warm on her bare legs. A moist-earth smell filled her nose.

Evangeline lay whimpering on her grandmother's cot. Her forehead felt hot. Tears leaked from her large, dark eyes, coalescing on her thick lashes and trickling down her cheeks. The beige sheets grew darker with her tears. She was a pretty six-year-old with her mother's mahogany eyes and long lashes. Her long legs came from her father. Ann whispered a prayer for him and Evangeline's brothers before she began the assessment.

"Vomiting? Diarrhea?" Ann asked.

The evening before Evangeline had picked at her dinner and Christine had put her to bed early. Joseta had given her acetaminophen at eleven. Evangeline usually slept with either Christine or Joseta.

"Her main complaint is her head," Christine said. "She calls it heat-ache."

Ann smiled and leaned close to listen to Evangeline's lungs. Evangeline smelled sweaty and sour. Her heart clipped along—the fever could explain that. Although well-nourished compared with the refugee children, she was thin by American standards. Her stomach felt soft. "When was her last acetaminophen?"

"An hour ago."

"That should be taking affect."

Evangeline sucked on her finger and whimpered.

"When her fever didn't come down after the medicine, I decided to wake you." Christine placed a damp rag on Evangeline's forehead, then fussed with the bedsheet.

"I'm glad you did." Ann searched for a rash or other clues. "Any odd exposures?"

"The candy from Scar," Christine said.

"Emit got some too. How is he?"

"He's riding with his *Data* today." Christine searched for words. "When my husband and sons were killed... I wonder if Evangeline was poisoned."

Ann's head spun. She heard they had disappeared, not that they were killed. Did she miss something? But Christine looked ragged and had moved on, so Ann didn't press the issue.

". . . that was awhile ago," Christine was saying. "Evangeline hasn't seemed sick until yesterday." She shook her head, as she combed her fingers through Evangeline's hair.

"I've been meaning to ask you. 99 says there's mold on the beans and the traders are selling beans they bought from the refugees. . ."

"I always wash beans and cook them well," Christine said. "We have enough propane. I don't have to collect firewood, so I don't skimp on cooking time."

Ann reconsidered all the patients she'd seen who might have symptoms related to the beans. Diarrhea? There was plenty of that. The adults were all healthy as far as she knew. But children were more sensitive. . . She'd check on Emit and talk to Robert. "I think we should take her to the medical tent."

Ann discussed the differential with Robert in the obstetrics ward. It was the only area where they could find some quiet. Joseta hovered over the gurney where Evangeline lay. Robert examined Evangeline, then fiddled with his stethoscope and the stuffed bear attached to the cord. "What about malaria?" he asked. "The fever-fever . . ."

"The thick smear was negative."

"One negative smear doesn't rule-rule out malaria," he reminded.

"Her lungs were clear. She isn't breathing fast. It's not pneumonia."

Evangeline needed a measles vaccine, but this was not measles—she didn't have the dry cough and runny nose that accompanied it.

"With the headache and fever, we should tap her," Robert stammered.

"No lumbar puncture needles here. Have you done one with a plain needle?"

Robert shook his head.

"The fluid just squirts out."

"Always something new," Robert said.

The spinal fluid was normal. In fact, everything was negative except for an elevated white count—15,000. Because of the leukocytosis, Robert was nervous about just watching her. "Chloramphenicol gives the best coverage."

Ann raised the issue of moldy beans.

Robert leaned on the gurney and rubbed his goatee. "Well there is *konzo*."

"What's that?"

"It's a toxin from eating too much cassava root that's poorly prepared. It was first described in Zaire in the 1930s. *Konzo* means tired legs. A neurotoxin. So she'd have neurologic symptoms. Other than being tired, her muscles felt strong. I'll recheck her reflexes."

"Does that cause a fever?" Ann asked.

"It starts with paralysis."

They talked it over with Dr. Philip who was covering inpatient. Although he never made eye contact, he was astute and happy to problem-solve the tough cases. Robert's photographic mind was an asset but limited to book learning and whatever had passed through Tulane during his fellowship year. Ann's crash course in tropical medicine at King Faisal helped, but here the patients seemed sicker. Perhaps the stress and poor nutrition had weakened their immune systems.

Dr. Philip spoke only French. "Keep malaria on your differential."

Ann, Evangeline and Joseta rode back to the compound. Joseta fussed with her granddaughter's hair and kissed her repeatedly. The sun had broken through the bank of gray clouds and warmed the car, making Ann feel sleepy. She found herself praying. . . *Dear Jesus, Christine and Joseta do not need another loss to add to their long list. Please. Please.*

Chapter 37

Ann and Edward struggled to keep their voices low because Joseta, Christine, and ill Evangeline slept on the other side of the wall. The goats bleated more than usual. Ann wondered if some predator was stalking them. Edward reviewed his cases. Then Ann tried to tell him about Evangeline, but he wasn't interested in the details of the case—it wasn't surgical.

"It sounds like you and Robert did a good job," he said and kissed her hand. "Can we stop working?" He pressed her palm against his groin. Soon they lost themselves in the depression above the clavicle, the mound of the breast, the concave of the pelvis, the musky scent of damp hair. They swayed and thrust. Hushed whispers gave way to whimpers and sighs. Sleep followed.

A gunshot cracked through the darkness. Ann bolted upright. "What was that?"

Edward put his hand on her knee and patted the sheets to find his t-shirt and shorts. Within seconds another shot blasted. Then someone pounded on the bedroom door.

Edward opened the door. A beam of light bounced off the floor. "I am headed out to find the guard," Margaux said in her husky voice. Ann pulled on her own top and shorts, located her headlamp and flip-flops, and followed them outside, then through the kitchen and common room. Everything was quiet, undisturbed. They crossed the veranda and hurried down the front walkway toward the road. The spotlight near the road was off. A truck clamored out of town, the muffler rattling.

Their guard bent over the motionless body. Ann aimed her headlamp, steadying her hand. Blood leaked from the hole between the other guard's eyes. She squatted down and reached for his neck. "Thready pulse," she said. Her own heart pummeled in her chest.

Edward crouched above her; his flashlight beamed on the scalp, white particles caught in the corkscrews of hair. "He's a goner. That's brain tissue."

Ann gulped, her legs weak.

Margaux coughed, wheezing from the jog. "They shot him, then shot out the streetlight."

"Damn. There goes our sleep for the night," Edward said.

Ann still stooped over the body. Edward pulled her to her feet and hugged her. Memories of Kigali flashed in her mind, the man lying in front of St. Michael, his foot a doorstop. The patient she transported whose breast was lobbed off. How long would these images haunt her? She wasn't expecting the same violence here at the camp.

"I am calling the Tanzanian police," Margaux said and headed back toward the compound.

Edward and Ann spoke with the guard, asking him to describe what had happened. They spent the rest of the night sorting through the logistics, notifying GH headquarters, checking on the others at the compound.

It took the Tanzanian police well over an hour to arrive. They were highly inefficient in taking a report. Ann brewed coffee and waited up with Margaux and Edward for two hours, wanting to be supportive, curious about how the police would respond and how the incident would affect their work, worried about the safety of everyone in the compound. She made a second pot of coffee.

Were they in danger?

Ann pointed out the bad muffler. It was likely the truck Christine had seen Innocent and Scar using at the market.

"We can't be sure," Edward said. "The vehicle was almost out of town by the time we got here."

Margaux sent Ann to bed. "The police are working with us. They have to. Basuko and Tanzania benefit from having the NGOs here. Their businesses are booming."

If Ann had understood the potential for violence before coming, she would never have volunteered for this mission. How motivated and excited she'd been after Edward's recruiting talk. How quickly she'd completed the GH card that evening and carefully taken it to the post office. How desperate she was to leave Milwaukee. . . The mission had morphed in unimaginable ways. Now she was in the thick of it and could not imagine leaving. Like Margaux and Edward, her skin was thickening. But despite the growing crust, she was gaining insights into her own motivations for choosing this work, as well as the motivations of others. Along with the danger came an adrenaline rush, the excitement of being on the front line.

Ann had two hours before she needed to dress for the day. At least she could rest her eyes. But her mind continued to examine the puzzle pieces. Scar was in the hospital. Christine had seen Scar and Innocent in the truck together, if the vehicle that left the scene had been their truck. Was Innocent the perpetrator? He had a weapon. Were the police sophisticated enough to identify exactly what kind of gun was used? Was the dead guard a Tutsi? The nuances in his physique were not so obvious. Would the police take this as seriously as Margaux suggested?

Exhausted from the worry, Ann flipped over and prayed herself to sleep. She fingered the glow-in-the-dark rosary from the nuns at the Beauraing orphanage. She remembered how the rosary had comforted her as a child. In the darkness, the luminescent rosary and a night-light had been her protection against the boogey men who loomed in the scary corners of her childhood bedroom.

Her sheets were damp when Christine shook her awake and handed her a cup of coffee.

Chapter 38

When Evangeline continued to spike fevers, despite three negative malaria smears, Dr. Philip encouraged Robert and Ann to start malaria treatment. Evangeline wasn't worse, but she wasn't better. She still fussed and acted uncomfortable. She remained at the compound, isolated from all the sickness that tromped through the medical tent. Christine spent much of her time tending to Evangeline. The other cook helped with food preparation and dinners grew bland.

Ann checked on them at the end of another hot and humid day in the clinic. Christine fanned Evangeline with a large banana leaf and gave her sips of purified water. If ice was available, Ann would have rubbed a cube along Evangeline's neck as well as her own. During hot summers in Wisconsin, she and her sisters had taken turns rubbing each other's foreheads and arms. Oh, for the frozen cubes now.

Ann felt Evangeline's forehead. Hot. "When was her last acetaminophen?"

"At noon."

"Let's give her some more."

Christine seemed happy for adult company, weary from spending the day with a fussy six-year-old. While Christine took a break, Ann administered the medicine, then settled Evangeline on her stomach. Evangeline whimpered into her pillow. Ann lifted the girl's cotton nightgown and traced circles and triangles on Evangeline's back with her fingers. A circle, then a triangle in the center. Another circle and a square. Ann recalled her own mother gently fingering the palm of her hand in church to quiet and soothe her when she was a restless and bored child. It was a reassuring gesture. Within five minutes, Evangeline stopped fidgeting and fell asleep.

Christine returned. She was fixated on whether Evangeline was poisoned. She worried that her neighbors back in Kigali might have given Evangeline something. "If they hated my family so. . ." Christine mused.

"What do you mean?" Ann asked, the timing didn't make sense.

"I believe my neighbors killed my boys and my husband. Evangeline watched them from under the bed." Christine related her concern matter-of-factly, as if she were bartering for potatoes at the market.

Ann didn't know what to say. Finally, she was hearing Christine's version which was different from Joseta's who'd said they'd disappeared. Ann started to say, "But Joseta said. . ." and stopped herself. Was Christine protecting her mother or was Joseta in denial about the events? What had Evangeline told her mother? Ann twisted the corner of the sheet. Either version was horrible. She'd eaten Easter Sunday dinner with Christine's family. Laughed with her boys. She forced her own breath in and out. "I'm sorry," she whispered. "I am so sorry."

Christine leaned forward and mopped her brow with the corner of her faded red and yellow kanga.

They sat in silence. Ann fanned herself, still wishing for ice cubes. Birds twittered in the garden. Finally, Ann summoned the courage to ask. "Did you tell your mother about Father Innocent?"

Christine looked at her lap and folded her hands, then she made eye contact with Ann. She exhaled slowly through pursed lips. "I couldn't."

Ann nodded.

Christine searched for words. "She's had so much." She sighed. "Data's abduction, then my husband and. . . it's been so hard on her."

"She's still hopeful about Vincent."

"She has to be." Christine refolded the sheet over Evangeline.

Ann felt an ache deep in her pelvis. It was hard to follow all the threads of the story, but she understood hope. She pinched at her leg as she remembered how desperately she had hoped that Rosie would open her eyes, would wake up. Ann and her family kept up the hope until the doctor's testing confirmed that Rosie's brain was dead. The day they turned off the ventilator Ann was filled with despair. She shivered at the memory of that day. It had dawned with a thick, gray fog obscuring all the familiar landmarks.

Ann's mother had hoped that she could beat her cancer, clung to a thread of hope until she had no strength left, too weak to say her goodbyes. Hope or denial? Either way both lives had ended bitterly.

Chapter 39

Joseta stood in the courtyard, staring at Christine's garden, when Ann stepped out of the outdoor shower. She had washed away the day's sweat and dissatisfaction, and the frustration that had come with the increasing injuries that presented to the medical tent. Joseta crouched down and pulled a weed, then stood up, mumbling to herself.

"How's Evangeline?" Ann asked.

Joseta glanced up, appearing surprised to see Ann. She rubbed the dirt from her hands. "Thank Jesus. Her fever broke."

"Wonderful," Ann said. Relief rushed through her. Evangeline had been sick for over a week days, eight long days.

"Yes, thank Jesus and the *umuganga gakondo*."

"What?"

"The witch doctor, a traditional healer."

"But Robert and I gave Evangeline antibiotics and anti-malarials."

Joseta's expression was flat, noncommittal. "Christine asked a Tanzanian healer to examine Evangeline." She adjusted the kanga on her shoulder; she had returned to traditional dress in the refugee camp, leaving her white nursing uniforms in Kigali.

"You're a nurse. How do you make sense of that?"

Joseta straightened and planted her hand on her left hip. Ann had seen this pose before. "Of course I believe both. Western medicines treat some things. But not everything. You and Robert did your medical tests to see if you could find a cause. You treated her. Wonderful. But some problems are beyond the power of medicine. Christine wanted to consult the healer in Basuko. I didn't stop her. Evangeline was very ill."

Ann bit her tongue. They had started the anti-malarials on day three despite the negative smears. They had followed Dr. Phillip's advice. Surely, malaria caused her illness and the medications had worked. Joseta was an excellent nurse. Ann had no concern about her knowledge or her judgment. But this surprised her. However, she thought it best not to argue. Perhaps she'd ask Joseta to explain her thinking later, another day, but not now. She seemed preoccupied, even testy, argumentative. "I'm glad she's better. Robert will be pleased."

Ann sat on the veranda after dinner. The guard paced back and forth, walking in and out of the pool of light cast by the overhead spotlight near the gate. The bulb had been replaced after much prodding from Margaux. The metal barrel of the guard's Kalashnikov reflected the lamp glow. Since the murder of their compatriot, the GH guards carried rifles while on duty. How things had changed. In Kigali Ann had gradually adjusted to stricter curfews, gave up walking, and asked staff or Father Innocent to drive her places.

She cringed at the thought of Innocent.

The drift toward tighter security was occurring here. Margaux prohibited expats and staff from walking unaccompanied around Basuko. It had felt like a safe town when they'd arrived. Now Ann found herself welcoming guards with guns, especially after the shooting of their guard. Like a frog in a kettle of water, she was acclimating to the increased heat.

The Tanzanian police had arrested someone. But Margaux worried that the police had grabbed a poor, powerless man in response to the NGO's outcry. The police needed to show their authority. They had responded with increased patrol; every hour or so they motored by. Scar had recovered from his collapsed lung and was discharged from the hospital, who knew what he was up to.

The beam of Ann's headlamp illuminated a page of *The Hobbit*. An English-speaking nurse who worked in the medical tent had given it to her. After finishing *Gorillas in the Mist*, Margaux had offered Ann some French novels, but Ann wanted to escape, not look up every fourth word in a French-English dictionary. Tiny gnats flitted in and out of the circle of light. Something larger landed on her arm. She smacked it and wiped the blood smear on her brown cotton pants. It was not the first stain.

Robert pulled up a plastic chair. "How's it going?" he stammered.

"The gnats are bugging me if you want to know the truth."

"I talked with Dr. Philip about poisoning. He said it's a common concern among Africans." Robert tripped over the final word.

"I'm glad he's working with us. Did he look you in the eye yet?"

Robert shook his head.

Ann swatted another bug, then went to her room for some Deet. When she returned, she handed the bottle to Robert. "Have some?"

Robert squirted the liquid into his hand and slapped it on his face like aftershave. The chemical smell grew strong as he smeared it up his forearms. "I've been thinking. When my grandfather was planting tea, I imagine he poured all kinds of compounds on the ground to manage weeds. Who knows what poisons the pickers were exposed to, and what poisons were absorbed by the tea bushes. Back in the 1950s they didn't care."

"Get this. Joseta told me Christine had a witch doctor see Evangeline, a *umuganga gakondo*. Her fever came down a few hours later."

Robert nodded. "Hmmm."

"Is that your response?" Ann shrugged. "I was hoping you'd shed some light."

"Didn't study that during my ID fellowship." Robert chuckled and grew silent. "Come to think of it, do we really know what made Evangeline better? Her malaria smears were never positive. We gave her our potions. She is better. We should be relieved."

Ann nodded. "Maybe my prayers helped. Joseta's too." Ann had arrived in Africa wanting to categorize things into black-and-white, good and bad. She was learning that was not possible, and that some things could not be explained by her rational mind. She wanted to manage the world with deductive or inductive reasoning, but she was grappling with more and more uncertainty.

They sat in darkness except for the street lamp near the road. A night calling bird sang from the mango tree off to the side. A response echoed in the distance. The clouds thinned and one by one the stars began to appear. Behind them, their compatriots in the common room listened to a local music station and played a board game.

"My grandfather detested religion," Robert said. "He told stories about how his workers consulted the traditional healers when they were ill. He called their prayers and rituals hocus-pocus. Told his workers they were wasting their hard-earned money." Robert combed his fingers through his hair. The hair at the nape of his neck now curled at his collar.

Robert was good company, easygoing. Ann felt lucky to have him on her team. She uncrossed her legs and smashed an insect feeding on her right ankle.

Margaux opened the door and stepped out onto the veranda. "It's a lovely evening. Finally, a break from the rain."

"The bugs are a pain."

"Join us, Margaux," Robert said. "You'll need to bring a chair."

Margaux carried out one of the chairs. She settled herself and lit a cigarette.

"Want some Deet?" Ann handed her the bottle.

Margaux set down her cigarette and squeezed the bottle into her palm. The chemical smell. She screwed on the cap and picked up her cigarette, taking a long draw.

"What are you talking about at the collaborative meeting?" Ann asked. Margaux attended a weekly meeting with all the NGOs working in the camp.

"We're overwhelmed with security and politics. The other NGOs are facing the same challenges we are. *Doctors of the World* had one of their local physicians kill some of the patients. They run the medical tent on the camp's north side." Margaux shook her head.

"More ethnic rivalries," Robert said.

"And I thought we had it bad. It wasn't someone from the outside?" Ann asked.

Margaux exhaled. Cigarette smoke floated across the veranda. Ann fanned her face. "The French are sending forces to southwestern Rwanda. They call it *Operation Turquoise*. They hope to stabilize the country. Halt the genocide."

"Aren't the French long supporters of the dead president's regime?"

"*Oui*," Margaux said.

"They're now calling it genocide?" Ann asked.

"No. Your country is hedging. The US spokesperson calls it 'acts of genocide.'" Margaux stomped out her cigarette and tossed the butt into the yard.

The International Red Cross estimated that 500,000 Rwandans were dead. But the US was stalling, saying there was no mandate to solve the world's problems, especially in Africa. There was no oil. No diamonds. The catastrophe did not affect US interests. The region had no value to the US.

"Word-word games," Robert said.

"I hope *Operation Turquoise* will help bring this mess to an end," Margaux said.

"But if the French have supported the president, won't that help-help the extremists finish off their job?" Robert stammered.

"I'm grateful to my country. France is the first international power to help." She swatted at her leg. "These bugs are irritating." She stood up. "I'm going to bed." The screen door banged after her.

"She must be sweeter than us," Ann said.

"I'm surprised the smoke didn't keep them away," Robert said without a falter. "She is a good boss."

Stars packed the sky. The Milky Way looked like a river. Ann's dad would be staring at a dimmer version; even in the Wisconsin countryside the stars were not as vivid. "Did you leave a girlfriend back home?" Ann asked. One of the OR nurses had been asking her about Robert.

Robert said nothing.

Ann continued. "A nurse from Stanford's NGO has the hots for you."

Robert shifted in his chair. He rubbed his goatee and whispered in a falter. "I'm not really into women."

Ann closed her mouth. She had not expected that from Robert. "I'm sorry." Was she so involved in herself that she'd missed the clues? "I'll quit encouraging her to be patient with your shyness."

"No, really," Robert stuttered, his voice barely audible. "Africans aren't friendly toward homosexuals. . . I don't want . . ." Robert started again, his manner grave. "There is a lot of prejudice about gays in Africa. I don't want it to get-get out. Please-please."

Ann leaned forward to hear. "It's safe with me."

Robert continued in a whisper with an occasional hesitation. "I had a relationship end badly during my ID fellowship. My parents never approved. I decided it was a good time to see the country and people my grandfather talked about. He was a great storyteller. When he died a year ago, my mother gave me his journals. Reading through them piqued my interest. He had, how shall I say it? A colonial mind-set. . . I felt the obligation to give back. It was the Rwandans who were responsible for his success. I thought it was a chance to use what I'd learned."

"Did you bring the journal with you?"

Robert nodded.

"Cool. I'd love to see it." Ann paused, then added, "I'll just say you left a girlfriend back in Belgium."

"Thanks," Robert said.

"Time for bed," Ann said. "Busy day tomorrow."

"Aren't they-they all?"

Ann said goodnight and walked around the building toward her bedroom. She kicked at the gravel. Robert was a great guy. She should have been more sensitive.

Chapter 40

The next morning a cloud hovered over the middle of the camp, like the vapors that covered Middle Earth in *The Hobbit*. It softened the camp's harsh realities. Stanford met the SUV on its first run. His cheeks were ruddy from his jog up the path from the orphanage. "There's a French actress. Arnaude Brun. I think I said it right. She's arriving sometime this morning. She and some French diplomat want to take fifty orphans to France. Robert, I need your help."

"What?" Robert asked. His face showed his displeasure.

"Help me choose which kids should go."

"No. We don't have time for an actress," Ann growled. "Look at the line."

"What side of the bed-bed did you get up on?" Robert teased.

Ann apologized and pointed to the queue of waiting patients that stretched at least ten meters, the end lost somewhere in the mist. Dr. Philip and the other Rwandan doctors would help, but Ann always liked having Robert around to consult. "Please, do your rounds as quickly as possible," she said in a sweet tone.

"Better," Robert said and followed Stanford to the orphanage.

Over the lunch hour, Ann visited 99 under his acacia tree. A bearded man led a donkey packed with burlap bags and leather satchels away from 99's tree. Several large, yellow gerry cans dangled from the straps. The gentleman nodded and continued south toward another refugee family. Ann worried that he might take advantage of 99. "What did he want?" she panted.

99 smiled and pulled a handful of coins from his pocket. "Sell oil and maize. Me bargain good price. Buy these." 99 pointed to a pile of root vegetables spread out on a burlap sack: Irish potatoes, sweet potatoes, and cassava. He

loaded them into the sack and tied the bag to a tree branch. The midday sun penetrated the tree's canopy in several spots, creating a dappled pattern on the dirt and remaining patches of grass.

"Why did you sell the oil and maize?" Ann asked.

"No like."

"Do others feel that way?"

99 nodded. "You have Coke?"

Ann pulled a bottle of Coke out of her pack.

99 took the bottle and put the top in his mouth, removing the cap with his teeth.

Ann cringed. "How can you do that?"

99 shrugged, then took a long drink, burping as he hobbled over to his stool. He settled himself and stuck out his feet.

Ann removed the dirty socks and unrolled the bandages. Soon, he would not need to cover the wound, but with the flies and dust, she didn't want to move too fast. His foot had healed slowly. "The oil will help you heal," she said.

"Yellow maize is animal food. Take long to cook—three days." 99 raised three fingers. "Use much fuel. White maize grind easy. Oil bring much coins."

Ann gathered that the refugees were unhappy with the food basket. They sold what they did not want to the Tanzanian traders, receiving precious cash. But how could they cook without oil? The pots were aluminum. Oil had fatty acids that were important for healing.

A scraping sound caught her attention; a rodent investigated the pots near the fire pit.

99 yelled and threw a stick, frightening the intruder away. He explained that the traders ground the maize, but the service was pricey. Cassava was the preferred flour for porridge. He rattled on, at times talking so fast he was hard to understand. "They cut rations. Important sell some things so I buy what I like."

"Who cut your rations?"

"Ask *burgomasters*," 99 said and shrugged. "They responsible."

Someone in charge had cut the refugees' food. That would have repercussions in the clinic; malnutrition was already a problem. Ann sighed. She unloaded two more bottles of Coke from her backpack and traipsed back to the medical tent.

As she squeezed her way through the waiting patients into the emergency area, she tried to remember the Mother Teresa quote Stanford had described—something about one—do what you can, one at a time.

Anyone heading to the orphanage had to pass the GH tent. Just as Ann and Robert tackled the afternoon's patients, a black Land Rover with silver trim rolled to a stop outside. The fog was long gone and the waves of heat beamed off the black chrome. The GH vehicle followed, and Margaux and Edward climbed out. They had arranged a tour of the medical tent for the actress and her entourage.

A brunette with big hair, red lipstick, and reflective sunglasses climbed out of the vehicle, flagged by a balding, middle-aged man dressed in brand-new outdoor gear. A well-dressed African followed. Several Land Rovers, filled with journalists carrying cameras and large microphones, pulled up. The blue jeans, Nikes, gortex rain jackets, quick-drying outdoor wear, and sunglasses stood in stark contrast to the colorful but worn and grimy clothing of the refugees waiting to be seen. The refugees gawked at the media circus—entertainment to pass the time.

The much-anticipated Arnaude Brun had arrived. Dressed in designer jeans, she wore a red tank top stuffed with breasts the size of the squash sold at the town market. Needless to say, Arnaude commanded the attention of all the men. Margaux looked frumpy with her gray pony tail, GH t-shirt, and well-worn jeans, but she never seemed concerned about her appearance. The only time Ann had seen her wear something other than that uniform was when they visited General Bagasora at the parliament in Kigali.

The group chatted for a few minutes and then Arnaude organized the men with tripods and cameras so the medical tent and the waiting refugees stood in the background. Edward was dressed in his scrubs. He ran into the outpatient area and borrowed Robert's patient. The three-year-old had a handsome face, but old machete scars embroidered his arms and the back of his neck like railroad tracks. Ann wanted to apologize to Robert for Edward's rudeness, but stopped herself.

When the cameras started rolling, Edward, his surgical mask dangling around his neck, stood between the actress and the French diplomat. The diplomat and well-dressed African had donned GH t-shirts. Ann could not hear what was said, but at one point Edward flipped the child around to show the scars on his neck and his extended arms. Ann's face burned. How could he? Did the child, who innocently displayed his scars, know he was being exploited? When the interview was done, Edward returned the patient to Robert without saying a word, jumped into the actress's Land Rover and rode down to the orphanage.

"You should go," Ann urged Robert. "Stanford wanted your help. Edward doesn't know the kids at the orphanage."

"I'm not much for the spotlight," Robert stammered.

"Go!" Ann urged.

Robert followed the entourage. Ann felt guilty interrupting patient care when the line of patients snaked so long, but she felt compelled to watch, obliged to observe Edward's arrogance. Who was this man she'd slept with? And what did the refugees think of these *wazungu*? Did they group her, Robert, Edward, and Margaux among the crazy whites, unable to distinguish them from the French entourage? Ann hoped not. She hoped that her efforts in the medical tent made her distinguishable to the few hundred refugees she'd cared for. But it was easy to generalize if you didn't recognize the nuances. Ann's old college landlord had said that black people were like Labradors, they all looked alike. But that wasn't true; generalizations about populations were fraught with miscalculations, even generalizations about animals. If Dian Fossey and her staff hadn't put in the time, they would not have learned that each gorilla had a unique nose print and personality.

Near the river, the group paused for more camera shots. Thankfully, the dead bodies were gone. Behind the actress and the diplomat, women stood knee-deep in the river, pounding clothes on large, gray and brown rocks as they did every day now that the river was clean. Colorful shirts, skirts, and pants were spread over the bushes and grass on the bank to dry. Children played at the water's edge; half were naked.

The actress and her train continued on. Robert lagged behind. When they entered the orphanage Ann returned to work. A sick feeling sat in her chest. She couldn't articulate the discomfort and didn't have time to sort it through.

At the end of the day, Stanford and Robert told Ann about the activities at the orphanage. They stood outside the tent. The smoke from dozens of cooking fires twirled upward. The laughter of the boys playing soccer was hard to ignore.

The actress had asked questions about the children and Edward had answered. "At first I tried to correct him," Stanford said. "But he frowned at me, so I shut up. He just made up their histories, and talked about how important it was for the children to have a good home. What a shooter. His French isn't that good. Sometimes I had to translate. Then I'd correct what he said."

"Robert, why didn't you jump in?" Ann asked. "Your French is excellent."

Robert's speech impediment was in full swing. "I'd open my mouth to talk and Edward cut me off. You know how I stutter when I get nervous."

Ann did. She tried not to rush in with a word when Robert was having trouble. But at the moment, she was furious with Edward; what an insensitive media hound. Such arrogance. Typical surgeon. She'd give him a piece of her mind.

"The worst part was when the actress looked over the children. It was like she was shopping for fruit. She examined their teeth and hands. The cameras were rolling the entire time. Some of the kids crawled under their cots." Stanford sighed and shifted his stance, uncrossing his feet and folding his arms. "I think they're coming to pick up the kids tomorrow."

The sick feeling still hung in Ann's chest. She worried about the children. Granted, they were likely going to a better life, but this appeared to be a media ploy by the French. She heard the ambivalence in Stanford's voice, the same ambivalence she'd had with Michelle's adoption back in Kigali. The actress examined the children in the same dehumanizing manner as the Ambassador's wife. And worst of all, she couldn't believe Edward turning the child's scars toward the cameras.

"Even though our conditions aren't the best, we take good care of the children," Stanford said. "It might be traumatic for some of them to fly off and live with white people."

"I didn't sign up for this," Robert lamented, fingering his goatee. "But some of the kids don't have parents."

"Maybe they do. Maybe their parents haven't found them yet," Ann interjected. "You've seen how adults stare at the photo board."

Robert nodded. "Still, we don't know that for sure. I guess it's in the best interest of the children to select the healthier ones. At least the ones who are talking."

Maybe Ann was overreacting. Robert had a point. Media ploy or not, the kids selected to go would have the chance of a better life. Who knew what would happen to the others, if camp authorities were redirecting food . . .

"Old Man might be a candidate, but I'd be sad to lose him," Robert said.

From the soccer field came cries: "Stanfor . . .Rober . . .Stanfor *viens jouer*."

Robert threw an arm around Stanford. "We'll deal with this tomorrow. It's time to play." They jogged toward the soccer players, who then surrounded them and slapped their backs.

Ann should rally the girls to play. Instead, she wandered toward the river. Long, lavender shadows stretched across the grass and the refugees' blue and black plastic tents. A cloud of mist had begun to coalesce over the reeds near the river. She walked through a patch of cool air and sat down on a smooth rock. The French adoption was yet another complicated event; nothing was all good or all bad, rather some tone of gray. Several bullfrogs serenaded the evening with baritone croaks. Ann's fingers started drumming out her song. *Da Da Da. Da Da Da.* It always lifted her spirits.

Chapter 41

You were obnoxious today," Ann said. She sat on Edward's bed watching him pump through his nightly exercise routine.

"Forty-eight. Forty-nine. Fifty." Edward huffed and sat up. "Seizing opportunities with the press is really important. We talk about the horrible things that are happening. The world learns. We bring attention to GH. Donations increase. There's always a bump with press attention. That's money to continue the good work you and I are doing."

"I get that. But did you have to be so rude to Stanford and Robert."

"I apologized." He flipped over and started pushups. Some bug fluttered against the screen, its assault became rhythmic.

"You were rude to Robert, cutting him off. The orphanage is his domain. And Stanford's."

"Neither of them are what you would call articulate." Edward pressed against the floor.

"You are being an ass."

"Twenty-nine, thirty." The halo from the candle's flame fluttered across his upper back. His muscles were well defined. He stood up. "Maybe I'm an ass, but I had that brunette actress, A-something, and the diplomat eating out of my hand." He started jumping jacks.

Ann's mood boiled. He could be a control freak, a perfectionist. She saw his point, but didn't want to admit it.

When he finished, he took a long draw from his water canister, wiped the back of his mouth with his hand, and sat on the floor next to the bed.

"I have another bone to pick." Ann folded her arms across her stomach and leaned forward. "Scar was discharged a few days ago. Now he's back out on the street. The shooting occurred while he was in the hospital, so he's not working alone. He's a Hutu extremist working against us, and we saved his life? I can't imagine he mended his ways. I don't get it."

"First of all, don't use the ethnic term." Edward said. "Secondly, remember your Hippocratic Oath."

Ann persisted, holding on like a dog with a savory bone. "Especially when you know one group has been so malicious. It just doesn't make sense."

"So you have the moral authority to play God?"

"I've never heard much God talk from you."

Edward moved to his knees, leaning against the mattress. "I care for patients. I provide good care. As good as I can, given the circumstances. In Somalia, we dealt with a variety of factions. We even created several entrances, served different groups on different days. It was a little crazy, but we could honestly say, 'We provide the best care we can for you and your people.' I believe we did."

"Margaux says they're discussing neutrality at the collaborative meeting. And the fact that ethnic rivalries are a problem across the camp."

"Margaux knows Global Health has a policy of neutrality. She's said nothing to me." Edward ran his fingers along Ann's leg, moving from her ankle to her knee. "It *is* a core issue for international aid." He said. "Especially in a conflict setting." He told her about amputating the leg of a Somali warlord who then wanted to repay him with confiscated bags of intravenous fluid. "We needed the fluid, but I refused. I didn't want to owe him." He fingered the hem of the leg of her shorts.

Ann stared at him. "That's different."

"Not really. . . It's all a delicate dance."

"I don't think you appreciate the nuance. You just fix up everyone regardless."

"I am not here to judge." He pulled Ann towards him, placing his hands on her thighs.

"You already said that. You're talking in circles."

"Keep your voice down," Edward whispered. "We'll have to agree to disagree."

"I know. But it's clear to me that we are just fixing up the Hu. . . the bad guys to continue what they started in Rwanda."

Edward rubbed his groin against her knee. "We left work several hours ago."

Ann sighed and laid her hands on his shoulders.

Edward moved his fingers between her legs. "Let's think about something else." He smiled up at her.

Ann held Edward's face between her hands. "I like you. I like that you'll argue with me."

Edward laid his head in her lap. Ann bowed over him, smelling his hair, the scent of shampoo. He lifted his head. "You do a good job of making your case." He bent down and kissed her thigh. "I like that about you."

Chapter 42

Ann and Stanford finished their on-call dinner of beans and plantains. So far, Ann hadn't keeled over from the beans or developed an unsteady gait. Stanford was still disheartened about the adoption of the orphans, so she'd encouraged him to join her on the night shift. They walked outside the medical tent for some air. Stars crowded the blue-black bowl of the sky and Ann pointed out the Southern Cross. "You have to be south of the equator to see it," she explained.

Stanford stared upward in amazement.

Ann's dad had told her to look for the Southern Cross. Three bright stars, the fourth, in the right arm, dimmer and sometimes a fifth between that arm and the bottom.

"Patient in labor," a nurse called.

Ann and Stanford hurried into the tent. In the labor area, a tall, thin, disheveled male stood next to a woman who moaned and writhed with each contraction. The man appeared twice her age, her husband or her father?

Ann lifted the woman's green-and-blue-print skirt, exposing her pregnant belly and showed Stanford how to press his hands to assess the baby's position. The usual thick firmness above the pubic bone was absent. "She's not vertex."

Stanford looked at Ann with confusion.

"The head's not down. She may need a section." Ann told Stanford to check for heart tones with the fetoscope.

His eyes widened as he counted the baby's heartbeat. "154."

"That's good. Let's do a vaginal check," Ann pulled on a glove. Before she bothered Edward, she wanted to know what she was dealing with.

The patient moaned, a deep guttural bleat, as Ann inserted fingers into the vagina. "No head. And it's not a butt. I think she's transverse."

Ann called the compound on the two-way radio. She imagined it buzzing next to the table where they played poker. Robert answered. Ann asked for Edward.

"Why do you need-need him?" Robert hesitated.

"I have a section. I think he'll want to be here."

Robert was silent.

"Robert, are you still there?"

"You know how he is when he plays poker," Robert spit out the words. "He's not in any shape to help. The beer-beer."

"Okay." Ann tightened her grip on the radio. "Will you come for the baby?"

"Sure."

"Heartbeats are good for now."

"I'll be there ASAP."

Ann shoved the radio into its holder. Touching it stung her fingers. Edward was wasted. She'd done twenty sections. Edward had complimented her on her technique. She wasn't fond of the Rwandan physician on call, but Robert was coming for the baby. "Stanford, it's you and me," she said in a tight voice.

"Can I first-assist?"

Ann nodded.

"Sweet."

Luckily, Joseta was on. Ann asked her to scrub in and circulate. Ann walked to the gurney, scrubbed, and gowned, she whispered a *Hail Mary*, then gave the signal. The nurse pushed Ketamine through a syringe into the patient's arm. The overhead light shone on the woman's taut belly; her breathing slowed but remained steady.

Stanford's copper-colored eyes were wide with expectation, a wisp of brown hair hung free from his surgical cap in the back. "This is my first C-section," he whispered eagerly.

"You'll do fine," Robert said as he slid in behind Stanford, gazing on like a proud teacher.

"Just do what I tell you." Ann's hands sweated inside her gloves, causing the powder to coalesce. Moisture beaded on her scalp. She picked up the scalpel. "Okay, let's go."

The woman's anatomy was easy. Joseta repositioned the overhead light, focusing the beam into the women's open abdomen. Stanford tried hard to help, but Ann adjusted his retractors on several occasions.

As expected, the baby lay sideways. Ann pried it out as if scooping the meat of an avocado from its shell. It demanded all her upper body strength.

Robert accepted the infant. "It's a boy," he said and carried it to the makeshift isolette.

Moving slowly and methodically, Ann peeled off the placenta, ligated all bleeders, checked for sponges, and began suturing up the uterus. The overhead light dimmed, wavered, and blinked off. Inky blackness surrounded them. "Damn," Ann said. The darkness was so complete her hands felt disconnected.

The nurse at the head of the gurney beamed a flashlight in Ann's direction. "Someone check the generator."

"I have my headlamp, but it's in my pocket," Ann said. "Stanford, do you think you could pull it out?"

"Sure." Shuffling, the sound of metal clanging to the floor. "Whoops, what did I hit?" Within a minute, Stanford's hands touched Ann's back.

"Lower. My right pocket."

Stanford reached under her gown and pressed against the curve of her hip, trying to locate her pants pocket. He retrieved her headlamp and switched it on. With a number of apologies, he stretched the band over her head. The light bounced over the woman's open abdomen.

"If they don't check the generator, I will," Joseta said impatiently; her voice came from several feet away. There were rustling noises; the strike of a match, the smell of sulfur, and a candle glowed, silhouetting the infant in his isolette, a wooden crate lined with a blanket.

Still no surgical lights.

"I'll see what's up." Joseta hurried out of the OR, curling her hand to protect the flame of a second candle.

Ann worked in her shaft of light. She could soon boast twenty-one C-sections. This one completed under the light of her headlamp.

There was no whimpering. She rose up on her toes to check. "Is the baby okay?"

In the halo of candlelight, Robert toweled off the baby. "He's not doing much."

"Stanford, go help Robert," Ann said.

"Here take my flashlight," the nurse standing at the head of the gurney said. She padded over toward Stanford; her flashlight's beam swung across the floor. Soon the isolette was bathed in golden light. Robert and Stanford threw immense shadows on the wall of the OR.

"Rub him hard," Robert said. "Along his spine. We want him to cry, move air in and out of his lungs."

Ann strained again to see what was happening. The baby lay in the circle of yellow light and Stanford's hands fluttered around him.

"Do you remember how to suction the mouth and nose?" Robert asked.

A few more stitches and Ann would be finished. "Tell me what's happening," she called.

"Cover him with the blanket to keep him warm." Robert's voice was calm. "Blow a few breaths into his mouth."

Swishes and clatters resonated around the isolette. "Don't tilt his head. Watch how I do it."

The seconds stretched out. Ann prayed this fiasco would have a happy conclusion. She completed an instrument tie and clipped the suture. If this baby lived, she'd be less critical of her colleagues, she'd grumble less about the dull food, she'd… Maybe there was foul play. Maybe that was why Joseta sounded miffed. Had someone interfered with the generators? Outside, the OR all seemed quiet. Ann lassoed another bite of skin with the needle, another knot. The nurse who had managed the anesthesia now blocked Ann's view of the baby. He'd looked good when she'd pulled him out. Ann's hands flew mechanically through another tie. Robert was more than competent. Her heart pounded in her ears. Sweat moistened her scalp and trickled down the back of her neck.

A cry ripped from the isolette.

"He's breathing. He's okay," Stanford called.

Ann knotted, then clipped the final suture and scurried over to the isolette. The baby's wrinkled face had a perturbed expression. His hands and feet writhed with his wail.

The overhead lights sputtered and beamed full force.

Relief coursed through Ann as she sighed.

Stanford's hands quivered as he swaddled a purple cable-knit blanket around the baby, then lifted him. Robert stood to his left, a broad smile stretched across his face. Ann wished she had a camera so she could capture this photo for Stanford—his broad grin, the first summer of his medical career and his first infant resuscitation. Stanford cradled the boy in the crook of his arm and touched his nose with a finger. "What a cutie," Stanford cooed. "I'm sure glad you figured out how to breathe."

Joseta had not returned.

The nurse wheeled the still-sleeping mother into the recovery area. Ann removed her surgical gloves, throwing them in the sink for washing and drying, and pulled off her cotton gown. She faced Stanford and Robert. "If we weren't here to do the C-section, this woman would have died. Don't forget that. And if you two hadn't kept your wits about you and resuscitated that baby, he'd be dead. Thanks for coming, Robert."

"Stanford did most of it. He did a great job."

The smile still extended across Stanford's face. His copper eyes danced as he carefully supported the infant's head. "Ten fingers and toes."

"Let's get some coffee," Ann suggested and they laid the baby in the isolette near his mother in the recovery area. "Robert, you want to join us?"

"I think I'll head back."

Ann saluted Robert as he left.

In the break room, Ann poured hot water into two green mugs labeled with the GH logo and handed Stanford the canister of Nescafe.

"Is it always like this?"

"Like what?"

"Being a doctor and delivering a baby. Do you always feel like your chest will burst?"

Ann shook her head. "It's a miracle. But it can become routine. I try to feel a little bit of the awe, to recognize the privilege. We've seen some horrible stuff. As a doctor, you see the best and the worst of life. I remind myself to celebrate the good times as much as I can."

They sipped their coffee. Stanford asked questions about caring for the infant.

A ruckus erupted in the emergency area.

"Let's see what's happening," Ann said matter-of-factly, and carried her mug with her.

Joseta stood near the entrance talking to a well-built Rwandan, at least six feet tall. He wore handcuffs and was flanked by two security guards. Both guards had pulled their rifles off their shoulders. One also held a pistol.

A baritone voice.

Ann froze about five meters from the group. She recognized the voice. The stance. She swallowed hard. Shivers marched up her spine. Her breath came in prickly bursts.

"You look pale," Stanford said. "Are you okay?"

Ann stared speechless and gestured toward Joseta. And Father Innocent.

"That's the priest who brings us food," Stanford said. "But he's not wearing his sunglasses."

Two more guards walked up with Scar.

"And the other guy. The one with the scar on his arm. He always has candy. They come once, twice a week."

Ann's heart thud in her chest. She tried to slow her breathing. Joseta looked in her direction. Ann had to say something. She couldn't run away.

Father Innocent's cheeks were hollow. He'd lost at least ten pounds. His shirt frayed at the collar and his trousers bagged. Stubble sprouted on his chin and cheeks. How long had it been since she'd seen him? Early April. Almost two months. Nothing about him looked priestly. He argued with the guards, spewing out Kinyarwanda words.

Ann tightened her grip around the coffee mug. She exhaled forcefully and closed the ten feet between them. Stanford followed close behind.

"Dr. Ann McLannly," Innocent said. "She can vouch for me too. And Stanford, how . . ."

"The outage?" Ann said dryly. "You were responsible."

Joseta stood, her arms akimbo, a position Ann had seen many times. "What?" Joseta said, then addressed the guards. "I told you, I've known this priest for years. He was the pastor at St. Michael parish in Kigali."

"You don't know what he's been up to . . ." The fear was gone. Ann felt the solid earth under her feet. She inhaled, ready to let Innocent have it.

"Actually, I found Scar near the generators," Joseta said. "The security guards found Father Innocent. He was wandering around the inpatient ward. He'd come to visit a former parishioner. I was just telling them that . . ."

"Why am I not surprised?" Ann interrupted. Her voice grew stronger as she spoke. It was a relief to confront him. "Joseta, you may not know this, but Father Innocent has been up to no good. Your revered pastor has been working against us. I'm sure he was helping Scar. Meddling with the generator. Interrupting our electricity. Let the guards do their duty. Believe me, we don't want to interfere. He is a dangerous man." Ann stared at the familiar pistol in the hand of the guard. She inhaled and exhaled. "A very dangerous man."

Innocent glared at Ann. His face contorted and his eyes burned with hatred. The same expression she'd seen in the ambulance. He snarled a string of Kinyarwanda. The only words Ann understood were "gutera ingunguru." Innocent curled his lips and spat in her direction. The spittle landed at her feet.

Ann stared toward the spot and braced herself. No one had ever spit at her. The only time she had encountered someone this angry was a patient on the psych ward, during residency training, a new admission who they'd eventually assigned to solitary confinement.

Innocent's gesture sliced like a machete. To think she had once liked kissing this man. This priest. That she had considered him a confidant. She tightened her shoulders to conceal the tremble in her chest.

Bubbles of saliva hung at the corner of his mouth. His lips were twisted as he continued his tirade.

"We've called the Tanzanian police," the guard who held the pistol said. "We'll hold him outside." He pushed Innocent through the entrance. The other guards followed with Scar. Innocent's rant grew muffled.

Joseta sized up Ann, then relaxed her arms. They hung at her sides. She chewed her lip, looked toward the entrance, then back at Ann. "Innocent said he came to visit Nzikobankunda. Do you remember her from the parish? She usually sat in front of us. She was so nice to me when Vincent was taken. She's been so sick. Innocent said he was delighted to see me, glad to know I had made it out of Kigali. . . He even asked me about Vincent." Joseta's teeth dug into her bottom lip.

"I'm sorry. I'm so sorry to tell you this."

Joseta stared back.

"Christine didn't tell you about Innocent?"

Joseta shook her head. Her eyes appeared moist.

Ann slipped her arm through Joseta's and walked her toward the break room. The stale air pressed around them. Ann needed some fresh air, but she also wanted to stay as far away from Innocent as she could. Stanford followed, saying nothing.

When Ann finished relating all the details, Joseta shook her head and straightened the mugs on the counter. "I am so disappointed." She wiped her eyes with the back of her hand and without another word she swiveled and left the room.

Sweat dripped from Ann's armpits. She undid her hair band and lassoed her hair again.

Stanford stared at her. "I thought they were good guys."

"Let's get some fresh air."

"Sure," Stanford said and followed Ann.

"I need air," she repeated. "We'll use the back entrance."

The coolness of the night was a welcome relief from the thick air inside the tent. Scents from the river contrasted with the hospital tent's tang of urine and vomit mixed with perspiration. The almost-full moon inched above the horizon, silhouetting the outlines of the refugees' tents and causing the plethora of stars to fade. In the distance, the occasional call of a goat or cow interrupted the stillness of the night beyond the medical tent.

Ann gave Stanford the thumbnail version of who Innocent was and how the perpetrators in Kigali seemed to be present in the camp. She skipped details about their personal relationship. She didn't want to burden Stanford. And she wanted to forget it all anyway.

"But they did good things for us at the orphanage. They brought food. Clothes."

"He was good to the orphans in Kigali too."

Stanford sighed. "How can someone be so good and so bad?"

Innocent and Scar were turned over to the police. Ann felt cautious relief. Hopefully the police would not just turn them free. Ann had repaired Scar. Hopefully, this time justice would be done. Hopefully, the police would take this seriously.

Chapter 43

By the time Ann returned to the compound, clouds had moved in. Rain pattered on the tin roof with a ping-ping. Edward awoke feverish and vomiting and Robert convinced him to stay at the compound and skip work for the morning, at least.

Ann sat on the edge of Edward's cot as he dry heaved into a bucket. Vomiting was her weakness; she squelched a gag with a hard swallow. He looked miserable, unshaven, a wrinkled t-shirt, the sour smell of body sweat and stale alcohol. Had he overdone it with the beer? He did like his beer. But that wouldn't cause a fever. She touched Edward's forehead with her hand. "You feel really hot. Let me check your temperature."

"Leave me alone," Edward barked.

Ann chewed her lip and refrained from commenting on his demeanor. "See if you can keep these down." She palmed two acetaminophen tablets into his hand and held out a glass of water. She set a jug of water on the floor next to his bed.

Edward sighed and rubbed his closed eyes. His cheeks were flushed, but there was no rash on the exposed skin of his abdomen or arms. She hardly recognized his room. Dirty clothes were scattered around. Three empty beer bottles and a Fanta bottle lay near his cot.

"Did you have a party in here? This is a pigsty," Ann said, then told herself to be more empathetic; he looked miserable.

Edward pulled his pillow over his head. "Just let me sleep. I don't need a mother."

"At least try to get the pills down with a few sips of water. You'll feel better. You don't want to get dehydrated."

In the common area, Margaux sorted through papers on the dining table in preparation for the morning's collaborative meeting. Christine had already left for the market. Outside, the rain continued its steady drizzle. Ann told Margaux about Innocent and Scar and the outage of the generator.

Margaux looked up. "Good to know." She sighed as she flipped through her papers, then she continued. "We're working hard to get the Tanzanian police to help us. International support beyond the French is still up in the air. Madeline Albright opposes any US involvement. She should know better after Bosnia. I think she's afraid of US opinion. Six dead US soldiers were dragged through the streets of Somalia last year."

Ann sat at the computer and scrolled through the online *New York Times*, trying to wind down enough to fall asleep. She drummed her fingers and stopped. A story about their camp, Batumba Camp in Tanzania. She read aloud, "*The largesse and the efficiency of the relief agencies are having the negative effect of making the people more dependent. The shops the people set up are not really necessary for their survival. The initiative is rapidly being eroded, and a 'gimme' attitude is taking over, especially among the children.*"

"We don't need this kind of press," Margaux whined.

Ann recalled her visits to 99, how the children hung on her, how, thanks to Stanford, she'd learned to welcome their touch. Perhaps the reporter had misinterpreted the children's desire for attention as she had early on.

"I'm not sure this is accurate. 99 told me they cut his food rations. He's selling his oil to buy vegetables. Of course, he's always asking for Coke."

Margaux stuffed folders into a satchel. "I'll see if other agencies have heard about changes in the food basket." She grabbed a large umbrella and headed out the front door.

Before going to bed, Ann listened outside Edward's door. Silence. She went to her room and stretched out on her mattress, adjusting the mosquito netting around her bed.

"Tee-hee, tee-hee."

Ann stared at the white mesh above her. A smile broke across her exhausted face. "I think something is under my bed?" she said in a loud tone.

"Tee-hee, tee-hee."

She rolled over and reached her hand beneath the bed. "This place has the strangest mice."

The giggling grew louder.

"Where are those mice? I don't want them to bite me." She batted the space.

More laughter and scrambling noises.

"I guess I'll have to tell Margaux. She must have left our bedroom door open again." Something swatted at Ann and she grabbed and pulled.

Evangeline squealed. "We're not mice." Another hand batted at Ann's wrist.

She scooted to the edge of her mattress and peered underneath. She held Evangeline's leg. Emit lay on his stomach, reaching toward Ann. "We're Tutsis," Emit said.

"You're what?"

"Tutsis," Emit repeated.

"What are you doing?"

"We're playing."

"Under my bed?"

Evangeline scooted out. Emit followed. They stood up. "We're playing hide from the Hutus," Emit said.

"Hutus want to kill us," Evangeline said.

"I want the Hutu and Tutsis to get along," Ann said, studying their smiling faces. Her nieces and nephews played cowboys and Indians. "I have to sleep now." She sent them out to play somewhere else, snickering to herself as she closed the door behind them. Sadness filled her as she settled onto her pillow. Their play was far too close to reality.

Before dinner, Robert and Ann checked on Edward. His hair lay plastered against his head; he'd not bathed or shaven all day. "It's you again." He rubbed his eyes. "Just let me sleep." The low sun sent shafts of light into the room. Outside, the goats bleated as their owner herded them into their pen for the night and called to a straggler.

"Edward, we're just trying to help-help you," Robert stammered.

"At least you finished the water," Ann said.

"Talk to us a minute-minute."

Edward opened his eyes and leaned up on his elbow. Ann positioned two pillows behind him.

She touched his head. "You feel like an oven. What else?"

"My head's the worst. But I ache all over." Edward fell back against the pillows.

"Christine said you ate something that didn't agree. At the meeting?"

Edward nodded. "That should be out of me by now. I had the runs last night. The vomiting stopped."

"What did you eat?" Robert asked.

"The Basuko mayor had several NGO medical directors to his office for a high-level meeting. We discussed water safety and latrines." Edward rolled his eyes. "I can tell you're impressed."

"At least you found your sense of humor," Ann said. "You were so grumpy before."

"Aren't you full of sympathy," Edward said. "You want to hear this?"

"Go on," Robert said.

"The mayor served soda in glass bottles. That's safe. And snacks. A dry-nut crispy something. I don't know what it was. I didn't eat much. Margaux ate some."

"She's fine," Ann said.

"Strange. If you aren't better-better tomorrow, we're taking you to the medical tent. We aren't taking no for an. . ."

"Yeah, right" Edward shrugged.

Chapter 44

In the morning, Stanford waited outside the medical tent as the SUV pulled up. The actress and her entourage were returning sometime that day. The list of the orphans to be adopted was folded in Stanford's shirt pocket. He was reconsidering some of the names he and Robert had selected earlier. Robert and Stanford disappeared into a cloud of mist as they hurried to the orphanage.

Edward had still complained of headache and fever, so Robert convinced him to stay at the compound.

After lunch, the motorcade of Land Rovers arrived, trailed by a yellow school bus that resembled one Ann had ridden during grade school. Too wide for the narrow path, the bus flattened the tall grasses. At a low spot near the river, the back tires spun in the mud, splattering the men who jumped out to push. Soon the bus labored on. At the orphanage, staff helped dozens of orphans climb onto the bus. Another two dozen toddlers and babies were carried by Rwandans who had been hired to accompany the orphans. The bus would drive them to Mwanza, Tanzania, where the children would be flown to France. A well-dressed African supervised the activities.

Despite ambivalent feelings about the whole endeavor, Ann watched. She was critical of everyone's intentions. Margaux and Edward had milked the publicity for GH. The actress and diplomat promoted themselves and their good deeds. The press covered it all like rabid dogs.

As the journalists documented the events, the refugees congregated to watch. The antics related to the adoption provided much-needed entertainment. With basic needs taken care of, the refugees' lives had grown boring. The women were the ones who cooked, lugged water, chopped wood, did laundry, and minded the children. The men had little to do. They, in particular, had traded misery for boredom and mundanity.

As the train of vehicles chugged out of the camp, several refugees ran behind, their palms open; some younger children followed suit. They cried out in Kinyarwanda, words Ann could not understand. One refugee who knew English yelled, "Money." A chorus of young voices repeated his cry.

Ann recalled the *New York Times* article about the "gimme" attitude. Maybe the reporter was right. What kind of monster were they creating?

At the end of the day, Ann headed outside. One of Stanford's soccer buddies kicked a black and white soccer ball between the goals. Another child toed a green ball. A third played with a purple ball. Where were the balls fashioned from plastic bags or banana leaves and twine? Ann counted a dozen brand-new balls on the field. She called to Robert and together they sprinted over to the soccer area.

"New balls?" she yelled at Stanford, who stood at the edge of the field inflating the balls with a bicycle pump.

"Donated by the actress," Stanford said, tossing a white ball with "France" printed in red in her direction. "Round up some girls to play with you."

Ann motioned to a group of girls sitting on the sidelines and kicked the ball toward the tallest one. The girl sent it back. Ann dribbled the ball around Robert who had darted in from the sidelines. "Find some boys to play with," she yelled. "This is the girls' game."

Robert threw up his hands and ran up to a group of small boys who sat on what remained of the grass. When GH had arrived, the grass stood long and lush. Thanks to the rainy season and foot traffic, the meadow had given way to a muddy field. Mud was tracked everywhere.

Ann taught the tall girl how to move the ball between her feet. Soccer wasn't popular when Ann was a child, but her nieces played. She had attended some of their games, learned the rules, and volunteered as an assistant coach. It had been an enjoyable way to stay active and have kids in her life. As she demonstrated how to move the ball, she forgot the day's frustrations. She side-kicked the ball to the tall girl who deftly moved it through the goals. Ann cheered and summoned three other girls to join them. Stanford threw her another ball and the girls took turns dribbling the balls down the field with minimal instruction from Ann. They were quick learners and had been watching the boys. She should have invited them to play earlier. The shortest girl back tackled the red ball, took possession, and started running the ball in the opposite direction.

"SUV's here," Robert called. Ann high-fived the tallest girl and jogged toward Robert. It felt good to breathe hard, the day's tensions dissipated; she needed to do this more often.

"Did-did you notice the boys I talked to?" Robert asked.

Ann shook her head.

"All the kids on the sideline were extremely thin. I tried to get them to play, but they wouldn't. I don't think they had the energy."

"Were they orphanage kids?" Ann asked.

Robert shook his head. "Kids from the camp. I'm worried they're not getting enough to eat."

"99 says his rations were cut."

"I believe-believe it. Something's not right."

When they checked on Edward, he was no better, so Ann and Robert hauled him back to the medical tent after dinner. He complained about his headache at every bump along the entire five kilometers.

Edward settled onto a gurney in the corner. "I feel like. . . like I've been run over. . . by one of those trucks. . . that barrel into town. Everything aches."

Robert prodded him with questions, a complete review of systems, with only a few hesitations. "Congested? Coughing?"

Edward grew cooperative, even appreciative of their efforts. The thermometer showed that he had a fever and his pulse was up.

"What medicine are you taking? Besides the ibuprofen and acetaminophen?"

"Nothing."

"What about your malaria prophylaxis?"

"I ran out."

"When?" Ann's hands flew to her head.

"In Kenya."

"Ran out in Kenya!" Ann's tone was parental. "You've taken *no* malaria prophylaxis on this mission? *That's six weeks.* Edward, what are you, what in the name of J. . . were you thinking?"

"We need-need to do a malaria smear," Robert said.

"I've done okay with Deet and my bed net. Lariam gives me horrible nightmares and I sunburn with doxy." He pulled the sheet over his head. "Please, just let me be."

"Quit acting like a child."

"Time to draw blood," Robert said in a steady voice.

Edward frowned and rolled out his lower lip, but stuck out his finger.

Robert wiped a finger with an alcohol-soaked cotton ball and jabbed it with a stylet.

"Ouch," Edward yelped.

"Sorry."

The lab tech was eating dinner, so Ann dropped a spot of blood on the glass slide and smeared it. They didn't do thin smears because *falciparum* was the only form of malaria. While she waited for it to dry, she talked with Joseta, who was working the night shift and using a lull to organize the medication cupboard.

"Edward's ill."

"I heard. He pushes himself." Joseta bent over and pulled a cardboard box from under a table. "Have I shown you my secret stash?" Joseta asked. "I keep it here, near registration. Such an obvious place, no one would think to look." Joseta directed Ann to count pills.

"One hundred amoxicillin as labeled. I'd add some gent for gram negative coverage." Ann wrote it down on a slip of paper.

Joseta handed her a box filled with pills in blister packs to count.

Before Ann started she asked, "Were you surprised to learn about Father Innocent?"

Joseta made the sign of the cross, then turned to look at Ann. "Disappointed. Vincent and I respected him. Even trusted him. He told me he'd see what he could do when Vincent went to prison. Now I wonder... You think someone is on your side... Maybe he turned him in," Joseta sighed and continued to organize the pill bottles.

Ann said nothing more and focused on counting. What could she say? She wanted to ask about Vincent, but held her tongue.

"There you are," Robert said. "Come look. The scope's centered on a classic view of the parasite."

Ann squinted into the eyepieces of the microscope. The individual red blood cells looked like scattered blue coins. A dark, irregular blue dot with a faint gray tail sat in the middle of one cell. To the right was a headphone structure, blue dots connected by a curvy line. "You should save these for Stanford."

They told Edward together. He took it in stride, swallowed the anti-malaria pills, and guzzled down a glass of water. If the parasite was sensitive to the drug, he would feel better quickly and his smear should clear in seven days.

Robert ticked through the instructions. "Back to the compound. No work for a few days. Take acetaminophen for your head and your fever. Drink lots of water in this heat. No alcohol," Robert spoke without faltering. "What did I forget?"

Ann shrugged. They helped Edward climb into the Toyota SUV. He winced.

"Doctors are the worst patients," Ann muttered to Robert. Then she slid into the backseat. It would be Ann's job to get Edward settled in his room, because Robert had decided to stay at the hospital to help with an ill child. With Edward's demeanor, she didn't savor the assignment.

Chapter 45

99 lay curled in a fetal position on a cot in triage. He moaned like a distressed cow. This was atypical of 99, *l'hôte d'accueille,* who made everyone feel welcome. A member of the security brigade had brought him into the medical tent after he'd collapsed in the latrines earlier that morning. His diarrhea was so bad that he'd messed in his trousers; he smelled atrocious. His skin had a yellow cast. He leaned over the side of the gurney; clutching his stomach, dry heaving toward the floor. Ann kicked a bucket in his direction and covered her nose, fighting off her own wave of nausea. She swallowed mechanically, stepping outside to regain her composure. It was another drizzly day; the rainy season held a prolonged clutch on the region. Edward was on day four of his malaria treatment. They'd been limping along without him.

When Ann returned, Joseta had pulled off 99's clothes and had handed him a wet washcloth to suck on. Ann offered to start the IV, to get her mind off the smell. Luckily, she pierced the vein in his forearm on her first try; 99 didn't flinch. If he was feeling well, he would have yelled at her—"Hey, you hurt me." Instead, silence.

Ann taped the IV in place and pushed a medication to help the spasm in his gut. A liter of lactated ringers flowed in, followed by a second at a slower drip. 99 slept most of the day.

99 was the first patient with severe diarrhea. Five adults and six children had presented with the same affliction by the end of the day. Ann was on call and admitted several more before midnight. Four children more presented with vomiting and diarrhea. They could not keep down ORS, oral rehydration salts. Given the number of sick children, and the disappearance of the on-call

Rwandan physician, Ann radioed the compound for help. Robert agreed to come in; Edward was still on his medicine and needed to sleep.

Robert arrived chipper, as if he'd had a full night's sleep, not just a couple of hours. He assessed the children. Their typically shiny, dark skin appeared pale and dull. He passed feeding tubes into the nostrils of three and started an IV on the fourth. Another family presented.

By 3:00 a.m. Ann wanted to collapse. She and Robert gathered in the break room. "I think this might be cholera," Robert said as he washed his hands. "I've never seen-seen it, but it comes on fast."

"Copious watery diarrhea. That's what I remember from lectures. I didn't see it in Kigali."

"The textbooks describe it as rice water. What's the source?" Robert asked.

"We have latrines." Ann said. "People shouldn't be pooping next to their drinking water."

Robert heated water in the electric pot. Ann yearned for brewed coffee. Nescafe just wasn't the same. She spooned a heaping teaspoon of powder into a mug, stirred, then perched on a stool.

"I just read my grandfather had a mistress here. Fathered a child."

Ann sat up and stared at Robert. "You have someone who shares some of your genetics somewhere in Rwanda?"

Robert nodded. "Not sure-sure. It was written on pages that were torn out and tucked under the cover of the journal. Like-like he was hiding it."

"Intriguing."

They mused about the child's history and life. He'd be older than Robert's mother. His mother had never mentioned anything about it. Either didn't know or just not something spoken about. A wave of energy enveloped Ann, the marvels of caffeine, biorhythms, and Robert's secret got her through the final hours. The night plodded on—a nightmare of IVs, oral rehydration packets, mopping up vomit and liquid stool.

They quarantined the patients with diarrhea off to one side and prepared stool specimens to send to a larger lab for analysis. Ann continued to thrust one foot in front of the other, bracing herself as she moved among the plethora of foul odors and unending need. When she had a moment that she was not focused on fluids and stool, passing NG tubes and starting IVs, checking inputs and outputs (Is and Os), she found herself thinking of home.

Tomorrow was the Fourth of July. Her father would set off firecrackers. Her brothers-in-law helped. Her mother would not be there to worry but her sisters would—what if dad or their husbands didn't move fast enough? What if one of the rockets exploded prematurely? Irene, her sister with Down syndrome, would clap and hoot at the display. Ann pushed through the exhaustion.

During her residency, she could never have imagined managing this many sick patients.

Outside, dawn splattered the sky fuchsia and silver. A gentle breeze blew soft on her skin, temporarily muting the toxic smells of the camp. Roosters crowed, goats bleated, and cows mooed. Gray smoke twirled upward from the cooking fires scattered among the refugee tents. Neither Ann nor Robert had gotten much sleep. Most days the work satisfied Ann, despite the pressing need. However, the night had seemed unending and particularly foul. Some patients were too far gone to resuscitate with fluids. In the morning, staff loaded the bodies into a pickup truck out back to be hauled to the mass grave.

Ann and Robert reported their cholera concerns to Margaux, who radioed headquarters. Within forty-eight hours, a large metal container arrived packed with all the necessities for treating cholera: cots, IV tubing and angio-catheters, liters of salt and sugar solutions, packets of ORS, feeding tubes of all sizes, boxes of gloves, buckets, and cases of bleach.

Margaux hired men to raise a separate tent. Bored refugees—children and old men—gathered around to watch the activity. The women were too busy standing in line for their food baskets, and performing their daily survival tasks, to care.

Once the white canvas stretched across the metal tent poles, Joseta took charge, putting several refugees to work. With her hands on her hips, she gave orders. "Set up the cots parallel to the walls. Leave a walkway in the middle. Children on the right. Adults on the left."

Margaux surveyed the setup. "Everyone needs to wash their hands and feet before entering."

"Bleach water," Ann said.

Joseta studied Ann. Joseta's eyes had a hollow look, a gloominess Ann had not seen earlier in the mission. But it did not hinder Joseta's competence. "Pans of bleach water at the entrance. Everyone removes their shoes and steps in."

"Next to the hand-washing stations," Ann said.

"That will be right here." Joseta lumbered over to the spot.

Margaux nodded her head in approval and instructed Robert and Ann to read the GH treatment protocols. "We'll be up and running by the time Edward recovers."

The sharp smell of bleach permeated the space. The key components of cholera treatment were isolation, hydration, and bleach. Patients received ORS by mouth. If the vomiting was profuse, the salt-sugar solution was administered by feeding tube. Intravenous fluids were reserved only for the severely dehydrated. This was different than Ann and Robert had done in the past. Once they mapped out the guidelines, Joseta and the local nurses ran the tent, freeing the physicians to provide the usual care. A doctor rounded each morning and evening.

In the meantime, Margaux contemplated the source of the cholera.

"What about the river?" Robert said.

"Folks take water from the river," Margaux said.

"They don't treat-treat it."

Margaux shoved her hand into her blue jeans pocket. "Bucket chlorination. I'll hire refugees to pass out chlorine at the river. I'll suggest that at the collaborative meeting."

Chapter 46

Help me pull the beds together," Ann said. "We are sleeping under the mosquito netting. I'm not taking chances." The metal legs scraped across the floor in Edward's room. Edward had returned to work and spent his second full day in the operating room. It was the first time Ann had stayed with him since his illness. Robert was on call.

"It's nice to know you care," Edward said. "You've been a little snippy."

Ann focused on arranging the mesh netting around them. "I blame myself for your malaria. Remember, we used to sleep outside the netting."

An insect buzzed and butted the screen. "That's ridiculous. Margaux put screens on the windows." Edward gestured toward the buzzing. It quieted when he extinguished the lamp.

Ann stretched out alongside him. "Are you taking your medicine?"

Edward pouted his lips and fiddled with the thin, leather cord around his neck. He had removed his wedding ring. He touched Ann's thigh with his left hand.

She worked to focus on their conversation. "Are you?"

"Are you my mother? Margaux is bad enough."

"Are you?"

Edward nodded, and fingered the waistband of Ann's soccer shorts.

Ann put her hand on top of his, holding it still. "We need to talk."

"You need to talk. I had other things in mind."

Ann continued. "I was really worried when you were sick."

"It's nice to know you cared." He touched her breast.

"Humor me. If we want this to work, we need to talk through our differences."

Edward rolled his eyes.

"Really." Ann sat up, crossing her legs. Edward cupped her foot.

"You have little feet. What's your shoe size?"

"Quit changing the subject. "I am worried . . ." She struggled about how to talk about his drinking.

Edward nodded, massaging the sole of her foot. He moved his hand up her leg. "So what are you trying to get off your pretty. . . ?" He leaned over and kissed her knee.

Ann stared at him. In the distance the neighbor's goats bleated.

Edward sat up. "What do I have to do to get to first base?"

"What's with the sports metaphors? I'm the one who likes baseball." His hands felt warm. She focused. He'd been too sick to talk.

Edward laughed. "I like when you're all business." He inched his fingers up her thigh.

"Beer. I think you drink too much."

Edward was silent. His gaze grew pensive. He tightened his lips and began to chew his cheek. He pulled back his hand and played with the cord around his neck.

"Your wedding ring is gone."

Edward nodded. His eyes grew moist.

Ann had tapped into something. This vulnerability was new. Edward stared at her. She couldn't appreciate the blueness of his eyes in the dark.

"What did I say?" Ann asked. "Please keep talking to me. I know I can be surly. . ." The silence hung heavy between them. Ann's chest rose and fell. In the distance, another goat bleated. Ann reached her hand toward Edward.

"I, I, I told you about the car accident." Edward touched his nose. "I was driving. My wife, Erica, was in the front seat, my son, Dean, in his car seat. . . in the back." Edward swallowed. He was biting back tears. His fingers covered his mouth.

Ann touched his hand.

"What I didn't tell you. . . I, I. . . had been drinking."

They sat in silence. Edward's words hung in the air–drinking. The light of the rising moon crept across the window ledge and spilled onto the floor. Ann studied Edward's face. The goats were still, but an insect droned against the screen. *Drinking*. . . She was right. He did have a problem. Ann could hear her own breathing. Edward let go of her hand and wiped his eyes with the corner of the sheet.

"You were drinking. . . You feel responsible for the accident?"

Edward nodded.

Ann sighed. Her eyes grew moist. She swallowed hard. Guilt. They were both burdened by it. She clasped his hand and debated whether or not to ask, then went ahead. "Why do you still drink?"

"Why don't I quit all together?"

"I have," Ann said, thinking of her own history.

"Maybe you're stronger than I. Smarter. I think I can control it. I limit it to poker games."

Ann said nothing.

"Margaux keeps an eye on me." Edward looked down, then sighed. He pulled Ann toward him.

She touched the cord around his neck. "Why?"

He inhaled. "Why did I take off the ring?" He ran his finger over her lips. "Annie, it's time for me to let go. Let go of Erica. She's dead. She's not coming back. It's time to move on." He kissed his finger and touched it to Ann's lips, then leaned toward her.

She felt the softness of his lips, the pressure of his hand against the back of her neck. She allowed herself to sink into the moment, to feel Edward holding her, kissing her.

It was not the setting Ann had envisioned for falling in love. As a gung-ho pre-med and medical student with no time for romance, she never imagined that her work would lead her here. . . to this man. . . to this place. But then people and events weren't all they seemed.

The moonlight grew brighter and an unearthly sweetness filled the room. Ann bent over and took him in her mouth. That night they fit together perfectly.

Over the next few hours, the shaft of moonlight marched from their beds to the desk. Ann spooned Edward, feeling the rise and fall of his chest. He snored softly. Some night bird hooted; another responded. Ann played chords with one hand–a lullaby. Her other was caught beneath Edward's chest. Slowly she played herself to sleep.

Pad, pad, pad. Ann startled awake. Boots on gravel. Just outside the window. Her heart galloped. Hair bristled on the back of her neck. Sweat beaded between her breasts. She slowed her breaths and stared toward the window. A shadow passed. More crunching gravel. A panting sound.

The voice of one of their guards.

A baritone responded. Close to the window.

Innocent? Was Father Innocent outside Edward's room? Stalking her in bed with Edward?

Boots grinding rocks. Pad, pad.

The guard again in Kinyarwanda.

Ann joggled Edward awake and pressed her finger to his lips. He rubbed his eyes. She pointed toward the window.

The commanding voice of the guard again, followed by sniffing.

Edward lifted the mesh netting and crept toward the window. Ann followed, pulling the sheet around her.

It took a minute for her eyes to adjust. In the pale moonlight a tall man stood talking to the guard who hunched over a black form. The guard whispered toward the blackness and stroked it.

"Silly," Edward whispered into her ear, his hands on her shoulders. "That's Confiance, the guard with his dog. They're just making rounds."

"The tall man," Ann whispered.

Edward peered through the window screen.

Ann felt Edward's arm around her. "Father Innocent Rwagasonza," she said, "the priest from Kigali." Ann's breath came in short spurts. She trembled inside; her skin was goose flesh.

Edward pulled her toward him, throwing both his arms around her. He rubbed her shoulders.

That anchored her. His body heat warmed her. Her breathing slowed a little.

Together they stood watching the two men and the dog. The moonlight reflected off the guard's Kalashnikov and the pistol fastened to Innocent's belt. They talked in hushed voices. Innocent stared toward the window of Edward's room. Said something to Confiance, pointed, then they walked around the building. They were lost from view.

"Should I check on them?" Edward said.

Ann found it hard to talk, her body still on high alert. The adrenaline pulsed. "Innocent. What did he want. . . was he looking for me?"

Edward shrugged. "The guard's handled it. I'll talk to Margaux in the morning."

They climbed back onto the bed. Edward spooned Ann and held her tight. His warm breath filled her ear. "You're shaking."

Ann clutched her pillow to her chest. Her heart still raced.

"What are you afraid of?" Edward whispered as he fingered her hair.

Ann mumbled into her pillow. Edward ran his palm along her spine, cupping her neck. He lifted her hair away from her face. They lay together for a while.

She needed to tell Edward. If he didn't know, if Margaux didn't know, they couldn't help her. She inhaled, then flipped around to look at him. "Father Innocent is the priest I knew in Kigali. Joseta and I went to his church. We were friends. He introduced me to the orphanage. He wanted me to sleep with him. . . I wouldn't." Ann rolled onto her back and stared up at the ceiling. "The police must have let him go. After they arrested him at the hospital they let him go . . ."

"From the other night?"

Ann nodded.

"I'll talk to Margaux." Edward lay balanced on his side, his hand on Ann's stomach.

"I don't know that there's much she can do." Ann's voice was weak.

"What did he do to you?"

"Nothing yet, but the fact that he's hanging around. . . There's a Kinyarwanda term when a woman rejects a man—throwing a bucket—*gutera*, to throw. He accused me of the worst —throwing an oil drum—*gutera ingunguru*."

"So you rejected him." Edward gave a half laugh. "Rejection's part of life."

Ann sighed. "He can't seem to let go of it."

"He wanted you to sleep with him and you wouldn't?" Edward's hand was warm on her stomach.

Ann nodded.

"What are you afraid of?"

Ann chewed her lips.

"Rape," Edward said. "Are you afraid . . ."

"My college roommate was raped. It was awful. I sat with her in the ER. Listened to her nightmares for months. The screams. I promised myself I'd do all I could to avoid. . . that. And the women here. . . Kigali."

Edward held Ann tight to his chest.

Chapter 47

Two weeks into the cholera nightmare, some patients, like 99, recovered after a few days of fluids. Others were not so lucky. Robert and Stanford lugged Francis, Stanford's soccer buddy, back from orphanage rounds. Robert clutched one of the newer soccer balls, the white ball with "France" printed in red. "I thought Francis would want this. His name. Well, sort of. He live-lives for soccer."

Together, they set the frail six-year-old on a cot as if they handled a hard-won trophy. Francis's dark brown eyes sunk into his skull and his dry lips stuck together. He whimpered.

Robert gently pinched his forearm. "Tenting," he said to Stanford. "See how his skin stands up? Severe dehydration—different from yours or mine." He demonstrated on his own forearm. As they examined Francis, a watery stool spurted from the boy's anus. Robert grabbed a towel embossed with Hilton Hotel. "Cholera," Robert said. "It runs like a faucet. Put on gloves."

"I'd like to stay with him," Stanford said. The boy vomited all over Stanford's pants.

After he changed into scrubs, Stanford helped Robert slip a feeding tube through Francis's right nostril. Once they taped the tube in place, Robert showed Stanford how to connect a syringe to the end and push in 30 cc of ORS every few minutes. "Fluids shut off the vomiting center in the brain," he explained, his voice steady. "We'll slowly replace what he's lost and try to keep up with what he's squirting out."

The watery diarrhea continued nonstop. The Hilton Hotel towel was replaced a half dozen times. The collisions of different segments of the world always stunned Ann. Did the guests at the Hilton ever imagine that the embroidered hand towel they used to dry their hands might someday diaper an African child with cholera? She'd stayed at Hiltons a few times for medical conferences, she'd never considered the possibility.

Stanford grimaced as he changed Francis's diaper again. This month and a half had provided many experiences for him. There was little glory in changing diapers, but he'd placed a feeding tube, started IVs, even assisted with a lumbar puncture, learning many critical skills. That morning, he insisted on tending to Francis.

After lunch Ann checked on Stanford and helped him calculate Francis's Is and Os. Enraged voices erupted outside the tent.

"*Ni kibazo*, it is a problem," someone shouted. A chorus of cries followed. The racket escalated.

Periodically irate patients stomped into the medical tent. Security routinely confiscated weapons at the entrance—machetes, sticks, mallets, clubs, even guns. They often managed groups of intoxicated men, usually after dark, but nothing this obnoxious, especially in broad daylight. "What's going on?" Ann asked. Memories of Kigali's street corners jammed her head.

From the mesh window of the cholera tent, an angry sky threatened the continuation of the morning's rain. The view faced the camp's registration shack, where several dozen men congregated, waving sticks and machetes. The commotion attracted others. Those who joined them brandished clubs, poles, hoes, and other homemade weapons. They fed off one another, and soon Ann could not see exactly how many had assembled. It was not clear what had provoked them. Other medical staff gathered at the mesh windows.

Joseta shooed the gawkers away. "You have work to do."

Edward materialized, gasping for breath as if he'd been running. His surgical cap covered his hair and his mask dangled around his neck. "Margaux just radioed," he said. "The Tanzanian police are on their way. We're supposed to stay inside."

Staff barraged him with questions.

He held up his hand. "I don't know any more. Take care of your patients. We've sent the rest away. You'll hear more when I know more." Edward turned and left.

Stanford returned to Francis, and Ann continued cholera rounds with Joseta, reviewing the specifics of each patient. There was an odor of bleach mixed with the stenches of diarrhea and vomit. Ann periodically sniffed her soap-scented skin to fill her nose with a more pleasant fragrance. She changed gloves with each patient. Thankfully, here at the camp, unlike in Kigali, they had a plentiful supply.

The patients who had died during the night had not yet been removed. They lay in the corner stacked like a cord of wood and covered with sheets. In the humid heat, their smell was noticeable. When the disturbance quieted, staff needed to haul them outside to the mass grave.

Bang.

A gunshot blasted outside. It was close.

Ann stood rigid.

Inside the tent, everyone grew still. Ann looked at Joseta, who gazed toward the mesh window; the feeding tube she was about to pass curled in her hand like a snake. Stanford sat next to Francis, clutching the 60 cc syringe attached to Francis's feeding tube, a worried expression on his face.

Bang. Bang. Bang. The blasts sounded just as close.

Shouts. The crack of clubs against wood. Screams. More gunshots.

Ann pursed her lips as she crouched down next to the gurney. Memories of Kigali flashed like a slide show—sitting in her bedroom with Sylvia the night the singing nuns were shot. There brick, mud, mortar, and concrete had separated her from the Kalashnikovs and pistols. Here in the cloth tent, where could they go for safety? Her palms grew sweaty as she clutched the metal frame of the gurney for support. They could not transfer patients to a safer place. There was no safer place, not here in the refugee camp. Of course, the medical facility would be a target for an angry mob. Seconds stretched to minutes. She shifted her position and then stood up again, her thighs achy from squatting. The bedlam outside the tent's thin canvas walls continued.

Edward returned with a calm air of authority; he'd removed his mask and surgical cap. "We're leaving," he said, his voice even. "Drop what you're doing and follow me."

Chaos roiled as staff tried to finish their duties. "What about the patients?" Ann asked.

"Leave your patient," Edward said firmly.

Ann looked toward Joseta. "You coming?"

Joseta nodded. "In a minute. I need to finish this." She busied herself with an IV, rearranging the tubing and changing the bag.

"Rwandan medical staff stay here." Edward said.

"Joseta is one of us," Ann said. "She needs to come." A gnawing filled Ann's stomach as she recalled the evacuation at the GH compound in Kigali. Expats only. None of the drivers, not even the cook, the director's girlfriend, were allowed to come along. Ann heard later that some of the American embassy folks had brought their pets on the plane. Pets permitted, but no Rwandans.

Something seemed wrong about that, colonial, even racist. At least Joseta was considered one of them, a gesture of solidarity, all the months they'd worked together. Granted, she'd been distant lately, but Ann could not leave Joseta behind. She waited, setting her clipboard in its box. She picked at the cuticle on her thumb.

"Ann, come. We don't have much time," Edward yelled.

Ann stared at him, a pleading look.

Edward persisted. "I'm not kidding. There's no time."

Ann scowled; gloom filled her heart. She bit at the cuticle and glanced around, several Rwandan nurses remained. Joseta was still engaged with a patient. Reluctantly, Ann did as she was told. At the tent's exit she called to Joseta, fingering the hem of the canvas, using it to blot the blood on her thumb. Then she hollered again, a hoarse cry, a squawk like a rodent caught in the clutches of a raptor. She scurried after Stanford and Edward, the gnawing in her stomach burned like hot acid.

The expats piled into the GH vehicle and the Toyota vroomed off. Joseta was not among them.

Ann folded her arms against her stomach and told Edward Joseta was missing.

"She can come in the other vehicle," Edward said.

The sigh that escaped from Ann's lips sounded like air released from a flattening tire.

Along the main road into the camp, near the registration and food distribution area, about a hundred yards from the medical tent, a large crowd of men and boys waved sticks, clubs, and machetes. The sky darkened as if it were dusk. Thunder clapped. The spotlight that lit the area at night was illuminated. Machete blades glistened in the light's beam. Several men commanded the group. One had a long scar on his right arm. Scar held a rifle. Next to him stood Father Innocent, waving his pistol.

The liquid in Ann's bowels gurgled. She clutched her abdomen and forced slow, steady breaths in and out of her lungs. She twisted to see if she could see Joseta in the vehicle behind them.

The GH driver veered down a side rode to avoid the mob. A kilometer farther, the bypass joined the main road. Ann couldn't see the other SUV. "Edward, radio the other driver and ask about Joseta," Ann said.

He tossed the walkie-talkie to her.

Ann pressed the button—no static. She flipped another button—nothing. "I think the battery's dead." She shook it and tried again. Nothing. She handed it back to Edward and stared out the window, chewing the nail of her thumb. Raindrops pelted the glass.

When they reached Basuko, the rain fell in sheets. Locals took shelter in entryways. A horse pulling a cart appeared to brace itself against the downpour; the driver held a yellow plastic tarp over his own head.

The town showed no hint of the unrest that roiled five kilometers away. As they piled out of the SUV, Margaux greeted them with a large, black umbrella. Several expats from other NGOs who worked in the medical tent had accompanied them.

Ann jumped out of the vehicle and ran to the second SUV. Raindrops stung her bare forearms. Cold drops pummeled her scalp and flattened her hair.

No Joseta.

"Can we go back?" she asked Edward. Large, dark-blue blotches saturated her scrubs. She held her hands to her forehead. Water dripped from her wrists and elbows. "She was only finishing a task for a patient."

Margaux held the compound door open and motioned for Ann to come inside.

"Can we go back for Joseta?" Ann asked again.

Margaux shook her head.

Ann hurried into the kitchen. Christine assembled a tray with Cokes and Fantas.

"Your mother stayed behind," Ann panted. "She was coming. The vehicle left without her." Christine threw a cloth in Ann's direction. Ann blotted her face. "I'm worried about your mom."

Christine shrugged. "You know Mama. She always manages to take care of herself."

Ann hurried to her room. She peeled off her wet scrubs and changed into a GH t-shirt and slacks. She was chilled. She rubbed her arms as she sat on her bed to collect her thoughts. Overhead, rain beat down on the roof, a deafening drumming. Joseta may be self-sufficient, but there were forces beyond Joseta's control. Could she take care of herself? Ann had accused Innocent in front of Joseta. Would he seek revenge? He had warned her to tell no one.

The glow-in-the-dark rosary that the nuns at Beauraing Orphanage had given her lay in the crate next to Ann's bed. She clutched it, whispered a prayer for Joseta, and tucked it into her pants pocket; she had to do something. The rain stopped as suddenly as it had started.

In the common room, expats huddled around the radio. Like a scene from the 1940s or 50s, everyone crowded together, their eyes glued on the black, rectangular talking box. The newscaster ticked through the top news of the hour: Conchita Martinez beat Martina Navratilova in the 101st Wimbledon Women's Tennis Tour. John Wayne Bobbitt and Kristina Elliot were arrested for domestic battery. The pre-trial hearings opened in Los Angeles against O J Simpson. Domestic violence in the US, but no mention of what was happening in the Batumba camp five kilometers away.

After the news, everyone stared toward Margaux and Edward like a class asking for direction. Edward suggested poker. Ann didn't know what else to do so she joined in, silently praying for Joseta's safety, fingering the rosary in her pocket. The group pulled chairs around the table, expanding the usual circle to include the expats from the other NGOs. Luckily, the newsprint with the different poker hands still hung on the compound wall.

Edward asked Robert to deal and directed Stanford to distribute the bottle caps. Edward asked if anyone wanted a beer.

"*Tu blagues*," Margaux said. "You *are* kidding. We don't know what the rest of the day holds. We need everyone thinking clearly."

Edward shrugged.

Margaux insisted they tune to the BBC channel during the game.

Ann chewed gum that she'd bought from a street vendor earlier in the week. She chomped out her anxiety about Joseta. With every bid, she touched the rosary in her pocket. She wanted to drum out a song with her fingers, but forced herself to study her poker hand. Evangeline wandered around the table and Ann invited her to help, scooting the chair back; the girl climbed on Ann's lap. She smelled of juice. Across the table, Christine minded her own hand, sipped a Coke, and did not seem worried about her mother.

Stanford was surprisingly good at poker, having played with friends in college. When Ann dealt, she called *Indian*. Edward groaned as he always did, but the expats unfamiliar with the game loved it, as did Evangeline and Emit. Emit won that hand and stood on his tiptoes to rake in the pile of bottle caps. The smile on his face stretched ear to ear. In the almost two months they'd played, both of the children had mastered the rules of *Indian* and learned the basic poker hands, hardly important life lessons, but they'd had fun.

When Robert took his turn, he called twos wild. Edward complained again, but Robert retorted without hesitation, "It makes it fun for the new players, Edward. Mind your cards."

Silently, Ann cheered Robert on.

In the late afternoon, the BBC carried news about the uprising. "This afternoon a violent crowd of 5,000 armed with machetes and sticks demanded that sixteen Hutu militiamen, rumored to be involved in the genocide in Rwanda, be allowed to stay in the Batumba refugee camp. Tanzanian police fired shots in the air to disperse the unwieldy crowd. Several of the militiamen were also armed. Foreign aid workers temporarily evacuated the camp."

"They got that right," one expat said.

Margaux excused herself and started making phone calls. The poker game ended before dinner. Although distant gunfire punctuated their poker plays and bets, Basuko had remained peaceful the entire day.

After dinner Ann telephoned her father, concerned the news of the camp's uprising might reach the US.

"Annie, I always love to hear from you," he said. "Tell me about your day."

Ann pressed the phone against her ear. Where to start? She'd chewed gum so hard her jaw ached. "There was some unrest in the camp. You might hear about it. I'm safe. We left and spent the day playing poker."

"Poker. That brings back memories. I used to play that with my WWII cronies."

She asked about his day.

"We missed you at our Fourth of July party. The fireworks were spectacular."

"You had help, I hope." She rubbed the muscle of her jaw.

He jabbered on, talking about the garden, how his friends prayed for her at daily mass, how her sister Coleen, Rosie's mother, seemed to be doing better. Next month was the one-year anniversary of Rosie's death. He reviewed the grandkids' plans for their county fair entries in August. "Remember when you won best cake of the fair with that Texas cake? What was the secret ingredient?"

Ann chuckled at the memory. "Tomato soup," she said.

His tone grew serious. "I have a medical question."

"What about?"

"Sometimes when I am working in the garden, my chest feels heavy. It goes away if I sit down."

Ann made him promise to make an appointment with his physician.

Chapter 48

The next morning, the registration center and food distribution buildings lay splintered and smoldering. Ribbons of gray smoke spiraled skyward. Wooden boards were already scavenged for firewood. Several refugee tents on the edge of the camp were shredded, their contents strewn about. Thousands had trampled the ground, their footprints stamped in the mud in between the large, gray puddles that reflected the shafts of sunlight that broke through the bank of gray clouds.

Ann's throat tightened. She'd witnessed the annihilation of Kigali. Margaux and Edward had worked in enough hotspots to have seen their share of destruction. But it was new for Robert and Stanford. Dismay replaced the hope in their eyes. No one spoke. The heavy clouds moved quickly, concealing the morning's sun for minutes at a time. Then a spot would open and beams of light would pour through. The stench of burning wood and plastic overpowered every other smell.

Would the Batumba camp end like King Faisal Hospital? Would looting chase the NGOs trying to provide aid away? The GH side of the Batumba Camp had been the target of the uprising. The other medical facilities had fared better. How would GH respond? What role had Scar and Innocent played? Ann had seen them in the crowd of hell-raisers the day before. Maybe it was time to leave; she'd served her six-month commitment.

When Ann reached the medical tent and saw the patients she felt differently, she could not abandon those in need. The battle of the day's weather, cloudy versus sunny, mimicked her mood—how to make sense of what had happened and what it meant for GH's work, for her future.

The tent suffered no structural damage, but angry refugees had raided the pharmacy, demanding that the Rwandan staff hand over much of the medication. Staff had done the best they could. Ann asked about Joseta.

"She's ill. Someone she called Father shot her. I think she knew him."

Ann rushed to the inpatient ward, her breaths quick and urgent. Father. Father Innocent. How could he? Fury flamed through her body.

Joseta lay on her side on the gurney, an IV dripped into her arm. The bag of fluid was almost empty. She appeared pale and groggy.

"What happened?" Ann asked. Her own heart stampeded in her chest. She'd been right. They should not have left without Joseta. She should have insisted they wait. "Who did this to you?"

Joseta mumbled nonsense.

Joseta's forehead felt hot. Beads of sweat bunched at her temples, her thin, gray hair exposed. Had Innocent done this? How could he? Ann recalled standing in the medical tent confronting Innocent in front of Joseta and listing off his "sins." He had spat at her.

Staff had admitted Joseta to the hospital during the night. But no one was available to operate. There was too much to do. At least someone had started an IV. Ann should be grateful for that.

Joseta's pulse raced. Her blood pressure read low. Someone had placed a bandage over the entrance wound on her abdomen, just to the left of her belly button. It was stained with foul-smelling liquid. No bowel sounds. Her stomach felt taut. A classic surgical abdomen. The bullet had probably nicked her bowel. Joseta needed surgery. Now.

Edward took Joseta to the OR within the hour. Ann wanted to scrub in and assist, but there was too much work to do. Instead, she radioed the compound to notify Christine about Joseta's imminent surgery. "Don't come yet. You can't see her anyway. I'll let you know when she's out. Edward's the surgeon."

Stanford found Ann biting back tears as she inventoried the mess in the pharmacy. "Francis is dead," he said. His voice sounded tight, his tears close to the surface. "One of the nurses put lactated ringers in the feeding tube. Robert told me you can't substitute LR for ORS. Your stomach needs sugar to absorb the salt." Stanford had witnessed many deaths, but Francis was one of his first actual patients.

"I'm sorry." Ann stood up and hugged him.

He shook his head. "I'm so . . ." He gripped her forearms. "I haven't cried here yet. I won't start now." He swallowed hard and stepped back, continuing to shake his head.

"It's okay to cry, you might feel better," Ann said. "When I was a student, a resident told me that it was good to put your emotions on hold so you can keep your wits about you, like pushing a button on one of those old phones, but you can't keep them on hold forever."

Stanford bit his lip. Tears started to leak from his eyes.

Ann put her arm on his shoulder. "You wanted to make him better. We're not always successful. It's a hard lesson. I'm so sorry." She pulled him in for another hug and recalled how devastated she'd felt when the hospital team in Milwaukee had turned off Rosie's ventilator. There had been a family conference, but her sister Coleen was upset and angry. Coleen refused to talk to Ann after that. At the funeral home and during the funeral, Coleen avoided her. Ann would walk into a room and Coleen moved to the opposite side or she left the room. It felt like everyone noticed the ice between them. Ann had sent her a card, but they had had no resolution before Ann left for Rwanda. Ann had not had the guts to phone her and there was still no response to Ann's emails. Ann vowed to keep reaching out.

Robert helped Stanford wrap Francis's body in the Star Wars sheet on which he had lain. With a shovel, they dug a grave near the orphanage. Stanford erected a marker out of a pile of stones and staked the red soccer ball imprinted with "France" on the top. Over the noon hour, Ann walked out to the gravesite.

One of the OR nurses found Ann as she tended to her afternoon slate of patients. "Dr. Edward needs you in the OR," the nurse said. Ann hurried to the scrub area. The nurse helped Ann tuck her hair under a cap and threw a sterile gown and gloves in her direction.

The smell of feces filled the operating room. Edward's arms were elbow-deep in Joseta's abdomen. The heart monitor beeped at a normal rate, which made Ann hopeful as she approached the table.

"You were right," Edward said. "The bullet penetrated her gut. She has peritonitis. I resected her bowel. I'm still irrigating."

Edward looked exhausted. Silver curls slipped from under his hair cover at the back of his neck. Ann wanted to touch them.

Edward continued. "Will you write orders? She'll need antibiotics."

"The pharmacy was raided."

"You might have to borrow antibiotics. Maybe one of the other NGOs."

The lump in Ann's throat made it hard to talk. "Of course," she croaked.

On the ward, none of the remaining antibiotics covered gram negatives or anaerobes. In the outpatient pharmacy, there were no antibiotics, period. But no one had thought of Joseta's hidden crate.

Ann anxiously riffled through the stash. Two vials of metronidazole. Great anaerobic coverage. For the bowel she also needed something to cover gram negatives. She prayed as she added the antibiotic to Joseta's IV. She printed the names of antibiotics with the appropriate bacterial coverage on a slip of paper and sent Stanford to the market in Basuko. A few of the vendors sold medications; hopefully someone would have what was needed. She asked Stanford to stop by the compound to pick up Christine and Evangeline and bring them to the medical tent on his return. After she radioed Christine about the plan, she focused on patients.

Big tears dripped from Evangeline's eyes as she watched the worry on her mother's face. Edward stood next to Joseta's gurney and explained to Christine and Evangeline what had happened and what he had done. Joseta was awake but groggy.

The nurses had rigged up a sheet that divided Joseta's bed from the rest of the inpatient ward. They had given her one of the few beds; most of the patients rested on grass mats. The space was tiny, but afforded a little privacy. Her mesh window faced the river. The air hung muggy with the sour smell of sweat and sickness. Christine fanned her mother with a piece of cardboard. Evangeline clutched her grandmother's hand. She began to sob. Ann bit her lip when Christine told Evangeline not to cry. "Be brave," Christine said.

Ann's older niece, Rosie's older sister, had cried, and cried. Coleen had picked up the sobbing eight-year-old and held her in her arms. Coleen had cried along with her daughter. To not be allowed to cry seemed cruel, with all that had happened in Evangeline's short life—the murder of her father and brothers, leaving her home, and now the injury of her grandmother. "Maybe she'd feel better if she cried," Ann whispered; she could not restrain herself. "I know it makes me feel better."

Evangeline raised her sad, mahogany eyes toward Ann.

Chapter 49

At the end of the day, Ann tromped out to see 99. It had been several days since she'd checked on him. Thankfully, he'd recovered from the cholera and resumed his old routines. She found him sitting on his stool leaning up against the acacia tree. Between his hands he batted a yellow soccer ball with "Coca Cola" printed in red. Deeper hollows carved his face beneath his cheekbones.

"*Mwiriweho*, good afternoon." The shade felt cool, pleasant. Ann unloaded three Cokes from her backpack. Christine had made it her responsibility to secure a steady stash for him.

He smiled and accepted them, popping off the lid of one bottle with his teeth as usual. Ann grimaced as she settled herself on the ground. Changing his behavior was hopeless.

"Me tired. This give me energy." He took a long swallow.

Ann gestured toward the new ball. "A gift?"

99 smiled and pointed to the printing. "Me love Coke. Everyone know."

Ann told him about Joseta's gunshot wound.

He studied Ann's face as she talked, his gaze longer than what was polite in the US. When she was done, he set down his bottle and said, "You sad. Me hear in voice and see." He pointed toward his own eyes.

Ann nodded. Wrapping her arms around her bent knees, she buried her face in her lap and allowed herself to absorb the coolness of the shade. She had raced from one task to another, one patient to the next all day. Her eyes grew damp as the dreadfulness of Joseta's situation settled in. Edward had done his best, but there were no guarantees.

"You worry about Joseta. She is a friend."

Ann nodded as a tightness formed in the back of her throat. She swallowed against it. She'd come to check on 99, not to burden him with her concerns. She rocked back and forth.

"Why fix up bad guys?" 99 asked.

Ann had not expected that. Here he was reading her mind—how did he do that? She sighed. "I've asked myself the same question. Edward says we must be neutral, practice neutrality."

99 shook his head and picked up his bottle again. After a long draw he said, "Big word. What mean?"

Ann explained. As she talked, she drew a circle in the dirt with a stick.

"You fix up bad guys. They keep do bad things." 99 shook his head. "Stupid."

Ann retraced the circle. 99 made it sound so simple. *Just stop.* A breeze rustled the canopy overhead. Several leaves floated to the ground. One landed in Ann's lap. She lifted it by its stem, twirling it in her fingers. 99 was right. Edward wouldn't hear it, he followed the GH policy—treat all comers, but Margaux understood the challenges neutrality was presenting. It was a point of discussion at the collaborative meeting. Ann dropped the leaf and drew a line bisecting the circle in the dirt.

A dozen meters away, several children kicked the new balls on the soccer field. The balls' gleaming whiteness was long gone. All were smeared with dirt, evidence of how welcome the gift had been. The laughter of the players captured 99's attention. He talked about how happy the children were with the balls and how kind the *wazungu* were to bring them. Ann made no mention of the layers of controversy about the actress's visit and the orphans' evacuation to France. But she had to admit, the balls outshone the homemade versions constructed from plastic bags, leaves, and string. The real balls didn't fall apart and the French diplomat had donated an air pump to inflate them. Perhaps the well-dressed African had suggested the gift.

Ann drew another line through the circle in the dirt. A roller bird fluttered out from the overhead canopy and startled her. She pointed it out to 99. It was her favorite local bird. During flight it rotated back and forth, true to its name. Its multicolored plumage, every pastel color of the rainbow, including lavender, showed luminous in the low angle of the afternoon sun. Ann stood up. She needed to check on Joseta before she caught a ride back to the compound with the other expats. She thanked 99 for the chat and jogged back to the tent.

Chapter 50

Ann struggled to secure the antibiotics to treat Joseta. With Stanford's purchase at the Basuko market, they scrounged together enough for five days of treatment. Ann paid a visit to the medical NGO on the north side of the camp. Margaux's counterpart, a thirty-something brunette bargained. "All I have is nine pills," the brunette director said. "I'll give you these, but you have to make Edward join me for a beer at the pub in Basuko. Later this week."

"You've worked with Edward?" Ann folded her arms across her chest.

The brunette tilted her chin. "What aid worker in Africa hasn't worked with Edward?" She laughed.

Ann stiffened. Edward was charismatic. Women noticed him. All the expat nurses had a crush on him. The Rwandan nurses liked him too. Then Ann found her humor. "So then, you know that no one makes Edward do anything."

The brunette laughed. "We were together in Bosnia." She ran her fingers through her long, loose curls. "He's a sweetheart," the brunette said.

That evening Ann sat tailor-fashion on the joined beds in Edward's room. Candlelight danced on the ceiling. Outside the room, insects cheeped. Edward stretched out on his mattress, his legs crossed at the ankles. He stared up at the mosquito netting. Ann asked about the brunette.

"Annie, you're jealous." He scratched the dimple on his chin

"So, you *were* together." Ann folded her arms, holding her ribs.

Edward gave Ann a long look, then a half smile. "I needed a warm body. . . to cuddle."

"So, I'll be known as your warm body in Basuko." She rocked back and forth, chewing her cheek.

Edward reached toward his neck and toyed with the leather cord, the wedding band still absent. Ann said nothing. He leaned up on his elbow and stroked her knee. "Annie, you mean much more to me."

Ann sighed and gazed toward some point on the ceiling, beyond the mosquito netting. He'd probably said that to the brunette too. He sounded so convincing. The candlelight softened the room's concrete block walls.

Edward sat up and caressed her cheek, then stroked her ear and its tiny gold hoop. His fingers were warm and soft. He traced her lips with his thumb.

Ann uncrossed her arms. So what about the brunette? He was with Ann tonight. He was hers for this mission, and he was right about needing someone to cuddle with in this hellhole. She leaned forward.

"Annie, you're special." Edward slipped his hand to the back of her neck and pulled her toward him. She inhaled his familiar smell. His arms enveloped her.

Joseta's surgical wound healed. Her temperature returned to normal. She started sitting on the side of the bed and dangling her legs. She hobbled to the bedside toilet. The odor of sickness faded. She asked if Evangeline could spend the afternoons with her and they read stories and played Rock, Paper, Scissors. Crayon drawings were duct taped to the tent canvas at the head of her bed.

In the afternoon, when Evangeline was not there, Ann asked Joseta about what she remembered. "After we left, who pointed the gun?"

"I can't remember." Joseta stared blankly, shaking her head. She leaned back against her pillow and pressed her hand to her forehead.

"One of the nurses said you addressed a priest."

"It's a blur."

"Do you remember anything?"

Joseta shrugged and stared blankly across the small room.

"Was it Father Innocent?"

Joseta said nothing, then whispered, "Vincent came to me. He said we'd be together soon."

Ann had cobbled together treatment for seven more days, twelve days total. But thirty-six hours after the last dose, Joseta's temperature shot up. A day later she fell into a coma.

Ann talked to the nurses and doctors who'd been left behind in the medical tent with Joseta during the uprising. One insisted that Joseta called out the name of a priest. But the nurse could not describe the individual. "We were overrun. Not long after you left."

Ann sat at Joseta's bedside. Her mind felt cloudy due to lack of sleep. Outside the mesh window it was dark. Occasionally, the bleat of a goat or a rooster's crow interrupted the silence of the night. Inside the tent, the air hung close, stuffy. A floral-patterned sheet hung over a string, separating Joseta's bed from the sleeping patients on the ward. A sporadic cry or whimper sounded from the restless ones. Evangeline's drawings still hung on the canvas wall, cheering the tiny space.

Ann had sent Christine home at 9:00 p.m. Christine needed sleep and Ann wanted some time alone with Joseta. Joseta had not responded for two days.

Ann called her name.

Nothing.

Ann rubbed her sternum, the cloth nightgown between her full breasts felt slightly damp.

Not even a grimace.

Joseta's breath remained steady until midnight. Ann gave in to sleep, resting her forehead on her folded arms on the mattress next to Joseta.

About 2:00 a.m., Joseta's respirations grew erratic. Ann jolted awake. She stood up and rubbed her eyes, peeking on the other side of the sheet that separated Joseta's space from the ward. No staff monitored the inpatients.

Ann returned to her chair and dropped a washcloth in the plastic basin of water that sat on the floor to her left. She wrung it out; water trickled back into the pan. She pressed the cool cloth to Joseta's forehead, then wiped around her mouth. She dampened it again and touched it to Joseta's cracked lips.

A long, coarse exhale.

"Joseta, are you talking to Vincent?" Ann whispered.

Silence. . . A ragged inhale.

"Is Vincent calling you?"

The exhale was a long rasp—the hum of Joseta's breath moving through her dry windpipe. Ann put down the cloth and pulled the glow-in-the-dark rosary the nuns at the Beauraing Orphanage had given her from her pocket. She'd not recited the rosary since childhood. It had been a comfort to her mother. Ten *Hail Mary's*, followed by the *Our Father*, repeated five times.

Ann pressed the larger bead between her thumb and forefinger and began: "*Our Father who art in heaven . . .thy will be done on earth as it is in heaven. . . give us this day our daily bread. . . and forgive us our trespasses as we forgive those . . .*" The repetition comforted Ann for the next hour.

Ann had sat with her mother during her final hours as well. "Pray the rosary," Ann's mother had murmured in a hoarse voice. Ann and her father had begun: "*Our Father . . .*"

Her mother lay in the hospital bed, her emaciated frame almost hidden in the fold of the sheets and maze of tubes and machines. Her arms were painted with black-and-blue patches, battle scars from the IVs and blood draws. Pictures from her younger grandchildren hung on the walls. Cards lined the window ledge. The room was hot—too hot—and dry.

She had been admitted to the hospital, hopeful that she'd get better. The same stuffiness, the same acrid smell of sickness had filled her large sterile room. The room was noisier than Joseta's. The tick of the heart monitor. The periodic whoosh of the NG tube's suction. The click of the IV machine. The *swoosh* of the oxygen.

Her mother wanted to be intubated. She wanted CPR. She sent several young medical assistants out of her room in tears. She wouldn't admit she was dying. She wouldn't talk about her funeral. She refused the priest who'd tried to administer Last Rights.

Ann's father dutifully fought to keep her alive, carrying out her wishes. Her final words to Ann were something about, "Ann, I am. . . disappointed with you . . ."

Ann's mother didn't want to be alone, but she complained about the chaos when her daughters, grandchildren, and husband were present. She whined and shushed them, even commanded the nurses to lower their voices. However, she was kind to Coleen. Coleen was the only family member who did not suffer the brunt of the anger. Even Irene was sent out the door sobbing at one point.

"You never could rub my back the way I wanted," she told her husband. During her final days, when she was too weak to talk, she moaned.

It was a relief when she became unconscious. Ann and her sisters convinced their father to sign the DNR/DNI papers. "They'll crack her ribs if they do compressions," Ann said. "Please, don't put her through that."

"But she wanted us to try."

"Dad, you're a veterinarian. What did you recommend for an old, arthritic horse?"

Her dad had stared at his wife, his eyes damp. Beyond the room's window, the water of Lake Michigan shimmered lapis lazuli in the sunlight.

"Dad, let her go in peace. It's time."

"But . . ." He reached into his pocket, pulled out a hanky.

"Don't put us through the torture. . . You don't want to look at her black-and-blue chest."

Ann and her father had stepped out when the nurse came to do a bath. That's when her mother died—during her bath. The plastic bowl of water sat on the bedside table when Ann and her father returned to the room. "At least someone was caring for her," Ann said to her father.

"I couldn't do anything right," her father said.

"None of us could."

When it was clear that Joseta was dying, they had stopped the two machines they'd used—the suction and oxygen. They were needed for post-op patients. At first a strange silence hung in the space. During her final hours, Rwandan staff, who worked the night shift, pulled back the sheet and checked on Joseta and Ann. Joseta would be missed.

Another labored and extended breath. The death rattle, her secretions pooled in the back of her throat.

Ann rested her hand on Joseta's abdomen. Joseta gasped. Ann's hand sank with the long, noisy expiration. "Is Vincent calling you?" Ann whispered.

Joseta had prayed for Vincent's release until the very end. She'd been hopeful. "Jesus, keep my beloved Vincent safe." Ann had heard that phrase several times. Joseta had whispered Vincent's name before she'd fallen into the coma.

Ann restarted the rosary. Prayer seemed like the best way to be with Joseta. Her faith had been so important to her. Christine had asked about having the *umuganga gakondo*, witch doctor, come, the same one that had healed Evangeline. Ann did not interfere, but she stepped out when he'd visited that afternoon.

With another *Hail Mary*, a wave of sadness overcame Ann. Moisture filled her eyes. Her chest felt tight. She couldn't button up her tears any longer. She leaned over and cried into the mattress, her forehead resting on her hands. She'd not wept for months. Sobs shook her body. Waves of grief. She cried for her mother. Despite all the grumbling, all the criticism, she was Ann's mother; she had brought Ann into the world, had championed Ann's decision to be a doctor, had been proud of her, introduced her as "my daughter, the real doctor." Somehow Coleen's PhD didn't count.

Ann sobbed for the injured patients she'd cared for—the fixables and unfixables. She cried for Rosie and all she could not do for her. "I'm sorry," she whispered into the sheet. "I'm so sorry," she said to Coleen. "Please forgive me." Her chest grew lighter as she clutched at Joseta's sheet, dabbing at her tears. She did not have a tissue and blew her nose into the pocket of her scrub top. She could change it later.

Another long, guttural gasp from Joseta. Silence. The smell of flatus.

Footsteps approached. Someone stood behind Ann. A firm hand rested on her shoulder. Edward handed Ann a white handkerchief.

Ann honked into it. "Thanks. I'm a mess."

"Just finished a case." Edward surveyed Joseta. "How is she? Her skin is cool."

Ann wiped her nose again. "Agonal breathing. Minutes pass and she doesn't take a breath. It won't be much longer." Ann folded the hanky. "I keep imagining Vincent is calling her."

"She was quite a woman. Quite a nurse."

"It's so sad."

Gray light now filled the mesh window. Edward pulled Ann to her feet and hugged her. He combed his fingers through her hair and kissed her on the forehead. "You meet some incredible people in this business."

Ann had wanted to blame Edward. If only he'd told the car to wait for Joseta the day of the raid. But he had the safety of the others to worry about. He'd done his best during the operation. He stood alongside her now.

Joseta's death was beyond his control, beyond Ann's control. Joseta had defended someone or something during the uprising. Ann had seen her do the same in Kigali. In the end, the lack of antibiotics sealed Joseta's fate. That would never have happened in the US.

Joseta died at 5:30 a.m. on July 11th as the sky lightened and the raucous roosters welcomed the day.

Ann washed Joseta's body. She'd seen an old nurse do that during her residency. "It pays respect to the deceased. It's the least we can do." It seemed appropriate. It bought time before Ann radioed Christine.

The water was cool as Ann wrung out the cloth. A ray of morning sunlight reflected on the surface of the water in the basin. A sunbeam. The water blessed by the morning's light. Holy water.

Ann wiped Joseta's forehead, her full, cracked lips. She lifted up the sheet, uncovering portions of her body. Her full breasts that had nursed her children. The ugly scar from the bullet. Her long legs. Her calloused feet. Ann's arms grew heavy as she worked, weighty. But she moved them with intention, with care. The *Memorare*, the prayer to the Virgin Mary filled her head. "*Remember oh most gracious Virgin Mary... anyone who fled to thy protection.*" Ann repeated it several times.

Ann wound the glow-in-the-dark rosary through Joseta's long fingers. She fingered the callous on her left, middle finger. She tucked a clean sheet around

Joseta. Christine would help her wrap and tie her. With the heat, they would bury Joseta later that day.

Ann killed more time. She did not want to awaken Christine until 7:00 a.m. She poured hot water from the electric teapot into a mug and spooned in the brown powder. She drank coffee. She'd grown used to the Nescafe.

After Edward finished rounds on his post-op cases, he joined her. The fragrance of the coffee, its strong bitter taste cut with a little powdered milk, revived Ann. She smiled at Edward through her damp eyes. "How do you make sense of all of the suffering, the loss?"

Edward looked at her, his half smile, the dimple. "You don't. You do your part to try to make a difference."

Later that morning, Ann helped Christine and Evangeline tie Joseta's hands and feet with strips of cloth. They secured the sheet around her body with more cloth strips. The odor of death was already present. A thick sweetness. A sweet, cloying smell.

The SUVs carried those who wanted to attend Joseta's burial back to the GH compound. Margaux had directed staff to dig a grave on the school property, beyond the garden in the back, where Joseta had often stood gazing at the distant hills.

A handful of the Rwandan nurses and doctors stood near the hole when Joseta was lowered into the ground. But only Ann and Evangeline wept. Christine wore a stony expression. Stanford stood silent, biting at his lip. Margaux looked on with concern and exhaustion. Edward and Robert had paid their respects in the medical tent and chose not to come to the gravesite.

That evening, over tea in chipped cups, Christine shared one of her mother's sayings. "Before we went to sleep she often said: *Aho kuba intumbi waba imva.*" Christine pursed her lips, then lifted the cup, blew the steam and took a sip. "It's better to be dead than to live like a dead person."

Joseta had been such a vital woman. After Vincent's abduction, she moved about with a new sorrowfulness, but she continued to be a committed nurse and colleague. Some part of her died when Vincent was jailed. The phrase gave Ann some comfort. If there was a God and a heaven, Joseta was certainly there with Vincent. Or praying for him to join her soon.

Chapter 51

The day after Joseta's burial, Stanford huffed toward the Toyota SUV wearing long pants and a dress shirt. A group of older orphan boys, Stanford's soccer buddies, jogged alongside. The tallest clutched a green and white soccer ball in one arm. Stanford stopped in front of the medical tent with a huff. The tallest boy, whose head reached Stanford's ear, threw his free arm around Stanford. The other five boys crowded in. Several wore t-shirts advertising a softball team in Nebraska. One was dressed in a pillowcase, a safari pattern. If Ann had a camera, it would be a perfect photo of their soccer team, a motley group.

"I'm leaving today," Stanford blurted. He pushed his bangs away from his copper-colored eyes and heaved, still breathless from the jog.

"That's why you're dressed up," Ann said.

"When-when did you find out?" Robert asked.

"Late last night. They told me to be ready first thing this morning. I'm glad I could say goodbye."

Robert bear hugged Stanford. "I'll miss you, little bro. Orphanage rounds won't be the same. I can't imagine how they'll manage."

"What will you do?" Edward asked.

"Refugees are flooding into Zaire because of *Opération Turquoise*. They want me to help with the orphans in one of the camps." Stanford's buddies stood close and watched him carefully.

"That's the other side of Rwanda. How are you getting there?"

"Land Rover," Stanford said. "I'm kind of excited about seeing another region. There's a big lake and volcanoes."

"Hopefully they won't erupt," Edward said. He shook Stanford's hand and headed into the tent.

"I'll miss you guys," Stanford said.

"You'll whip them into shape," Ann said. "It's been great having you here."

"Robert, will you play soccer with my pals?" Stanford asked, looking toward the group.

"Of course," Robert said. Robert made the effort to touch each of the boys. Then he grabbed the green and white ball from the tallest boy and threw it back to him. The boy caught it and smiled.

The day was beginning to heat up. The morning's sun now shone where they stood, and Stanford and his soccer pals moved into the shade at the side of the tent. The boys would miss him terribly. Did they understand that Stanford was leaving for good? Their lives would soon be marked by yet another loss.

Ann hugged Stanford. He smelled of cologne. "You'll be a great doctor. Keep in touch when you get back to school." She would miss him; teaching and mentoring him had helped her, had grounded her, had reminded her about the tremendous privilege she had as a physician, the opportunity to participate in the lives of her patients, through good and bad.

Stanford said his goodbyes to the rest of the hospital staff and then hurried back to the orphanage. His entourage trailed after him.

"I'm going to miss him," Robert said.

Ann nodded in silence.

Chapter 52

After another long day at the medical tent, the expats bumped back to the compound. Stanford had left three days earlier. Ann climbed out of the SUV ready for a shower. Edward greeted her. "Change your clothes and meet me here. Five minutes max." Edward had spent the afternoon at the NGO meeting and was already dressed in jeans and a t-shirt. "I have a surprise. Hurry."

"I'm exhausted," Ann said. Some of the fun of working had left with Stanford.

"You'll like the surprise."

The screen door banged behind Ann as she stepped onto the veranda and pulled her hair into a ponytail. Edward handed her a bandana. "Tie this around your eyes."

"Can I trust you?" Ann teased.

Edward knotted the bandana at the back of Ann's head and took her hand. "A step down here." They walked along the stone pathway. "We're going through the gate. Now to the right." The gate clanged behind them. The breeze lifted the wisps of hair at her temples. As a kid she'd played blind with her sisters. Irene had loved the game. Ann preferred to be the helper.

A horse clip-clopped along with a cart. The smell of horse lasted for a minute or more. They walked through town. The buzz of voices. Edward held her hand firmly. It grew easier to depend on his guidance. They turned up a side street to the right. A car motored by.

"Where are you taking me?"

"It's a surprise."

The fragrance of a blooming bush, then an animal smell and bleats as hooves crunched the dirt and gravel surface of the road. "Goats? Are they goats?" Ann asked.

"The farm girl comes through." Edward laughed. "Another block and we'll be there." The cries of the goats faded as they trotted away.

Edward directed Ann to the right and the texture under her gym shoes changed. The air felt cooler, darker. They had walked into a building. The smells gave no clue. The space around her felt more constricted then widened.

"We're here." Edward undid the knot and the bandana fell away. Ann stood blinking in a medium-sized room. An upright piano stood against the far wall.

"Where are we?"

Edward put his hand on Ann's shoulder. "When I was at the mayor's, before I got sick, I learned this school had a piano. This afternoon I checked it out to see if we could borrow it."

"You arranged for me to play?"

Edward nodded.

"How sweet." Ann threw her arms around his neck and hugged him. He understood how much she missed playing. She stared at the dimple on his chin through her damp eyes.

Edward kissed her on the forehead. "I've never heard you play."

Ann sat down and adjusted the stool. Wood scraped tile as Edward pulled a chair next to her. Ann stretched her fingers over the keyboard trying to decide what to play. If she'd known, she would have brought the sheet music the Beauraing nuns had given her when she left.

"What's the song you like? The one you taught the children at the orphanage."

Ann's fingers found the cords. *Da Da Da. Da...* the notes of the introduction to the *Children of Sanchez*.

"What a beginning," Edward murmured.

Ann continued to play. Energy rushed from her fingers into her chest. The song charged the space as a peacefulness settled into her abdomen and pelvis. She sat solidly on the stool. The music grounded her. There were only the notes, the melody. The weariness of the day fell away. She ended with a flourish.

Edward applauded, his claps echoing in the empty room. Ann's fingers promptly began *The Happy Farmer* by Robert Schumann, an upbeat tune she had learned as a child. "My dad's favorite," she said when she finished.

"Do you know *Annie's Song*? I've always liked it." Edward leaned over and kissed her on the cheek. "I have more reasons to like it now."

Ann's hands reached across the black and white keys as she sang. Edward joined in. He started in tune, but ended off-key. They laughed when they finished.

"I won't ask you to join my chorus."

He fingered the gold ring in her earlobe. "We make our music in other ways." His breath was warm against her cheek.

Ann played several more songs. For the next hour, the piano and room belonged only to them. The compound, the medical tent, and the day's lineup of sick and injured patients seemed like a different country, a different world.

"It's getting dark. We should go," Edward said.

They returned to the compound hand in hand. Ann stepped with a lightness, her heart surrounded by a halo of warmth.

Chapter 53

At the beginning of the third week of July, a wooden skeleton framed the damaged registration building. Increasing numbers of traumatic injuries sought help at the medical tent. Many arrived too late to repair. Ann slogged through her days. She had not seen 99 for three days, so armed with a fresh supply of Coke, she hiked toward his tree over the lunch hour.

The rainy season had finally lifted and the late-morning sun beat down. Children streamed toward her. They held out their hands; some grabbed for her pants pockets. Their smiles shone beneath the grime that covered their faces and laminated their t-shirts and shorts, adding a sheen to the cloth of their clothes. Only a few had been scrubbed clean by their mothers. Bathing and laundering meant a trip to the river. Most families managed to do that once a week at the most.

Initially, Ann's response to the crowding children had been fear. She had no candy, no gum, nothing to give—what did they want? But Stanford had modeled a different response. He had reached out and touched the children, held the hands of some, let others grab his forearms, allowed them to hang onto his shirt or pants. He secured his forearms against his pockets, blocking any hands from reaching inside. "They just want physical contact," he'd told her. Ann smiled at the thought of Stanford. By now, he should have arrived in Zaire, hopefully without a hitch.

The children practiced their English as they walked with her. "Hello. How are you, Dr. Ann. Good morning. Goodbye. Hi. Bye bye."

Two large-winged black birds with white feathers on their upper backs flew from their roost as Ann and her entourage approached 99's camp. Three pecked the ground near his belongings. A sick feeling settled in Ann's stomach as she noticed the putrid smell. She sent three older children back to the medical tent to get Robert or Edward. She and the other children continued toward the tree.

Ann smelled 99 before she identified him. She spun on her heels and retched. The hot, bitter bile burned her throat and tongue. She composed herself and apologized to the children.

A vulture poked inside 99's rib cage. It paused and stared toward Ann, his inky-black, jeweled eye protruding from a gray skin-covered head. His beak, the same color of gray, was filled with spongy, pink lung.

Ann wanted to cover the eyes of the children. She wanted to send them away. They didn't need to see 99 like this. Their friend, this kind and gentle man. They had seen enough death. She searched for something to cover him until help came.

Edward arrived breathless from the jog. The three children followed.

"99's dead," Ann said. She had dragged over 99's bed mat. "Help me wrap him."

A puddle of dried blood pooled beneath him. Together, Edward and Ann flipped 99 over. The bullet wound sat beneath his left shoulder blade. The back of his white t-shirt had a hole and was stained red. Rivulets of blood had dried on his trousers and matted his kinky black hair. Large flies buzzed and feasted like ants in honey.

"How could someone shoot him?" Ann choked on her words. *Who could hurt 99? Everyone loved him, especially the children.* Tears clogged Ann's throat. *Who would do this? Who could be so cruel?*

"He's been dead for a while. It must have occurred last night."

Ann wrapped her hands around her stomach in a defensive posture. "This neutrality stance is ridiculous," she said. "It just doesn't make sense." She scraped her sandal through the dirt. "Extremists killed Joseta. Our guard was shot. The Tanzanian police are no help. Scar and Father Innocent run free." Ann swallowed her tears; she couldn't cry, not in front of the children, but she continued her rant. "And now 99."

The children watched cautiously at the edge of the shade.

Ann fumed on about neutrality.

Edward said little.

It took awhile. The hot sun beat down. Despite his slight frame, 99 was heavy. Ann and Edward paused to rest. At one point, a vulture dive-bombed them. The smell made her eyes water. The flies swarmed. A mirage of silver ripples spread in front of them as they made their way toward the medical tent. Several times, silver shimmered, as if they needed to step through a puddle of water, then when they reached the place, it was only dirt, any hint of something more had disappeared.

Robert greeted them at the entrance of the tent. Staff secured a sheet for burial and helped Ann wrap 99's body in the same manner she'd prepared Joseta. She had to help—it felt like the only way to pay respect to 99's life.

A pickup truck transported him to the mass grave thirty meters behind the medical tent. Hundreds of Rwandan refugees had been buried there. Those who'd sought help at the medical tent too late to be cured. The weak and frail. Ann stared at the gaping hole in the red earth. Dozens of children and adults whose immune systems were not able to fight off pneumonia, malaria, cellulitis, meningitis—even with the antibiotics GH had supplied—rested there. She pinched her nose against the stench. Hundreds more had died from cholera. With that epidemic, Margaux had hired the backhoe to dig a second grave.

With dry eyes, Ann helped Robert fling 99 in with the other bodies. A thump confirmed his landing. They scooped up handfuls of dirt and grabbed bunches of dried grass, throwing that in as well. They covered their noses with their forearms against the horrendous stink of death mixed with the tang of sickness—vomit, defecation, and sweat. All merged in the hot air.

Ann and the other doctors had documented all the deaths on the Mortality Summary Form: age, gender, and cause of death—diarrhea, bloody diarrhea, acute respiratory infection, fever unknown, suspect malaria or measles, suspect meningitis, war injury, malnutrition, and other. Sometimes Ann recited the categories in her sleep.

It seemed irreverent to simply toss 99 in without a prayer. Ann folded her hands and recited the *Our Father*. One of the older boys said several sentences in Kinyarwanda and then started singing. The other children joined in. It was a song Ann had heard 99 sing with the children. When they were finished, the children applauded and wandered back toward the camp.

Robert wore the same distraught look that Ann felt. 99 deserved a wail, a collective wail. But neither Robert nor Ann said anything. Like the Rwandans, they had begun to cry inside. Their eyes were dry.

They gazed across the expanse beyond the graves. The sun had passed its zenith, but gripped the afternoon with the strength of sharp teeth. "Why would someone shoot 99? In the back? Murder him?" She looked at Robert. Sweat trickled between her shoulder blades. No wind offered relief.

Robert stared at her and said nothing.

At home, Ann rarely attended the funeral mass of a patient. She usually mailed a sympathy card. There was a distance. The preservation of the body by the mortuary. She might see the embalmed body at the visitation, pay respects to family if she knew them well. There was the prayer card, the tradition of flowers, or donations to some charity.

Ann and her father had planned every step for her mother's service. More than two hundred people shook Ann's hand at the funeral home. Several dozen bouquets perfumed the two adjoining rooms. Ann's brothers-in-law were pallbearers. At the end of the funeral mass, she sang the Ave Maria, her mother's favorite song. She made it through with only a quiver in her voice.

Here in Africa it was all so final. There had been so much death. The mourning period was abbreviated, almost nonexistent. With Joseta, they had dug a grave for her near their compound. But once she was covered with dirt, everyone had returned to work, even Christine.

99 touched many with his jovial manner. He knew no stranger. Like Ann's sister, Irene, he charmed most who met him. He made so many smile, even the staff and expats who did not know him. Ann would miss his lisp, his toothy, ear-to-ear grin, his pleasure with a bottle of Coke, uncapping it with his teeth.

The driver of the truck called to them. "You want a ride back to the tent?" Robert asked.

Ann looked at Robert. "I need to walk."

Robert nodded and climbed into the truck; they *vroomed* off.

Ann had hoped to leave all the senseless killing in Kigali, but the victimization continued here. Lawlessness ruled the camp. Worse yet, there would be no justice. She meandered back toward the tent. She picked up a plastic bag caught in a bush and filled it with trash—a used condom, an empty packet of Oral Rehydration Solution, a broken blue flip-flop. Soon, her bag could hold no more.

Stopping the extremists seemed like an impossible task. Ann wiped perspiration from her forehead with her wrist. She adjusted her sunglasses. The intense sun burned her nose and cheeks. She should have worn her hat.

Maybe it was time to leave. The murders of Joseta and 99 felt personal. Was Father Innocent slowly killing off everyone she loved? She didn't have the strength to do this anymore.

Chapter 54

That evening Ann followed Margaux out to the veranda after dinner. Margaux retrieved a cigarette and tossed her pack of *Impalas* toward Ann. Ann caught it and threw the pack back. It landed in Margaux's lap. Margaux chuckled.

"I quit." Ann sucked in a breath. "I can't do this anymore."

"You quit the cigs or you're leaving?" Margaux coughed, then blew her nose in a tissue.

"I've done my six months. I was hanging on. I felt a commitment to Joseta and Stanford. An obligation to you and Edward. Robert." Ann ran her fingers through her hair. "I'm done. I'm exhausted. Am I a coward? I am not sure I'm doing any good."

"You've had a rough first mission." Margaux lit her cigarette.

Ann nodded and stared at her lap. She perched on the edge of a chair.

Margaux sucked on a cigarette, then coughed violently.

"You shouldn't smoke with your cold."

Margaux frowned, then swallowed a sip of whiskey. "I'm your boss and you're telling me what to do?"

Ann shrugged. "It's been tough. Maybe it's time to face my family in Milwaukee. What I know is that I can't handle any more death. Joseta. 99. All the patients from cholera."

Margaux studied Ann.

Three vehicles bumped over the speed bumps in front of the school.

"Lots of traffic tonight," Ann said.

"The camp's census is well over a quarter mil, even with the uprising. Now fifteen NGOs are trying to manage this crisis. My headache today, in addition to this *laryngite*, is that Paul Kagame, the Tutsi rebel leader, continues to accuse the NGOs of supporting the *génocidaires*. He wants us to close the camp and send the refugees back to Rwanda."

"Edward won't like that," Ann said.

"He doesn't know yet. We haven't talked."

"He had cases all day and call tonight."

Margaux drew on her cigarette, then had another coughing spell. She ground her cigarette into the patio stone with her heel.

"Would I leave from Kigali or Tanzania?"

"I am headed to Kigali in a week to talk with the International Red Cross. I'll survey the situation there. See if the city is ready to accept the refugees and report back to our collaborative group." Margaux pulled another cigarette from her pack and tapped it on her palm. "You can ride with me."

"Is the airport open?"

"Any day."

Ann wanted something more definitive.

In her room she searched for her mother's locket among her things. She recalled packing it carefully when she left Kigali, but couldn't remember what safe place she'd put it in.

Things had been so confusing when she'd left Milwaukee. She'd resented everyone. In Rwanda, she'd gained some sympathy for what her dad had been through. But was she ready to deal with her angry sister? Sure, Coleen was devastated with the death of Rosie, but did she have to blame Ann? Ann had come here to get some perspective. Instead, she'd gotten more death. More loss.

Chapter 55

The next day during the last hour of daylight, Ann asked Edward to walk with her. They followed a goat path up a hill on the edge of town that Ann had discovered early on. At the top one could look at the expanse of the camp. She'd visited it regularly until the guard was shot and Margaux had prohibited everyone from walking alone. Some days when she was at the compound after a night of call, she took the children on "adventures." The path led up a grassy hillock that left her panting by the time she'd reached the top, but the view always gave her perspective.

They walked in silence. Overhead a raptor played on the air waves. Ann sorted through how to tell Edward she needed to leave. She didn't want him to think she was a coward.

Goats bleated in the distance. Two thirds up, Edward grabbed Ann's hand and pulled her through the steepest part of the climb. "You're getting out of shape, Annie."

They sat side by side on a flat, gray rock. The changing light tinted the sky and the clouds reflected the hues like an artist's pastel palette. Twittering birds filled the branches of an ancient wind-strangled tree. In the distance, the tarps and the tin shacks of the camp shimmered in the angled rays of sunlight.

Edward talked about his day. Five cases. After ten minutes, Ann interrupted him. "I need to tell you something."

Edward said nothing for a minute, staring at the tree. Then he sighed. "I'm sorry, I've been talking. . . I should have asked if there was something on your mind when you suggested we come up here." He laid his hand over hers.

Ann studied the tree, the birds darting and chattering. "I'm going home."

Edward said nothing.

"I feel like a failure. I just can't do this anymore."

Edward sighed and then pulled Ann into his chest and buried his face in her hair. "I'll miss you kid."

They sat together. He smelled of the OR—disinfectant, soap mixed with perspiration. "It's been great. I know you're frustrated. We've disagreed. Of course, I'm always right and you're wrong."

Ann chuckled, but continued with her serious vein. "I left home too soon after my mother's death."

"I'll miss you, Annie." Edward squeezed her harder. "Really. . ." There was a quiver in his voice.

Ann's own tears sat at the back of her throat. She gulped against the knot.

Edward continued. "Maybe we'll work together. . . on another mission. . . This *is* my calling."

The fragrance of some flower filled Ann's nose. A flock of birds swooped out of the tree, creating a vibrating black cape as they headed toward the setting sun. "I know," Ann said and squeezed his hand. "I know."

Edward's lips brushed her forehead. "You're tired. You need to finish things. . . at home."

"I'm not sure."

In the camp, the smoke from the cooking fires hovered like a sheet of thin, gray silk. The toxic stench was undetectable. The refugees, the size of ants, moved through their evening routines, the dirt on their clothes invisible, the colors vivid like photos in a travel brochure. The details faded in the dimming light. Ann and Edward sat arm in arm and watched the light bleed from the sky as long as they could.

Chapter 56

The sunny days dried out the camp, but magnified the stench of the latrines and unwashed bodies. During the last week of July, Ann watched the setting sun slash swaths of purple across the tents and tarps as the refugee families cooked dinner. The western sky was ablaze with gold, purple, and mauve.

The GH vehicle kicked up dirt and gravel as it pulled away from the medical tent, carrying the expats back to the compound for the night. It would be a lonely call night again without Stanford. Although he'd been gone more than two weeks, Ann still missed him. Call had been more fun with him asking questions and helping. Margaux was checking into flight options for Ann. She'd return to the US through either Tanzania or Kigali.

Ann ambled into the break room. Starting call so exhausted wasn't good. Maybe food would help. She tied her hair with a clasp, then washed her hands and blotted them on her scrub pants. Someone had walked off with the towel. She ladled cassava leaf soup into a bowl. She perched on a stool, inhaled the spicy fragrance, and blew at a spoonful. The absences hung like a huge hole in her chest. Without 99, Joseta, and Stanford, Ann felt empty. Last night Edward and Margaux had argued on the veranda about the future of GH's effort at the camp. Edward was grumpy when he finally came to bed.

"Woman giving birth. Hurry," a nurse called.

Ann gulped down her soup; no telling when she'd have another chance to eat.

She rushed into the delivery area. The young woman pushed out two babies in rapid succession. Ann was occupied for several hours stabilizing the smaller twin. She thought about calling Robert, but he'd had a brutal call night the night before and needed his sleep. Dr. Philip, the Rwandan physician, was on call. He broke away from his inpatient duties to help her. He thought the one baby was septic and suggested starting antibiotics.

Ann returned to the break room for a cup of coffee. Her watch read 12:20.

"Machete wound," the nurse called.

Ann hurried into the emergency area. Two Rwandans rolled the victim from the tipoy onto a gurney. The camp's ambulance service functioned well and provided financial support to a number of refugees who rotated the responsibility.

As she pulled on gloves, she prepared herself for yet another victim. How many machete wounds had she sewn up? She stepped up to the patient's side. A well-proportioned Rwandan male struggled for breath. Blood trickled from the machete wound on his back. Ann called for oxygen and put her stethoscope on the ebony skin, just above the wound. No breath sounds on the right. A pneumothorax. The gash was low enough that it might have pierced a kidney. He'd need a catheter to check for hematuria. Blood in the urine could wait. She'd address his breathing first.

"Bring oxygen and a chest tube," she said. She circled the gurney to listen to his heart and check his blood pressure herself. She'd learned to recheck the nurses, especially at night. Leaning forward, she prepared to rest her stethoscope on the patient's chest. The smell of sweat filled her nose. She gazed into the anguished face of Father Innocent.

"Help me," he mouthed. His eyes squinted shut. Sweat beaded on his temples as he labored for every breath. Ann pressed the oxygen mask to his face and pulled the rubber band over his head. He'd shaved his head since she'd last seen him standing outside, near registration, during the uprising at the camp. She connected the tubing to the tank and turned the knob. The oxygen canister grunted, then whooshed. The oxygen should make his breathing easier.

Innocent lay with his eyes closed. She wondered if he'd recognized her.

He grunted, then thrashed on the cart. He fell still. He might have had a seizure from the lack of oxygen. She needed to work fast. Her palms sweated inside her gloves. Her mouth felt like sandpaper. She asked the tipoy carriers to help her position Innocent so she could investigate his machete wound.

The bleeding had stopped. With her gloved pointer finger she inspected the injury. The rib was intact, no step off indicating a fracture. She'd seal it for now and suture it later. She put her stethoscope to the affected side. Still no breath sounds. He needed a chest tube. The tube would allow his right lung to expand to its full capacity. Ann swabbed Betadine on the entrance wound, wiped it clean, smeared it with antibiotic gel, and covered it with four-by-four gauze. The nurse ripped the tape for her. Ann pressed it to his chest, sealing any leak.

The oxygen tank groaned as noisy as always. Ann studied Innocent's face, the sharp line of his jaw. His lips pursed inside the mask. Perspiration slicked his forehead and dripped from his scalp. Father Innocent, the pastor of St. Michael, garbed in his white and gold vestments, his regal air at Easter. How he loved the high drama of the liturgy, sang in his melodic baritone, inspired parishioners with rousing sermons. He'd doted on his flock at Easter, the last day she'd worshiped at St. Michael. Joseta had revered him, confided in him about Vincent's abduction. Innocent had appeared to care.

Ann took the chest tube from the nurse and tore open the paper package. She grasped the plastic tube and spread the paper like a sterile field alongside Innocent's chest. She paused; her legs felt rooted to the ground beneath her feet. His chest rose and fell, the right side moved less than the left. If Edward were here, he would tell her to get busy.

Ann wanted to talk to Innocent. She wanted to understand why he did what he did, his motivations. In his current condition, would he hear her? Would the nurse think she was crazy? The nurse who was on spoke French, no English.

Ann recalled their talks on the parsonage veranda. "Innocent, you were confident in your opinions. You'd lived in the US. You helped me understand Rwanda. You walked me through my culture shock. You were my friend. I was homesick. Our talks were my touchstone during my early months in Kigali."

Ann touched his right side. She counted ribs with her gloved fingers. Kinky black hair covered his muscular chest. "You pressured me to sleep with you. Did you know Sylvia encouraged me? Gave me condoms? Thank God, I didn't. Thank God, I kept my boundaries."

A, B, Cs—airway, breathing, circulation—the Advanced Life Support mantra echoed in Ann's head. Innocent's airway was secure, but his breathing was hampered by the collapsed lung. She needed to act now. Why was she stalling? Edward would tell her, "We care for all of our patients. We don't take sides." But Edward was not on call. The nurse would do what Ann told her. Staff was used to triaging fixable and too-sick-to-fix. A shiver rushed up Ann's spine and she swallowed hard.

There was the yard at St. Michael church, the buzzards silently circling overhead, signaling the horror that lay among the blades of grass. "I'll never forget the creak of the church door as it blew back and forth in the breeze. It bumped up against the foot of one of your parishioners. One of your beloved parishioners was the door stop. Overhead, the arm of the Jesus statue held a bloody dress. Innocent, why did you turn over your parishioners? Some priests protected their flocks. What about the elders? You listened to them after mass, visited them in their homes. Took them Communion, the Body of Christ. How could you? The parents you reassured. The children you touched on their heads and shoulders, during the kiss of peace. How could you?"

The nurse looked at Ann quizzically. A wave of nausea moved through. She'd been nauseated the evening she'd learned about the slaughter at St. Michael's. Another shiver settled at the base of her neck.

"Lift his arm up," Ann said to the nurse.

His hand lay open; the fingers bent slightly, the pink palms cupped but empty. There was the back of the ambulance. The pistol in Innocent's hand. "Hatred spewed from your mouth. Rage filled your eyes. I was shocked. Your look and words were like daggers—*gutera ingunguru*. Did you hate me because I rejected you? Did I reject your manhood? You are a priest. I tried to honor your vows. The vows you made. Sacred vows."

Innocent's eyes fluttered open momentarily. His look was distant, glazed. The lack of oxygen from his collapsed lung had affected his mentation.

If she was going to save him, she needed to act now—identify the rib, swab the skin with betadine, cut through the layers with the scalpel, burrow up over the rib with her finger, and insert the tube. Her hand with the chest tube trembled.

The nurse stared at Ann, waiting for direction.

The air inside the medical tent hung heavy, the day's heat still caught inside. The smells of ammonia mixed with sweat. Ann fanned herself with her gloved palm. She tightened her grip around the chest tube in her hand. The Hippocratic Oath, not to play God. To treat all, regardless.

Ann worked her fingers along the right side of Father Innocent's ribs and counted. She'd done this dozens of times. She remembered caring for Scar. Edward had made her do it. She'd done it reluctantly, questioned herself.

The nurse opened the scalpel and suture kit. The oxygen tank rumbled, unbearably noisy. "Innocent, you threatened me. Threatened me. Threatened. . . What were you plotting when you drove by the compound? Why did you shoot our guard? What were you looking for when you stood outside Edward's bedroom window, visited with our guard in the early hours of the morning? Were you jealous because I was sleeping with Edward? Were you looking for me? Did you want to hurt me? How vulnerable you are now.

"What I don't understand is your loyalty to orphans, the nuns at Beauraing. Like the Pied Piper, you and Scar stole WFP food bags and gave them to Stanford's orphans. How can someone do such good and such bad?"

Ann bit her lip as she studied Innocent's face. Her heart raced. "The kindness doesn't negate your threats to me. Your harm to those I loved. Did you shoot Joseta during the raid? If you didn't, why didn't you protect her? She and Vincent worshiped you. And what about 99?

"*Gutera ingunguru.* Would you have raped me? I was afraid. I am afraid." Sweat moistened the nape of Ann's neck and trickled down between her shoulder blades.

For a moment Innocent's eyelids fluttered open and his gaze seemed to lock hers. A pleading. Ann fingered the chest tube. The nurse still steadied Innocent's arm. Why should she put in the tube? Dr. Philip was already in bed. If she weren't here in the emergency area at this moment, there would be no one to insert the chest tube. 99 had said, "You are stupid to keep fixing up the bad guys. They keep doing bad things."

Could she do it? Edward was not here. The nurse would do what Ann asked. She set down the tube and lifted her stethoscope from around her neck. She bent over and placed its diaphragm on Innocent's chest, just over his heart. *Lub dub, Lub dub*, a pause. *Lub dub*, another pause. She slid the scope to his lungs. Breath sounds on the left. Nothing on the right. Her own stomach gurgled. She forced a breath out and straightened, reaching toward the oxygen tank. Her hand hovered over the knob for several seconds. Then with an inhale Ann grasped it. She twisted the knob to the right.

Silence.

Ann exhaled. "We won't waste the oxygen. He's an unfixable," she said in French. "Wheel him to the corner of the tent."

The nurse looked at her and tightened her lips into a compressed line. "*Oui,*" she said.

The gurney's wheels squeaked across the floor. Ann wrapped the unused chest tube in the paper.

Chapter 57

In the morning, Ann returned to the compound exhausted. She needed to tell someone about Innocent. As she fixed the mosquito netting around her cot, she considered who might understand. Robert. Maybe Christine, she'd been a nursing student. Did she owe Edward an explanation? They'd gotten sloppy about checking out the mortality reports.

Dr. Philip had gone to bed shortly before midnight. Innocent had arrived twenty minutes later. At 5:00 a.m. Philip returned refreshed and ready for his coffee. Ann showed him Innocent's corpse rolled in a sheet, waiting to be carried to the mass grave. Philip looked at Innocent's face and shrugged. He did not recognize the priest. "All we can do is our best," Philip had said.

Was that an absolution? Ann had worked through the night with a short coffee break at four. She contemplated the Rwandan physician's absence between midnight and five as she mixed a heaping teaspoon of Nescafe into the steaming water. She needed it strong—very strong. It seemed unprofessional to abandon patients, but all of the Rwandan doctors went to sleep in the middle of the night. They stopped what they were doing, left patients waiting, and went to bed.

Getting their sleep was probably survival. Ann had worked at the camp for over two months. Everything seemed to be falling apart, much like Kigali. She could leave. The Rwandan physicians had nowhere else to go. Dr. Philip had to pace himself.

Ann rested her head against her pillow and closed her eyes. That night she had taken a step in stopping the violence. One small step. She felt better about going home. She was ready. The sounds of the distant traffic lulled her to sleep.

Ann awoke at noon. She showered in the outdoor lean-to, allowing the warm water to drum on her back as long as she dared. After toweling off, she wiped the vapor from the cracked mirror with her palm. She studied her freckled face. More freckles had sprouted despite her careful applications of sunscreen. Several gray hairs coiled upward at her temple. Too many to pluck. She felt old, especially after last night.

Christine had returned from market. She stood in the courtyard hanging laundry. Evangeline sorted oranges into crates against the compound's wall. Two chickens lay on the ground, their feet tied together with string. They squawked and beat their wings, creating clouds of dust.

"Dinner?" Ann asked.

"Do you want to help me? After I hang the clothes?"

"I've seen enough blood."

Christine secured a GH t-shirt to the rope strung across the courtyard with two clothes pins.

"A good day for drying clothes," Ann said. The sun warmed her face. She watched Evangeline bent over the crate, occupied with her task. ". . . I wish your mother was here."

"I do too," Christine said and lifted blue jeans from the wicker basket. "How was call?"

Ann sighed. "Your mother wouldn't be happy with me. She was so good at treating all comers. Without judgment." Ann swallowed, trying to find the words. "Last night Father Innocent came in with a machete wound."

Christine stopped, her arms poised above the clothesline. She rotated to look at Ann.

"I wish your mother were here so I could tell her about it."

"She was very fond of him." Christine folded her arms across her chest.

"He's a complicated man. . . I, I decided not to help him. I felt bad, but at the same time I'm relieved. I was afraid of him."

Christine stood silent, studying Ann's face, wiping her palms on the blue paisley cloth of her kanga. Finally Christine said, "He's been hurting people. You think he. . . he shot mother."

Ann nodded. "Your mother and others. But your mother had a bigger heart than me. She would have forgiven him. Taken care of him, regardless. I couldn't."

Christine held her hands to her lips.

"I know he was responsible for the death of our guard and probably 99.

He threatened me. I couldn't just fix him up. . . let him continue his monstrous work."

Christine bent over and pinned an orange kanga on the line. Then she pressed her fingers together and scrutinized Ann. She had her mother's piercing gray-brown eyes. She sighed, then lowered her arms and planted her hands on her hips. Ann had seen Joseta assume the identical stance when she meant business. Christine inhaled and exhaled, then said, "My mother would understand."

"Thanks." An orange butterfly floated toward Ann and landed on her forearm. It lifted its front feet up and down and rested its mouth on Ann's skin with a tiny pinch.

Both Ann and Christine watched it. Evangeline skipped over to touch it. The butterfly didn't move.

"It likes the salt on my skin," Ann said.

"Can you put it on my arm?" Evangeline asked. "I want the flybutter to kiss me."

Christine laughed. "Butter-fly. Butter comes first."

"Butter-fly." Evangeline said with purpose.

"I've seen them land in pools of piss," Christine said.

"The urine has minerals and salts."

The butterfly floated away.

Ann wanted to understand how Christine bore all her loss: her husband, sons, her school career on hold, her mother. . . Ann blurted out, "How do you do it? How do you keep going with all that has happened?"

Christine did not look at her as she hung the final skirt on the line. "Do I have a choice?" she said. She bent over and picked up the basket, heading toward the house, then twisted, "And my offer to help with the chickens?"

Ann turned her head to the right and left with vehemence. "Been there done that. Helped my grandpa as a kid. Thanks, but I've seen enough death."

That evening Edward was on call. Ann played French Scrabble with Robert and the children. After the kids went to bed, she told Robert about Innocent.

"What do you want from me?" He scratched his goatee, then folded his hands together.

"I'm not sure."

"Would I have done what you did? No. But then, I've not been here as long as you, and the priest was not threatening me."

Ann sighed. She didn't need his forgiveness. She didn't even need his approval. At the time, she'd felt confident in her decision. It was done. Why was she doubting her actions?

Chapter 58

Ann sat on Edward's bed, her legs crossed. He lifted up the mosquito netting and crawled on to the other bed. The fan sighed overhead like a wheezy old man.

Ann took a deep breath. "I wanted you to know that Father Innocent came in when I was on call yesterday. He had a chest wound. He was really sick. He needed a chest tube. I chose not to insert one."

Edward stared at her. "How do you feel about that?"

"Okay," Ann said.

"You know I don't agree with your decision."

"I know."

"You're leaving, so I can't really fire you."

"I am telling you because I want to be accountable to you."

"We've talked about neutrality."

Ann nodded.

"Sometimes you do things in the field that you wouldn't do at home. It seems like the right thing to do at the time. Or it is your only option. Your tools are limited, so you have to get creative. Those episodes follow you home. They haunt you. You question them. But you do work them out over time."

They sat in silence.

Finally, Ann asked, "Will it prevent me from accepting another assignment with GH?"

Edward shook his head. "It's between you and me."

Ann said nothing. An insect knocked against the screen nearest the candle.

"I like you Annie. You are a good doctor. We've disagreed about the neutrality."

"Can we agree to disagree?"

Edward smiled. "When are you leaving?" He touched her bare knee.

"I'm waiting to find out which airport is open."

"I'll miss you."

She'd miss him, miss sleeping with him. She'd never expected someone like him during this mission.

Edward blew out the candle and they spooned each other, sleeping soundly.

Loud banging awoke Ann sometime after midnight. One of the guards called through the door, "Phone. Ann. Phone."

"What time is it?" Edward asked, his voice heavy from sleep.

"It's for me," Ann said. She located her headlamp, slipped on her flip-flops, and pulled on one of Edward's shirts. She plodded into the courtyard and followed the guard into the common room. "What time is it?" she asked.

"*Enye*, four." The guard pointed toward the phone.

Ann picked up the satellite phone. "This is Ann."

"Dad was admitted to the hospital after the stress test. I thought you'd want to know." It was Coleen, Rosie's mother, the psychotherapist. Ann had not talked to her for a year.

"They cathed him?"

"I think so."

"I'm leaving soon. What's next?"

"I don't know. I'm not a doctor. Not a medical doctor."

"He must have had a significant blockage."

"Something like that. They talked about a cabbage…surgery, it sounds like a vegetable, but I know it's not. It would be nice to have you here. To translate. He's an active man. He overdoes it on the farm, in his garden. He keeps so busy, especially since mom died…" Her voice drifted. A child cried in the background.

"Are you still there?"

"Yep. I've got one of the neighbor kids with me today. She's a handful."

"What time is it there?"

"Five in the afternoon."

"You must mean a C-A-B-G, coronary artery bypass graft, heart surgery."

"Maybe."

"How are you?" Ann asked.

Silence... It lasted long enough that Ann was getting ready to ask if she was there.

Then... "It's getting a little easier."

Ann sighed. "I can't imagine." Silence. The awkwardness continued. "It's good to hear your voice. I've prayed for you."

"Thanks."

Ann hated to hear about her dad. "I'm waiting to figure out which airport I can fly out of. It's a long story."

"It would be great if you could come."

"I'll be there."

"Irene's written you a letter or colored you a picture every day. We haven't mailed them. Dad's saved them. They fill three grocery bags."

Ann smiled, industrious Irene.

Ann held onto the phone before setting it in its cradle. She was ready to go home. It was time to make peace with her sister. They'd had a conversation. Time had healed her anger toward her dad, her feelings toward her sister. All she'd seen had taught her about loss. It was time.

That evening she talked to Margaux, who was irritable and still coughing. She'd taken Ann's advice to cut back on her cigarettes after Edward, Robert, and Ann had given her a hard time.

Margaux tapped the edge of her whiskey glass. "I'm told the Kigali airport is opening this week." Without her cigarettes she did a lot of tapping.

"I need to go."

"Let me check tomorrow."

"It'd be nice to see Kigali before I leave. Maybe even visit Beauraing orphanage."

Chapter 59

Unnerving silence overwhelmed Margaux and Ann's trip back to Kigali. Even the birds seemed to observe some code of quiet. Patches of charred grass, untended crops, and destroyed homes smudged the landscape, the owners largely absent. Few people tromped or biked along the roadside. Instead, three-by-three inch white cards littered the road like confetti. Each card contained a photo, name, and ethnicity. Were the owners alive or dead? Had Ann cared for them in Kigali? Did they make it to the Batumba camp? During a stretch break, Ann picked one up and wiped off the damp eucalyptus leaves and smears of red clay.

"What's the name?" Margaux asked.

"Christian Harimana." Ann said. "Tutsi." She rubbed the card like someone might rub a talisman. Where was this twenty-something male? "I hope he was one of the lucky ones," she murmured.

Kigali still burned with the evidence of the unlucky. Three months had lapsed since mid-May. The smell of barbequed flesh filled the air. A fine layer of ash dusted everything. Dogs outnumbered people. Pups chased after their mothers. Their barking became white noise.

The loudspeakers in the neighborhoods hung mute. Destruction marked the houses and buildings in many neighborhoods, including their own—shattered windows, walls pock-marked like Swiss cheese, gates and sign posts twisted and bent, doors axed open. Squatters had taken up residence in several of the embassies and the grade school on the corner. The singing nuns' convent lay in rubble. Ann replayed the night the nuns were shot like an unforgettable bad dream. The gunshots, then the remaining scratchy alto. The baritone who sang several bars of the hymn followed by a spiteful laugh. The baritone and the laugh—Father Innocent. She had missed it at the time.

The GH compound stood empty, the front door missing and the ground-floor windows smashed. The metal gate lay in the yard covered with feces. Until May, it had served as such a safe haven. How soon after they left was it ransacked? Margaux had been wise to move them to the refugee camp.

John Friend, the American, had weathered the months at the Seventh Day Adventist compound in Kigali. Only two windows had been shot out in his church. In early July, RPF leader, Paul Kagame, secured the city without international assistance. The UN was present as a peacekeeping force, but they had no weapons and could not fight. When Rwanda was no longer friendly to the Hutu or their sympathizers, many had fled to Zaire, where Stanford worked.

John welcomed Margaux and Ann with hugs. He showed them to their rooms. "Wa-ash off the du-ust and gri-ime," he said in a Texas drawl that stretched single syllable words into two. After a supper of beans and rice, he ushered them into his living room, lit candles given the erratic electricity, and served Margaux scotch straight up.

"Where did you find this?" she asked.

John smiled. "Sorry, ice is impossible."

"*Merci, merci*," Margaux said, then tried to manage her disappointment when he asked her not to smoke in the house.

John and Ann shared a Fanta. Over the months, he had secured supplies for several orphanages, including Beauraing. "The nuns and all the children are fine," he said. "Many orphanages were not so lucky."

Ann shivered and studied her glass. The tiny bubbles migrated toward the top of the orange soda.

"Brutal stories." John moved his head from side to side. "The manager at Hotel des Mille Collines protected over a thousand refugees. The UN finally evacuated them. It took a few tries. I think the refugees were bused to Tanzania. Maybe your camp... NGOs are setting up camps all over. And ..."

Margaux interrupted what might have been a monologue. John was a talker. "The Hutu extremists are organizing our camp."

Ann was surprised to hear the ethnic term.

Margaux continued, "Paul Kagame wants us to shut down the camp. He wants the refugees to come back. Now that I'm here, I'm not so sure." She sipped her scotch and rubbed her fingers together.

"Lots of work to do," John said. "Some progress though." He raised his eyebrows in Margaux's direction.

"You're an optimist." Margaux tapped her fingers as if she had a nervous tic. "I'm not sure we should continue our work in the camp. We're just feeding and sewing up the perpetrators. But if we pull out, we'll cause lots of suffering." She looked toward Ann, who sat in a chair to the left of the window.

The candle flame near Ann flickered due to an air leak in the rim around the window glass. At home, the air leak would be cold during the winter months. Here it only made the flame burn harder. The smell of burning wax was pleasant. "It's complicated," Ann shrugged. "No easy answers."

"Welcome to life," John said. "Especially international work. The cultural nuances are a real challenge at times."

"I've decided the neutrality in the camps is misguided," Margaux said. "Of course, Edward and I disagree."

This was the first time Ann had heard Margaux give her opinion so definitively. Ann recalled the heated discussion she and Edward had had. Ann did not feel the need to mention Innocent's death. Most of the time, she felt confident that she'd done the right thing. She feared for her safety. She knew she'd never be able to live with herself if she'd put in the tube and watched him heal and go on to murder someone else, even rape her. Perhaps she was playing God. But at the time, it seemed like the best thing to do. Maybe she'd think differently at home.

Out the window, a street lamp sputtered on. The electricity was back on in the *secteur*. Within the lantern's glow the street stood eerily silent.

"Do you all know the old Rwandan saying, 'It takes over a thousand people to undress a naked man'?" John offered.

Margaux shook her head. "I need a cig." She excused herself and went outside into the courtyard to smoke.

"She still smokes like a chimney," John said.

"Some things don't change." Ann shrugged. "All of us rode her hard when she was sick, but when she recovered. . ."

John smiled. "Old dogs. . . old tricks. She's a gem." He excused himself to phone his family in the US.

Ann considered the impossibility—undressing a naked man. The relentless challenges of this mission. The overwhelming realities. The endless need. She had jumped from the mess at home into this. One overwhelming situation into another. She thought of Innocent. Had she done more harm than good? She set down her glass and drummed her fingers on her knees. Soon Chuck Mangione's *Children of Sanchez* played in her head. Frustration flowed from her fingers.

Outside the window, the street lamp's pool of silver light spotlighted the broken curb. A dog and her pups wandered through the luminous circle. The mission had seemed so straightforward—help the victims. Address their medical needs. It turned out to be much more complicated. Nothing was what it seemed.

Margaux returned. "It's quiet out there." She lifted her scotch from the coffee table and slid back into her corner of the couch.

John returned from his phone call and chattered on, his southern drawl singsong, comforting despite the topics. He talked about the killings. Wealthy men had paid other men to kill. It had been a nine-to-five job. A way to put food on the table when other jobs—teacher, farmer, mechanic—became impossible due to the society's collapse.

John offered Ann a car and driver so she could visit the orphanage. "The nuns at Beauraing ask about you," John said. "They talked about you after you left. 'She's gutsy for a first-time volunteer.'"

Margaux smiled toward Ann. "She'll come back. She's wired for aid work." She swirled the amber liquid in her glass. "You'll get home and realize you don't fit in. One of your friends will complain how a flat tire ruined her day and you'll think back to one of your days here."

"Life in the US will feel small," John said.

"I can't manage to stay in France for more than a month," Margaux said. "I see my friends and then back I come."

Ann couldn't know for sure. There was Edward. Edward. She recalled their final evening in his room, their decision to agree to disagree, her final night in his bed, his gentleness. Ann would miss him, but she needed to deal with her family; she couldn't put it off any longer. She would take care of her father and make peace with Coleen. She was ready.

Margaux and John sat on the couch, bantering like old friends.

The Parliament building where Ann and Margaux had visited General Bagasora was not far from where they stayed. Situated on a hilltop, it overlooked the Supreme Court and the other government buildings. Pockmarks from bullets and grenades dotted the façade. Bomb blasts had left holes like gaping wounds. The driver told her that Bagasora was accused of planning the genocide.

Not only buildings and homes carried scars, but the few men, women, and children who walked the streets wore their losses—missing arms, hands, or legs. A girl missing her left ear with a thick scar marring her cheek stood on a corner selling Chiclets from a cardboard box. She was alive, but physically disfigured. What internal ghosts haunted her and the other survivors? Could they become whole again? How could the new government heal the country? How could the country and people possibly recover and rebuild?

As if reading her thoughts, the driver said, "Survival is not always the better choice." He explained that it was the month of *Gicurasi*, a time of sadness and sickness. The change from heavy rains to dry weather often brought illness. The long months of dryness killed off the weaker animals. "Sometimes nature takes care of things."

The grassy field, where a small herd of goats had grazed and children had played soccer, held a cremation pyre. Incinerated bones and fragments of cloth protruded from the piles of black char. From the road, Ann identified skulls and long bones—femur, tibia, and humerus—legs and arms. Well-nourished dogs and their pups enjoyed a continuous feast.

The refugee camp was still assembled on the King Faisal hospital property. It had grown since Ann's last visit and resembled Batumba—tents packed into a compressed space, cooking fires with ribbons of smoke, unwashed bodies milling around. The hospital's brick building had several mortar holes. The balconies were packed with people. John had said that the property had become a safe haven for 6000 refugees, several thousand beyond the census when Ann left. *Médecins Sans Frontières* (MSF) had arrived in late May, a couple of weeks after GH pulled out. MSF struggled to make it function as a hospital again. "I'm sure they'd take you back," John had said.

But Ann was heading home. The UN guard at the gate refused to let them pass. Just as well.

Ann did not ask to drive by Joseta's, but they motored past St. Michael's on the way to the orphanage. Father Innocent's church and parsonage were vacated, the corpses gone. Several mounds of freshly turned red-brown earth rose in the yard behind the church. The door of the parsonage stood open, creaking in a breeze that also rustled the dry leaves of the eucalyptus and bougainvilleas.

Ann recalled the blackness of Innocent's skin and the pinkness of his palms touching all the children at the handshake of peace, touching her. A shiver shimmied up her spine. She had done what she needed to do. But she carried her action with her. She sucked in a breath and pressed away the memory with a string of *Hail Marys. Hail Mary full of grace, blessed art though among women. . . Pray for us sinners now and at the hour of our death.*

She could think of no other response. Perhaps that was the purpose of prayer, when nothing made sense in the world, when you lacked control over the events that overwhelmed you, prayer was the one response that was possible. You could offer your hopes to the possibility of someone, something, some force greater than yourself. Prayer was about hope.

Down the street, the Beauraing Orphanage stood untouched just as John had reported. Ann sighed with relief as she hurried through the bamboo gate, expecting 99 to greet her and ask for a Coke. She whispered a prayer for him as she rapped on the pink door.

One of the Rwandan nuns opened it, recognizing Ann. She repeated Ann's name several times, a lilt in her tone. A number of the children flocked around Ann and reached to touch her, many new faces among them. They looked happy but thin. The familiar scents of juice, diapers, and porridge were strangely pleasant. The children and nuns had weathered the genocide. Miraculous.

"Where is Sister Mary Joseph?" Ann asked.

The nun's hands flew to her lips. "She's ill," she whispered. "She'll be delighted to see you."

Ann gasped. "I'm glad I came."

She followed the nun into a section of the orphanage she'd never entered, the nuns' sleeping quarters. Sister Mary Joseph looked pale and weak but smiled when she saw Ann. She murmured something and Ann leaned close to hear. Sister's warm breath was stale, and the smell of powder blanketed the acrid scent of sickness. Her attempt to speak resulted in a bout of horrific coughing. When Sister regained her composure, the nun offered Sister Mary Joseph a sip of water.

"I should have brought my stethoscope," Ann said.

Sister rasped. "*Mon amie*, I am glad to see you. God bless you." Sister tried to sit up but fell back against her pillows. Ann and the Rwandan nun pulled Sister into a more comfortable position for talking by adjusting her pillows. Sister touched her fingers to her forehead, then her shoulders, and her heart, making the sign of the cross in Ann's direction.

Ann bowed her head as the nuns recited the *Our Father*, the *Hail Mary*, and thanked God for Ann's safe return from the camp. The Rwandan nun prayed for the continued safety of the orphanage. Ann listened patiently, finding reassurance in the Catholic rituals. Maybe they were their own version of witchcraft, efforts to stave off the darkness, customs to preserve hope. Nevertheless, Ann found them to be a source of comfort.

Sister Mary Joseph hacked again, her cough much worse than Ann remembered.

"Who is checking on you?" Ann asked.

Sister Mary Joseph tried to respond, but no words came out.

"John brought the MSF doctor," the Rwandan nun said. "He gave her some pills. Sister says that she is old and ready when her time comes."

Ann winced.

"Let's take her outside. I'll get the wheelchair."

Ann held Sister Mary Joseph's hand while the Rwandan nun retrieved a squeaky contraption and wheeled it to the bedside. Together they helped Sister

Mary Joseph pivot onto the seat; her frame felt bird-like. Ann propped a pillow behind her while the nun removed Sister's white cotton bonnet and adjusted her veil. Ann swallowed her shock at Sister's thin, wispy hair. It resembled her mother's head after chemotherapy.

Outside, the distant hills shimmered emerald green in the afternoon sun but for several broad patches of black scar. A burnt-flesh smell hung beneath the spicy fragrance of the eucalyptus. No one picked tea. The nun said that the fields had been planted with land mines.

In the back of the yard, the grove of spiky banana trees stood tall, unharmed. A long stem of lime-green bananas curled skyward like a servant extending its fingers toward the heavens. The rustling of the banana leaves mixed with the children's laughter as they played a game of tag. A soft breeze tousled Ann's hair as she watched the children. The gift of play.

In the far corner of the yard stood several mounds of fresh red earth, each marked with two whitewashed boards nailed together. There were no names. Ann did not recall the graves and asked about them.

"We've lost a lot of children," the nun said. "Children arrived malnourished and sick. We could only keep them clean and fed in their final days. After you left, we had very little medical help until MSF came to King Faisal."

The children ran up, then stood quiet for a few minutes, inspecting Sister Mary Joseph's wheelchair, staring at Ann and the nun, who sat on wooden chairs sipping tea. In time, the children wandered off, kicking at the grass and chasing the yellow butterflies who fed on a nearby patch of white honeysuckle-like flowers. Soon, they resumed their game of tag.

"I'll let the two of you alone to talk," the nun said.

Ann set her china cup on a small plastic table and took Sister Mary Joseph's frail hand in hers. "I thought you might want to know that Father Innocent is dead."

Sister Mary Joseph nodded. "We assumed he was dead or in prison," Sister rasped. "The RPF has started to arrest the extremists."

Ann swallowed hard. "He came in with a knife wound. I was on call. I could have saved him."

Sister squeezed Ann's hand. Her palm felt warm and dry.

"I didn't." The words fell out.

Sister continued to press Ann's hand.

"I'm not sure I did the right thing."

"He was loyal to us," Sister whispered. "And he did some horrible things."

"Why?" Ann asked. "Why the complicity with the killers?"

Sister Mary Joseph coughed, and Ann helped her take a sip of tea. A light breeze raised Sister's veil. "A big question," Sister Mary Joseph rasped. "An angel and devil wrestle for control in each of us." She began to hack again. Ann gave her another swallow of tea. "Perhaps he wanted to impress the archbishop. Perhaps he owed the government favors. Power corrupts."

They sat in silence. The angel and devil wrestle for control. Ann was far from perfect, but her angel had helped her prepare to return to Wisconsin.

In the yard, the children played with abandon. Their game of tag morphed into swinging statues. They had no awareness of all that had happened, the trauma that each had likely suffered was forgotten, at least for the moment. It gave Ann a small thread of hope.

She played the piano before she left. Her fingers flew across the black and white keys, which were still in tune. She hammered out her mother's favorite song, the *Ave Maria*. Then she played several tunes from the *Sound of Music*. The children watched; two of the younger ones squeezed next to her on the piano bench and several of the older ones sang along.

Ann's plane was one of the first to leave the Kigali airport when it reopened. Her route home connected through Paris. *Operation Turquoise*, the French intervention, had opened the air highway between Rwanda and France. At the end of the month, the first US troops would arrive to secure the Kigali airport for an expanded international aid effort.

This time, the view from the plane was marked with devastation. Every downtown building sported evidence of destruction, several blasted-out windows at a minimum. The amount of work to reconstruct the city and heal the people, if that was possible, loomed large. Outside the city, charred fields stained the once impossibly green hillsides with large sections of scar and ruin.

Ann remembered the unpruned tea bushes, the weedy fields filled with rotting vegetables, and the numerous piles of fresh earth that she'd seen up close from the Toyota's window during her return to Kigali. Scenes of bodies piled like sacks of grain flashed in her head like a strobe light. The faces of some of her patients, stoic and afraid. The wounds—intentional, placed to torture, carved without thought about the pain and suffering that was inflicted. 99 lying on the ground in his own pool of caked blood. Innocent gasping for breath—would his death haunt her?

The smells, the unforgettable stench of death—would she ever blow it out? Rub it out? It seemed stuck forever.

The memories pressed around her. Frail Sister Mary Joseph sharing her wisdom. The locals and the expats who had worked side by side, laughed with her, cried, and complained, stood together in silence. They had helped her negotiate practicing medicine on unfamiliar ground. She fingered the thin gold chain of her mother's locket. She'd put it on for the trip home. During her seven months, she'd witnessed the human capacity for both goodness and evil.

As the plane climbed, the scars to the land grew less noticeable and, once again, the overwhelming greenness of the hills impressed her. The staircases of green pushed against their forested caps. The soft mounds of the green mountains were populated by gorillas and birds that Ann had never had the time to visit. She prayed for Vincent, hoping he'd not suffered unbearably at the hands of his jailers and that he was at peace. She prayed for Joseta and 99. Prayer was all she had.

Two gray volcano cones came into view; Stanford worked somewhere near them. The crushing green hemmed the brilliantly blue sky. From ten, and then twenty thousand feet all appeared tranquil, the horrors that had come to pass imperceptible. She was heading the wrong direction to see the Tanzania landscape, but she imagined the camp and the graves where Joseta, 99, and even Innocent were now part of the earth.

It would take awhile to make sense of all she had seen and done. She had no regrets about leaving. She'd put in her time. She'd miss her co-workers, miss Edward. But she worried about her father's health and needed to concentrate on him and her life in Milwaukee.

Suddenly, a presence settled near her shoulder. She looked up toward the steward call button and the overhead light and reached to the spot two feet above her shoulder, expecting to feel something. Instead, she grasped a blast of cold air from the vent. She pulled her fleece around her shoulders.

Outside, the plane was suspended in a bank of billowy white clouds.

Historical Note

This novel takes place during the Rwandan Genocide. Between April and July 1994 more than 800,000 Rwandans were murdered by their neighbors. After President Habyarimana's plane crash, extremists in the government launched planned killings and tried to wipe out the Tutsi race. Hutus tortured and raped Tutsi men, women, and children, as well as Tutsi sympathizers. Well-to-do Hutus bought their way out of the savagery, but many poor Hutus showed up to do their "work" day and night with machetes and clubs. For the first time in many months, they had a job and could provide for their families. For one hundred days, murder and rape were occupations. The rape survivors often contracted AIDS, giving birth to a generation of AIDS babies.

Like Father Innocent, many priests and ministers were accused of handing their communities over to the killers. Other religious leaders struggled to protect their parishioners and tried to stop the slaughter. The International Red Cross was one of a handful of NGOs that remained in Kigali, as did a Seventh Day Adventist volunteer who intervened in the decimation of one orphanage. MSF arrived in late May and reopened King Faisal hospital.

Rwanda's social fabric disintegrated, leaving survivors afraid to trust those around them. The United Nations, Europe, and the United States finally responded after the RPF secured Kigali in July 1994. President Clinton visited in 1998, apologizing for the West's delayed response and acknowledging the devastation that resulted. He did not say that Rwanda was not a priority because, as a land-locked country, without oil or minerals, the US had little interest.

RPF rebel leader Paul Kagame became president and accused international aid organizations of providing safe havens for the killers in the refugee camps.

Hutu-extremists organized the refugee camps in Zaire, now Congo, and attacked Kagame's fledgling government for two years. International aid agencies faced an impossible decision— to deliver aid under the mercy of the génocidaires or to abandon the refugees. Aid organizations matured during the crisis, learning lessons in Rwanda that shape their work today: the importance of speaking out against injustice, the challenges of strict neutrality, and an awareness of the many unintended consequences that accompany the provision of aid.

When refugees and internally displaced persons returned to their homes, the killers and victims had to figure out how to live together as neighbors. Through the ancient process *gacaca*, where community members gather and talk out their gripes and differences, Rwandans spoke to each other and figured out how to cohabitate. Trials were held and over 100,000 were imprisoned. It was not a perfect reconciliation, but Rwanda has moved on. Genocide memorials stand in most cities and towns and annual remembrances remind Rwandans and tourists about the 1994 horrors. The flag was changed from red, yellow, and green to yellow, green, and blue after the genocide due to the association of the former colors with the genocide's brutality.

This is also a story about resilience. Time heals. Hard work brings recovery. Rwanda is a country in a hurry. Roads are paved, new building construction is underway, and Rwanda is a 21st century country. Children are educated. Tourists pay hundreds of dollars to book tours to visit Dian Fossey's gorillas. They fly into the remodeled Kigali airport, rent land cruisers, and stay at upscale hotels. Rwandan guides now lead the gorilla expeditions, which benefit the local economy with jobs, lifting many into the middle class. Men from the community serve as porters, supplementing their family incomes. Because fighting during the genocide encroached on the gorillas' territory, their population declined, but they, too, have recovered, and today their numbers flourish.

Across the border, in the Congo, formerly Zaire, a country with immense resources, a civil war with incomprehensible savagery is still waged. Militias rape, mutilate, and kill civilians. Since 1998 more than five million have died from violence, hunger, and disease. Little international attention has been focused there. Famine rages in Somalia in part because one religious group wants dominance over the population. It is a complicated world; there are no easy answers, but one tenet is true:

> *There will be no humanity without forgiveness. There will be no forgiveness without justice, but justice will be impossible without humanity.*
>
> —Quotation in the Kigali genocide museum

Discussion Questions

1. Why did Ann decide to volunteer with Global Health? What are your thoughts about her reasons and the motivations of other characters about their international aid work (Dr. Robert, Dr. Edward, Margaux)? If you have done international volunteer work what were your motivations for doing so?

2. Do you agree with Ann's decision to remain in Kigali, Rwanda, when her co-workers decided it was better to leave? What would you have done in that situation?

3. What do you think about the Colonel's decision to sterilize the patients on whom he performed a C-section without consent? What were his reasons? Ann did not agree with him, but did what she was told. What would you have done in that situation? What are the unintended consequences of their actions?

4. What do you know about the Hutu/Tutsi conflict in Rwanda? What other ethnic conflicts have resulted in humanitarian crises? What are the ways that ethnic conflicts have been resolved or stopped in those situations?

5. Neutrality is an important principle for many international aid organizations. What are the positive and negative consequences of this approach during the Rwanda genocide? How has neutrality played out in other international ethnic crises? If you have done international work, what has been your own experience?

6. Visiting a culture not your own, especially a low-resource country, is a tremendous learning opportunity and gives you perspective on the values and routines you take for granted at home. What did Ann learn during her time in Rwanda and Tanzania? If you have traveled, reflect on your own experiences and what you learned about yourself and your culture from that trip. What traditions or patterns may enhance your approaches at home?

7. The Hutus settled in the refugee camps and changed the power balance. Paul Kagame and others accused the NGOs of supporting the Hutus who were the main perpetrators of the genocide. In this story, what was the evidence of the Hutu infiltration? As an aid worker how might you monitor whether or not this was happening in a refugee camp?

8. What do you think about the French actress and diplomat who facilitated the adoption of the children in the refugee camp? What might be the unintended consequences of this effort?

9. How did the aid workers in this story cope with the stress? What are the ramifications to the ways they coped? If you have worked internationally, how have you coped? What advice would you give a new international health volunteer about self-care before s/he begins a mission? How did Joseta and Christine manage their losses and their lives? How does your approach compare and contrast with Joseta and Christine's approaches?

10. What do you think about Ann's decision not to help Father Innocent when he came into the Emergency Department in the camp? Was she wrong? What would you have done in that situation? If you have worked internationally are their things that you did that you regret, or would do differently if you could do them over again?

11. Some churches were helpful to victims and some supported the perpetrators in the Rwandan genocide. What are your thoughts about the role of the church in political conflicts? What other international conflicts have had religious overtones?

12. Traditions around birth, illness, and death in other countries may be different from what you have experienced at home. What surprised you about birth and death traditions in this story? Poisoning is often considered to be a cause of illness in Africa. What are the issues in a

developing country that may make poisoning a reality? (See Chapter 39.) Consulting witch doctors is a common practice, especially in rural areas. As a western trained healer, how might you understand and work with a local witch doctor. If you have worked internationally, what were your experiences and what did you learn from these approaches?

13. A reconciliation process was used to create a peaceful country after the genocide. Many people were tried and went to prison, but an ancient process called *gacaca*, where community members gather and talk out their gripes and differences, was also employed. Rwandans spoke to each other and figured out how to cohabitate. Neighbors who were victims had to figure out how to live next door to their perpetrators. How does this differ from what might have happened in the US, which uses the legal system to settle differences?

Acknowledgments

Thanks to all who helped birth this story. Writing mentors: Cynthia Bend, Coleen Johnston, and Catherine Friend. Editors: Gary Gilmer and Patti Frazee. Steve Swanson for sharing his experience. Readers of this story: Deborah Rine, Kristen Wixted, Therese Pautz, Cindy Howard, Tim Pera, Pam Orren, Cecelia Erickson, Marj Helmer, Jean Wiley, Kristine Heim and those I've forgotten to mention. And to the teachers and students at the Loft Literary Center in Minneapolis and Women Writing for (a) Change in Cincinnati for teaching an English major and physician how to write.

Special thanks to Leslie Matton-Flynn of Cup and Spiral Books, writing pal and graphic designer.

Research for this book included books, journal and magazine articles, movies, and blogs. Helpful book resources in no particular order: *We Wish to Inform You That Tomorrow We Will be Killed with Our Families*, Philip Gourevitch; *Leave None to Tell the Story*, Alison Des Forges; *In the Kingdom of Gorillas: Fragile Species in a Dangerous Land*, Bill Weber & Amy Vedder; *Land of a Thousand Hills*, Rosamond Halsey Carr & Ann Howard Halsey; Machete Season: The Killers in Rwanda Speak, Jean Hatzfeld ; Shake Hands with the Devil, Roméo Dallaire; God Sleeps in Rwanda, Joseph Sebarenzi; A People Betrayed: The Role of the West in Rwanda's Genocide, Linda Melvern; *Blue Sweater*, Jacqueline Novogratz; *An Ordinary Man*, Paul Rusesabagina; *A Problem from Hell: America and the Age of Genocide*, Samantha Power. Helpful movies: *Hotel Rwanda*, *Ghosts of Rwanda*, *Sometime in April*, *Rwanda: Do Scars Ever Fade*, *In the Tall Grass*.

About the Author

Dr. Therese Zink is a family physician, teacher, and leader in family medicine and global health education. She established the Global Health residency track in the Department of Family Medicine at the University of Minnesota to help young doctors make wise choices about how they practice internationally. She has cared for patients, conducted research, and taught primarily in the Midwest, incorporating international health work throughout her career. Her award-winning stories on doctoring have been published in literary and medical journals, as well as anthologies. Inspired by her work with patients and students, Zink edited two anthologies: *The Country Doctor Revisited: A 21st Century Reader* (Kent State University, 2010), stories, poems and essays about rural health care today and *Becoming a Doctor: Reflections by Minnesota Medical Students* (Univeristy of Minnesota, 2011), a literary portrait of the many steps along the path to becoming a physician. Her own collection, *Confessions of a Sin Eater* (2012), includes stories that explore her journey and the privilege and burden of doctoring. Zink believes that holding the patient's story is an important part of healing, and understanding how that story may intersect with one's own is crucial to personal and professional growth. www.theresezink.com

Dr. Ann McLannly Global Health book

Follow Dr. Ann McLannly, a thirty-something physician, who volunteers with Global Health in international hotspots around the world. Ann and her colleagues navigate landscapes and cultures during conflicts that garnered little media attention when they occurred. The nuances and challenges of the international crises are revealed as Ann and her colleagues confront their own fears and moral dilemmas. Like the Global Health volunteers enmeshed with forces beyond their control, your adrenaline will pump and you will become addicted to the intrigue, romance, and the challenge of practicing medicine on unfamiliar ground.

Coming *Mission Chechnya* and *Mission Palestine*. To learn more visit www.theresezink.com

25770982R00167

Made in the USA
Charleston, SC
14 January 2014